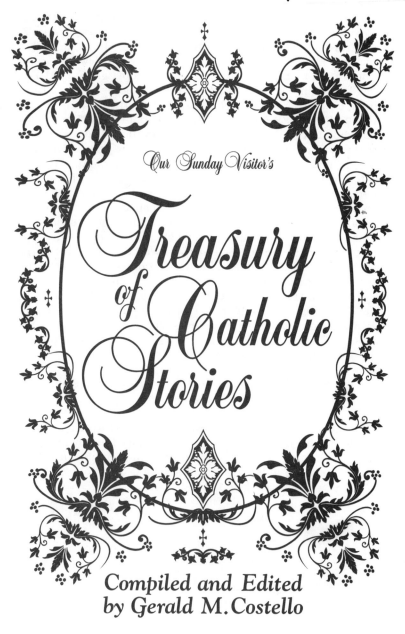

Our Sunday Visitor's

Treasury of Catholic Stories

Compiled and Edited
by Gerald M. Costello

Our Sunday Visitor Publishing Division
Our Sunday Visitor, Inc.
Huntington, Indiana 46750

947

Dedicated to twelve extraordinary grandchildren — Nicole and Ray Rishty; Bobby and Teresa Marx; Kevin, Chris, Katy, Kyle, Carly, and Clare Costello; Patty and Charlie Costello — who all love a good story, especially if it's told by Grandma Jane.

Acknowledgments

Many people helped me to put this anthology together, none more so than my good friends at Our Sunday Visitor. That's especially true of Bob Lockwood, president and publisher, who developed the concept for the book to begin with and whose thoughts about its contents have been invaluable, and Greg Erlandson, editor in chief, whose preliminary contacts ultimately got us all together. Editors Jim Manney (initially) and then Henry O'Brien were unfailingly helpful and constructive with their comments and suggestions. In addition Henry, who is OSV's managing editor of religious books, kept tons of organizational details in respectable order, a task that had me hanging on the ropes. For that, special thanks. And the same to OSV's associate publisher, Msgr. Owen F. Campion, whose interest in the book from start to finish has been a constant source of encouragement.

Working on the book reacquainted me, after all these years, with the satisfactions (and occasional frustrations) of library research. Heartfelt thanks to many dedicated staff people at the New York Public Library, the Walsh Library and the Immaculate Conception Seminary Library, both at Seton Hall University, South Orange, New Jersey, and the Hesburgh Library at the University of Notre Dame, Notre Dame, Indiana, for their help. Particular thanks to Charlotte Ames of the Notre Dame library not only for her interest in and suggestions about the project but for some timely technical assistance, proving in the process that you *can* teach an old dog new computerized research tricks. A few of them, anyway.

I am indebted, as always, to John Cardinal O'Connor, Archbishop of New York, not simply for his generous comments about this book but for his long-standing friendship. The same holds for Archbishop Edwin F. O'Brien, Archbishop for the Military Services, U.S.A., and Father John Catoir, former director of The Christophers and now executive director of Eva's Village and Sheltering Program, Paterson, New Jersey.

Historians R. Scott Appleby and Jay P. Dolan of the University of Notre Dame graciously gave of their time to review the scope of this book and offer suggestions for material that might be included.

Then there were friends who suggested or provided topics for the book, reviewed sections, or simply provided encouraging words along the way. With apologies to any who have been inadvertently omitted, my thanks to them: Anne Buckley, Sally Cropper, Julie Crum, William Sadlier Dinger, Msgr. Peter G. Finn, Father Benedict J. Groeschel, c.f.r., Father Boniface Hanley, OFM, Bill Holub, Msgr.

Kenneth E. Lasch, Tom Lorsung, Bishop James F. McCarthy, the late Bishop John G. Nolan, Father Joseph A. O'Hare, S.J., Father Val Peter, John Plouff, W. King Pound, Stephanie Raha, Charles Schubert, Anthony Verga, Eileen White, Monica Yehle, and Mark Zimmermann.

Thanks, certainly, to those publishers and others without whose material (whether in public domain or copyrighted) this work could not have been possible. Although every effort has been made to obtain permission where required, there are some excerpts in this volume whose copyright holders (if any) could not be determined or tracked down. A list of publishers and their works appears near the end of this book under "Special Acknowledgments."

And finally, as she has so many times in the past, my wife, Jane, put up with a significant amount of disruption in our lives so this book could be completed. She has my thanks, my admiration, and my everlasting love.

GERALD M. COSTELLO

Table of Contents

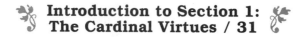

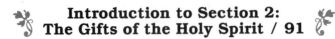

**Introduction to Section 2:
The Gifts of the Holy Spirit / 91**

Foreword

The hunger for heroes and heroines never abates. I was not a particularly pious child, and my announcement in my mid-teens that I intended one day to become a priest was met with shocked silence by my parents, and raucous guffaws by my sisters and brother. Yet much of the inspiration came from reading or being told the stories of the canonized, those meriting canonization, and those who, while their causes for sainthood will perhaps never be pursued, stirred my soul as did the tale of anyone who had already made the grade and had been officially designated a saint. They lured me to be far more and far better than I could ever have dreamed of becoming.

Jerry Costello tells their stories straightforwardly and succinctly, but always with a flair. My own seminary was St. Charles Borromeo in Philadelphia. Hence, I was delighted to find St. Charles in this treasury of Catholic stories. I recall being amazed that despite his extraordinary self-denial in favor of the poor and their crucial needs, someone made so bold as to try to assassinate Charles Borromeo in his own cathedral in Milan.

Did Constantine really see a cross in the sky? Did he hear the words "In this sign you will conquer"? Certainly, he was convinced of the vision himself, and the conviction played no small part in his victory. Was the Maid of Orléans, Joan of Arc, truly a saint, despite her insistence against the "authority" of the bishop that her "voices" must be obeyed above all else? I remember taking part in Shaw's play about her many eons ago. There was not the slightest question in my mind about her heroic sanctity. Who could read of Isaac Jogues's having his fingers chewed off while his heart burned with love for those who tortured him thus, without longing for martyrdom himself? In virtually our own day, can anyone who has visited El Salvador and has even a superficial understanding of what Archbishop Romero confronted not be inspired by his heroism?

One after another, as though building a magnificent cathedral, Jerry Costello relates inimitably the poignant stories of hero following upon hero, heroine upon heroine, from Augustine of the fourth and fifth centuries to Maximilian Kolbe of the twentieth; of Dorothy Day of New York to Mother Teresa of Calcutta; of Patrick the doer to Thomas Aquinas the thinker; of Maria Goretti's forgiving her attacker to Kateri Tekakwitha's bearing insults with a gentle smile.

Not content to tell us his often winsome stories of an extraordinary array of holy men and women, the author gives us insightful expositions of Church teachings frequently referenced, but not always understood — for example, the cardinal virtues, the gifts of the Holy Spirit, the corporal works of mercy, the spiritual works of mercy. At the same time Costello adds a very special touch, setting the stage for the heroics of St. Boniface, for example: "The crowd was spoiling for a good show."

I am delighted by any measure with *Our Sunday Visitor's Treasury of Catholic Stories*. More, the people I preach to day after day and Sunday after Sunday will be pleased more than somewhat when they hear me repeat, if in my own less elegant terms, these wonderful stories that will entrance the youngest and eldest. They are sheer gift.

✠ JOHN CARDINAL O'CONNOR
ARCHBISHOP OF NEW YORK
APRIL 1999

Preface

This book is filled with stories, one hundred twenty-six of them, all different. But they all have one thing in common, too.

Each one springs from the same story — not *a* story, but *the* story, the greatest story ever told, the story of Jesus Christ.

Those who told it first told it best, and it is as spellbinding to us today as it was to those who heard it then, nearly two thousand years before our time. It still grips us — with its drama, its humanity, its never-failing love, and its never-ending promise.

Within it are dozens of episodes, stories within the story, narratives that continue to entrance and inspire us, and to motivate our lives. The story of Jesus was so powerful that in time it would give rise to every story in this book — and to more, *millions* more, stories beyond counting. Including our own.

Here — as told by Luke, the New Testament's most gifted storyteller — are some of the moments in that story that we treasure most. Read the words again, and let them come alive in your heart. They set the stage for all that follows.

The Annunciation (Luke 1:26-38) • In the sixth month the angel Gabriel was sent from God to a city of Galilee named Nazareth, to a virgin betrothed to a man whose name was Joseph, of the house of David; and the virgin's name was Mary. And he came to her and said, "Hail, full of grace, the Lord is with you!" But she was greatly troubled at the saying, and considered in her mind what sort of greeting this might be. And the angel said to her, "Do not be afraid, Mary, for you have found favor with God. And behold, you will conceive in your womb and bear a son, and you shall call his name Jesus. He will be great, and will be called the Son of the Most High; and the Lord God will give to him the throne of his father David, and he will reign over the house of Jacob for ever; and of his kingdom there will be no end." And Mary said to the angel, "How can this be, since I have no husband?" And the angel said to her, "The Holy Spirit will come upon you, and the power of the Most High will overshadow you; therefore the child to be born will be called holy, the Son of God. And behold, your kinswoman Elizabeth in her old age has also conceived a son; and this is the sixth month with her who was called barren. For with God nothing will be impossible." And Mary said, "Behold, I am the handmaid of the Lord; let it be [done] to me according to your word." And the angel departed from her.

The Birth of Jesus (Luke 2:1-19) • In those days a decree went out from Caesar Augustus that all the world should be enrolled. This was the first enrollment, when Quirinius was governor of Syria. And all went to be enrolled, each to his own city. And Joseph also went up from Galilee, from the city of Nazareth, to Judea, to the city of David, which is called Bethlehem, because he was of the house and lineage of David, to be enrolled with Mary his betrothed, who was with child. And while they were there, the time came for her to be delivered. And she gave birth to her first-born son and wrapped him in swaddling cloths, and laid him in a manger, because there was no place for them in the inn.

And in that region there were shepherds out in the field, keeping watch over their flock by night. And an angel of the Lord appeared to them, and the glory of the Lord shone around them, and they were filled with fear. And the angel said to them, "Be not afraid; for behold, I bring you good news of a great joy which will come to all the people; for to you is born this day in the city of David a Savior, who is Christ the Lord. And this will be a sign for you: you will find a babe wrapped in swaddling cloths and lying in a manger." And suddenly there was with the angel a multitude of the heavenly host praising God and saying, "Glory to God in the highest, and on earth peace among men with whom he is pleased!"

When the angels went away from them into heaven, the shepherds said to one another, "Let us go over to Bethlehem and see this thing that has happened, which the Lord has made known to us." And they went with haste, and found Mary and Joseph, and the babe lying in a manger. And when they saw it they made known the saying which had been told them concerning this child; and all who heard it wondered at what the shepherds told them. But Mary kept all these things, pondering them in her heart.

The Baptism of Jesus (Luke 3:1-3, 15-22) • In the fifteenth year of the reign of Tiberius Caesar, Pontius Pilate being governor of Judea, and Herod being tetrarch of Galilee, and his brother Philip tetrarch of the region of Ituraea and Trachonitis, and Lysanias tetrarch of Abilene, in the high-priesthood of Annas and Caiaphas, the word of God came to John the son of Zechariah in the wilderness; and he went into all the region about the Jordan, preaching a baptism of repentance for the forgiveness of sins. . . .

As the people were in expectation, and all men questioned in their hearts concerning John, whether perhaps he were the Christ, John answered them all, "I baptize you with water; but he who is mightier than I is coming, the thong of whose sandals I am not worthy to untie; he will baptize you with the Holy Spirit and with fire. His winnowing fork is in his hand, to clear his threshing floor, and to gather the wheat into his granary, but the chaff he will burn with unquenchable fire."

So, with many other exhortations, he preached good news to the people. But Herod the tetrarch, who had been reproved by him for Herodias, his brother's wife, and for all the evil things that Herod had done, added this to them all, that he shut up John in prison.

Now when all the people were baptized, and when Jesus also had been baptized and was praying, the heaven was opened, and the Holy Spirit descended upon him in bodily form, as a dove, and a voice came from heaven, "Thou art my beloved Son; with thee I am well pleased."

Jesus Begins His Ministry (Luke 4:14-21) • And Jesus returned in the power of the Spirit into Galilee, and a report concerning him went out through all the surrounding country. And he taught in their synagogues, being glorified by all.

And he came to Nazareth, where he had been brought up; and he went to the synagogue, as his custom was, on the sabbath day. And he stood up to read; and there was given to him the book of the prophet Isaiah. He opened the book and found the place where it was written, "The Spirit of the Lord is upon me, because he has anointed me to preach good news to the poor. He has sent me to proclaim release to the captives and recovering of sight to the blind, to set at liberty those who are oppressed, to proclaim the acceptable year of the Lord." And he closed the book, and gave it back to the attendant, and sat down; and the eyes of all in the synagogue were fixed on him. And he began to say to them, "Today this scripture has been fulfilled in your hearing."

Jesus Chooses the Twelve Apostles (Luke 6:12-31) • In these days he went out into the hills to pray; and all night he continued in prayer to God. And when it was day, he called his disciples, and chose from them twelve, whom he named apostles; Simon, whom he named Peter, and Andrew his brother, and James and John, and Philip, and Bartholomew, and Matthew, and Thomas, and James the son of Alphaeus, and Simon who was called the Zealot, and Judas the son of James, and Judas Iscariot, who became a traitor.

And he came down with them and stood on a level place, with a great crowd of his disciples and a great multitude of people from all Judea and Jerusalem and the seacoast of Tyre and Sidon, who came to hear him and to be healed of their diseases; and those who were troubled with unclean spirits were cured. And all the crowd sought to touch him, for power came forth from him and healed them all.

And he lifted up his eyes on his disciples and said:

"Blessed are you poor, for yours is the kingdom of God.

"Blessed are you that hunger now, for you shall be satisfied.

"Blessed are you that weep now, for you shall laugh.

"Blessed are you when men hate you, and when they exclude

you and revile you, and cast out your name as evil, on account of the Son of man! Rejoice in that day, and leap for joy, for behold, your reward is great in heaven; for so their fathers did to the prophets.

"But woe to you that are rich, for you have received your consolation.

"Woe to you that are full now, for you shall hunger.

"Woe to you that laugh now, for you shall mourn and weep.

"Woe to you, when all men speak well of you, for so their fathers did to the false prophets.

"But I say to you that hear, Love your enemies, do good to those who hate you, bless those who curse you, pray for those who abuse you. To him who strikes you on the cheek, offer the other also; and from him who takes away your cloak do not withhold your coat as well. Give to every one who begs from you; and of him who takes away your goods do not ask [for] them again. And as you wish that men would do to you, do so to them."

The Last Supper (Luke 22:14-20, 39-42) • And when the hour came, he sat at table, and the apostles with him. And he said to them, "I have earnestly desired to eat this passover with you before I suffer; for I tell you I shall not eat it until it is fulfilled in the kingdom of God." And he took a cup, and when he had given thanks he said, "Take this, and divide it among yourselves; for I tell you that from now on I shall not drink of the fruit of the vine until the kingdom of God comes." And he took bread, and when he had given thanks he broke it and gave it to them, saying, "This is my body which is given for you. Do this in remembrance of me." And likewise the cup after supper, saying, "This cup which is poured out for you is the new covenant in my blood. . . ."

And he came out, and went, as was his custom, to the Mount of Olives; and the disciples followed him. And when he came to the place he said to them, "Pray that you may not enter into temptation." And he withdrew from them about a stone's throw, and knelt down and prayed, "Father, if thou art willing, remove this cup from me; nevertheless not my will, but thine, be done."

The Crucifixion and Death of Jesus (Luke 23:13-25, 32-34, 39-46) • Pilate then called together the chief priests and the rulers and the people, and said to them, "You brought me this man as one who was perverting the people; and after examining him before you, behold, I did not find this man guilty of any of your charges against him; neither did Herod, for he sent him back to us. Behold, nothing deserving death has been done by him; I will therefore chastise him and release him."

But they all cried out together, "Away with this man, and release to us Barabbas" — a man who had been thrown into prison for an insurrection started in the city, and for murder. Pilate addressed them once more, desiring to release Jesus; but they shouted out, "Crucify, crucify him!" A third time he said to them, "Why, what evil has he done? I have found in him no crime deserving death; I will therefore chastise him and release him." But they were urgent, demanding with loud cries that he should be crucified. And their voices prevailed. So Pilate gave sentence that their demand should be granted. He released the man who had been thrown into prison for insurrection and murder, whom they asked for; but Jesus he delivered up to their will. . . .

Two others also, who were criminals, were led away to be put to death with him. And when they came to the place which is called The Skull, there they crucified him, and the criminals, one on the right and one on the left. And Jesus said, "Father, forgive them; for they know not what they do." And they cast lots to divide his garments. . . .

One of the criminals who were hanged railed at him, saying, "Are you not the Christ? Save yourself and us!" But the other rebuked him, saying, "Do you not fear God, since you are under the same sentence of condemnation? And we indeed justly; for we are receiving the due reward of our deeds; but this man has done nothing wrong." And he said, "Jesus, remember me when you come in your kingly power." And he said to him, "Truly, I say to you, today you will be with me in Paradise."

It was now about the sixth hour, and there was darkness over the whole land until the ninth hour, while the sun's light failed; and the curtain of the temple was torn in two. Then Jesus, crying with a loud voice, said, "Father, into thy hands I commit my spirit!" And having said this he breathed his last.

The Resurrection of Jesus (Luke 24:1-8, 33-39, 44-53) • But on the first day of the week, at early dawn, they [the women who had come from Galilee with Jesus] went to the tomb, taking the spices which they had prepared. And they found the stone rolled away from the tomb, but when they went in they did not find the body. While they were perplexed about this, behold, two men stood by them in dazzling apparel; and as they were frightened and bowed their faces to the ground, the men said to them, "Why do you seek the living among the dead? He is not here, but has risen. Remember how he told you, while he was still in Galilee, that the Son of man must be delivered into the hands of sinful men, and be crucified, and on the third day rise." And they remembered his words, . . .

[The two friends of Jesus who encountered him on the road to Emmaus] rose that same hour and returned to Jerusalem; and they found the eleven gathered together and those who were with them, who said, "The Lord has risen indeed, and has appeared to Simon!"

Then they told what had happened on the road, and how he was known to them in the breaking of the bread.

As they were saying this, Jesus himself stood among them, and said to them, "Peace to you." But they were startled and frightened, and supposed that they saw a spirit. And he said to them, "Why are you troubled, and why do questionings rise in your hearts? See my hands and my feet, that it is I myself; handle me, and see; for a spirit has not flesh and bones as you see that I have." . . .

Then he said to them, "These are my words which I spoke to you, while I was still with you, that everything written about me in the law of Moses and the prophets and the psalms must be fulfilled." Then he opened their minds to understand the scriptures, and said to them, "Thus it is written, that the Christ should suffer and on the third day rise from the dead, and that repentance and forgiveness of sins should be preached in his name to all nations, beginning from Jerusalem. You are witnesses of these things. And behold, I send the promise of my Father upon you; but stay in the city, until you are clothed with power from on high."

Then he led them out as far as Bethany, and lifting up his hands he blessed them. While he blessed them, he parted from them and was carried up into heaven. And they worshiped him, and returned to Jerusalem with great joy, and were continually in the temple blessing God.

Editor's General Introduction

"Tell me a story."

Those four little words spell out an invitation — a difficult one to turn down, for most of us. And thank heaven that's still the case. Because even in an age when children are swamped with technologically generated entertainment, available at their beck and call, nothing beats an old-fashioned story — told (preferably) by one grown-up to one child. Stories can delight or they can frighten, they can entertain or they can teach, they can soothe or they can excite. Almost always, though, they stretch the imagination. That's one reason that they're so appealing, to storyteller and listener alike.

Teachers love stories, as well they might. They know there's no better way to get a lesson across. Obviously this is nothing new. In the ancient world, entire civilizations owed their survival to stories passed along from one generation to the next. The Greeks understood that fables made life's little lessons more memorable, and the Romans had a phrase that summarized the educational value of storytelling: *Verba movent, exempla trahent* ("Words influence, examples attract").

And oh, how those examples have attracted Catholics, millions and millions of them, down through the centuries! The faith has been nourished beyond description by the stories Catholics tell one another — beginning with the greatest story of all, the story of Jesus. But literally, that story is only the beginning. The story of Jesus and the others that followed spread the faith around the world, speeding its growth in good times and keeping its flame alive in bad.

There *is* something about stories and the Catholic faith that seems perfect together, a connection that many commentators have noted. Three contemporary authors, in particular, have explored the subject at some length in recent years.

"Jesus obviously was a natural storyteller and those who followed him picked up the habit," Father William J. Bausch once wrote. "The real work of spreading the Good News fell to accounts of Jesus, his disciples, and a whole array of saints. Legends, tales, epics, and myths were the embodiments of deep truths. Stories told of how people actually lived the Gospel."

John Shea has written engagingly of "the perennial Christian strategy," which he said consists of three simple steps:

1. Gather the folks.
2. Break the bread.
3. Tell the stories.

"As Christians," he continued, "we have inherited ancient stories that carry the faith convictions of our people. Although these stories may start with 'long ago,' they end with 'right now.' " They help us, he added, as we confront the mysteries of life and death: "We gather together and tell stories of God to calm our terror and hold our hope on high."

Father Andrew Greeley adds the convincing point that, for Catholics, stories are inextricably intertwined with the sacramental character of the Church, with the ceremonies that mark "the critical landmarks of life." The sacraments of reconciliation and anointing of the sick, he says, "embed in ritual and mystery the deeply held Catholic story of second chances."

For all these reasons and more, stories traditionally have been a staple in the lesson plans of Catholic teachers, in parochial schools and religious instruction classes alike. Stories of the saints, especially, enthralled and inspired generations of students with accounts of bravery, piety, and care for others. Writing in *America* magazine in 1997, Jesuit Father James F. Keenan remembered from his school days that "the generosity of Elizabeth of Hungary, the wisdom of Thomas Aquinas, the courage and prudence of Thomas More, the courage and wisdom of Catherine of Alexandria, the charity of St. Thérèse of Lisieux and St. Catherine of Siena, the faith of St. Paul, the hard-won courage of St. Peter were tangible presentations of virtues." And for good measure, one might add, they helped to drill home some basic understanding of this mysterious Church — the same Church that somehow linked each of us, insignificant though we might be, to these storied heroes.

Time has brought change, not always for the better. By all accounts, stories of the saints no longer enjoy that kind of prominence in the classroom today. Evidence suggests, too, that the basics of the faith are often the *mysteries* of the faith, when they should not be — on matters as elementary as the Ten Commandments, standard prayers, and the Real Presence of Jesus in the Eucharist. Catholic students seem to be embracing the social Gospel as never before, which is surely to the good. But there is more to the Gospel than that, and it begins with a knowledge of and commitment to the Christian faith.

The American bishops received an eye-opening report in this regard at their Spring 1997 meeting in Kansas City, Missouri, when a committee on religious education cited "recurring deficiencies" in textbooks for Catholic students — in areas that included the Trinity, the divinity of Jesus, the sacraments, and the concept of sin.

If younger Catholics are not as well grounded in the faith as they should be, the fault goes far beyond the classroom itself. Parents, after all, remain a child's primary educators; it's up to them to do something about it if they believe the child's religious education is defective or incomplete. Nor is the classroom the only place where religious training takes place. At the Kansas City bishops' meeting, one prominent archbishop said the inadequacies reported in some religious textbooks were the same ones that people complained about in the preaching they heard.

That might help to account for the fact that the problem of religious confusion among Catholics is not limited to students. All too many adults, too, fail to understand the basic teachings of their faith. Witness recent polls showing that many Catholics either have doubts that Jesus is truly present in the Blessed Sacrament, or aren't sure just what they're supposed to believe.

This is not to suggest that the Church in the United States produced better Catholics two or three or four generations ago. It *is* meant to suggest, however, that the Church of that time produced Catholics who were better informed about its basic teachings. This, in turn, enabled them to understand more perfectly not only the joys of their faith but also the demands — even the sacrifices — that it might require of them. If that spirit and knowledge of years past could somehow be combined with the commitment to social action that helps define today's Church, this generation of Catholics could engage the world with a newly energized source of spiritual strength.

This book represents a contribution — a modest one, perhaps, but a contribution nonetheless — in that direction. It presents stories in the Catholic tradition, from the earliest days of the Church right up to the present, and they're meant for young and old alike. They are stories about martyrs and miracles, popes and kings, missionaries and preachers, clergy and laypeople. In a real sense, they constitute the narrative tradition of the Church.

They come from a wide variety of sources, ranging from century-old textbooks to contemporary magazines and newspapers. More than a few qualify as legends, meaning that the truths they convey might depend more on faith than on fact. That's all right. There are times, Cardinal Newman observed a century and a half ago, when the heart is reached not through reason but by imagination. In our own time, Father Greeley has reminded us that Catholicism is "willing to risk" stories that might seem fanciful to others, out of our conviction "that God discloses himself in the objects and events and persons of ordinary life."

Whether centuries old or thoroughly up to date, these stories are arranged in a way that will remind readers of some values we all should hold dear — namely:

1. The four cardinal virtues: temperance, prudence, justice, and fortitude.

2. The seven gifts of the Holy Spirit: wisdom, understanding, counsel, strength, knowledge, piety, and fear of the Lord.

3. The seven corporal works of mercy: feeding the hungry, giving drink to the thirsty, clothing the naked, visiting the imprisoned, sheltering the homeless, visiting the sick, and burying the dead.

4. The seven spiritual works of mercy: counseling the doubtful, instructing the ignorant, admonishing sinners, comforting the afflicted, forgiving offenses, bearing wrongs patiently, and praying for the living and the dead.

What sets all of these stories apart is their moral purpose. In the past they helped to foster an awareness of Catholic heritage in young people, calling them to a life of faith and virtue. A new generation will benefit not only from a fresh reading of the classic tales of old but also stories of the Church's more recent heroes — men and women such as Dorothy Day, St. Maximilian Kolbe, Pope John XXIII, Bishop Walsh of Maryknoll, the martyred religious women of El Salvador, Cardinal Bernardin, Mother Teresa, and Pope John Paul II. Their lives remind us that in every age, God sends special people whose extraordinary example helps to reinvigorate the Church and to inspire the rest of us to holiness.

Here, then, is *Our Sunday Visitor's Treasury of Catholic Stories*, presented in hopes of fostering an awareness of Catholic heritage, of teaching Catholics and their friends about the Church, and of calling individual Catholics and their families to a life of faith. It all began with that magic four-word invitation: "Tell me a story." It continues, now, with four more magic words: "Once upon a time . . ."

Introduction to Section 1:
The Cardinal Virtues

The cardinal virtues.

There's an old-fashioned ring to that phrase, isn't there? Make that *refreshingly* old-fashioned, so that "old-fashioned" won't be confused with "outdated." For the virtues are enduring. They're always in season, and always will be.

Something in those words, "the cardinal virtues," suggests all that is positive: stability, judgment, trust, decency. And for extra measure, good old common sense. All the right things, in other words, that just don't ever — or never *should* — go out of style.

Old the cardinal virtues certainly are. They go back to the classic Greek philosophers, who, centuries before the birth of Jesus, proposed them as cornerstones of right living. They make their first scriptural appearance in the Book of Wisdom, in which a Jewish sage incorporated positive aspects of Greek thought in his text for Hebrew readers — readers who were increasingly on the move, traveling ever further from their traditional homeland. Wherever you go, the Wisdom sage wrote, in whatever company you find yourself, remember that certain standards of conduct, certain ways of life, will always apply.

And thus we find him speaking of wisdom herself: ". . . The fruits of her works are virtues; for she teaches moderation and prudence, justice and fortitude, and nothing in life is more useful for men than these" (Wisdom 8:7).

What a teacher he was! Let his lesson sink in: *Nothing in life* could be more useful than maintaining these tried-and-true values. These, indeed, are the cardinal virtues: temperance (moderation) and prudence, justice and fortitude — just as the Greeks defined them, just as Jewish readers dispersed throughout the Mediterranean world absorbed them, just as Christian thought has honored them down through the centuries.

Why "cardinal" virtues, you may ask? It stems from that word's original derivation, from the word *cardo,* which literally means "hinge." Thus, something that is cardinal is of critical importance; it is something on which everything else might — well, *hinge.* In this case other human virtues hinge on these, the cardinal virtues. They're the ones that are the most important for us to consider; if we ignore them we're missing the message that our Christian faith wants us most to hear.

Virtue itself comes from *virtus,* meaning power. All of the virtues give us the *power* to do good and avoid evil. In traditional Catholic teaching, the "theological virtues" — faith, hope, and charity — are usually spoken of as "infused," given to us by God, and in one way or another they govern our relationship with the Lord. The *cardinal virtues* are something else, however. They have to do with the way we interact with other people. Living a virtuous life in this sense means dealing with life in the right way: temperately, prudently, justly, courageously.

That's a tall order. But the Church has always taught that the cardinal virtues can be learned, that with practice and prayer sincere Catholics can act just as the virtues dispose them to. The first step in doing that is to get a better fix on the virtues themselves.

Return to that "old-fashioned" idea for a minute. Think, if you will, of a traditional old-style bank building, one that looks like someone's idea of a classical Greek temple. Picture the four columns in front, and fix them in your mind as temperance, prudence, justice, and fortitude. Obviously they interact with one another. They must, since they have a common goal (in this case, the very practical business of holding up the roof). But each has its own identity as well. Think of them in that way, too — each as a tower of strength in itself.

The Church's premier teachers have explained the virtues to us — even the great St. Thomas Aquinas himself, who thought them so important that he wrote: "Every moral question can be reduced to the consideration of the virtues." But our perception of the virtues isn't limited to the classroom experience. The real lesson involved in learning about the virtues comes in putting them into use, in living them. That's why the examples set for us by the great men and women of the Church — its saints, canonized or not; its doers of mighty deeds — are so important. That's why the stories about what these people did mean so much to us, and why they're worth holding on to. Beyond their sheer dramatic appeal, they teach us something vital about life as it should be lived. Is any other lesson quite as important?

Before the stories begin, take a moment to consider the cardinal virtues on an individual basis.

Temperance. Easy enough, right? Taking care not to drink too much? Well, yes, but that's only part of it. An important part, to be sure, as some of the stories in the opening section suggest — one, for instance, on Matt Talbot, the Dublin workingman who turned from alcohol to a life of penitential service to the Lord, and another on Archbishop John Ireland, the Minnesota prelate whose relentless campaigns against excessive drinking earned him the title of "The Apostle of Temperance."

The real meaning of this virtue is much broader. "Self-control" comes close to capturing it, but again it's not the whole story. Temperance indeed lets us keep our physical desires in check, particularly those involving food and drink, as well as sexual activity. Beyond that, though, the temperate person will practice moderation and balance in *all* things. Temperance becomes a way of life — as it was for the Blessed Mother, who accepted everything, even her approaching death, in humility and patience; as it became for St. Peter, finally embracing his certain martyrdom, and as it was lived every day by St. Frances of Rome, a generous and loving woman whose life was always directed to a heavenly reward.

Prudence. Here's another virtue whose meaning tends to become a bit confused, thanks in part to public misunderstanding of the word. Think back to the popular comic portrayal of former President George Bush on *Saturday Night Live* — the one in which the actor taking the part of the president rejected any adventurous suggestion on the grounds that "it wouldn't be prudent." It was a humorous takeoff on Bush's own press-conference responses, of course, but it helped to perpetuate the idea that the prudent person is timid or overly cautious.

Not so. Prudence enables us to discern, to choose the proper course of behavior in a given situation. Here another popular reference might help. Remember the Spike Lee-Danny Aiello film that caused such a sensation a few years ago? *Do the Right Thing* was both its title and its enduring message. And that, in a phrase, is what prudence directs us to do — the right thing, making the right decision, because it is what God expects of us.

There's nothing timid or overly cautious about the men and women whose stories are told here — and who habitually did the right thing. In a special way that's true of St. Francis of Assisi, the beloved saint whose popularity inspired stories beyond counting, and, much closer to our own time, of Pope John XXIII. This good man, who spent most of his ecclesiastical career in the prudent circles of Vatican diplomacy, stunned the world by convoking the Second Vatican Council — a decision that proved to be not only "the right thing" but one that would change the face of the Church forever.

Justice. We're on more solid ground here as far as understanding is concerned; the meaning of justice as one of the virtues and its general perception by the public are one and the same. Justice demands that we be fair and righteous in our conduct, that in all our actions we respect the rights of others.

The ancient philosophers considered justice in the sense of "giving every man his due," true enough as far as it goes. Scripture put a fuller face on it, notably in the book of the prophet Amos. No one spoke more forcefully or more bluntly on the matter than Amos, who railed against the wealthy idlers and hypocrites of the Northern Kingdom, "You who oppress the weak and abuse the needy" (Amos 4:1). Enough of empty worship, of offerings made in vain, and the worthless sacrifice of animals, he said; instead, "let justice surge like water, and goodness like an unfailing stream" (Amos 5:24).

Theologians differentiate between the various forms of justice, several of which are depicted in these stories. The Emperor Constantine, for example, finally recognized the rights of Christians by allowing them to worship freely. One hundred years ago Pope Leo XIII ushered in a new era of Church teaching on social justice, and within our own lifetime Archbishop Oscar Romero became a martyr because he sought justice for the poor people of El Salvador.

Fortitude. Again, no problem here. To be a good Catholic, an effective Christian, one must be strong in the faith, a concept clear to us all. The virtue of fortitude gives us a strength of soul that enables us to overcome all the dangers of life that confront us, and to remain steadfast for the Lord.

This entire book — and much more — might easily be filled with stories of men and women who were models of fortitude for the faith, people not afraid to stand up and be counted. Some of those who were finally chosen are likely to be familiar: St. Lawrence, being put to death in a gridiron over an open flame, telling his torturers to turn him over, since he was already "done" on one side; the heroic Joan of Arc, whose bravery surpassed that of all her captors, and certainly that of those who did her in. What greater examples of fortitude might there be than the North American Martyrs, the seventeenth-century Jesuits who suffered ghastly torture as they tried to minister to the Hurons and Iroquois?

And finally, for courage of a different sort, there was Archbishop John Hughes, who let the anti-Catholics of his day know that he was fed up with their "twaddle" and called out parishioners by the thousands to protect their churches from physical harm. Today's tabloid headlines would probably call him a stand-up guy. In New York City, some one hundred fifty years ago, all Catholics stood a bit taller too — because John Hughes's courage gave them strength of their own.

A Mother Goes Home to Her Son

The 'Legend of the Madonna' Describes Mary's Earthly Farewell

From the earliest days of Christianity, Mary has been a singular model for all followers of Jesus. Mary, the Mother of Christ and the Mother of the Church, practiced all the virtues perfectly and served as the example, down through the centuries, for all who have followed her.

The Blessed Virgin had no concern for earthly pleasures. Instead she gladly yielded to the will of God and embraced all that was given her — joy and sorrow, laughter and tears — in patience and love.

That would have been true, certainly, at the time of her death — the beginning of the heavenly journey that would reunite her with her beloved Son. The ancient and reverent "legend of the Madonna" recounted here — a pious tale that reflects the unique devotion that early Christians felt for Christ's Mother — describes Mary's willing acceptance of the end of her earthly life. The story prompted countless generations of earlier Catholics, young and old, to turn from the trifling attractions of the world to thoughts of eternal life in the Lord.

Story retold from traditional sources.

Mary's last days on earth were spent in the house of John, on Mount Sion, where she awaited with love and patience the time when she would rejoin her Son.

One day an angel, dazzling in a white gown, appeared to her with a startling message:

"Hail, O Mary, blessed by him who gave salvation to Israel! I bring you a branch of palm gathered in Paradise; command that it be carried before your bier. In three days your soul shall leave your body and you shall enter into Paradise, where your Son awaits your coming."

Mary hardly knew what to say, but she quickly found her voice.

"If I have found grace in your eyes," she said, "tell me first your name. Then grant that the Apostles, my brothers, may be reunited with me before I die, so that I may give up my soul to God in their presence. And then I pray that my soul will not be frightened by any spirit of darkness, nor any evil angel be allowed to have power over me."

"Why ask my name?" the angel replied. "It is the Great and the Wonderful. And yes, all the Apostles will be reunited with you this day. He who in former times transported the prophet Habbakuk from Judea to Jerusalem by the hair of his head can just as easily bring the Apostles here. Finally, don't be afraid of the evil spirit. Aren't you the one who bruised his head, and destroyed his kingdom?"

With that, the angel vanished from sight, departing into heaven. But the palm branch he left behind glowed from every leaf, and sparkled as bright as starlight. Mary lighted the lamps and waited for the hour that was to come.

And at that very moment John, who was preaching at Ephesus, and Peter, who was preaching at Antioch — and all the Apostles, dispersed in different parts of the world — were suddenly caught up as by a miraculous power, and found themselves at Mary's door. She was astonished when she saw them, but blessed them and thanked the Lord. She gave John the shining palm left by the angel, asking him to carry it in front of her at the time of her burial. After kneeling down and leading them all in prayer, Mary went to bed to compose herself for death. And John wept bitter tears of sadness.

That night — as Peter stood at the head of Mary's bed, and John at its foot — a mighty sound filled the house, and delicious perfumes filled the chamber. Then Jesus himself appeared, accompanied by angels, patriarchs, and prophets. They gathered around the bed of the Virgin, singing hymns of joy. And Jesus spoke:

"Arise, my beloved! Receive the crown that is destined for you."

And Mary, answering, said:

"My heart is ready, for it was written of me that I should do your will." Then all the angels and blessed spirits who accompanied Jesus began to sing and rejoice.

And the soul of Mary left her body and was received into the arms of her Son, and together they ascended into heaven.

The Apostles looked up, saying, "O most prudent Virgin, remember us when you come to glory." Then they laid the body of the Virgin in a tomb in the Valley of Jehoshaphat.

On the third day Jesus said to the angels, "What honor shall I confer on her who was my mother on earth?" And they answered, "Lord, let not that body which was your temple ever see corruption, but place her beside you on your throne in heaven."

Jesus consented, and the Archangel Michael brought the soul of Our Lady to him. The Lord said, "Rise up, my dove, my undefiled, for you shall not remain in the darkness of the grave, nor shall you ever see corruption." Immediately the soul of Mary rejoined her body, and she rose up glorious from the tomb, ascending into heaven — surrounded and welcomed by troops of angels, blowing their silver trumpets, touching their golden lutes, singing and rejoicing as they sang: "Who is she who rises as the morning, fair as the moon, clear as the sun, and terrible as an army with banners?"

'...Upon This Rock'

St. Peter's Human Failings Only Enhanced His Greatness

It's easy for Christians to see themselves reflected in St. Peter. Despite his closeness to Jesus, he was prone to the same human failings that afflict the followers of Christ today.

How many times did he miss Jesus' message (and how many times did Jesus patiently explain it all over again)? How many times did he play the fool, even attempting to walk on water because that's what his Lord had done? How many times did he prove himself weak and inadequate, to the point of denying his Master — yes, three times over, and yes, before the cock had crowed?

And with it all, the homely goodness of Peter would prevail. His human imperfections ultimately magnified his inner strength, revealing the depth of his virtues. It would be Peter, after all, who showed the other disciples the only path they could follow. When Jesus asked the disciples, "But who do you say that I am?" it was Peter who answered: "You are the Messiah, the Son of the living God" (Matthew 16:15-16). When Jesus asked the Twelve if they would join the other followers who were leaving him, Peter was the one who spoke up: "Master, to whom shall we go? You have the words of eternal life" (John 6:68). And when Jesus laid the foundation for his Church, it was Peter to whom he turned: "... You are Peter, and upon this rock I will build my church, and the gates of the netherworld shall not prevail against it. I will give you the keys to the kingdom of heaven. Whatever you bind on earth shall be bound in heaven; and whatever you loose on earth shall be loosed in heaven" (Matthew 16:19-20).

Christians revered Peter from the earliest days of the Church. Here are two of the stories about him that his followers held close to their hearts. They still do the same today.

First story based on Acts 12:3-19;
second story retold from traditional sources.

1. An Angel Frees Peter From His Prison Bonds

The night was bleak, the atmosphere chill. For the third time in his life Peter found himself in prison, and this time seemed sure to be the last. Herod Agrippa, the king, had unleashed a reign of terror against Judea's fledgling Christian community. Many were thrown into jail, and an executioner's sword had slain James, the brother of John. Peter was next on the list, marked for the same fate.

All the followers of Jesus were praying for the safety of the man left by the Lord to lead them, but his jailers left no hope for his escape. Sixteen soldiers formed Peter's personal guard, with shifts of four men on duty at all times — two at his side, inside the dungeon cell, two more at the gate. And for good measure, iron chains bound Peter to the cold floor. Fitful sleep came to him from time to time, providing a moment's respite from his anguish; but even as he dozed, Peter knew that in the morning he faced certain death.

Then, in the middle of the night, he was startled by a light so bright that it filled the cell with a brilliant glow. Suddenly an angel of the Lord was at his side, tapping him awake.

"Get up quickly," the angel said. "Put on your belt and sandals. Put on your cloak and follow me." Amazed, Peter saw that the chains had fallen from his wrists. He did as the angel commanded and was astonished as they passed one guard after another. The iron gate leading to the city opened miraculously for them, and as they walked toward an alleyway the angel vanished as mysteriously as he had appeared.

Recovering his senses, Peter realized he had been rescued by the Lord. He slipped through the night to the house of Mary, the mother of John who was also called Mark, knowing that many of the disciples would be there. A maid, overjoyed to hear his voice at the gate, rushed to tell the others that Peter was there — only to be told that she must be out of her mind! But Peter persisted with his knocking and soon stood among his friends, letting them know that the Lord had set him free. Then he withdrew to a safer place of refuge.

At daybreak the jail where Peter had been held was the scene of riot and commotion. A search turned up no sign of the former prisoner, and Herod ordered the guards who had been on duty to be put to death.

2. Peter Returns to Rome, And to the Glory of Martyrdom

It was no time for anyone who called himself a Christian to be in Rome. It was the year 64, in the time of the Emperor Nero, a madman who was intent on making followers of Jesus the scapegoats for the fire that had devastated the city in July. The warning signals were all up, and some Christians were making their way out of the city. One of them was their leader, Peter, yielding to the pleas of friends to save himself.

He was barely two miles from Rome, on the old Appian Way, when who should appear before him but the Lord himself. Peter was dumbfounded.

"Domine, quo vadis?" he stammered. "Lord, whither goest thou?"

"I go to Rome," Jesus replied sadly, "to be crucified a second time."

In an instant, Peter understood the Lord's message. He knew he must quickly return to Rome.

There he resumed his teaching and his ministry to all, his life in constant danger. The atrocities Roman officials committed against the Christians — on Nero's direct orders — defied belief. Some were sewn inside animal skins to be torn to pieces by dogs. Some were crucified. Still others were covered with tar and then set afire — simply to provide torchlight for the emperor's garden. Nero himself drove through this mad scene, disguised as a charioteer.

Finally Peter was captured, along with Paul, and thrown into the Mamertine Prison. Even there he continued to preach the message of salvation through Jesus — so convincingly that his two guards, as well as many fellow prisoners, were converted.

Finally he was sentenced to death by crucifixion in the Circus of Caligula, at the foot of the Vatican. At the last moment, Peter hesitated.

"I cannot meet death as the Master did," he told his executioners. "Place the cross upside down."

The guards agreed to this last request, and in that cruel fashion Peter went in glory to rejoin the Lord.

Earthquake and Volcano

The Veil of St. Agatha Saves a Frightened City

Living a life of heroic virtue is surely a sign of sanctity, and just as surely the phrase applies in a special way to St. Agatha (d. 251), virgin and martyr.

In these words — preserved just as they appeared in a Catholic text published in Boston more than a century ago — earlier generations learned how this young Sicilian woman, subject to unspeakable tortures, nonetheless remained virtuous throughout her ordeal. In whatever style it is told, the story of St. Agatha still teaches a lasting lesson: by fixing her mind on the heavenly kingdom that would be hers, she let that vision guide her every thought and action.

Even in the hands of her captors, understanding the fate that awaited her, she prayed: "Jesus Christ, Lord of all, thou seest my heart, thou knowest my desires. Do thou alone possess all that I am. I am thy sheep: make me worthy to overcome the devil."

The miracles associated with St. Agatha apparently continued beyond her lifetime. A year or so after her death, when Mount Etna erupted in volcanic fury, fiery streams of lava approached the outskirts of Catania. Frightened citizens took the veil of Agatha from her tomb, hooked the end of it on a lance, and advanced toward the flames in procession. As they drew near, the flow stopped and the city was saved — and, as legend has it, all the unbaptized who witnessed the miracle were converted on the spot.

Story from *A Handbook of Christian Symbols and Stories of the Saints*, by Clara Erskine Clement, Ticknor and Co., 1886 (republished by Gale Research Co., 1971).

The Emperor Decius strangled his predecessor, Philip; and desiring to make it appear that he did this because Philip was a Christian, and not for his own advancement, he instituted great persecutions of the Christians throughout his empire. He made Quintianus king of Sicily.

Here, at Catania, dwelt Agatha, a maiden of great beauty, whom Quintianus tempted with presents, flattery, and promises, without success. He then gave her to Frondisia, who was a courtesan with nine daughters, all as wicked as possible, and promised her great riches if she would subdue Agatha to his wishes. Frondisia attempted to influence Agatha by every means in her power for thirty-three days; but Agatha remained fixed in her purity, and her faith in Jesus.

At the end of that time Frondisia said to Quintianus, "Sooner shall that sword at thy side become like liquid lead, and the rocks dissolve and flow like water, than the heart of this damsel be subdued to thy will."

Then Quintianus in fury commanded her to be brought, and attempted to move her by threats; but she said, "If thou shouldst throw me to the wild beasts, the power of Christ would render them weak as lambs; if thou shouldst kindle a fire to consume me, the angels would quench it with their dews from heaven; if thou shouldst tear me with scourges the Holy Spirit within me would render thy tortures harmless." Then the tyrant ordered her to be beaten, and her bosom to be torn with shears. After that she was thrown into a dark dungeon.

At midnight there came an aged man bearing a vase of ointment, and a youth with a torch. It was St. Peter and an angel, but Agatha did not know them; and the light that filled the dungeon so frightened the guards that they fled, leaving the door open.

Then one said to the maiden, "Arise and fly." Then St. Peter healed her wounds with celestial ointment, and vanished from her sight.

The rage of Quintianus not being satisfied, he sent for her again, and was astonished at the wonderful cure of her wounds. "Who hath healed thee?" asked he; she replied, "He, whom I confess and adore with my heart and with my lips, hath sent his Apostle, and helped me, and delivered me."

Then Quintianus ordered her to be burned; and as she was thrown in the fire, a great earthquake shook the city, and the people ran to the palace, crying, "This has fallen upon us because of the sufferings of this Christian damsel"; and they threatened to burn Quintianus if he did not desist. So he ordered her to be taken from the flames, and she was borne again to prison, scorched, and in great agony. Here she entreated God to release her and take her to heaven; which prayer was heard, for immediately she died.

Tower of Strength

'I Am Prepared for the Worst,' Said St. Lawrence

The story of St. Lawrence (d. 258) is one that was familiar to all Catholic schoolchildren in generations past. And the chilling, even frightening, account of his heroic martyrdom — right down to the courageous taunt he offered to his executioners — invariably left a lasting impression on those who heard it.

It was this same account of Lawrence's death that became part of the Church's tradition even within the lifetime of his contemporaries, some of whom ascribed the conversion of the entire city of Rome to his prayers. As early as the fourth century his followers honored him by building a chapel at his burial site, and to this day he is remembered by name in the first Eucharistic Prayer of the Mass.

Story from *Little Lives of the Great Saints*, by John O'Kane
Murray, P. J. Kenedy & Sons, 1910.

When St. Sixtus became pope in 257, he ordained Lawrence deacon; and, though he was yet young, the pontiff appointed him first among the seven deacons, who served in the Church of the Eternal City. He thus became the pope's archdeacon. This was a charge of great importance, to which was annexed the care of the treasury of the Church and the distribution of its revenues among the poor.

In the year 257 the Emperor Valerian published his bloody edicts against the Catholic Church. He foolishly flattered himself that its destruction was merely a question of time and rigorous persecution, not knowing it to be the work of the Almighty. His plan was as simple as it was stupid and blindly brutal. He would cut off the shepherds and disperse the flocks; and hence he began his barbarously elaborate scheme by ordering all bishops, priests, and deacons to be put to death.

Lawrence was full of joy, for he had just heard that he should soon be called to God. But a pressing duty was to be performed. He set out immediately to seek the poor widows and orphans, and gave them all the money that he had in his keeping. He even sold the sacred vessels to increase the sum. This was also given to the poor.

"Bring your concealed treasures to light," a Roman official demanded of St. Lawrence. "The emperor has need of them for the support of his army."

"The Church," calmly replied St. Lawrence, "is, in truth, rich; nor has the emperor any treasure equal to its possessions. I will take pleasure in showing you a valuable part; but allow me a little time to set everything in order and to make an inventory."

Lawrence went all over the city, seeking out from street to street the poor who were supported by the charity of the Church. He knew where to go, and well the poor knew him. On the third day he had his *treasures* gathered together. He placed them in rows before the church, and they consisted of hundreds of the aged, the decrepit, the blind, the lame, the maimed, the lepers, widows, virgins, and young orphans.

He then proceeded to the residence of the prefect, and invited him to come and see the treasures of the Church. The haughty official was astonished to behold such a number of poor wretches. To him it was a sickening sight that aroused anger, fury, and disappointment.

"What are you displeased at?" exclaimed the dauntless Lawrence. "Behold the treasures I promised you! I have even added to them the gems and precious stones — those widows and consecrated virgins who form the Church's crown. It has no other riches. Take these and use them for the advantage of Rome, the emperor, and yourself."

The enraged prefect, no longer able to control himself, cried out: "Do you thus mock me? Are the ensigns of Roman power to be thus insulted? I know that you wish to die. This is your foolish vanity. But you will not take leave of life so soon as you imagine. I will see to that. I will protract your tortures. Your death shall be slow and bitter. You shall die by inches."

The saint was stripped, and his naked body torn with a kind of whips called scorpions. After this severe scourging, plates of red-hot iron were applied to his bleeding sides. Lawrence, in spite of such appalling treatment, presented a joyful countenance, while the prefect raged with the fury of a wild beast. He could not comprehend how any human being could cheerfully endure such punishment. He even accused the martyr of being a magician, and threatened that unless he at once sacrificed to the gods he would add to his torments.

"Your torments," answered St. Lawrence, "will have an end, and I do not fear them. Do what you will to me. I am prepared for the worst."

The prefect at once ordered him to be beaten with leaden plummets, and soon his whole body was a bruised and torn mass. The saint prayed to God to receive his soul; but a voice from heaven, which was heard by all who stood around, told him that he had yet much to suffer.

Lawrence was next placed on a rack, and his suffering body stretched so that every limb was dislocated. His flesh was torn with hooks, but he did not flinch. Calm and cheerful, he prayed and suffered. An angel was seen to wipe his face and bleeding shoulders, and the sight of the blessed spirit converted one of the soldiers, who went up to the saint and asked to be baptized.

The frantic prefect now ordered a large gridiron to be procured. It was soon in readiness, and live coals, partly extinguished, were thrown under it that the martyr might be slowly burned. He was placed naked upon this iron bed, and bound with chains over a slow fire. His flesh was soon broiled, and little by little the cruel heat was forcing its way into his very heart and bowels. A light beautiful to behold shone from his face, and his burning body exhaled a most sweet odor. The martyr, says St. Augustine, felt not the torments of the persecutor, so strong and vivid was his desire of possessing Christ. Thus in the midst of appalling torments he enjoyed that peace which the world cannot give — the peace of God.

Turning to the prefect, St. Lawrence said to him, with a cheerful smile: "Let my body now be turned; one side is broiled enough."

The cruel prefect ordered him to be turned. It was done, and the saint said, "Eat now, for it is well done." The prefect again insulted him; but the martyr continued in earnest prayer, with sighs and tears imploring the divine mercy with his last breath for the conversion of the city of Rome. Having finished his prayer, a ray of immortality seemed to light up his manly countenance; he lifted his eyes toward heaven, and his pure, holy, and heroic spirit went to receive the shining reward promised to those who suffer persecution for the sake of justice and religion.

A Cross in the Sky

Constantine's Heavenly Vision Spurs Him to Victory

The colorful life of the Roman Emperor Constantine (c. 285-337) inspired a host of stories and legends, many of which persist to this day. The son of Emperor Constantius and St. Helena, discoverer of the True Cross (see Section 2), he was said to have had a vision of the Apostles Peter and Paul that would eventually draw him to the faith, and when he founded the city that bears his name — Constantinople — he was reported to have marked out its boundaries with the same lance that pierced Christ's side.

But the best-known tale about Constantine is the one of the cross in the sky, told here by Father Edward Curran, a priest of the Brooklyn diocese who in the 1930s published a collection of stories designed to strengthen the faith of schoolchildren. Whatever historians may care to believe about the miracle, the fact is that Constantine won this all-important battle over his rival Maxentius, became emperor, and finally ushered in an era of justice for Christians by ending persecution and placing them under the protection of the empire.

Story from *Great Moments in Catholic History:*
100 Memorable Events in Catholic History Told in Picture and Story, by Rev. Edward Lodge Curran, Grosset & Dunlap, 1937.

Constantine the Great was born in Servia. His father was Constantius, a Roman officer, who became emperor of Rome in 305. His mother was Helena.

At the time of his father's death Constantine was with the Roman army in Britain. The popularity and bravery of Constantine made him loved by the men of the army, captains as well as spearmen. With great shouts and cheering the soldiers selected him to succeed his father as emperor of Rome. His brother-in-law, Licinius, was already emperor in the East.

Constantine immediately marched toward Rome in order to take over his position as emperor. Meanwhile a man named Maxentius, the wicked son of Maximian, one of the cruelest emperors who ever persecuted the Church, proclaimed that *he* was emperor of Rome.

Northern Italy hailed Constantine as emperor. He then marched against the army of Maxentius. Suddenly, on the march, Constantine fixed his eyes upon the sky. A strange sight appeared before him. He saw a Cross. On the Cross he saw some Latin words: *"In Hoc Signo Vinces."*

He was not far from Rome. He was near the Milvian Bridge, where the troops of Maxentius were waiting to destroy him and prevent him from becoming emperor. The message of the Cross caused him to proceed courageously. He no longer feared. His tired troops became inspired. "In this sign," said the Cross, "thou shalt conquer."

Pledging his loyalty to the Cross, which he recognized as the Cross of Christ, Constantine marched on to defeat the troops of Maxentius. By the battle of the Milvian Bridge, on October 28, 312, Constantine the Great became Roman emperor in the West.

He had marched beneath the Cross of Christ and conquered. Other emperors had tried to destroy the Cross and were themselves destroyed. The victory of Constantine brought freedom and peace to the Catholic Church.

Constantine read and studied. He did not hasten his conversion. Toward the close of his life, he was baptized and received into the Church by Pope Sylvester I.

The Cross of Christ had conquered for Constantine at the Milvian Bridge. In the sign of the Cross we Catholics can conquer everything in life.

Giver of Good Things

St. Nicholas Proves Himself Generous and Just

Historians don't have all that much to say about St. Nicholas of Myra (fourth century), because the facts are admittedly hard to come by. But the storytellers — ah, that's something else! History's shortcomings are more than made up in legend and lore, and over the centuries the bishop who was Nicholas of Myra has been transformed into Jolly Old St. Nick.

That there was such a bishop is beyond doubt; Nicholas has been venerated in the East (and especially in Russia, which considers him its patron saint) since the sixth century. The Western Church has revered him for a thousand years, and generations of children have thought of him as the merry if somewhat mysterious friend who leaves gifts in memory of the baby Jesus at Christmas.

Tradition supplies us amply with what history does not tell, as these little stories from an old text illustrate. Nicholas's generosity comes to the fore in the legend of the gifts of gold he leaves as dowry for the daughters of a former nobleman, now impoverished. And his determination to head off the execution of three innocent men reveals another side of Nicholas: his thirst for justice in the name of the Lord.

Selection from *A Handbook of Christian Symbols and Stories of the Saints*, by Clara Erskine Clement, Ticknor and Co., 1886 (republished by Gale Research Co., 1971).

According to legend Nicholas was born of illustrious Christian parents, after they had been many years married without having children; and it was thought that this son was given by God as a reward for the alms that they had bestowed upon the Church and the poor, as well as for the prayers they had offered. Their home was in Panthera, a city of Lycia in Asia Minor. The very day of his birth this wonderful child arose in his bath, and joining his hands, praised God that he had brought him into the world.

On account of his holy dispositions his parents early dedicated him to the service of the Church. While still young, Nicholas lost both father and mother; and he regarded himself as but God's steward over the vast wealth he inherited.

A certain nobleman of Panthera, who was very rich, lost all his property, and became so destitute that he could not provide for his three daughters, and he feared that he should be driven to sacrifice their virtue for money to keep them from starvation. The daughters were filled with grief, and having no bread knew not where to look for aid.

Now Nicholas heard of this, and resolved to relieve them. So he took a good sum of gold, and tied it in a handkerchief, and went to the house by night to try how he could give it to them and not be himself seen. As he lingered near the dwelling, the moon shone out brightly and showed an open window. Then Nicholas threw the gold inside the house and hastened away. The money fell at the feet of the unhappy father; and with it he portioned his eldest daughter, and she was married. Again Nicholas did the same, and the second daughter received this sum.

But now the nobleman resolved to watch, in order to know who was thus kind to him; and when Nicholas went the third time, he seized him by his robe, saying "O Nicholas! Servant of God! Why seek to hide thyself?" Then Nicholas made him promise that he would tell no man. This was but one of the many charities that he practiced in Panthera.

At length he determined to go to Palestine. On the voyage a sailor fell overboard and was drowned, but St. Nicholas restored his life; and when a storm arose, and they were about to perish, the sailors fell at his feet and implored him to save them; and when he prayed, the storm ceased.

After his return from Palestine Nicholas dwelt in the city of Myra, where he was unknown, and he lived in great humility. At length the bishop of Myra died; and a revelation was made to the clergy to the effect that the first man who should come to the church the next morning would be the man whom God had chosen for their bishop. So when Nicholas came early to the church to pray, as was his custom, the clergy led him into the church and consecrated him bishop.

He showed himself well worthy of his new dignity in every way, but especially by his charities, which were beyond account. At one time a dreadful famine prevailed in his diocese; and when he heard that ships were in the port of Myra laden with wheat, he requested the captains to give him a hundred hogsheads of wheat out of each vessel. But they dared not do this; for the grain was measured at Alexandria, and would be again measured at Constantinople, where they were to deliver it. Then Nicholas said that if they obeyed him, it would happen by the grace of God that their cargoes should not be diminished. So they complied; and when they arrived at the granary of the emperor they found as much wheat in their ships as when they left Alexandria. And moreover, that which they gave St. Nicholas was miraculously increased; for he fed the people so that they had enough to eat, and still sufficient remained to sow their fields for the next year.

At one time Constantine sent certain tribunes to put down a rebellion in Phrygia. On their journey they stopped at Myra, and Nicholas invited them to his table; but as they were about to sit down, he heard that the prefect of the city was preparing to execute three innocent men, and the people were greatly moved thereat. Then Nicholas hastened to the place of execution, followed by his guests.

When they arrived, the men were already kneeling, with their eyes bound, and the executioner was ready with his sword. St. Nicholas seized the sword and commanded the men to be released. The tribunes looked on in wonder, but no one dared to resist the good bishop. Even the prefect sought his pardon, which he granted after much hesitation. After this, when the tribunes went on their way, they did not forget St. Nicholas.

A Favorite Among Saints

Stories About Francis of Assisi Inspire a Singular Devotion

When Catholics are asked to name their favorite saint, they seem to agree on their choice to a remarkable degree. The winner, of course, is St. Francis of Assisi, whose appeal endures from century to century.

It's easy to see why. The popular image we have of Francis (c. 1181-1226) is that of an eminently good and selfless man, embodying all the virtues, totally in tune with his God and with the world around him. And wonder of wonders, the image turns out to be true. That helps to account for his lasting popularity: Francis appeals to people of our time every bit as much as he did to those of his own.

Part of that appeal is based on his simplicity, but that word must be understood in its proper sense. Francis did not choose a simple way of life for its own sake. Rather, he did so — as all truly prudent people do — to enable him to be possessed by God completely, without distraction; to choose every action in a way that would bring him closer to the Lord.

Legends sprang up about Francis even in his own lifetime, all of them designed to exalt him as a holy man constantly uniting himself with Christ. Here are some of the best-known stories, beginning with an account of Francis' journey to Rome, in 1209, to seek papal approval of his somewhat revolutionary plans for religious life. Pope Innocent III was hesitant about saying yes — until a dream helped to open his eyes. The next three stories are taken from the Fioretti — *the "Little Flowers" of St. Francis, a collection of tales and legends that appeared about one hundred fifty years after his death. The section closes with two famous Franciscan prayers — Francis' own "The Canticle of Brother Sun," as well as "The Prayer of St. Francis," recited in his name today by followers the world over.*

Stories 1, 2, and 4 and prayers from *Brother Francis*, edited
by Lawrence Cunningham, Harper & Row, 1972; story 3
from *The Little Flowers of St. Francis of Assisi*, St. Anthony
Guild Press, 1958.

1. The Pope's Dream

Catholic that he was, Francis insisted on seeking the approval of this new form of life from Pope Innocent III. In 1209 he set out with his by now twelve followers for Rome.

Innocent was understandably reluctant when Francis first presented his case. Rome is, after all, the seat of prudence, and when a comparatively unknown youth enters the papal chambers seeking universal approval of a novel form of religious life, the prudent thing would seem to be to ignore him and his idea. And it appears that Innocent acted prudently.

But even popes sleep and even popes dream, and during the night after his interview with Francis, Innocent dreamt a strange dream. He saw the huge Roman basilica of St. John Lateran, the Mother Church of Christendom, quaking on its ancient foundations, threatening to lean over and fall as a great tree before a storm. Suddenly a little man appeared and threw his thin body against the toppling structure and alone held it up before the nameless furies threatening it. The face of the little man was plain: it was that of Innocent's petitioner of the day before.

It would not be prudent for a pope to change a decision on the basis of a dream, but he sent for Francis, and listened to him far more carefully. Like every other human being, Innocent was touched by the personality before him. But because prudence subordinates personalities to principles, Innocent consulted his advisers. They concluded with the pope that Francis' revolutionary ideas had merit and further to deny their validity would be to deny that one could live a life described as ideal in the Gospels. Innocent gave his verbal endorsement and promised more definite approval if Francis' plan proved practical.

2. Converting the Sultan

Francis, fired by his zeal for Christ and a desire for martyrdom, once took twelve holy companions and journeyed across the ocean to go directly to the sultan of Egypt. When he arrived at the territory of the Saracens, the passes were guarded by ferociously cruel men who allowed no Christian to pass alive. However, it pleased God to save them all from death, but they were beaten, bound, and taken in chains to the sultan.

Before the sultan, St. Francis, filled with the Holy Spirit, preached the faith of Christ so fervently that he was even prepared to be tested by fire. The sultan was quite touched by this devotion, by his steadfast faith, and by the utter unworldliness that he saw in him. St. Francis would not accept any gift, even though he was the poorest of men. He was concerned only to suffer willingly for his faith. The sultan, as a result of this, listened to him willingly, granted both St. Francis and his companions permission to preach where they wished, and invited him to come often to see him. The sultan also gave them a safe-conduct pass so that they would not be harmed by his followers.

Armed with this permission, St. Francis sent his companions two by two to different parts of the country to preach the faith of Christ. He chose one area and with a brother went there. On arrival, they stopped at an inn to rest. At the inn there was a woman, beautiful in body but tainted in soul, who tempted St. Francis to sin. St. Francis said, "I accept your proposition. Let us be off to bed." She led him to a room, and St. Francis said to her, "I will show you a beautiful bed." There was a great fire there in the fireplace, and St. Francis, rapt by the Spirit, stripped off his clothes and entered the fire and then invited the girl to likewise undress and come join him in that beautiful spot. St. Francis stood in that fire for a long time with a smiling face and was neither burned nor even scorched. The girl was so overcome by this miracle and so penitent in her heart for her sin that she not only repented her evil but converted perfectly to the faith of Christ and, through her, many other souls were saved in that area.

After a bit, St. Francis realized that he could do no more in those parts and, through the intervention of divine guidance, decided to send all of his companions back to the Christian lands. All together they went back to the sultan to make their good-byes. The sultan said to him, "Francis, I would most happily embrace the faith of Christ, but I fear to do so now. For if those about me heard of it, they would kill not only me but you and all your companions. Since there is so much good that you can do and there are so many grave duties that I must discharge, I am unwilling to provoke either your death or mine. So tell me what I must do to be saved, and I will follow your advice as best I can."

St. Francis responded, "My Lord, I must go now and return to my country. After my return, when by the grace of God my death has come, and I have gone to heaven, I will send you two friars who will come to you to baptize you in the name of Christ, and so you will be saved. My Lord Jesus Christ has revealed this to me. In the interim, free yourself from all entanglements so that when the grace of God comes, he may find you devout and faithful." This the sultan promised, and this he did.

After this, St. Francis and his companions returned to their land, and after a time Francis died and rendered his soul to God. The sultan, informed of the death, set guards at all the frontiers with instructions that if two men should come with clothing similar to that of St. Francis, they should be brought to the sultan without the least delay to bring him the promised salvation. In the meantime St.

Francis appeared to two friars and told them to go across the ocean to the sultan and bring him the long-sought-after salvation. They immediately complied, and the guards on seeing them brought them to the sultan. The sultan received them with great joy and said, "Now I know that the good God has sent his servants for my salvation, just as St. Francis promised me after his divine revelation." Receiving the instruction of the faith of Christ, he was baptized by the Brothers and regenerated in Christ. The sultan later died, and his soul was saved by the merits and intervention of St. Francis.

3. Preaching to the Flock

Going by the prompting of the Holy Spirit, without taking thought of the way or the road, St. Francis came to a village called Savurniano. And he began to preach, but first of all he commanded the swallows who were singing that they should keep silence, until he had done preaching; and the swallows obeyed him. And he preached with so much fervor that all the men and women in that village were minded to go forth and abandon the village. But St. Francis suffered them not, and said to them: "Do not be in haste, and do not go hence, and I will order that which you must do, for the salvation of your souls"; and then he thought of his Third Order, for the salvation of the whole world. And he left them much comforted, and well-disposed to penance; and he departed thence, and went by Cannaio and Bevagno.

And passing along, in fervor of soul, he lifted up his eyes and saw many trees standing by the way, and filled with a countless multitude of little birds; at which St. Francis wondered, and said to his companions: "Wait a little for me in the road, and I will go and preach to my sisters the birds." And he entered into the field, and began to preach to the birds that were on the ground. And suddenly those that were in the trees came around him, and together they all remained silent, so long as it pleased St. Francis to speak; and even after he had finished they would not depart until he had given them his blessing. And according to Brother Masseo afterward related to Brother James of La Massa, St. Francis went among them and touched them with his cloak, and none of them moved.

The substance of the sermon was this: "My little sisters, the birds, you are much beholden to God your Creator, and in all places you ought to praise him, because he has given you liberty to fly about in all places, and has given you double and triple raiment. Know also that he preserved your race in the ark of Noah that your species might not perish. And again, you are beholden to him for the element of air, which he has appointed for you; and for this also, that you neither sow nor reap, but God feeds you, and gives you the brooks and fountains for your drink, the mountains and valleys also for your refuge, and the tall trees wherein to make your nests. And since you know neither how to sew nor to spin, God clothes you, you and your young ones. Wherefore your Creator loves you much, since he has bestowed on you so many benefits. And therefore beware, my little sisters, of the sin of ingratitude, and study always to please God."

As St. Francis spoke thus to them, all the multitude of these birds opened their beaks, and stretched out their necks; and opening their wings, and reverently bowing their heads to the earth, by their acts and by their songs they showed that the words of the Holy Father gave them the greatest delight.

And St. Francis rejoiced, and was glad with them, and marveled much at such a multitude of birds, and at their beautiful variety, and their attention and familiarity; for all which he devoutly praised their Creator in them. Finally, having finished his sermon, St. Francis made the sign of the Cross over them, and gave them leave to depart; and thereupon all those birds arose in the air, with wonderful singing; and after the fashion of the sign of the Cross that St. Francis had made over them, they divided themselves into four parts; and one part flew toward the east, and another to the west, another to the south, and another to the north, and all departing went their way singing wonderful songs; signifying by this, that as St. Francis, standard-bearer of the Cross of Christ, had preached to them, and made on them the sign of the Cross, after which they had divided themselves, going to the four parts of the world; so the preaching of the Cross of Christ, renewed by St. Francis, should be carried by him and by his Brothers to the whole world; and that these Brothers, after the fashion of the birds, should possess nothing of their own in this world, but commit their lives solely to the providence of God.

In the praise of Christ. Amen.

4. Brother Wolf

While St. Francis was staying in the town of Gubbio, there appeared a huge wolf. It was so ferocious and terrible that it devoured not only animals but also men. The citizens of the town were so terrified that they always went out fully armed as if ready to go to war. But, despite this, they were helpless, especially when a single man met the wolf. Because of their fear, nobody would even venture out of the house.

Because of this, St. Francis (who felt great pity for the people) made up his mind to go and find the wolf, even though everyone told him not to. Still, making the sign of the Cross, he went out one day with his companions, putting his trust in God.

His companions hung back, but St. Francis took the road leading to the place where the wolf was often found. A number of people followed in order to see a miracle, and when the open-mouthed wolf approached St. Francis, the saint made the sign of the Cross over the wolf and called out to him, "Come to me, Brother Wolf, and I order you, in the name of Christ, neither to harm me nor the others."

Incredible as it seems, the moment St. Francis made the sign of the Cross, the wolf closed his mouth and stopped dead in his tracks. When he heard the order, he came meekly to the feet of St. Francis and lay down.

Then St. Francis spoke to him, "Brother Wolf, you have done much damage in these parts and committed great crimes by maiming and killing God's creatures without his permission. You haven't stopped at this but also maimed and killed men who are made in the likeness of God. You ought to be treated like a robber and a murderer and handed over to the hangman. The people hate and curse you, and this land is an enemy to you. But, Brother Wolf, I want to make peace between you and these people. If you will stop harming them, they, in turn, will forgive you, and neither men nor dogs will pester you in the future."

When St. Francis said this, the wolf showed his agreement with the words of the saint by signaling with his body and tail and ears and with a nod of his head showed his compliance. Then St. Francis said, "Brother Wolf, since you are ready to make peace and keep your word, I promise that these people will give you enough to eat during your life so that you need not starve. I understand that you did these evil things because of hunger. Since I have begged this favor, Brother Wolf, you must promise me to harm neither animal nor man. Do you promise this?" And the wolf, with a nod of his head, promised.

Then St. Francis said, "Brother Wolf, I want you to give me a sign that you have promised so I can have faith in you." St. Francis put out his hand as a sign of their pact and the wolf lifted its paw and tamely put it in the hand of St. Francis, giving the best sign of faith that he could. Then St. Francis said, "Brother Wolf, I command you in the name of Jesus Christ to come with me without fear, and we can go and make peace in the name of God." And the wolf obediently followed him as a meek lamb would.

The citizens of the town were stupefied. The news spread everywhere, and in a moment the people — young and old, men and women — lined the piazza to see St. Francis with the wolf. When St. Francis saw the crowd, he stepped forward and began to preach to them. He told them that God permitted such evils because of sinfulness and that they should fear the pain of eternal damnation more than a wolf, who can only kill their bodies. He said that they should fear the opening of the jaws of hell more than the jaws of a simple animal. "Be converted, beloved of God, and do penance for your sins, and God will free you from the wolf today and the gates of hell tomorrow."

When he had finished his talk, St. Francis said, "Listen to me, my brothers. Brother Wolf, who is here before you, has promised and sworn peace with you now and in the future; he will do you no harm if you will give him a bit to eat. And I promise that he will keep his end of the bargain." The people unanimously promised to feed him daily. Then St. Francis said to the wolf, "And you, Brother Wolf, do you promise to keep the peace and not harm the animals or men or any other creature?" And the wolf, kneeling down with head bowed, made signs with his tail and ears to indicate that he wished to keep the pact.

St. Francis said, "Brother Wolf, I want you to make the sign of agreement that you made outside the city gate here among the people so that you will show that you will not betray the pact that I have made in your name." And the wolf put his right paw in the hand of St. Francis. With this, and because of all the other things they had seen, the people began to praise God in the heavens for sending them St. Francis and for freeing them from the ravages of the once-wild wolf.

After this the wolf lived in Gubbio for two years. He went daily from house to house without harm or being harmed. The people fed him and he was such a familiar sight that the dogs didn't even bark at him. Finally, after two years, Brother Wolf died of old age. The people mourned him, because he had been a familiar sight among them and was a constant reminder of the virtue and holiness of St. Francis.

To the praise of Christ. Amen.

The Canticle of Brother Sun
(Translated from the Italian by Lawrence Cunningham)
Most High, omnipotent, good Lord,
To you alone belong praise and glory,
Honor, and blessing.
No man is worthy to breathe thy name.
Be praised, my Lord, for all your creatures.
In the first place for the blessed Brother Sun,
Who gives us the day and enlightens us through you.
He is beautiful and radiant with his great splendor,
Giving witness of thee, Most Omnipotent One.
Be praised, my Lord, for Sister Moon and the stars
Formed by you so bright, precious, and beautiful.
Be praised, my Lord, for Brother Wind
And the airy skies, so cloudy and serene;
For every weather, be praised, for it is life-giving.
Be praised, my Lord, for Sister Water,
So necessary yet so humble, precious, and chaste.

Be praised, my Lord, for Brother Fire,
Who lights up the night.
He is beautiful and carefree, robust, and fierce.
Be praised, my Lord, for our sister, Mother Earth,
Who nourishes and watches us
While bringing forth abundance of fruits with colored flowers
And herbs.
Be praised, my Lord, for those who pardon through your love
And bear weakness and trial.
Blessed are those who endure in peace,
For they will be crowned by you, Most High.
Be praised, my Lord, for our sister, Bodily Death,
Whom no living man can escape.
Woe to those who die in sin.
Blessed are those who discover thy holy will.
The second death will do them no harm.
Praise and bless my Lord.
Render thanks.
Serve him with great humility.
Amen.

The Prayer of St. Francis*
Lord, make me an instrument of your peace.
Where there is hatred, let me sow love.
Where there is injury . . . pardon.
Where there is discord . . . unity.
Where there is doubt . . . faith.
Where there is error . . . truth.
Where there is despair . . . hope.
Where there is sadness . . . joy.
Where there is darkness . . . light.
O Divine Master, grant that I may not so much seek
To be consoled . . . as to console.
To be understood . . . as to understand.
To be loved . . . as to love.
For:
It is in giving . . . that we receive.
It is in pardoning . . . that we are pardoned.
It is in dying . . . that we are born to eternal life.
Amen.

---

*This well-known prayer, often ascribed to Francis, was written by an unknown person in this century. The prayer is also identified with The Christophers.

Visions, Saints, and a Guardian Angel

The Remarkable Story of St. Frances of Rome

All the comforts of her day were available to St. Frances of Rome (1384-1440), but they held little if any attraction for her. The wife of a wealthy nobleman, she shunned the pleasures of Roman society in favor of a temperate life centered on prayer and acts of charity. She also became a trusted adviser of Pope Eugenius IV.

This brief account of her good works focuses on the unique and personal association Frances experienced with her guardian angel, a relationship that developed a year after the death of her favorite son. There were other supernatural connections as well: mystical visions, long periods of ecstatic prayer (especially after receiving Communion), divine messages that told of future events. She also possessed an uncanny ability to perceive the presence of angels.

Through it all, she lived a life of spartan simplicity, devoting herself to the care of others to an extraordinary degree. As one biographer wrote: "Her ordinary food was dry bread. Secretly she would exchange with beggars good food for their hard crusts; her drink was water, and her cup a human skull."

Selection from *Married Saints*, by Selden P. Delany, The Newman Press, 1950; copyright 1935 by Longmans Green and Co., (first printing 1935; reprinted 1950).

A year after the death of her favorite son, Evangelista, while Frances was praying in her private oratory, a bright light suddenly shone before her and she saw the departed child accompanied by an archangel. The boy told her of his happiness in heaven and foretold the approaching death of his sister Agnese, which actually happened as he had foretold. He consoled his mother, however, by informing her that the archangel who accompanied him was henceforth to be her guide. For twenty-three years this archangel was nearly always visible to Frances, though invisible to those about her. He assumed the form of a beautiful child of eight or thereabouts and indicated his wishes by touching her shoulder or, when she needed restraining, striking her on the cheek. When she committed a fault, the angel vanished, but returned when she made her confession. In the last epoch of her life this angel was succeeded by another of still higher dignity.

The revelations that St. Frances enjoyed usually came by way of mystical vision. She beheld saints and angels, as we have already seen. When she recovered from the plague after her family had given up hope, she had a vision of hell so terrible that she could never speak of it without tears. She also saw clearly into the meaning of many contemporary historical events and what would be their ultimate results.

The times in which she lived were replete with calamities and distresses: civil war, pestilence, famine, brigandage, and the wanton destruction of property filled the hearts of the Roman people with anxiety and terror.

Yet Frances went about the streets of that stricken city, tranquil and unharmed. Not only was she universally respected for her works of mercy, her miracles, and her extraordinary virtue; but as her heart was in heaven, she had nothing to fear on earth. She looked not on the things that were seen, but on the things that were not seen. Her gaze was fixed on the unchanging eternal realities.

The year 1434 was marked by unusual misfortunes. The Holy Father, Eugenius IV, was in exile. As he had taken the side of the Florentines in their war with Philip, duke of Milan, Philip in revenge had stirred up against the pope many of the bishops, assembled in the Council of Basel. They even dared to summon the pope to appear before the Council as an accused criminal.

On the night of the fourteenth of October, Frances was in an ecstasy in her oratory. The Mother of God appeared to her and gave her instructions to be transmitted to the pope at Bologna. The next day Frances called on her confessor Dom Giovanni, and besought him to go at once to Bologna to carry out the orders of Our Lady. He demurred, saying that his journey would be useless; that he would only compromise Frances and himself; and that the pope would look upon him as a fool and a dupe.

However, as Frances insisted, he went and was received cordially by the pope, who approved of all the requests that Frances had sent, and gave orders that they be carried out.

When Dom Giovanni returned and began to describe to her the results of his mission, she interrupted him, saying:

"It is I, if you please, who will recount to you the events of your journey. I was with you in spirit; and I know all that has happened."

She narrated the facts exactly as they had taken place, among them the recovery of a member of the party from an illness, due to the prayers of Frances.

Frances spent long vigils in prayer for the Church. Her prophets and saints revealed to her the dangers of the present and future. She was finally spurred to action, first under the inspiration of St. Thomas the Apostle, and then under that of St. Gregory the Great; and she dictated to her confessor some letters to the pope. She urged the Holy Father not to let himself be deceived or trust to appearances or insist on little things; that he seek not his own advantage, but give attention rather to the flock that had been committed to him and for which he would have to render an account.

On the thirteenth of August 1439, Frances perceived a change in the visage and bearing of her guardian angel. His face flowed with joy as he said:

"I am going to weave a veil of a hundred strands, then another of sixty, then another of thirty."

One hundred ninety days after the vision, the angel had completed his task. The face of Frances was seen to shine with an unearthly light. The end of her strenuous and agitated life was at hand. Her last words were:

"The angel has finished his task: he beckons me to follow him."

The Maid of Orléans

St. Joan of Arc Dies a Hero's Death

The story of St. Joan of Arc (1412-1431) is one of the most improbable in the Church's great library. After all, who would believe that a teenage girl, inspired by heavenly voices and clad in the armor of a knight, could possibly lead a French army against the British, free the besieged city of Orléans, and see to the coronation of Charles VII as king of France?

And yet these are precisely the things that happened because of the courage and faith of this young peasant girl. She heard the messages of her favorite saints — St. Michael, St. Margaret, St. Catherine — and, donning the uniform of a soldier, turned the face of history. But one day, fighting at Compiègne, she was captured and turned over to the British. The end of her story would be marked by tragedy: a trumped-up trial, and cruel execution at the stake.

This account of Joan's final days follows her capture by Burgundian troops and her transfer to the British. A heroine on the battlefield, she fell victim to the dark forces of intrigue and treachery that ultimately sealed her fate. Still, redemption would ultimately come. Those involved in her trial quickly fell from grace, and the English cause eventually collapsed. Less than twenty-five years after her death Joan was officially ruled innocent of all charges, and she was finally canonized a saint — as loyal French people knew her to be all along — in 1920.

Selection from *St. Joan of Arc*, by Margaret and Matthew Bunson, Our Sunday Visitor, Inc., 1992.

Months of agony began for Joan as preparations for her trial got under way in Rouen on January 3, 1431. The purpose of her judges was to make the entire farce — the ridiculous, insane mockery of truth — look legal. Joan was held in Bouvreuil Castle, chained twenty-four hours a day to a block of wood. Her guards insulted her and laughed at her, and others, including King Henry VI of England, visited her to make fun of her condition. Her cell was cold and windowless.

After weeks of questions and sermons, Joan's trial started officially on March 24, 1431, with seventy separate charges read against her. All of them were odd, including one about her use of male clothing, and another that attacked the fact that the voices spoke to her in French. The judges apparently felt that saints and angels only spoke English. If the voices had talked in English, Joan, of course, would not have understood a word. These and other peculiar charges were eventually reduced to twelve, all designed to label her a witch. She collapsed as a result of her treatment and became seriously ill.

Not wanting Joan to die in their care, the judges had her nursed back to health. They threatened her with torture while she was recovering, and the judges even took a vote on the use of torture. Two supported the use of fire and hideous machines, but ten opposed such cruelty.

On May 23, Joan was told that she would be handed over to the state officials for execution. She finally agreed, out of exhaustion and hopelessness, to deny that her voices were from God. Forced to wear women's clothing, Joan soon discovered that her jailers had stolen her skirts and blouses. They left behind a suit of men's clothes, and she was forced to put on those garments. The English, delighted that she had fallen into their trap, declared that she had once again taken up her old ways of witchcraft and heresy. The male clothing was a sign, they announced.

Joan, in turn, faced her enemies with a sudden fierce power that made them uneasy. She informed them that her voices had scolded her for denying them, and that she would die before she would give in again. Torture, death by flames, anything that the English and the Burgundians could hand out would be better than admitting to lies. Struck by her anger, the judges signed the death warrant of Joan of Arc.

She had taken the worst that they could give her, and she had triumphed, as anyone who suffers innocently or at the hands of evil men wins out in the end. Joan weighed heaven against their threats and their promises, and she accepted the will of God. He alone allowed such men to live and to prosper. He alone would bring her to his side. The men might plot and take their revenge, but death awaited them too in time, and the grave would not hide their evil.

On the morning of May 30, 1431, Joan was granted the right to make her last confession. This did not make any sense at all! If Joan was a witch and a heretic, why would she want to go to confession? Why would a court that had condemned her as a witch and a heretic allow her to make such a confession? Joan also received Holy Communion, which would never have been given to a "witch" who traded in lies and magic.

After she was led to the Place du Vieux-Marché, where she heard one last sermon, Joan was tied to a stake and her sentence was read aloud. As the men piled wood around her and lighted the flames, a Dominican priest held up a crucifix so that she could end her life with this vision before her. The priest shouted through the flames and the smoke that she would soon be in paradise.

As the flames began to blister her flesh, and as her small body slowly disappeared in the fire and billows of dark smoke, the men who had plotted her death found little joy in it. One English soldier who had been waiting to put a log on her death pyre — the mound of wood and flames — turned away in horror as he was convinced that he saw Joan's soul rise out of the flames in the form of a white dove. The learned judges took to their beds in remorse, and others fled the scene with dread. The executioner said later that Joan's heart had not burned in the fire but was intact when the ashes were removed.

Throughout France a silent moan emerged from the lips of the people when word came of her execution by fire. Many of her comrades-in-arms had probably believed that she would be ransomed by the king. The simple people turned from their leaders in disgust and horror, knowing that the Maid of Orléans had been sacrificed for the greed and ambitions of men.

'And Then — ?'

St. Philip Neri Asks the Ultimate Question

St. Philip Neri (1515-1595) was, most of all, a happy man. He sometimes asked God to temper his joy, afraid that he might die of sheer pleasure. He conveyed this sense of happiness and well-being to those around him in the streets of Rome. As one biographer wrote: "His touch gave health of body; his very look calmed souls in trouble and drove away temptations. He was gay, genial, and irresistibly winning; neither insult nor wrong could dim the brightness of his joy."

This was, of course, no empty giddiness; rather it was the delight that comes to those who know God's way and make it their own. They are the ones who possess prudence in its fullness, examining every conscious act with an eye on the final prize. This charming story about St. Philip Neri — retold here in the classic style of another era — illustrates the point.

Story from *Catholic Anecdotes*, by the Brothers of the
Christian Schools; translated from the French by Mrs. J.
Sadlier; D. & J. Sadlier & Co., 1885.

People are wont to busy themselves a great deal about their future, that is to say, about making a position for themselves in the world, and choosing a state that will best ensure their success in life; unhappily, they do not always think enough of the true future, which is eternal.

A young man named Spazzara, who lived in Rome in the sixteenth century, went one day to St. Philip Neri, and entered into long details about the study of law, which he had just commenced. He described the course that he meant to pursue in order to obtain the degree of doctor.

"And then — ?" demanded the saint. "Then," replied the young man, much encouraged, "I will plead causes, and I hope successfully."

"And then — ?" added the saint, again. "And then, people will begin to speak of me, and I shall enjoy a reputation."

"And then — ?" continued St. Philip Neri, smiling. "And then"

— answered the young man, a little embarrassed, "and then — oh! I shall live at my ease, and I shall be happy."

"And what then — ?" "Well! Then, — I shall end by dying."

"And then," resumed the saint, raising his voice, "and then, what shall you do when your own trial comes, when you shall be yourself the accused, Satan the accuser, and the Almighty God your judge?"

The young man, who little expected such a conclusion, hung his head and began to consider within himself. A short time after, he renounced the study of law, and endeavored, by consecrating his life to the service of God, to prepare seriously for that final, *what then*? That is to say, that awful judgment, which shall be followed by eternity.

Let us do the same, my dear young friends, and we shall never repent of it.

North American Martyrs

The Heroism of St. Isaac Jogues
and His Companions Lives On

Eight French Jesuit missionaries martyred between 1642 and 1649 in what is now upstate New York and southeastern Canada wrote a heroic chapter in the colonization of North America, and shrines in their memory — one in Canada, one in Auriesville, New York — testify to their greatness. The eight North American Martyrs — layman René Goupil and Fathers Isaac Jogues, Jean Lalande, Jean de Brébeuf, Antoine Daniel, Gabriel Lalemant, Charles Garnier, and Noël Chabanel — were canonized in 1930.

In The American Catholic Experience *(Doubleday & Co., Inc., 1985), historian Jay P. Dolan movingly describes their impact: ". . . Their heroic exploits and bloody martyrdoms became part of popular Catholic folklore. Growing up Catholic in the early twentieth century meant reading the lives of these missionaries and hearing tales about their heroism among the Indians. A young Catholic boy or girl did not have to look to Europe for saintly models. They were right there in the forests of New France, and the exploits of Brébeuf, Jogues, and Marquette inspired a number of young people to go and do likewise in China, Latin America, and other missionary regions around the world. What people remembered of the French mission was not the Indian conversions, but the Jesuit heroism."*

Father Jogues (1607-1646), known to the Indians as Ondessonk, suffered unspeakable pain and torture. After running a gauntlet of Iroquois, he was fastened to a post where his thumb was severed. His captors chewed his other fingers to the bone, and flaming brands repeatedly seared his body. He lived in captivity like an animal for a year before escaping, and, with great difficulty, made his way back to France. His ordeal had left its mark; his fellow Jesuits failed at first to recognize him. Pope Urban VIII gave him permission to offer Mass with his mutilated hands, and he was treated as a hero. Yet he returned to America, to his mission — this time to his death.

Excerpts from *Saint Among Savages: The Life of Isaac Jogues*, by Francis Talbot, S.J., Harper & Brothers Publishers, 1935.

1. St. Isaac Returns to France

Something about this poor, starved-looking man impressed the Brother. He thought he had better speak to the Father rector, and so went over to the sacristy. He found the rector partly vested for Mass; nevertheless, he whispered to him that there was a poor man in the parlor who wanted to see him right away because he could not wait and had news of the Fathers in Canada. The rector said the man had to wait until after Mass, and continued vesting. The thing troubled him; the Brother had said it was a "poor" man from Canada. "It may be that the man is in a hurry," he thought to himself. "He may be in want and may need some help." Taking off his alb and his amice, he went to the parlor.

The room was shrouded in darkness. The Father rector could see only the dim outline of the visitor, and asked him if he had come from Canada, as the Brother related. Yes, the man answered, he had been in Canada. Do you know the Fathers there? Very well. Father Vimont? Yes. Father de Brébeuf? Extremely well. And Father Jogues, did you know Father Isaac Jogues?

"I knew him very well indeed," Isaac answered.

"We have had word that he was captured by the Iroquois. Do you know, is he dead? Or is he still captive? Have those barbarians not murdered him?" the Father rector inquired.

"He is at liberty," he said, with a queer gulp. "Reverend Father," Isaac broke into tears, "it is he who speaks to you."

He fell on his knees, at the rector's feet, kissed his hand, begged his blessing. A cold shiver passed through the Father rector. Then a burst of joy. He lifted Isaac from his knees, threw his arms about him, kissed him on both cheeks. With a loud voice, which rumbled strangely through the quiet corridor at that hour of sacred silence, he welcomed him and brought him to the community room. The Brother porter, the other Brothers, the Fathers, startled by the excited voices, came hastening into the room. They gathered about Father Isaac; they embraced him and kissed him; they were so overjoyed that they could only gasp sounds, scarcely could they find words.

2. A Martyr's Death

About sundown, when the shadows were lengthening over the village, there came a young brave to the cabin. He sought out

Ondessonk and invited him to visit another lodge where there were people who wished to eat and talk with him. Jogues recognized the man as belonging to the Bear clan, a man who had been somewhat hostile. To refuse this brave would be interpreted as an act of great discourtesy and would betray a suspicion that might breed greater ill feeling. Spurning an invitation to eat in a cabin was an insult not easily forgiven. Besides, Jogues thought, to show fear of this brave would be cowardly.

The smoky half-light of the October evening lingered over the cabins and the tang of autumn was cool in the air as Jogues emerged into the open. He and Honatteniate [his "sworn brother"] followed their guide till they arrived before the long house where their guide turned to pause with a stolid and expressionless stare. Jogues did not hesitate for long. Suspicion or fear, either one would give the Mohawk an advantage over him.

Casually, then, he placed his hand against the stiff skin that hung down from the lintel and pushed it inward so that he might enter. A blast of warm, smelly air assailed him. Through the heavy gloom and smoke he glimpsed the fires gleaming down the center of the long, narrow room, and saw the people dimly shadowed about them. He shoved with his shoulder against the shaggy skin and bent his head under the low doorway. He saw and knew no more.

Behind the doorpost a warrior stood, with a tomahawk poised ready to strike. The bowed head of Ondessonk came forward around the edge of the skin curtain. Honatteniate leaped into the entry, thrusting out his arm to ward off the blow he saw crashing down. The tomahawk slashed his forearm and thudded upon the head of Ondessonk. The guide sent Honatteniate reeling into a corner and with another blow the murderer smashed the skull of Ondessonk. Father Jogues lay as he fell, crumpled at the doorway of the lodge. The moment was still. No one spoke. The braves leaned over the bleeding head and the prostrate form. They whispered in awed tones that Ondessonk was dead.

A Bishop of Iron Will

Archbishop Hughes's Strategy
Wards Off the Know-Nothings

Long before the term became fashionable, Archbishop John Hughes (1797-1864) was politically incorrect. He said exactly what was on his mind, stood up resolutely for the Church and the rights of individual Catholics, and rarely if ever backed down from a good fight. He was less concerned with pleasing other people than he was with doing what he saw as right.

As the first archbishop of New York and one of the leading public figures of his day, he had to take on, among others, the violently anti-Catholic Nativists — the Know-Nothings, as generations of history students would remember them. In their own time, however — and in the time of Archbishop Hughes — they presented a grave threat to law and order, and to religious liberty.

This account, by a contemporary, describes the bishop's alarm at the Nativists' brutality and riotous behavior in Philadelphia — and his determination that, at all costs, their thuggery would not be repeated in New York. To make sure of that, he was able to call on some impressive reserves: thousands of Catholic men willing to defend their churches, with their lives if necessary; the ability to stand toe-to-toe with the mayor of New York, telling him how he would run things if he were in charge of the city, and — perhaps most important of all — a will of pure iron.

Excerpt from *Life of the Most Reverend John Hughes, D.D.,*
First Archbishop of New York, by John R. G. Hassard, D.
Appleton and Co., 1866.

A good priest who had escaped from Philadelphia advised Bishop Hughes to publish an address urging the Catholics to keep the peace. But the bishop thought the time for meekness and inaction had passed. He was ready for a desperate struggle if the mob forced one upon him.

At his direction, each church in the city was occupied by an armed force numbering in the hundreds or even thousands. Yet he was careful to warn his people against striking the first blow, or doing the least unlawful act to provoke a riot.

"We know," he wrote in his newspaper, *The Freeman's Journal*, "the nature of a mob, especially a mob of church-burners, convent-sackers, and grave-robbers; that with it a firm front is the best peace-maker, and that to let it know that, be the authorities as supine as they pleased, the scenes of Philadelphia could not be renewed with impunity in New York, would do more for order than all the twaddle that could be poured out by all the papers in the country."

A delegation of Nativists was expected to arrive in New York from Philadelphia, and a meeting of their political brethren was called in City Hall Park, to give them a suitable reception and escort them through the streets. Bishop Hughes felt that a crisis was at hand; if this meeting were held, he believed that nothing could save New York from the disorder that had disgraced Philadelphia. An extra *Freeman's Journal* was immediately issued, warning the Irish to keep away from all public meetings, especially the proposed meeting in the park. The bishop also visited the mayor, Robert H. Morris, and advised him to prevent the demonstration.

"Are you afraid," asked the mayor, "that some of your churches will be burned?"

"No sir, but I am afraid that some of *yours* will be burned. We can protect our own. I come to warn you for your own good."

"Do you think, bishop, that your people would attack the procession?"

"I do not, but the Nativists want to provoke a Catholic riot. If they can do it in no other way, I believe they would not scruple to attack the procession themselves, for the sake of making it appear that the Catholics had assailed them."

"What then would you have me do?"

"I did not come to tell you what to do. I am a churchman, not the mayor of New York. But if I *were* the mayor, I would examine the laws of the state, and see if there were not attached to the police force a battery of artillery, and a company or so of infantry, and a squadron of horse; and I think I should find that there were; and if so, I should call them out.

"Moreover, I should send for Mr. Harper, the mayor-elect, who has been chosen by the votes of this party. I should remind him that these men are his supporters; I should warn him that if they carry out their design, there will be a riot; and I should urge him to use his influence in preventing this public reception of the delegates."

How far the mayor may have been influenced by this conversation I do not pretend to say, but there was no demonstration on the arrival of the Philadelphia Nativists, and no disturbance in New York.

'The Pope of the Workingman'

Leo XIII Pioneered the Field of Social Justice

With the European community undergoing intense political upheaval for much of the nineteenth century, the Vatican turned inward and away from the modern world. Blaming the turmoil on new trends in political thought and changes in the social order, the Church distanced itself from progress, from liberalism, and indeed from modern civilization.

Then came Pope Leo XIII (1810-1903). Elected pope in 1878, the longtime archbishop of Perugia gradually embarked on a course that would change all of that. He understood that the Church had an obligation to reach out to the world around it. A pioneer not only in social justice but in ecumenism as well, he led the Church into the twentieth century — and into a new era. In doing so, he allied the Church firmly with working families, helping to stem a wave of anticlericalism growing among the lower classes. It was a change that could have come about sooner, to be sure, but it represented such a marked departure from the old order that Leo would be known during his lifetime — and beyond — as "The Pope of the Workingman."

His 1891 encyclical Rerum Novarum *("Of New Things") is one of the universally recognized landmarks of the Church's teaching on social justice. In the privileged surroundings of his youth there may have been little evidence of the direction his social thought would take, but as this charming story indicates, the priesthood seemed to beckon to him early in life.*

Adapted from *The Great White Shepherd of Christendom*,
edited by Charles J. O'Malley, J. S. Hyland & Co., 1903.

While still very young, Joachim Pecci — the future Pope Leo XIII — began to display a great fondness for study that his mother interpreted as a sure sign of the priestly vocation she desired for him.

One day Count Ludovico Pecci, the boy's father, took him for a walk and, from a distant hillside, pointed out the locations of Aquino and Monte Cassino.

Our Sunday Visitor's

"What!" exclaimed Joachim. "Aquino, where St. Thomas the Doctor was born, and Monte Cassino, where he learned to read and write! Papa, may I go there too to learn to read and write?"

Count Ludovico came back from the hike with mixed emotions. The boy's wish to study as St. Thomas did was somewhat at odds with the career the father had in mind for him.

"I wanted to make a general of him," he confided to his wife, the countess.

"Well," she replied, "you might have started something else. You may even make a pope of him!"

'Let Us Go to Father Ireland . . .'

A Temperance Society Gets Its Start in a Most Unlikely Place

Temperance broadly defined — the case, usually, when it's discussed as a virtue — involves the moderate or reasonable use of the physical appetites. But it was temperance of a different sort — or, rather, something much more specific — that was often on the mind of Archbishop John Ireland of St. Paul, Minnesota (1838-1918). A major influence on the development of the Church in the United States, the archbishop deplored the evils of drunkenness so often (and so effectively) that he became known as "the American apostle of temperance."

He was never, strictly speaking, a prohibitionist, but he railed against the "liquor traffic" and the deadly harm it had inflicted upon his people, particularly on his beloved fellow Irish. He held audiences spellbound across the country with heartrending tales of families reduced to tatters because a breadwinner had wasted his wages in the grog shop. He warned of ruined homes, of pauperism, of vice and crime — all brought on by drink. His hardworking countrymen responded with mixed feelings at best, but every now and then, they surprised him — just as they did when a group of them one day beseeched him to help them stop their drinking. He had been reluctant to launch a temperance organization, concerned about seeming to impose on others an obligation that wasn't, strictly speaking, a binding one. But this request was something special. And it had sprung up from the most unlikely place.

Selection from *John Ireland and the American Catholic Church*, by Marvin R. O'Connell, Minnesota Historical Society Press, 1988.

What the bishop did not choose to do himself he would not prevent one of his subjects from doing, and the temperance cause in the diocese of St. Paul did have its rebirth. Many years later Ireland told, with suitably dramatic flourishes, how it happened:

"Seven good, generous — too generous — men were assembled together on a Friday evening in a very popular saloon on Minnesota Street. They drank and treated one another; but a gleam of good Christian sense dawned upon their minds and one said: 'We ought to stop lest we be ruined.'

"Another said: 'Let us go and see Father Ireland, and organize a temperance society,' and a petition with seven names upon it was actually gotten up in that saloon, and candidly the keeper of the saloon was one of the signers. The writing was a little tremulous.

"One was commissioned to bring me the petition, and as he opened the door of my room he was not very steady on his limbs, and he nearly fell, but he soon recovered himself and said: 'I have a petition for you.' I read the petition and without a moment's hesitation said: 'Yes, a society will be organized.'"

At four o'clock on the following Sunday afternoon an organizational meeting was held in the cathedral clubrooms. "Fifty men signed the pledge, and the Father Mathew society was born."

Fire in His Soul

Matt Talbot's Spiritual Journey Took On Breathtaking Dimensions

Archbishop Ireland had preached against intemperance because he saw how many lives could be ruined by drink. Matt Talbot knew the problem, too — from the inside out.

Matt Talbot (1856-1925), born to a poor Dublin family, left school at the age of twelve and went to work for a wine merchant — and promptly became the victim of drink. He went on to other menial jobs, always a willing and dependable worker — but always a slave to alcohol.

His Catholic training had left its mark, though. Even in the depths of his drinking days he made it a point to get to Mass each week, and when, in his late twenties, he finally decided to take the pledge, he prayed to the Blessed Sacrament for divine help.

That decision began a spiritual journey of breathtaking dimensions, one that would last the rest of his life. Turning his heart and mind completely over to God, he left a legacy of faith that continues to amaze us today, three quarters of a century after his death.

Adapted from *Matt Talbot, The Irish Worker's Glory*, by Rev. James F. Cassidy, Burns, Oates & Washbourne Ltd., 1934.

Eucharistic visits laid the foundations of Matt Talbot's spiritual life, and he was convinced that there were diabolical efforts to keep him out of church. Twice an unseen force tried to hold him back physically from Mass, but to no avail. Talbot triumphed through the magnetism of divine love.

On another occasion he was assailed several times by the demon of despair, who sought to keep him from receiving Communion by the vivid presentation of the lure of drink and the futility of seeking to escape it. This time he struggled for three hours before overcoming temptation, and his victory proved to be momentous. Never again did he have to battle against such assaults.

When he could, he tried to convey to others the meaning of the

Eucharist in his life. A lonely woman once told him how depressed she felt because a dear brother had left for America, but she found his reply short on sympathetic consolation. "Lonely!" he exclaimed. "How could you be lonely? That's nonsense, and Our Lord in his tabernacle."

Talbot's penitential practices were extreme. To nearly constant prayer he added the most rigid self-denial. For fourteen years he wore mortifying chains and ropes around his body. He imposed on himself special fasts during the year and, in general, ate little more than was necessary for the preservation of life. He slept on a wooden pillow, and prayed and read on bare knees. He never married, and gave away most of his salary — especially to the missions, a favorite charity.

A near-invalid for the last two years of his life, Matt Talbot still tried to maintain his spiritual rigors as best he could. Even the final act of his life involved an act of sacrifice; he died on a Dublin street on June 7, 1925, on his way to morning Mass at the Dominican church.

'A Council!'

The Holy Spirit Inspires Pope John XXIII

The world still remembers him as Good Pope John. That's as it should be. Pope John XXIII (1881-1963) stands as one of the most beloved figures of the twentieth century, perhaps even in the entire history of the Church.

His great knack was for putting people at ease, including himself. Stories abound of his simplicity, his lack of pretense. Some of the best ones were gathered for publication not long after his death — in Wit and Wisdom of Good Pope John, *collected by Henri Fesquet (P. J. Kenedy & Sons, 1964), and* The Humor and Warmth of Pope John XXIII, *by Louis Michaels (Pocket Books, Inc., 1965). Readers probably remember some of the gems:*

• "When the body gets worn out," Pope John said about the aging process, "the soul gets in shape."

• Loving companionship, he broke the old tradition in that popes ate alone by inviting his secretary, Monsignor Loris Capovilla, to dine with him. But, he later confided to a friend: "I get no pleasure out of eating alone with Capovilla. He eats like a canary."

• Before receiving President and Mrs. Kennedy, Pope John asked an aide how he should address the president's wife. Either "Mrs. Kennedy" or "Madame" would be correct, the aide responded. The pope switched from one to the other, undecided to the last moment. He resolved the dilemma when she walked in by spreading his arms wide and exclaiming, "Jacqueline!"

• A diplomat new to the Holy See asked Pope John how many people worked at the Vatican. The pope gave his answer without batting an eye: "About half!"

• A letter to Pope John from twelve-year-old Bruno said, "I am undecided. I want to be either a policeman or the pope. What do you think?" "My little Bruno," the pope replied, "learn how to be a policeman, because that cannot be improvised. Anybody can be pope; the proof of this is that I have become one."

• If poking fun at himself helped to make a point, he did it. Of the prison that the papacy actually was, he hesitated not a moment in telling Boston's Cardinal Richard Cushing, "Sono nel sacco qui" — "I'm in a bag here."

Not quite true, not entirely. Pope John's papacy would change

the Church, and the world, for all time. That was because this "tran-
sition pope" — as he was supposed to be — convened Vatican Coun-
cil II, the four-year convocation of bishops (1962-1965) that changed
the way the Church thought of itself, and the way all of us thought of
it too. For almost all of his priestly career, John XXIII had exercised
the prudent ministry of a Vatican diplomat. And here he was, near-
ing the age of eighty, setting in motion the deliberations that would
result in a revolutionary new understanding of the Church. In his
well-known allusion, he said he simply wanted to open the Church's
window to let in a little fresh air. He would elaborate on that later:

"The idea of the Council did not ripen in me as the fruit of long
meditation, but came forth like the flower of an unexpected spring."

There was, of course, a bit more to it than that. Here's the way
it was recounted by Time *magazine's man at the Council, Robert*
Blair Kaiser.

Selection from *Pope, Council and World: The Story of Vatican*
II, by Robert Blair Kaiser, The Macmillan Co., 1963.

The initial image of the pope as a good-humored, informal, winning, harmless old gentleman was, as events proved, very incomplete. After scarcely a month in office, John had an inspiration that was to astonish, to stir, and to challenge the Church and the world.

Significantly, the inspiration came in a global context. Cardinal Domenico Tardini, in his capacity as pro-Secretary of State, had come to John's apartment high on the fourth floor of the Vatican Palace and begun to riffle through his daily reports to the pope. The Vatican diplomatic corps is nothing if not diligent, and its communiqués about matters ecclesiastical and political pour into Rome every day. In that second week of January in 1959, France had just given the mantle of presidential power to General Charles de Gaulle. The people of Soviet Russia were cheering over the government's successful launching of a 3,245-pound rocket into orbit around the moon. And in Cuba, a bearded leftist named Fidel Castro smashed the dictatorship of Fulgencio Batista. In Italy, the Catholic Demochristian Party wanted to make an alliance with the Socialists. From Rio de Janeiro came a disturbing study of the people pouring into that city and the anonymity and squalor of the *favelas* they lived in.

What to do? Tardini, raised to the purple by John, but a Vatican figure for decades, droned on. What to do? John rose and walked slowly over to his window overlooking Rome. A light rain slanted down across St. Peter's Square, dimming the view beyond the Tiber.

Tardini was finishing his report . . . on Africa now, where new nations were springing up like mushrooms. The Congo missions. The Algerian revolt. A bishop's report on vast possibilities, on a new set of problems. Progress. Agitation. Dissension.

John could plainly see that the whole world "was plunged in serious distress and agitation, deepened in dissension and threats." The Church, he thought, should come to a confrontation with the world. But how? In Rome, the Curia had learned to keep the world apart, to play the politics of preservation. The faith was a pearl, meant to be guarded from outside contamination. John thought of it as a seed, meant to grow and have influence on Bologna and Bombay, Chicago and Cambrai, Montreal and Warsaw and Mwanza.

All of a sudden, the thought came to him (he said later it was an inspiration of the Holy Spirit): Get help from Bologna and Bombay, Chicago and Cambrai, Montreal and Warsaw and Mwanza and all the other bishops of every land.

"A council!"

Tardini's assent to this proposal was "immediate and exultant," according to John's first recorded report of that meeting, and, according to another later report given by John, "restrained but nevertheless positive." As a matter of record, however, Tardini told persons in the Curia that John would soon forget he had even mentioned a council.

John didn't forget. Some days later, on the second day of the Church Unity Octave, a week dedicated by many Christian bodies to prayer for world religious unity, John's feeling became a certitude. He said Mass in his private Chapel of the Holy Family, and afterward he knelt in thanksgiving and meditated on the seventeenth chapter of St. John's Gospel — "That they all may be one, as thou, Father, in me, and I in thee; that they also may be one in us; that the world may believe that thou hast sent me. . . ."

Thus, right from the start it would be a council with a triple finality. First, for human unity and peace. Second, for Christian unity, a necessary step to that goal. Third, internal renewal of the Church, a necessary step to Christian unity.

The Conscience of El Salvador

Archbishop Romero Became a Martyr for His People

The stature of Archbishop Oscar Romero (1917-1980) continues to grow day by day, nearly two decades after he was assassinated while offering Mass in a hospital chapel. The archbishop of San Salvador, capital city of El Salvador in Central America, was silenced because he had become a tireless and — to the ruling totalitarian junta — dangerous crusader for human rights and social justice. But if being alive means to live in the hearts of the people, he is with us still.

Archbishop Romero was fearless because he was united with his people. Once he said: "Christ invites us not to fear persecution because, believe me, brothers and sisters, those who are committed to the poor must risk the same fate as the poor, and in El Salvador we know what the fate of the poor signifies: to disappear, to be tortured, to be captive, and to be found dead."

The archbishop shared fully the fate of those he served. In this account of how that happened, British author Mary Craig describes the mounting crisis between Archbishop Romero and government officials, and takes up the story as he began the last day of his life.

Selection from *Six Modern Martyrs*, by Mary Craig, The Crossroad Publishing Co., 1985.

Only the last act remained to be played, and the curtain had already risen on it. On Monday morning Archbishop Romero went to confession; he was to say the 6:00 P.M. evening Mass in the chapel of the cancer hospital where he lived. "I want to feel clean in the presence of the Lord," he told his confessor.

The Mass was for the mother of a friend, and unwisely its time and location had been announced in the press. "Though I walk in the valley of the shadow of death, yet will I fear no evil, for thou art with me," he read aloud from the Twenty-third Psalm; and the Gospel reading took up this theme of death and resurrection: "The hour has come for the Son of Man to be glorified. . . . Unless the grain of wheat falls to the ground and dies, it remains only a grain. But if it dies, it bears much fruit. . . ."

As he always did, the archbishop based his homily on the readings:

"You have just heard the Gospel of Christ that one must not love oneself to the point of refusing to become involved in the risks of life that history demands of us; and that those who fend off danger will lose their lives. But whoever, out of love for Christ, gives himself to the service of others, will live, like the grain of wheat that dies, but only seems to die. If it did not die it would remain alone. Only in undoing itself does it produce the harvest."

When he had finished speaking, a shot rang out. Romero died instantly, shot through a main artery. And in the uproar that was let loose, the assailant or assailants made their escape.

The news spread like a brush fire, and the Salvadorans were stricken. Thousands waited to see the body as it lay in the basilica, and when on the Wednesday it was moved to the cathedral, the weeping crowds filed past the glass-topped coffin, touching it, pressing against it. With difficulty, and at enormous risk to themselves, *campesinos* poured into the city, queuing in the blazing sun for their turn to take a last look at the man they had known as *Monseñor*.

To the anguished question "Why did he have to die?" the people replied as one: "Because he loved the poor." In the cathedral, Father Cesar Jerez, provincial of the Jesuits in Central America, made the same comment. And *The Times* of London in an editorial on the day following Romero's death backed this view. Romero "was killed because he had become a symbol of the need for human rights and social justice." In the last weeks of his life he had become a real threat to the junta, as he appealed to President Carter for an arms embargo, and to the military to stop the terror. Worse, perhaps, he had begun to shake international confidence in the regime's credibility.

Naturally the junta professed themselves shaken by the murder, and proclaimed three days of official mourning for "this most vile of crimes." As messages of sympathy and of condemnation of the violence began to flood into the archdiocesan offices, other bishops were united in horror. They excommunicated the murderers and praised their dead colleague as one who "remained faithful to his motto of speaking the truth in an effort to build true peace and justice." They spoke of the context of "violence that reaches the limits of madness" and praised Romero's tireless campaign against "institutionalized injustice and abuses against human rights and the inalienable dignity of man." This had gained him the esteem of friends and strangers alike, they admitted, though it had also "aroused the animosity of those who felt uncomfortable from the force of his evangelical word and witness. For being faithful to the Word, he fell, like the great prophets."

And as the thousands gathered on the Sunday morning in the cathedral square, a sinister epilogue was being prepared. Members of the popular organizations were getting ready to march to the square, where a sea of humanity already heaved and swayed. About two hundred fifty thousand people, among them *campesinos,* had come by bus, by lorry, or on foot. There were no crush barriers, no police to keep order, only a handful of Boy Scouts.

Mass had already begun on the steps of the cathedral when suddenly the air was filled with the thunder of an explosion. Shots rang out, and the thousands panicked and stampeded, fleeing into the surrounding streets and into the cathedral, screaming, praying, shouting. Most, probably all, of the fifty who died that morning, died of heart failure or asphyxiation, or were trampled under foot.

The archbishop's body was hastily lowered into its tomb. That afternoon an official broadcast placed the blame for the disaster on the popular organizations, but hardly anyone believed that version of events. There were too many witnesses who could give it the lie. Few people doubted that the bomb that caused the panic had been flung from the National Palace on the far side of the cathedral square.

That evening, twenty-four of the foreign mourners met at the archdiocesan offices. They issued a statement, signed by eight bishops and sixteen others, in which they rejected outright the government version of the day's events. In their statement they paid glorious tribute to the murdered archbishop:

"For defending the life of his people and striving for a society of justice and peace, he was murdered, like Christ, at the moment of offertory. From the very beginning of his ministry he had to witness the blood of martyrdom, the suffering of his people. That blood and that pain strengthened him in his determination to be the faithful and understanding shepherd who never abandoned his flock, who lent them his voice and who gave his life for them."

A Priest on Skid Row

A City Tale of Sin and Repentance

Good storytellers abound in the priesthood, and the great ones are worth their weight in gold. One of the very best is Father William J. Bausch of the Trenton (New Jersey) diocese, whose books frequently remind us of the role of stories in arriving at profound and heartfelt truths.

"Jesus obviously was a natural storyteller," he wrote in the preface of More Telling Stories, Compelling Stories *(Twenty-Third Publications), "and those who followed him picked up the habit. . . . The real work of spreading the Good News fell to accounts of Jesus, his disciples, and a whole array of saints. Legends, tales, epics, and myths were the embodiment of deep truths. Stories told of how people actually* lived *the Gospel."*

Here's the story of the way a priest lived the temperance gospel — the hard way, on Skid Row. Father Bausch — who presents it just as it was originally told by Brennan Manning, then a Franciscan (Third Order Regular) priest — calls it "a story of sin, grace, repentance, sharing, and celebration."

Story from *Storytelling: Imagination and Faith*, by William J. Bausch, Twenty-Third Publications, 1984 (originally in *The Wisdom of Accepted Tenderness*, by Brennan Manning, Dimension Books, 1978).

A few years ago, I lay desperately sick on a motel floor in a southern city. I learned later that within a few hours, if left unattended, I would have gone into alcoholic convulsions and might have died. At that point in time I did not know I was an alcoholic. I crawled to the telephone but was shaking and quivering so badly that I could not dial. Finally, I managed one digit and got the operator. "Please help me," I pleaded. "Call Alcoholics Anonymous." She took my name and address. Within ten minutes a man walked in the door. I had never seen him before and he had no idea who I was. But he had the Breath of the Father on his face and an immense reverence for my life. He scooped me up in his arms and raced me to a detox center. There began the agony of withdrawal. Anyone who has been down both sides of the street will tell you that withdrawal from alcohol can be no less severe than withdrawal from heroin.

To avoid bursting into tears, I will spare the reader that odyssey of shame and pain, unbearable guilt, remorse and humiliation. But the stranger brought me back to life. His words might sound corny to you, like tired old clichés. But they were words of life to me. This fallen-away Catholic who had not been to the eucharistic table in years told me that the Father loved me, that God had not abandoned me, that the Lord would draw good from what had happened (etiam peccatis). He told me that right now the name of the game isn't guilt and fear and shame but survival. He told me to forget about what I had lost and focus on what I had left.

He gave me an article from an American Medical Association journal explaining alcoholism as a biopsychological sickness, that an alcoholic is a biological freak who cannot stop drinking once he takes the first drink. The stranger told me to feel no more guilt than if I were recovering from some other disease like cancer or diabetes. Above all else, he affirmed me in my emptiness and loved me in my loneliness. Again and again he told me of the Father's love; how, when his children stumble and fall, he does not scold them but scoops them up and comforts them. Later I learned that my benefactor was an itinerant laborer who shaped up daily at Manpower, a local employment agency. He put cardboard in his work shoes to cover the holes. Yet, when I was able to eat, he bought me my first dinner at McDonald's. For seven days and seven nights, he breathed life into me physically and spiritually and asked nothing in return. Later I learned that he had lost his family and fortune through drinking. In his loneliness he turns on his little TV at midnight and talks to John Wayne, hoping he will talk back. Every night before bed he spends fifteen minutes reading a meditation book, praises God for his mercy, thanks him for what he has left, prays for all alcoholics, then goes to his window, raises the shade, and blesses the world.

Two years later I returned to the same southern city. My friend still lived there, but I had no address or telephone number. So I called A.A. In one of life's tragic ironies, I learned that he was on Skid Row. He had been twelve-stepping too often (i.e., the twelfth step of the A.A. program is bringing the message of recovery to practicing alcoholics). There is a buzz word with the A.A. community — HALT. Don't let yourself get too hungry, angry, lonely, or tired or you will be very vulnerable to that first drink. My friend was burned out from helping others and went back on the sauce.

As I drove through Skid Row, I spotted a man in a doorway

who I thought was my friend. He wasn't. Just another drunk wino who was neither sober nor drunk. Just dry. He hadn't had a drink in twenty-four hours and his hands trembled violently. He reached out and asked, "Hey, man, can you gimme a dollar to get some wine?"

I knelt down before him and took his hands in mine. I looked into his eyes. They filled with tears. I leaned over and kissed his hands. He began to cry. He didn't want a dollar. He wanted what I wanted two years earlier lying on the motel floor — to be accepted in his brokenness, to be affirmed in his worthlessness, to be loved in his loneliness. He wanted to be relieved of what Mother Teresa of Calcutta, with her vast personal experience of human misery, says is the worst suffering of all — the feeling of not being accepted or wanted. I never located my friend.

Several days later I was celebrating the Eucharist for a group of recovering alcoholics. Midway through the homily, my friend walked in the door. My heart skipped. But he disappeared during the distribution of Communion and did not return. Two days later, I received a letter from him that read in part: "Two nights ago in my own clumsy way I prayed for the right to belong, just to belong among you at the holy Mass of Jesus. You will never know what you did for me last week on Skid Row. You didn't see me, but I saw you. I was standing just a few feet away in a storefront window. When I saw you kneel down and kiss that wino's hands, you wiped away from my eyes the blank stare of the breathing dead. When I saw you really cared, my heart began to grow wings, small wings, feeble wings, but wings. I threw my bottle of . . . wine down the sewer. Your tenderness and understanding breathed life into me, and I want you to know that. You released me from my shadow world of panic, fear, and self-hatred. God, what a lonely prison I was living in. Father Brennan, if you should ever wonder who Ben Shaw is, remember I am someone you know very well, I am every man you meet and every woman you meet. . . . Am I also you?"

His letter ends, "Wherever I go, sober by the grace of God one day at a time, I will thank God for you."

All the Good Things

A Sister's Classroom Exercise Left a Lasting Impression

A gifted teacher combines knowledge of the subject at hand with proven educational techniques to impart a lesson in a way that leaves a lasting impression. When all that happens, learning takes place. But sometimes something more is called for, too.

That's how it was several years ago with Sister Helen Mrosla, OSF, when she was teaching in Saint Mary's School in Morris, Minnesota. To deal with a difficult situation one day she made what turned out to be a prudent decision — "prudent" in this case meaning the proper course of behavior in a given situation.

That definition, by the way, sounds exactly like a classroom exercise. The way Sister Helen handled it was something else entirely, as you'll see here.

This story originally appeared in *Proteus: A Journal of Ideas*, Spring, 1991, Shippensburg University. Reprinted in the October 1991 *Reader's Digest* and in *Chicken Soup for the Soul*, by Jack Canfield and Mark Victor Hansen, Health Communications, Inc., 1993.

He was in the third grade class I taught at Saint Mary's School in Morris, Minnesota. All thirty-four of my students were dear to me, but Mark Eklund was one in a million. Very neat in appearance, he had that happy-to-be-alive attitude that made even his occasional mischievousness delightful.

Mark also talked incessantly. I tried to remind him again and again that talking without permission was not acceptable. What impressed me so much, though, was the sincere response every time I had to correct him for misbehaving. "Thank you for correcting me, Sister!" I didn't know what to make of it at first, but before long I became accustomed to hearing it many times a day.

One morning my patience was growing thin when Mark talked once too often. I made a novice-teacher's mistake. I looked at Mark and said, "If you say one more word, I am going to tape your mouth shut!"

It wasn't ten seconds later when Chuck blurted out, "Mark is talking again." I hadn't asked any of the students to help me watch Mark, but since I had stated the punishment in front of the class, I had to act on it.

I remember the scene as if it had occurred this morning. I walked to my desk, very deliberately opened the drawer, and took out a roll of masking tape. Without saying a word, I proceeded to Mark's desk, tore off two pieces of tape, and made a big X with them over his mouth. I then returned to the front of the room.

As I glanced at Mark to see how he was doing, he winked at me. That did it! I started laughing. The entire class cheered as I walked back to Mark's desk, removed the tape and shrugged my shoulders. His first words were, "Thank you for correcting me, Sister."

At the end of the year I was asked to teach junior high math. The years flew by, and before I knew it Mark was in my classroom again. He was more handsome than ever and just as polite. Since he had to listen carefully to my instruction in the "new math," he did not talk as much in ninth grade.

One Friday things just didn't feel right. We had worked hard on a new concept all week, and I sensed that the students were growing frustrated with themselves — and edgy with one another. I had to stop this crankiness before it got out of hand. So I asked them to list the names of the other students in the room on two sheets of paper, leaving a space between each name. Then I told them to think of the nicest thing they could say about each of their classmates and write it down.

It took the remainder of the class period to finish the assignment, but as the students left the room, each one handed me his or her paper. Chuck smiled. Mark said, "Thank you for teaching me, Sister. Have a good weekend."

That Saturday, I wrote down the name of each student on a separate sheet of paper, and I listed what everyone else had said about that individual. On Monday I gave each student his or her own list. Some of them ran two pages. Before long, the entire class was smiling. "Really?" I heard whispered. "I never knew that meant so much to anyone!" "I didn't know others liked me so much!"

No one ever mentioned those papers in class again. I never knew if they discussed them after class or with their parents, but it didn't matter. The exercise had accomplished its purpose. The students were happy with themselves and one another again.

The group of students moved on. Several years later, after I had returned from a vacation, my parents met me at the airport. As we were driving home, Mother asked the usual questions about the trip: How the weather was, my experiences in general. There was a slight lull in the conversation. Mother gave Dad a sideways glance and simply said, "Dad?" My father cleared his throat. "The Eklunds called last night," he began.

"Really?" I said. "I haven't heard from them for several years. I wonder how Mark is."

Dad responded quietly. "Mark was killed in Vietnam," he said. "The funeral is tomorrow, and his parents would like it if you could attend." To this day I can still point to the exact spot on I-494 where Dad told me about Mark.

I had never seen a serviceman in a military coffin before. Mark looked so handsome, so mature. All I could think at that moment was, Mark, I would give all the masking tape in the world if only you could talk to me.

The church was packed with Mark's friends. Chuck's sister sang "The Battle Hymn of the Republic." Why did it have to rain on the day of the funeral? It was difficult enough at the graveside. The pastor said the usual prayers and the bugler played taps. One by one those who loved Mark took a last walk by the coffin and sprinkled it with holy water.

I was the last one to bless the coffin. As I stood there, one of the soldiers who had acted as a pallbearer came up to me. "Were you Mark's math teacher?" he asked. I nodded as I continued to stare at the coffin. "Mark talked about you a lot," he said.

After the funeral most of Mark's former classmates headed to Chuck's farmhouse for lunch. Mark's mother and father were there, obviously waiting for me. "We want to show you something," his father said, taking a wallet out of his pocket. "They found this on Mark when he was killed. We thought you might recognize it."

Opening the billfold, he carefully removed two worn pieces of notebook paper that had obviously been taped, folded and refolded many times. I knew without looking that the papers were the ones on which I had listed all the good things each of Mark's classmates had said about him. "Thank you so much for doing that," Mark's mother said. "As you can see, Mark treasured it."

Mark's classmates started to gather around us. Chuck smiled rather sheepishly and said, "I still have my list. It's in the top drawer of my desk at home." John's wife said, "John asked me to put his in our wedding album." "I have mine, too," Marilyn said. "It's in my diary." Then Vicki, another classmate, reached into her pocketbook, took out her wallet, and showed her worn and frazzled list to the group. "I carry this with me at all times," Vicki said without batting an eyelash. "I think we all saved our lists."

That's when I finally sat down and cried. I cried for Mark and all his friends who would never see him again.

Introduction to Section 2:
The Gifts of the Holy Spirit

If you knew your catechism in the old days — your Baltimore Catechism, that is — you knew that the seven gifts of the Holy Spirit were wisdom, understanding, counsel, strength (or fortitude), knowledge, piety, and fear of the Lord. You knew, too, that the gifts were "infused with sanctifying grace," because "the Holy Ghost [Spirit] dwells in the souls of the just and he is never present without his gifts."

It was all there in Question Number 125.

Then you could learn more by going on to Question 126.

"How do the Gifts of the Holy Ghost help us?

". . . By making us more alert to discern and more ready to do the will of God.

"(a) The difference between the virtues and the Gifts of the Holy Ghost consists in this: that the virtues help us to follow the guidance of our reason and faith, and the gifts help us to follow readily the inspirations of the Holy Spirit."

It was a tall order for young minds to grasp and hold on to, but somehow (perhaps it was the seemingly endless repetition of the questions and answers) many of us did. For millions of Catholic schoolchildren (and those in religious instruction classes, too) the gifts of the Holy Spirit were almost tangible presences, along with so many other items presented to us, no-nonsense style, in the old catechism.

The near disappearance of those worn little catechism booklets signals the fact that fewer young people today are learning about the gifts of the Holy Spirit, since they're not that well advertised anywhere else. Years ago children could rattle off all seven in an instant. Today most probably don't even know they exist.

That's too bad, because they haven't gone anywhere. They're still with us. They're right there, for example, in the *new* catechism — the *Catechism of the Catholic Church*, published in 1994 and a popular best-seller ever since. After listing them, in the old familiar lineup, the catechism advises (in section 1831): "They belong in their fullness to Christ, Son of David. They complete and perfect the virtues of those who receive them. They make the faithful docile in readily obeying divine inspirations."

Or the short form: They help those who are properly disposed to lead better Christian lives.

How did people first learn about the gifts of the Holy Spirit? Where do they come from?

Once again, they go back to Old Testament times, to the prophet

Isaiah, who wrote: "But a shoot shall sprout from the stump of Jesse, and from his roots a bud shall blossom. The spirit of the Lord shall rest upon him: a spirit of *wisdom* and of *understanding*, a spirit of *counsel* and of *strength*, a spirit of *knowledge* and of *fear of the Lord*, and his delight shall be the *fear of the Lord*" (Isaiah 11:1-3). (The Greek and Latin texts of Isaiah translated the first use of "fear of the Lord" as "piety," thus providing the traditional seven gifts of the spirit. Italics have been added here for emphasis.)

This is one of the traditional messianic prophecies, of course, the text teaching that the spirit of the prophets will be bestowed on the Messiah. Another prophet, Joel, later makes it clear that in the New Age and the Day of Yahweh — the time of the Messiah — this same spirit will be available to all: "Then afterward I will pour out my spirit upon all mankind. Your sons and daughters shall prophesy, your old men shall dream dreams, your young men shall see visions" (Joel 3:1).

Jesus' lengthy Last Supper discourses in John's Gospel contain several references to the strengthening presence of the Spirit (or Advocate) and in his appearance to the disciples after his resurrection, we read, also in John: "[Jesus] said to them again, 'Peace be with you. As the Father has sent me, so I send you.' And when he had said this, he breathed on them and said to them, 'Receive the Holy Spirit. Whose sins you forgive are forgiven them, and whose sins you retain are retained' " (John 20:21-23).

Finally, what more dramatic evidence of the gifts of the Holy Spirit than their manifestation on the day of Pentecost? "When the time for Pentecost was fulfilled, they were all in one place together. And suddenly there came from the sky a noise like a strong driving wind, and it filled the entire house in which they were. Then there appeared to them tongues as of fire, which parted and came to rest on each one of them. And they were all filled with the holy Spirit and began to speak in different tongues, as the Spirit enabled them to proclaim" (Acts 2:1-4).

Our understanding of how these gifts apply to us as individual Christians is hardly new. Early Church writers, at least as far back as St. Justin Martyr (c. 100-165), identified the "spirits" mentioned in Isaiah as gifts of the Holy Spirit, possessed in their fullness by Jesus and available to all his followers, "according to their merits." And so the prayers of the Church, especially at the time of confirmation and again at the ordination of deacons, still ask specifically that the Lord send these seven gifts as a sign of his favor.

In one way or another, the gifts of the Holy Spirit have been a favorite theme of Christian storytellers — some of whom have pointed out that the number seven is hardly accidental. During the Middle Ages, especially, that figure was seen as something mystical, a sign of perfection. Thus there were seven sacraments, seven days of the week, seven penitential psalms, seven deadly sins, and so on. Some famous cathedrals, including those at Chartres and Rheims, were built with seven chapels. (And, as this book will later note, the Church also lists the works of mercy, both corporal and spiritual, in groups of seven.)

What do the gifts of the Holy Spirit have to do with us today? The stories that follow might offer some answers — suggesting, perhaps, that not only have the gifts been with us all these years but that they are still here, still available in abundance to those who seek them. When the Spirit comes upon someone today, the experience will hardly be as dramatic as it was for the disciples at Pentecost, or even as fascinating as it was for those about whom the stories were written. Retelling these tales now shows how the gifts were manifested at different times in the life of the Church. They teach a good deal about a group of special men and women, and how they were affected by the gifts of the Spirit. In the process they might invite us to think about ourselves as well.

Wisdom. Few Old Testament topics have been addressed as eloquently — or as frequently — as wisdom, given in such measure to the great King Solomon. One example, from the Book of Wisdom, is this passage, written as though it were Solomon himself speaking:

"Therefore I prayed, and prudence was given me; I pleaded, and the spirit of Wisdom came to me. I preferred her to scepter and throne, and deemed riches nothing in comparison with her, nor did I liken any priceless gem to her; because all gold, in view of her, is a little sand, and before her, silver is to be accounted mire" (Wisdom 7:7-9).

Considered as a gift of the Holy Spirit, wisdom enables us to make sound judgments regarding all important matters in life — that is, all those matters that deal with our final end. The stories here describe men and women who did precisely that: St. Ignatius of Antioch, for example, a martyr of great heroism, or St. Catherine of Siena, whose genius persuaded a pope that it was time for him to return to Rome. Others include St. Ignatius Loyola, whose Jesuit followers gained an enduring reputation for intellectual achievement and faithfulness to the Holy See, and Cardinal John Henry Newman, one of the most learned men of his time, whose conversion to Catholicism stunned the world.

Understanding. This gift is a perfect counterpart to wisdom, as Scripture reminds us in the original story of King Solomon. The Lord was so pleased that the king had asked for an understanding heart that he promised: "I do as you requested. I give you a heart so wise and understanding that there has never been anyone like you up to now, and after you there will come no one to equal you" (1 Kings 3:12).

Understanding enables us first to apprehend revealed truth, and then to follow it — a concept caught perfectly in the psalmist's prayer: "Your hands have made me and fashioned me; give me discernment [understanding] that I may learn your commands" (Psalm 119:73).

The subjects of the stories here display understanding hearts, too — among them St. Augustine, who perceived a great lesson in the seaside game of a young child, or the Mexican bishop who understood that a miracle had taken place, thus helping to lead the world to Our Lady of Guadalupe.

Counsel. The Spirit's gift of counsel — the ability to choose in all things the path most likely to lead to one's sanctification — is at the heart of the stories told here of holy people whose faith defined their lives. In various ways the counsel they provided helped others toward their own salvation.

That was true in extraordinary fashion of St. John Vianney, the nineteenth-century Curé of Ars in France, who had no equal as a counselor — and consoler — of penitents. As improbable as it might seem, he spent up to eighteen hours a day, every day, in the confessional, hearing the confessions of the throngs of visitors who streamed into the small village of Ars. His divine gift was not only that of counsel but also one of miraculous perception: he could read the hearts and souls of the penitents who came to him. It is impossible to imagine that these gifts, along with his personal insights and remarkable patience, did not put thousands directly on the road to heaven.

Strength. Possessing the fortitude to resist temptations and overcome danger is another sign of the Spirit's favor; countless saints and other holy people in the Church's long history provide us with examples to that effect.

Consider some of them here: St. Christopher, whose sheer physical strength enabled him to carry a most unlikely burden through a rushing stream; St. Leo the Great, whose moral courage turned back Attila the Hun and saved Rome.

Closer to our own time are two American chaplains whose strength of character made them heroes not only to the men they served but to the entire nation as well: Father Francis P. Duffy, the New York priest who epitomized the courage of the "Fighting 69th" Regiment in World War I, and a man he helped lead to the priesthood — Father John P. Washington, one of the famed Four Chaplains who gave up their life jackets to save others when their ship was torpedoed during World War II.

Knowledge. The Scriptures repeatedly assure us that knowledge — along with wisdom and understanding — is a gift more valuable than we might even imagine. Thus we read, for example, in the Old Testament: "A wise man is more powerful than a strong man, and a man of knowledge than a man of might" (Proverbs 24:5). But under no circumstances is knowledge to be squandered; it comes from God and is to be used toward his glory and directed to our own salvation.

Knowledge was a hallmark of the men whose stories appear here. They range in time from the fourth century to the twentieth; from the story of St. Jerome — that brilliant and at times curmudgeonly scholar whose chief legacy was the translation into Latin of the Bible — to that of G. K. Chesterton, who put his towering mind and gentle humor entirely in the service of Christ and his Church.

Piety. How many pious people has the Lord sent, over the centuries, to serve as examples for the rest of us? The number must surely run into the millions: men and women whose piety, or godliness, is strong enough to convince others to love religion and its devotional practices. And all Catholics must know some of them personally — good people whose lives genuinely inspire those around them.

Some familiar stories are retold here — the origins, for example, of the rosary, of the scapular, of the First Friday devotion.

Fear of the Lord. The phrase, unfortunately, is more often misunderstood than not. Typically it conjures up an image of someone cringing in fright at the thought of God's judgment, fearful and anxious of what might lie ahead. But the reality is something different. "Fear of the Lord" is an appreciation of all that God is, a sense of awe and wonder at the boundless extent of his goodness and might.

The phrase is often used in the Bible's Wisdom Literature — most notably in the first chapter of Sirach, where it is repeated word for word ten times, and is used most familiarly in verse 12: "The beginning of wisdom is fear of the Lord, which is formed with the faithful in the womb." In other words, without fear of the Lord there is no wisdom in the true sense — no sense at all of what is truly important in this life, no understanding of what awaits us in the next.

Six stories attempt to capture the essence of the gift, and perhaps none does it better than that of Sister Thea Bowman. Sister Thea, who died in 1990 after an agonizing struggle with cancer, lived a life of wonder and excitement at the greatness of God. She had an incomparable gift of getting others to share it with her. How she accomplished just that with the entire body of the nation's bishops — even in the throes of her final illness — makes for a memorable story, and a reminder that the fear of the Lord can be a powerful gift indeed.

Quick as a Flash

St. Paul Helped to Change the World —
Once He Understood

The thought of one person being able to change the world in this day and age is almost beyond our imagining. We're all too dependent on one another, on the technology we've created, for that to happen. And yet in his own time St. Paul (d.c. 67), to a large degree, did just that — arguably more so than anyone else since Jesus lived among us on earth.

He was the missioner extraordinary, of course, spreading the Good News about Jesus throughout most of the known world. Jew, Gentile, those in pagan lands — they all responded to this man and his words, to the strength of his convictions, the love in his heart, the force of his personality.

That would have been accomplishment enough for anyone else. But for Paul it was only the beginning. The incomparable letters he wrote unveiled his vision of the divine plan and gave the young Church its shape and direction, leaving a lasting imprint that endures today.

Now consider this: none of this would have happened, none of it would have been possible, had not the Holy Spirit blessed Paul with the gift of understanding —understanding about Jesus, understanding about his followers, understanding about what must be done.

And all of that began to happen in an instant. Just like this . . .

Adapted from Acts 9:1-30.

His name was Saul — a Roman citizen, born at Tarsus in Cilicia, instructed early on in the Mosaic law. Few could match him when it came to persecuting the new faith in Jesus, and he did so with a vengeance. He dragged Christians out of their homes, bound them with chains, and thrust them into prison. He even applied for a commission to take up all the Jews in Damascus who confessed Jesus Christ, planning to bring them to Jerusalem — where they would serve as an example to others.

But his life underwent a dramatic change while he was on his way to Damascus. He and his party were suddenly surrounded by a blinding light from heaven, brighter even than the sun. The stunning surprise of it all literally knocked Saul off his feet. He fell to the ground and heard a mysterious voice: "Saul, Saul, why are you persecuting me?"

"Who are you, sir?" he asked.

"I am Jesus, whom you are persecuting," came the reply. "Now get up and go into the city, and you will be told what you must do."

The experience transformed Saul and baffled his companions, who had heard the voice yet saw no one at all. Trembling and astonished, Saul followed the command he had received — even though he could not see and had to be led by hand into Damascus. There he stayed for three days before a holy man named Ananias came to him — on "the street called Straight" (Acts 9:11). In a house there Ananias laid hands on Saul and proclaimed: "Saul, my brother, the Lord has sent me, Jesus who appeared to you on the way by which you came, that you may regain your sight and be filled with the Holy Spirit."

All at once something like scales fell from Saul's eyes and he regained his sight, and, after he had eaten, recovered his strength as well. He stayed for some days in Damascus, proclaiming Jesus in the synagogue and confounding the Jews as he did so. Eventually they conspired to kill him, but he and his disciples learned of the plot. His friends lowered Saul in a basket through an opening in the wall, after which he made his way to Jerusalem. There he became known also as Paul (cf. Acts 13:9) and reported on his mystifying conversion. "He moved about freely with them in Jerusalem, and spoke out boldly in the name of the Lord" (Acts 9:28).

In the Lap of the Lord

The Life of St. Ignatius of Antioch,
Begun in Glory, Ended in Martyrdom

Catholics everywhere owe a debt to St. Ignatius of Antioch (c. 35-107) for a unique gift: their name. It is this heroic saint, known for his wisdom and fidelity, who is generally credited with being the first to use the word "Catholic" to describe the new faith community that grew up around the followers of the crucified Christ.

"Wheresoever the bishop shall appear," Ignatius wrote in his epistle to the people of Smyrna, "there let the people be, even as where Jesus is, there is the Catholic Church." His epistles give historians a special insight into the lives of the first Christians and the depth of the wisdom of the earliest Church Fathers.

What St. Ignatius meant by using the world "Catholic" is both simple and profound: the Church, universal in place, scope, and time, is a community of believers called together not by men and women but by the Lord himself.

Story adapted from *Anecdotes and Examples Illustrating the Catholic Catechism*, selected and arranged by Rev. Francis Spirago, Benziger Brothers, 1904.

St. Ignatius, bishop of Antioch, had a special reverence for the holy name of Jesus, and with good reason. According to tradition, it was young Ignatius, then barely more than a toddler, who was held by Jesus as he taught his disciples a lesson. Do you remember the story?

On the way to Capharnaum the Apostles were quibbling among themselves, wondering who would be the greatest in the kingdom of heaven. When they entered the city, Jesus called a young boy to come to his side and, taking him by the hand, set him in the midst of his followers. Then Jesus told them:

"Amen, I say to you, unless you turn and become like children, you will not enter the kingdom of heaven. Whoever humbles himself like this child is the greatest in the kingdom of heaven. And whoever receives one child such as this in my name receives me" (Matthew 18:3-5).

According to an old legend, the child whom Jesus called to his side was Ignatius, who in later years would run to the spot, kiss the ground, and tell his companions, "Here is the place Jesus took me in his arms and embraced me."

What is known about Ignatius beyond a doubt is that he grew to be a very holy man — a priest first, and then bishop of Antioch, an important community where St. Peter himself had once taught the faithful. Under Ignatius' leadership, the entire population soon became Christians.

The Emperor Trajan, passing through Antioch on an expedition, found the Roman temples deserted and demanded to know who was responsible. The governor had a ready answer: it was Ignatius, the Christian bishop. Trajan summoned the bishop and asked if he were indeed the "evil spirit" who had sown such discord in the city.

"He cannot be called an evil spirit," Ignatius replied, "who hears God in his heart."

"I suppose you mean Jesus of Nazareth," said the emperor.

"Indeed," Ignatius said, proceeding to proclaim the folly of worshiping heathen gods.

The emperor, turning furious, cut him off with two fearsome words: *"Ad leonem"* — "[Cast him] to the lions."

Ignatius was seized and taken to meet his fate in Rome. Christians there tried to save him, but he wrote them and asked them not to interfere. He would not be denied, he said, the crown of martyrdom. In the amphitheater, facing the lions that soon would tear him apart, he prayed aloud: "The name of Jesus shall never depart from my lips, and even if it were to do so, it cannot be obliterated from my heart."

Pious legend further has it that those who recovered Ignatius' remains found his heart — and on it was inscribed, just as the saint had foretold, the holy name of Jesus.

The Christ-Bearer

An Old Legend Tells How St. Christopher Got His Name

Almost every collection of stories about the saints — even those that go back for generations — includes this one. It's still popular today, and here it's told by one of the master storytellers of our own time, Father William J. Bausch.

Little is known about St. Christopher that goes beyond the realm of legend, and it was for that reason that his feast day (July 25) was dropped from the Roman calendar in 1969. That doesn't mean, however, that the Church had decided that Christopher was "no longer a saint" (as popular understanding had it at the time), or that he can no longer be regarded as the patron saint of travelers, especially motorists. No reason, either, that readers shouldn't continue to enjoy this timeless tale of how St. Christopher (literally, "the Christ-bearer") got his name.

Story from *Storytelling: Imagination and Faith*, by William J. Bausch, Twenty-Third Publications, 1984 (originally in *The Wisdom of Accepted Tenderness*, by Brennan Manning, Dimension Books, 1978).

Christopher was a mild and gentle giant of a man who served the king of Canaan faithfully. Though he cared deeply for his lord, the king, he dreamed of serving the strongest master in the world. Taking leave of Canaan, he traveled until he came to the castle of the one said to be the greatest ruler of the world. When the king saw the size and strength of Christopher, he made him second in command and invited him to dwell in his court.

One day when a minstrel was entertaining the king, he sang a song about the devil. Whenever the name of the devil was mentioned, the king made the sign of the Cross. Christopher asked the king about his actions.

"It is to ward off the devil," the king answered.

"Do you fear his power?" asked Christopher.

"Ah, yes," said the king, "he has great might."

Christopher shook his head sadly. "I must leave you, my lord, for I have a great desire to serve the most powerful one in this world. It seems the devil is that one."

Christopher began his search for the devil, wandering until he met a great company of knights. The leader of the knights, a man who appeared cruel and horrible, approached him and asked him what he wanted. "I am in search of the devil to be my master," said Christopher evenly.

"I am the one you seek," said the terrible knight. Christopher immediately bowed before the devil and promised his allegiance.

A bit later, as the company of knights walked together, they came upon a cross standing at an intersection. Immediately the devil turned to the side, taking his followers in a circuitous route until he finally came back to the highway.

"Why did we take this route?" asked Christopher.

At first the devil was reluctant to answer, but Christopher persisted. "There was once a man called Christ who was killed on a cross," the devil explained. "When I see his sign, I am afraid and attempt to avoid it."

"Then he is greater and more powerful than you," said Christopher. "I see that I have yet to find the one who is the greatest lord on the earth. I will leave you to find Christ, whoever he is."

Christopher began a long search for the one people called Jesus, the Christ. At last he came upon a pious hermit who welcomed him and began to teach him about Jesus. One day the hermit spoke to Christopher. "You are not ready to serve Christ. In order to do this you must fast."

Christopher said, "It is most difficult for me to fast. Ask me to do something else."

"You must wake early in the morning and pray long hours each day," the hermit said.

"Please," said Christopher, "find me a task more to my ability. I am not a man who can pray for long periods of time."

The hermit thought for a moment before he spoke again. "You are indeed tall and strong. You shall live by the river and carry across anyone who comes in need. In that way you will serve Jesus. I hope that Our Lord Christ will one day show himself to you."

So Christopher began his life of service at the river, where the current was strong. There, with the help of a huge pole, he carried rich and poor alike over the treacherous river.

One day as he slept in his lodge by the river, Christopher heard the voice of a child calling, "Christopher, come carry me over." When he looked outside, he saw no one. Back in his lodge, he again heard the voice call. Again his search was unsuccessful. The third time he went outside, he found a child who begged Christopher to carry him over the river.

The giant took the child on his shoulders and began his walk across the river. As the water rushed against his body, the weight of the child was almost too much to bear. The farther he walked, the more the water swelled, and the heavier the child rested on his shoulders. For the first time in his life, the giant Christopher was gripped with a fear of death. At last, using all his might, Christopher reached land and put the child down.

Lying nearly exhausted, Christopher spoke to the child. "I was in great trouble in the water. I felt as if I had the weight of the whole world on my shoulders."

Then the child spoke. "Indeed you have borne a great burden, Christopher. I am Jesus Christ, the king you serve in your work. This day you have carried not only the whole world but the one who created the world. In order that you might know what I say is true, place your staff in the earth by the house, and tomorrow it will bear flowers and fruit." Then the child disappeared.

The next morning Christopher walked outside, and there he found his staff bearing flowers, leaves, and dates. Christopher now knew that he served the greatest and most powerful master in the world.

The Power of Prayer

St. Aphraates's Holy Water
Saved a Crop From a Plague of Locusts

The use of holy water is an ancient sign of piety; references to it go back to the earliest days of the Church.

Water itself, of course, has traditionally held a central place in liturgical practice. It has always been regarded as a symbol of cleansing, and is used as such in the sacrament of baptism. "Holy water" — that is, water blessed by a priest — is described as a sacramental: a sign introduced by the Church as a reminder of the sacraments given to us by Christ.

This story of the way St. Aphraates used holy water to save a farmer's fields is one of many in the same vein, passed along to its listeners as a reminder of the saving power of God. Here it is, as it was told long ago.

Story adapted from *Catholic Anecdotes*, by the Brothers of
the Christian Schools; translated from the French by Mrs. J.
Sadlier; D. & J. Sadlier & Co., 1885.

St. Aphraates, an ancient hermit, came from his native Persia to live near Antioch, the capital of Syria. As it happens, that area is periodically ravaged by hordes of locusts, which cover the land like a cloud and then settle in the fields, devouring the crops and causing illness with their pestilence. One year this plague came upon the land once again, this time with a horrible intensity.

A poor man went to St. Aphraates. "Father," he said, "we are lost. The locusts are coming. They will eat up my field of wheat, and it is all I have to feed my wife and children — and to pay the emperor's taxes besides. Man of God, have pity on me!"

"My good man," Aphraates replied, "I can do nothing of myself; it is only God who can work a miracle in your behalf. Nevertheless, if you have confidence, bring me a pitcher of water."

The poor laborer went out and quickly returned with the water. St. Aphraates dipped his hand in it, said a prayer over it, and blessed it. Then he gave it to the man, telling him to take the pitcher and sprinkle a little of the holy water it contained all around his field.

The man did so exactly, and before long it became clear just how miraculous the holy water would prove to be. The locusts arrived, and in a moment darkened the air and covered the country to a great distance. But not one crossed the limits of the farmer's field; any that went in that direction were thrown back as if by an invisible force.

The crop on that field would turn out to be most abundant that year, convincing everyone of the sanctity of Aphraates — not to mention the virtue of holy water.

A Sign of Faith

Even in Death, St. Cecilia Testified to Her Belief

Many stories of the early martyrs testify to the superhuman strength these men and women displayed in the face of dreadful torture. How much is fact, and how much is pious legend? We'll probably never know. What we should remember is this: the tortures and executions were real in the days of the early Church, and so were the martyrs. The details are less important than the fact of their sacrifice, often under heroic circumstances.

So it is with St. Cecilia (d. 177). Little is known of her life beyond what legend and tradition tell us, but this patroness of Church music has been regarded as a saint since the time of the sixth century. Here the story of her incredible fortitude is retold to make a point about the Blessed Trinity.

Story adapted from *Catechism in Stories*, by Rev. Lawrence
G. Lovasik, SVD, The Bruce Publishing Co., 1956.

On the evening of her wedding day, the music of the marriage hymn ringing in her ears, Cecilia, a rich, beautiful, and noble Roman maiden, renewed the vow by which she had consecrated her virginity to God. The heart of her young husband, Valerian, was moved by her words and he received baptism — as did his brother, Tiburtius. But the joy of the moment would not last. Within a very short time all three would be called on to seal their faith with their blood.

The charge against Cecilia was simple enough: she was accused of being a Christian, a dangerous offense in those days. But the threats of the pagan prefect failed to weaken her love for Christ.

"Do you know," she exclaimed, "that I am the bride of my Lord Jesus Christ?"

Her captors decided on a horrible fate: death by suffocation. She was confined a full day and night to a hot-air bath, heated to seven times its usual temperature. But, to the wonderment of her guards, the heat had no power over her body. Very well, then; an executioner would sever her head from her body. Three times his trembling hands delivered the three blows allowed by law, and yet she lived on.

Cecilia spent the next two days and two nights on the rough floor of her bath — fully conscious, her head nearly severed, joyfully awaiting her crown. Then on the third day her agony was over, and the virgin saint gave back her pure spirit to Christ. The Christians buried her just as she lay in death, her head facing the floor — *and three fingers of her right hand and one finger of her left hand set forward, as a proof of her faith in the truth that there is only one God in three divine persons.* About the year 300 her body was exhumed and found in the same position — incorrupt.

'On the Day Called Sunday...'

Early Mass Described by St. Justin Martyr Sounds Much Like Our Own

St. Justin Martyr (c. 100-165), one of the great theologians and teach-ers of the early Church, was especially skilled in uniting faith with reason — so successful in influencing other Romans to turn to Chris-tianity that he was martyred by the emperor. There's an irony there, since Justin labored diligently to free the Christians of his day from the waves of mindless persecutions that threatened them so fre-quently.

He did so in brilliant fashion in his First Apology, *a lengthy letter written, probably between 151 and 155, to the Emperor Anto-ninus Pius to plead the Christian cause. Opening with a bold appeal to justice, he went on to refute some of the many slanders against Christianity, continued with a well-ordered exposition of Christian theology, and concluded with a description of some of the rites of worship practiced by followers of the new faith.*

It is his account of the Sunday service, in which Christians com-memorated the sacrifice of Jesus, that has so fascinated Catholics of our own day. His description of what we know as the Mass is easily recognizable: the readings, the Gospel, homily, creed, preparation of the gifts, Eucharistic Prayer, distribution of Communion, and a collec-tion to aid the poor. Remember that this was written only one hun-dred twenty-five years or so after Jesus died on the Cross. It should give us a new appreciation of the rich heritage we share.

Taken from the *First Apology*, St. Justin Martyr, c. 151-155.

And on the day called Sunday, all who live in cities or in the country gather together in one place, and the memoirs of the Apostles or the writings of the prophets are read, as long as time permits; then, when the reader has ceased, the president verbally instructs and exhorts to the imitation of these good things.

Then we all rise together and pray and as we said before, when our prayer is ended, bread and wine and water are brought, and the president in like manner offers prayers and thanksgivings, according to his ability, and the people assent, saying, "Amen."

There is a distribution to each and a participation of that over which thanks have been given, and to those who are absent a portion is sent by the deacons. And they who are well to do and willing give what each thinks fit. And what is collected is deposited with the president, who aids the orphans and widows, and those who through sickness or any other cause are in want.

Sunday is the day on which we all hold our common assembly, because it is the first day on which God, having wrought a change in the darkness and matter, made the world, and Jesus Christ our Savior on the same day rose from the dead.

The True Cross

St. Helena's Dogged Persistence Led to Its Discovery

Many aspects of the discovery of the True Cross by St. Helena (c. 250-330) are, technically speaking, unverifiable, but historians are able to vouch for key elements of the story.

Helena was indeed the mother of the Emperor Constantine, the first emperor to give the Church the full protection of Roman law. And in 326 she did undertake a pilgrimage to the Holy Land, where her gifts helped to finance the construction of several major churches, including that of the Holy Sepulchre.

History is less clear on details of the recovery of the True Cross, although the story as told here is the one that has persisted for many generations. (Another legend embellishes this account significantly, tracing the wood of the Cross not only to the doorway of Solomon's Temple but back to a Tree of Life venerated by David and Moses and planted by Adam himself.)

At any rate, St. Helena did report finding the True Cross and ensured that relics were sent to Constantinople and Rome while others were left in Jerusalem. In dealing with this matter over the centuries, many Catholics have been content to let faith supply those answers that history cannot.

Story adapted from *Little Pictorial Lives of the Saints*,
Benziger Brothers, Inc., 1925.

With his edict having restored peace to the Church, Constantine wanted to give further glory to the Lord by building a magnificent church in Jerusalem. Accordingly his mother, Helena, undertook a journey to the Holy Land in 326 — even though she was nearing the age of eighty at the time. She had a number of things she hoped to accomplish, none more important than the discovery of the True Cross of Jesus.

Helena found that no marker indicated its final resting place, nor was there any traditional understanding — even among the city's Christians — as to where it might be.

In fact, it lay beneath a pile of rubble, deliberately placed there by pagans to hide the site of Jesus' tomb. Atop the rubble, adding to the concealment, stood a temple to Venus. Nearby was a statue of Jupiter, on the very spot where the Savior had risen from the dead.

Helena consulted many of those she met in Jerusalem, ultimately discovering that in Jesus' time it was the custom to bury next to the victim those instruments that might have been used in his execution. Thus, she reasoned, if she could find the sepulchre she would find the Cross as well. She set about having the statues destroyed, the temple torn down, the rubble removed — and finally, at a great depth, came upon the tomb itself. Nearby was a breathtaking discovery: three crosses, three nails, and even the sign that had been affixed atop Jesus' Cross!

One of the three crosses had to be that of the Lord, but which one? Bishop Macarius thought he might have a way to find out. A well-known woman of the city was extremely ill; why not bring the three crosses to her side? If one of the three brought about her cure, that would surely be the Cross on which Jesus had died. And that is just what happened: two crosses were pressed to the woman and produced no effect at all, but the third Cross — the *True* Cross — resulted in an immediate and complete recovery.

Overjoyed, Helena built a church on the spot, installing the Cross there with great veneration. Later she carried part of it to her son, then at Constantinople, and still later took another piece to Rome. It was enshrined in the church that she built, Holy Cross in Jerusalem *(Santa Croce in Gerusalemme)*, and remains there to this day.

The sign that had been atop the Cross of Jesus — the one that had mockingly described him as "Jesus of Nazareth, King of the Jews" — was also taken to Rome, hidden away in a lead box until its rediscovery in 1492. Many chips were removed from the original True Cross over the years, to be given to devout persons, and yet the Cross itself never grew smaller — a wonder attested to by St. Cyril of Jerusalem twenty-five years later.

And the three nails? "One the Empress Helena placed in the crown of Constantine; another she made into a bit for his horse; the third she threw into a whirlpool in the Adriatic — and immediately the sea was calm."

'I Am a Christian'

St. Jerome Shared His Knowledge
of the Bible With All the Church

As a young man, St. Jerome (c. 347-420) lived the good life of his day. Raised in comfortable surroundings near what is now Trieste, he was educated in Rome, did some traveling, dabbled a bit at this and that. He had been baptized and was attentive to his faith, but remained inordinately fond of the classic Latin works he had studied: Cicero, Virgil, Terence.

He was in his mid-twenties when he sailed to the East, planning vaguely to devote himself to Christ. But in Antioch, he became ill while staying at the home of a friend, and then had a dream — or was it a vision? —that would turn his life around. Firmly resolving to pay more attention to things that were sacred, he went off to live as a hermit, learning Hebrew in the process.

The language would stand him in good stead. Returning to Rome, he became secretary to Pope Damasus, who commissioned him to undertake a translation of the Bible. Unhappy with Rome's political climate following the death of Damasus in 484, Jerome settled in Bethlehem — where he would spend the rest of his life heading a monastic community, serving as a Father confessor to visitors from all over the world, and producing not only the classic Latin translation of the Bible (in the case of the Old Testament, from the original Hebrew) but also scores of commentaries and other scholarly texts. The Church honors him as its patron of Scripture study.

One more point: by reputation, St. Jerome comes down to us as the grumpy old man of his day. He was said to be intemperate, and harsh on those with whom he disagreed. But that attitude of hostility seems to have been reserved for his intellectual and theological foes — in Jerome's view, the "enemies of the Church." Those who sincerely sought his priestly counsel were never turned away.

Story adapted from traditional sources.

Jerome interrupted his journey to Jerusalem to stay for a time at Antioch, where he was the guest of the priest Evagrios. The scholar was not traveling lightly; he had with him the library he had assembled at Rome. And it was that library, he later confessed, that occupied his mind day and night. If he fasted, it was to prepare for a reading of Cicero; if he spent the night in vigil, it was only to prepare him to pick up the writings of Plautus — "unhappy man that I was!" as he expressed it in later years.

But then illness intervened, making his stopover in Antioch longer than he had planned. It turned out to be a deadly fever, one that had already taken the lives of two members of Evagrios's household, and Jerome was treated with extra care and kindness. Not only did he pull through; an experience he underwent when the fever was at its height would change his life forever.

At that point the illness had left Jerome weak and emaciated. His body was icy cold and, as he later told the story, "they were getting ready to bury me."

And then it happened: the ecstasy, or miracle — or perhaps nothing more than a fever-induced dream. In it Jerome found himself in some kind of court, facing an unseen judge whose countenance was hidden behind a dazzling bright light. The judge had a question for Jerome: What is your religion?

"I am a Christian," he answered.

"You lie," was the judge's stern answer. "You are a Ciceronian, not a Christian. Where your treasure is, there your heart is also!"

Stunned, Jerome then heard an order that he be flogged. His cries for mercy fell between lashes of the whip.

Finally others in the dream took up his cause, begging the judge to forgive Jerome his youthful indiscretions and give him the chance to do penance. Only if he goes back to his habits of worldly reading, they pleaded, should there be cause for further punishment.

Jerome himself was ready to promise much more.

"Lord!" he exclaimed. "If ever I own profane books again, or if I read them, it will mean that I have denied you!"

With that, Jerome was dismissed — and soon after found himself waking up. Had it only been a dream? If it was, what would account for the bruises on Jerome's body — or the trembling that lingered from his ordeal?

One way or the other, the experience had a lasting effect. From that day forward, Jerome devoted himself only to the Lord — and his works would reach out to the whole world.

Lessons for a Lifetime

St. Augustine, Who Never Stopped Learning, Still Teaches the World Today

Countless generations have known St. Augustine (354-430) as one of the most influential thinkers in history. Father and Doctor of the Church, he has left a permanent imprint on the theology and spirituality of individual Catholics and the Church as a whole since his own time.

And for almost that long, Catholics have loved to hear stories about this remarkable saint. The first one here is a charming tale, a pious legend that for centuries has given children an idea of what knowledge is all about. It takes advantage of the old encounter-by-the-seashore approach, a device that storytellers of old found useful to command their listeners' attention right from the start. The setting is easy to visualize and the dramatic setup takes place in a moment. (In another well-known seaside tale, St. Justin had a chance meeting at the shore with an old man — who opened his eyes to the wisdom of God.)

This time it's a young boy who leads the way. He manages to leave the great Augustine with the understanding that in this life neither he — nor any of us — will ever have all the answers.

The second story, the one of St. Augustine's conversion, is one of the Church's best known, in good measure because of Augustine's own account of it in his Confessions. *It came about for many reasons, among them the persistence of the prayers of his mother, St. Monica, and the power of the preaching of a teacher he respected, St. Ambrose. It came about, too, because Augustine finally began to realize the extent of the Lord's goodness and greatness. He himself described how that happened:*

"I asked the earth, and it said, 'I am not he!' All things confessed the same. I asked the sea and the deeps, and among living animals the things that creep, and they answered, 'We are not your God! Seek you higher than us!' . . . I asked the heavens, the sun, the moon, and the stars: 'We are not the God whom you seek,' they said. To all the things that stand around the doors of my flesh I said, 'Tell me of my God!' . . . With a mighty voice they cried out, 'He made us!' My question was the gaze that I turned on them; their answer was their beauty."

First story adapted from *Catholic Anecdotes*, by the Brothers
of the Christian Schools; translated from the French by
Mrs. J. Sadlier; D. & J. Sadlier & Co., 1885; second story
from *Saints and Their Stories*, by Mary Montgomery,
Harper & Row, 1988.

1. And a Child Shall Lead

One day St. Augustine was walking along the shore of the
Mediterranean Sea, meditating on the mystery of the Holy Trinity.
He hoped to understand it more fully so he could explain it in a
work he was about to compose.

He was lost in his thoughts when he came across a little boy
playing at the side of the sea. The young lad was running back and
forth, using a shell to carry water from the sea into a hole he had
dug in the sand.

"What's that you're doing, young friend?" Augustine asked.

"I'm trying to put all the water from the sea into this little hole,"
the boy replied.

Augustine smiled. "But that's impossible," he said gently. "Can't
you see that the hole is too small, and the sea too large?"

"So you think I can't do it?" the boy asked, looking up directly
at Augustine. "Let me assure you of this: it will be easier for me to
put all the water of the sea into this little hole than it will be for you
to comprehend or explain the doctrine of the Holy Trinity!"

No sooner had the boy spoken these words than he disappeared — an angel, in fact, who had taken the form of a child to give
St. Augustine this important lesson. The learned doctor thanked
God for such a favor, and gave himself no further trouble trying to
penetrate inscrutable mysteries.

2. St. Augustine Opens His Heart to God

In Tagaste, North Africa, old men sat around the market square.
They enjoyed the warm sun, but they didn't much care for a boy
named Augustine. When he and his rowdy friends walked by, one
of the old men shook his head. "Augustine will come to no good
end," he warned. "He leads other boys astray. They steal and skip
school and play pranks just the way Augustine does."

"What that boy needs is a whipping," another of the old men
grumbled. "But he'll never get it. His tongue is so quick and his
mind is so clever that he can talk his way out of anything."

Augustine's mother, Monica, knew that her son was a problem. Even though she often scolded him, his behavior didn't change.
He kept right on getting himself and others into trouble. The only

Our Sunday Visitor's

thing left to do was pray for him. And she did a great deal of that.

Monica was a Christian, but her husband was a pagan. His name was Patricius, and he was a Roman official in Tagaste. At home, Patricius was grouchy and bad-tempered. Mostly he thought about himself and how he could get elected to higher office. He did very little to help his wife raise their three children.

One of Monica's greatest hopes was that Augustine would accept her Christian faith. But he refused to even listen to her beliefs. "Your religion holds no interest for me," he told her angrily. "I don't want to hear about it anymore."

School didn't interest Augustine either. Even though he was very bright, he failed in his subjects. "What will we do with Augustine?" his worried mother often asked her husband. "What ever will become of him?"

Augustine's parents finally decided to send their son to a school twenty miles away. The school was in the town of Madaura and there things began to change. Again, Augustine became a leader. But now his leadership was in schoolwork, not in troublemaking. He still loved games and sports. He still loved having a good time. The difference in Augustine was that he also took an interest in his studies. Soon he was at the top of his class and was especially good at speaking and writing.

Augustine finished his studies at Madaura and went on to the university at Carthage. Before long, he was a very well-known student. Whenever his name was mentioned, people would nod and say, "Augustine is our most famous speaker and writer. No one will give you an argument about that."

While Augustine was at the university, he became interested in religion. But the religion that interested him was not Christianity. It was a religion called Manichaeism. Manichaeans believed there were two gods: one of good and one of evil. They thought these forces of good and evil had equal power and battled each other for victory.

Augustine became a Manichaean, which greatly troubled his Christian mother. "How can you follow such a religion?" she asked again and again. "Don't you even hear me when I tell you that there is only one God? This one true God sent his Son, Jesus, to show us how to live."

Even though Augustine loved and respected his mother, he refused to change his mind. No matter how much she argued and cried and prayed, Augustine held on to his beliefs and ignored hers.

After Augustine finished his studies at the university, he became a teacher. His first job was in his hometown of Tagaste. While teaching there, Augustine became dissatisfied with his religion. He gave up Manichaeism, but that left him with an empty feeling. He kept searching for something to believe in. Still, he did not want to think about being a Christian.

After a time, Augustine grew restless in Tagaste and went to live in Rome, where life was difficult for a foreigner. Augustine was poor and lonely and often sick. When he tried to start a school, the students cheated him out of money they owed for classes.

Augustine was offered a teaching job in Milan, a city in northern Italy. He gladly took the job. Soon he became well known for his speaking. But one man in the city was even better known than Augustine. He was the bishop of Milan, who would one day be known as St. Ambrose.

After Augustine heard Bishop Ambrose preach, he wanted to know more about his beliefs. The bishop agreed to meet with Augustine, but only for a short time. "I am kept busy caring for the needy and reading the Scriptures to those who can't read for themselves," he told Augustine. "You are a scholar who can read for yourself. But do not read the Scriptures for their beautiful writing. Read instead for their beautiful ideas."

Augustine began studying the Bible. He came to believe in what it said, but he was not yet ready to become a Christian. It was too hard for him to change his life and live the way Jesus asked him to. "I want to be good," he said, "only not just yet."

Meanwhile, Augustine's mother had come to live in Milan. Even though she was often angry and upset with her son, she never stopped loving him. As Augustine learned more about the Christian faith, he understood that his mother's love and God's love were alike: both were unending.

Finally, Augustine decided to become a Christian. He was baptized by Bishop Ambrose on Holy Saturday in the year 387. No one was happier or more proud than Augustine's mother, Monica.

A short time later, Monica died. Augustine was heartbroken to lose the mother who had loved him so greatly. She was so faithful to her beliefs and so dedicated in her love that we know her today as St. Monica.

Augustine returned to Africa and became a priest. He went on to become bishop of the important city of Hippo. Besides being a great preacher and teacher, he was a fine writer. A lot of his writings spoke out against the false beliefs held by many people of the time. One of his most famous books is called *Confessions*. In it he tells about his own search for God and how he came to love Jesus and the Christian way of life. He writes: "You have made us for yourself, O Lord, and our hearts will find no rest until they rest in you."

Since his death long ago, Augustine's writings have had a great influence in the Church in every period of history. He is honored both as a saint and as a Doctor of the Church.

'The Man of God'

St. Alexis Lived as a Humble Beggar — In His Family's Palatial Home

Even though much of what legend tells us about the life of St. Alexis (d. 417) cannot be historically confirmed, he commanded a remarkable following that extended over the course of many centuries. How did it all begin? No one knows for sure, but not many years after his death, an unknown writer set down the unlikely story of Alexis' life — how he rejected the great wealth to which he was born in Rome, ran off to Syria, and years later returned unrecognized to his own home, living out his days as a beggar.

The story caught on. People of his generation (and those that followed) loved it so much that they referred to Alexis simply as "The Man of God." His followers saw in him the reflection not only of great wisdom but of all the gifts of the Holy Spirit combined. They entrusted religious communities to him (including the nursing congregation commonly called the Alexian Brothers).

But there were cautions, too, against using his life of superhuman sacrifice as a model. Commenting on St. Alexis in his own classic work Butler's Lives of the Saints, *Father Alban Butler wrote: "The extraordinary paths in which the Holy Ghost is pleased sometimes to conduct certain privileged souls are rather to be admired than imitated."*

Selection adapted from *Catechism in Stories*, by Rev. Lawrence G. Lovasik, SVD, The Bruce Publishing Co., 1956.

Euphemianus, a Roman citizen of great wealth, had a son named Alexis whom he loved very much. He lavished attention on the young man, but there was a problem: Alexis had become a Christian, and insisted in giving away his things to the poor. Seeing Alexis so casually dispose of his belongings irritated his father, who took the problem to his friends: what could he do?

They were sure they had the answer. Marry off the lad, the friends told Euphemianus; he'll soon forget his ill-advised charities. Taking their advice, Euphemianus went ahead with wedding preparations for Alexis — who recoiled at the thought. His protests went unheeded, however, and the wedding day came. That night, as the feast was at its height, Alexis disappeared.

The young man went far away — to a small town in Syria, where he became a beggar. Over the years he attracted the love of the townspeople, because whatever he collected from his begging he turned over to the poor. Not only generous but kind and loving as well, he eventually became known far and wide as a holy man. His growing fame bothered Alexis, however, and one night — just as he had all those years earlier in Rome — he vanished without a trace.

Months later he turned up — to the same Roman house he had fled as a bridegroom long ago. He was in tatters, but the servants of the house, recognizing him as a holy man (but not as their own Alexis), found room for him underneath the palace stairs.

There he lived for seventeen years, begging and still helping the poor. But one morning he failed to appear at the kitchen door for his alms of bread. The servants found him dying in his hovel beneath the stairs. At his request, the wealthy woman who headed the house came to see him. When she looked down at him, he uttered his last words: "I am Alexis, your son."

The mother broke out in tears, embracing him. In time the house of Euphemianus became a church under the patronage of St. Alexis, of whom it was said: "It was through the gifts of the Holy Spirit that Alexis received the wisdom and understanding to give up worldly possessions in order to obtain heavenly treasures. The Holy Spirit gave him the courage and strength he needed to make these sacrifices. The same Holy Spirit filled his soul with childlike fear of God and true piety."

The Man Who Saved Rome

St. Leo's Eloquence and Strength
Turned Back Attila the Hun

Popes have been confronting the tyrants of the world for centuries, reminding them that all earthly might fades in time while strength of the soul endures. It's a tradition that goes back at least as far as Pope St. Leo the Great (pope from 440-461), who faced down the rampaging Attila the Hun near the city of Mantua in 452 and persuaded him to spare Rome.

Leo was armed only with his eloquence and the courage of his convictions, but they succeeded where the armed force of others had failed. It wasn't long before the tale was embellished; legend soon had it that Attila turned back in terror when he saw a vision of Sts. Peter and Paul standing behind Pope Leo, ready to confront him with a heavenly host.

Actually, no legend was needed. St. Leo's own strength of soul had done the trick. Here's the way Catholic schoolchildren learned the lesson earlier in this century.

Story from *Great Moments in Catholic History:*
100 Memorable Events in Catholic History Told in Picture
and Story, by Rev. Edward Lodge Curran, Grosset &
Dunlap, 1937.

Many times the Christian civilization of the world has been threatened with destruction. Today evil forces from Soviet Russia threaten to destroy it. Again and again, the Church has had to save civilization.

In the time of Pope St. Leo the Great (440-461), word came to Rome that the Huns under Attila, "The Scourge of God," were on their way southward. The citizens of Italy were terrified. His troops had been defeated in France, at the town of Châlons on the River Marne. A Roman general named Aetius had turned him back after a fierce battle.

The "Scourge of God" was infuriated. He would have his revenge on Rome. As a barbarian he hated civilization. Schools and homes and farms and works of art would be destroyed.

Over the Alps Attila swept with his horsemen and foot soldiers. The bodies of men and women slaughtered in northern Italy were the only things left in the towns that he took and destroyed.

The citizens of Venetia abandoned their town and fled to some islands in the Adriatic Sea. There, out of their fishing villages, the modern beautiful city of Venice arose.

On and on, nearer to Rome, killing men and women and children, destroying buildings, burning farms, Attila, the "Scourge of God," at last came face-to-face with Pope Leo, the Vicar of Christ, in Mantua.

The face of Attila was cruel. The face of Pope Leo was kindly. Around Attila were thousands of his warriors armed with their swords of conquest. Around Leo were a few Christian citizens from Rome, armed with the truth of Christ.

The man of war looked and listened to the man of peace. Strange words of Christ, the Prince of Peace, broke upon the ears of Attila. "All that take the sword shall perish with the sword."

He shuddered as he heard how not even the Roman emperors were able to destroy Christianity. The shouts of his warriors died out. His eyes grew wide with wonderment.

There were other countries he could conquer. He gave his orders. He marched away — back to the north and east from whence he came. Pope Leo had conquered. Once again Christianity had saved civilization from the destroyer.

Gregory the Great

His Influence on the Life of the Church Knew No Bounds

The Church does not easily bestow the appellation "great" on its popes. Of the two hundred sixty-four men who have sat in the chair of Peter, only two have been so recognized. The first was Pope Leo the Great; the second was his successor (by some one hundred thirty years), Pope Gregory the Great (540-604).

For all practical purposes, the influence of Pope Gregory I was limitless. His musical initiatives led to what we still refer to as Gregorian chant. He was the first pontiff to describe himself as "servant of the servants of God." His lives of the early saints, his homilies on the Gospel, his comprehensive study of the Book of Job — all these mark him as a scholar of the first order. And the legacy of his evangelization lives on today; it was Gregory who commissioned St. Augustine of Canterbury to convert the people of England.

His interest in those far-off isles might have been stirred by a chance encounter with a group of young men visiting Rome from England before Gregory had become pope. As the first of these three brief tales indicates, he was fascinated by their distinctive appearance, and used some Latin word games — linking "Angles" with "Angels," "Aelli" with "Alleluia" and so forth — to perceive in their visit something of the hand of God.

All three of these stories are taken directly from the first known biography of Gregory, written by an anonymous monk of Whitby (England) about a hundred years after the pope's death. The other stories tell of Gregory's attempts to avoid his election as pope, and of a miracle at Mass that convinced a doubter of the Real Presence of Jesus. All three tales show that even at that early date, Gregory's followers recognized his special quality. And even to this day, it's a quality we still call "great."

Excerpts adapted from *The Earliest Life of Gregory the Great*, by an Anonymous Monk of Whitby; text, translation, and notes by Bertram Colgrave, The University of Kansas Press, 1968.

1. Visitors From England

There is a story told by the faithful that before Gregory became pope, there came to Rome certain people of our nation, fair-skinned and light-haired. When he heard of their arrival, he was eager to see them; being prompted by a fortunate intuition, being puzzled by their new and unusual appearance, and, above all, being inspired by God, he received them and asked what race they belonged to.

They answered, "The people we belong to are called Angles." "Angels of God," he replied.

Then he asked further, "What is the name of the king of that people?"

They said, "Aelli," whereupon he said, "Alleluia, God's praise must be heard there."

Then he asked the name of their own tribe, to that they answered, "Deire," and he replied, "They shall flee from the wrath of God to the faith."

2. Let This Cup Pass

When Gregory was elected by the people of God to the pastoral office and the apostolic dignity already mentioned, he fled from it with great humility and very anxiously sought a place to hide in. But he was watched with such care that even the entrance gates of the city were surrounded by guards on every side; so he is said to have persuaded some merchants to take him out, hidden in a cask. He then immediately sought out a hiding place in the depths of the bushes, where he lay hidden.

But after he had been there for three days and nights, the watchmen at the heavenly gates forthwith declared his whereabouts. For the people of God did not elect someone else, as he had hoped, but gave themselves up to fasting and supplication day and night, praying earnestly that God would show them where he was. Then for three whole nights there appeared to them a very bright column of light that penetrated the forest so that its top reached up to the sky. . . . When his hiding place was revealed, he was found and led to the sacred office.

3. A Miracle at Mass

There is an ancient story that once a certain matron in Rome was making her oblations and had brought them to Gregory; the saint received them and consecrated them into the most holy Body of Christ the Victim. When she came to receive it from the hands of the man of God and heard him say, "The Body of Our Lord Jesus Christ preserve thy soul," she began to smile. When the man of God saw this, he closed his hand as it reached her mouth, not wishing to give her the holy Body of the Lord; then he placed it on the altar and decided to hide it with his vestment.

When Mass was finished, he called her up and asked why she laughed when she should have communicated.

She answered, "I made those loaves with my own hands and you said they were the Body of the Lord."

Then he at once bade all the people of God in the church to pray together with him that Christ the Son of the living God would deign to show whether the most holy sacrifice was, as he said, truly his Body in order to strengthen the faith of her who did not believe in this sacrament. When he had finished speaking, the saint found that what he had placed on the altar was like the fragment of a little finger and covered with blood. He called the unbelieving woman to behold the marvelous sight and when she saw it she was utterly dumbfounded.

Then the saint said, "Now look with bodily eyes on what you were before too blind to see with your spiritual eyes and learn to believe on him who said, 'Except ye eat the flesh of the Son of Man and drink his blood, ye have no life in you.' "

He again urged those who were in church to pray that he who deigned to show them the mercy they had asked for would also deign to change the sacred Body back into its natural form; this they ventured to pray for and also for the lack of faith of the incredulous matron. When they had done as he bade them, he made her communicate, now that she believed him who said that "he that eateth my flesh and drinketh my blood dwelleth in me and I in him."

St. Brendan the Voyager

His Journeys Stirred Dreams of Distant Lands

Irish partisans have long challenged the assumption that Columbus was the "discoverer" of the New World, pointing to the explorations of St. Brendan (c. 489-583) as proof — well, at least an indication — that the Irish got there first.

Whether St. Brendan was, in fact, the first European to reach America will probably never be known for a fact. What is known, however, is that St. Brendan, a man of indomitable courage, came on the scene at a time when the world needed brave men who could think about life, seek the truth about God, and also understand the laws of science. This is the story of what we know of St. Brendan, who answered that call so gallantly that we remember him today.

Adapted from *Lives of the Saints You Should Know*,
by Margaret and Matthew Bunson, Our Sunday
Visitor, Inc., 1994.

Was there really an Irish saint called Brendan, and was he quite the dashing hero he's made out to be? Oh, yes, and more than hero he was a missioner extraordinary, not to mention a navigator of exceptional skill. And there was indeed an incredible sea journey that he led, one that lasted for seven years. How far he and his companions traveled, and in what sort of vessel, is a matter for ongoing debate, but sail he did.

No one knows exactly why Brendan went off as he did. Perhaps he and his men simply wanted to see for themselves what waited over the distant horizon. But knowing Brendan's life story, it seems likely that he and his companions — holy men all, committed to the faith — went in search of souls to be saved.

A priest who built monasteries and then moved on, he was a restless sort who never stayed in one place for long. Eventually he began to explore the wilderness, on land and sea, taking a band of companions with him.

On his seven-year voyage, he and his men were supposedly looking for the "Land of Paradise," and where the search took them is still unknown. Some historians believe that Brendan traveled only as far as the outermost islands of Ireland. Some records show that he and his fellow monks landed on islands off the coast of Africa — the Canaries, Madeiras, or the Azores. The most startling destination given by some historians is North America. They point to the fact that part of Chesapeake Bay on the east coast of the United States was once called "Greater Ireland." Shawnee Indian legends also tell of a group of white men landing in their territory many years ago.

One day the sail of Brendan's ship became visible on the Irish horizon, and the people flocked to the shore to see who was landing. They were amazed when the group identified themselves, and runners raced across the land to announce their return.

Brendan and his fellow voyagers told of their discoveries and described the places, people, plants, and animals they had seen during their seven-year trip. He was not content, however, to sit on his laurels; he knew there was work to be done in the world.

With his monks he set out again, building more monasteries throughout Ireland. He is known to have visited the Hebrides, Scotland, Wales, and even Brittany, on Europe's mainland. He also spent three years in Britain, but returned to Ireland before going home to the Lord.

The rule of the spiritual life that he established at Clonfert Monastery was supposedly dictated to him by an angel, and it was maintained in the monastery for centuries. While he was a holy man, a priest dedicated to the service of God and the Church, Brendan brought something else to his vocation: a spirit of curiosity, of adventure, of wanting to know the secrets of the unexplored world.

Above all, he brought faith to his voyages and explorations. It took genuine courage and belief in the providence of God to sail out into the unknown in those days. Brendan's life became an Irish epic, repeated over and over to new generations around the hearth fires.

The Flame of Learning

'Saving Civilization' With the Monks of Ireland

Catholic schoolchildren have known for a long time that the monks of Ireland kept the flame of learning alive during the Dark Ages, holding the barbarians at bay while they preserved old books and produced new ones for the generations who would follow. America's reading public came to a new appreciation of that contribution in recent years, thanks to a best-selling book titled How the Irish Saved Civilization *by Thomas Cahill.*

His subtitle is The Untold Story of Ireland's Heroic Role from the Fall of Rome to the Rise of Medieval Europe, *and he tells that story in a riveting, refreshing style. But there's reverence in the story, too: an appreciation of work, worship, and sacrifice, all done in the name of knowledge used in service of the Lord.*

At a time when old centers of learning were disappearing, when the ancient empire was fading from memory and a new, illiterate Europe was rising on its ruins, literary culture was alive and well in the monasteries of Ireland. Monks like Columcille and Columbanus, and others who followed their example, led their countrymen off in every direction, including the southeast, and mainland Europe — to establish new monasteries, and, in the process, to ensure the continuation of a literary tradition.

Did the Irish really "save civilization"? Yes, indeed. See how effortlessly Thomas Cahill sums it up here.

Excerpt from *How the Irish Saved Civilization*, by Thomas Cahill, Anchor Books, Doubleday & Co., Inc., 1995.

There is much we do not know about these Irish exiles. Their clay-and-wattle buildings have long since disappeared, and even most of their precious books have perished. But what they knew — the Bible and the literatures of Greece, Rome, and Ireland — we know, because they passed these things on to us. The Hebrew Bible would have been saved without them, transmitted to our time by scattered communities of Jews. The Greek Bible, the Greek commentaries, and much of the literature of ancient Greece were well enough preserved at Byzantium, and might be still available to us *somewhere* — if we had the interest to seek them out. But Latin literature would almost surely have been lost without the Irish, and illiterate Europe would hardly have developed its great national literatures without the example of Irish, the first vernacular literature to be written down. Beyond that, there would have perished in the West not only literacy but all the habits of mind that encourage thought. And when Islam began its medieval expansion, it would have encountered scant resistance to its plans — just scattered tribes of animists, ready for a new identity.

Whether this state of affairs would have been better or worse than what did happen, I leave to the reader to ponder. But what is certain is that the White Martyrs, clothed like druids in distinctive white wool robes, fanned out cheerfully across Europe, founding monasteries that would become in time the cities of Lumièges, Auxerre, Laon, Luxeuil, Liège, Trier, Würzburg, Regensburg, Rheinau, Reichenau, Salzburg, Vienna, Saint-Gall, Bobbio, Fiesole, and Lucca, to name but a few. "The weight of the Irish influence on the continent," admits James Westfall Thompson, "is incalculable. . . ."

As late as 870 Heiric of Auxerre can still exclaim in his *Life of Saint Germanus*: "Almost all of Ireland, despising the sea, is migrating to our shores with a herd of philosophers!"

By this point, the transmission of European civilization was assured. Wherever they went, the Irish brought with them their books, many unseen in Europe for centuries, and tied to their waists as signs of triumph, just as Irish heroes had once tied to their waists their enemies' heads. Wherever they went, they brought their love of learning and their skills in bookmaking. In the bays and valleys of their exile, they reestablished literacy and breathed new life into the exhausted literary culture of Europe.

And that is how the Irish saved civilization.

A Sign of Holiness

Our Blessed Mother Presents
the Scapular to St. Simon Stock

A half-century ago any Catholic schoolchild could have described a scapular, but today — in the United States, at least — its use has fallen off sharply. And so, for those who don't know (or don't exactly remember), the scapular consists of two small pieces of cloth connected by pieces of string so that it may be pulled over one's head and then worn front and back. A sacramental (a symbol of religious devotion), it is a modified version of an outer garment dating from the Middle Ages, worn in response to Our Blessed Mother's promise of a happy death to those who use it.

The scapular comes to us from St. Simon Stock (c. 1165-1265), who, as prior general of the Carmelites, asked for Mary's protection of the order. She appeared to him in 1251, presenting the scapular along with the pledge that "whosoever dies in the habit shall be saved." The devotion spread and has endured for centuries. Church leaders have traditionally endorsed the practice — with the proviso that the wearer of a scapular should not automatically expect to die in a state of grace, but must merit it by living a good life.

Story from *Little Pictorial Lives of the Saints*,
Benziger Brothers, Inc., 1925.

Simon was born in the county of Kent, England, and left his home when he was but twelve years of age, to live as a hermit in the hollow trunk of a tree, whence he was known as Simon of the Stock. Here he passed twenty years in penance and prayer, and learned from Our Lady that he was to join a religious order not then known in England. He waited in patience till the White Friars came, and then entered the Order of Our Lady of Mount Carmel.

His great holiness moved his brethren in the general chapter held at Aylesford, near Rochester, in 1245, to choose him prior general of the order. In the many persecutions raised against the new religious, Simon went with filial confidence to the Blessed Mother of

God. As he knelt in prayer in the White Friars' convent at Cambridge, on July 16, 1251, she appeared before him and presented him with the scapular, in assurance of her protection. The devotion to the blessed habit spread quickly throughout the Christian world. Pope after pope enriched it with indulgences, and miracles innumerable put their seal upon its efficacy. The first of them was worked at Winchester on a man dying in despair, who at once asked for the sacraments, when the scapular was laid upon him by St. Simon Stock.

In the year 1636, M. de Guge, a cornet in a cavalry regiment, was mortally wounded at the engagement of Tehin, a bullet having lodged near his heart. He was then in a state of grievous sin, but had time to make his confession, and with his own hands wrote his last testament. When this was done, the surgeon probed his wound and the bullet was found to have driven his scapular into his heart. On its being withdrawn, he presently expired, making profound acts of gratitude to the Blessed Virgin, who had prolonged his life miraculously, and thus preserved him from eternal death. St. Simon Stock died at Bordeaux, in 1265.

The Rosary

Our Lady Asked St. Dominic to Promote This 'Most Dear' Devotion

Many Catholics know that St. Dominic (c. 1170-1221) is credited with beginning the devotion of the rosary, but here again legend, tradition, faith, and history mix in a somewhat inconclusive way.

To begin with, many cultures and several religions have used prayer beads of one sort or another, in some cases long before the time of Dominic. Earlier, Christian laypeople were encouraged to pray the Our Father one hundred fifty times, as a way of matching the hundred fifty Psalms chanted by the more literate monks and nuns.

But when St. Dominic began to promote widespread use of the rosary early in the thirteenth century — as he undeniably did — the devotion quickly became popular and spread throughout Europe. The meditations on the fifteen mysteries (divided evenly into categories of joyful, sorrowful, and glorious) served to remind Catholics of important incidents in the lives of Jesus and Mary — just as they do today.

Did the rosary come directly to St. Dominic from Our Lady? History has nothing to say on the matter, but the story remains etched in the hearts of people today — indicating, perhaps, that once again faith has supplied an answer.

Story from *Catechism in Stories*, by Rev. Lawrence G. Lovasik, SVD, The Bruce Publishing Co., 1956.

St. Dominic was a noble young Spaniard who lived in the thirteenth century. In early youth he made a vow of chastity that he was able to declare on his deathbed he had never violated. He burned with zeal for the salvation of souls. The sad state of morality in France, which he observed when he passed through that country with his bishop, determined him to found the Order of Preachers.

The Albigensians were the communists of that day. They pillaged churches and murdered priests, while they rejected morality and despised all authority. St. Dominic dedicated himself to the work of saving the souls of these people. He went about preaching. Three times during each night of prayer he scourged himself. He made little headway.

He appealed to the Blessed Virgin. The heavens opened, and the Mother of God, holding a rosary in her hand, appeared in dazzling brightness to her servant and said, "Be of good courage, Dominic; the fruit of your labor shall be abundant. The remedy for the evils you lament will be the meditation on the life, death, and glory of my Son, uniting thereto the recitation of the angelic salutation by which the mystery of the Redemption was announced to the world."

Having explained the devotion of the rosary, she continued, "This devotion you are to spread by your preaching is a practice most dear to my Son and to me. It is a most powerful means of putting away heresy, extinguishing vice, propagating virtue, imploring the divine mercy, and obtaining my protection. I desire that you always promote this manner of prayer. The faithful will obtain by it innumerable graces, and will always find me ready to aid them in their wants. This is the precious gift that I leave to you and your children."

Full of gratitude, Dominic went to the city of Toulouse. The people, by a mysterious call, had already assembled in the church. Dominic ascended the pulpit and preached about the devotion revealed from heaven. For a while the people paid little attention to him. A violent storm arose, lightning lit up the church, and peals of thunder resounded. A statue of the Blessed Virgin began to move, pointing to heaven and then to Dominic as if imploring the people to listen to him. The hearts of the people were touched. The victory was gained. The people begged to be taught this wonderful devotion. Historians tell us that more than a hundred thousand people returned to the true fold.

First Fridays

A Holy Practice Grew
Through Devotion to the Sacred Heart

Others before her had encouraged devotion to the Sacred Heart of Jesus — St. Bernard of Clairvaux, for one, and St. Francis de Sales — but it was only after the supernatural experiences of St. Margaret Mary Alacoque (1647-1690) that it became widely popular.

St. Margaret Mary, a member of the Visitandine Order, began receiving visions of Our Lord in 1673 — visions in which he appeared with his Sacred Heart visible, surrounded by a crown of thorns and flames. Among the promises he made was that of a happy death to those who received Communion on nine consecutive first Fridays of the month; the practice quickly gained a wide following and continues in our own time.

St. Margaret Mary's life had its unhappy moments. Crippled as a child, she endured cruel and insensitive treatment from her family. Later, after her visions had taken place, she was subject to severe criticism from other members of her community. Their criticism only strengthened her resolve to persevere, however, and eventually she won their apology — and their friendship.

Story from *Catechism in Stories*, by Rev. Lawrence G.
Lovasik, SVD, The Bruce Publishing Co., 1956.

In 1647 there was born a child in France, named Margaret Mary Alacoque, who was to be the means of spreading devotion to the Sacred Heart. Since her one desire was to give her life to the service of God, she entered the convent of the Visitation Sisters. There her love for the Blessed Sacrament became so strong that it was only with difficulty that she could tear herself away from the Divine Presence. She used to tell Our Lord that she wished to be consumed with love for him as a candle is consumed while burning.

Once while she was rapt in prayer before the altar, Our Lord appeared to her. He showed himself in glory with his five wounds shining like five brilliant suns, and his Sacred Heart like a furnace of fire. He told her how much he loves all mankind and how he feels the ingratitude they show him by forgetting him. He appeared to her a second and a third time in 1675. On the last occasion he said, *"Behold this heart that has loved men so much that it has spared nothing to testify to them its love; and in return I receive from most of them only ingratitude by their irreverences and their sacrileges and by the coldness and contempt they have for me in the Sacrament of Love."*

She told all these things to her confessor, the Blessed Claude de la Colombière, who made her write down an account of what she saw and heard.

One of the devotions that Our Lord taught St. Margaret Mary was the Holy Hour of Reparation. Our Savior in his agony in the Garden of Olives went over to his Apostles Peter, James, and John, to seek a little consolation from them; but he found them asleep. He said to them, "What? Could you not watch one hour with me? Watch and pray that you enter not into temptation." In memory of this, Jesus asked the saint to honor his Sacred Heart by rising every Thursday night at eleven o'clock and by prostrating herself for an hour before him in the Blessed Sacrament. During the hour she was to implore God's mercy for poor sinners and try to sweeten the bitterness he felt when his Apostles slept during his agony in the garden.

Among the ten promises he made to St. Margaret Mary is "The Great Promise": *"I promise thee in the excessive mercy of my heart that my all-powerful love will grant to all those who go to Holy Communion on the first Friday in nine consecutive months, the grace of final penitence: they shall not die in my disfavor nor without receiving their sacraments; my divine heart shall be their safe refuge in this last moment."*

St. Margaret Mary died on October 17, 1690.

A Shower of Roses

Our Lady of Guadalupe Provided
the Sign the Bishop Sought

The relatively unknown player in one of the Church's best-known and best-loved stories — that of Our Lady of Guadalupe — had a far more important role in it than one might imagine. If Bishop Juan de Zumárraga had not asked for a sign, the miracle of the Blessed Mother's appearance to Juan Diego near Mexico City in 1531 might have slipped into relative obscurity. Juan had been to see the bishop twice to tell him of his visions, and his aides were beginning to tire of this poor peasant with his fanciful tales.

But the third time proved to be the charm. After Juan told Mary, who appeared to him once again, that the bishop had asked for a sign of her presence, she sent him back with a cloakful of fresh roses. When the bishop saw them — along with the miraculous portrait of the Virgin on Juan's cloak — he understood that the vision was undeniably real, and gave permission for a church to be built on the site just as Our Lady had requested. The rest is history — and story par excellence.

Story from *The Grace of Guadalupe*, by Frances Parkinson
Keyes, Julian Messner, Inc., 1941.

After the Queen of Heaven had given him her orders, Juan took the road toward the causeway that leads directly to Mexico City. He was already tranquil and confident of a happy outcome, and he carried with great care the contents of his *tilma* (cloak), being watchful that nothing should slip from his hands and meanwhile rejoicing in the fragrance of the beautiful flowers.

When he arrived at the palace of the bishop, the prelate's majordomo and other servants came out to meet him. He asked them to say that he desired to see the bishop. But none of them wished to do so. Accordingly, they made him wait for a long time. But when they saw how patiently he stood there, with hanging head, waiting to be called, and how closely he was guarding something that he seemed to be holding in his robe, they approached him, in order to find out what he had and satisfy their curiosity.

When Juan Diego saw that he could not conceal the fact that he was carrying something and that on account of this burden the servants intended to pester him, he gave them a glimpse of what he had. Seeing that this was a great variety of Castilian roses and knowing that this was not the time when such flowers normally blossomed, the servants were greatly astonished, and all the more so because the flowers were in such full bloom and were so fragrant and so beautiful.

Discomfited, they went to tell the bishop what they beheld and to say that the Indian who had been there so many times before again wished to see him. When he heard this, the bishop was convinced that they must have seen something of the sign that in its entirety would bear witness to that for which the Indian had asked. So he immediately ordered that Juan Diego should be brought into his presence.

As soon as the man entered the room, he bowed down, as he had done before, and told the bishop again everything that he had seen and heard, besides delivering his message. "Your Excellency," he said, "I did that which you asked. I told my Mistress, the Queen of Heaven, Holy Mary, Mother of God, that you required a sign in order that you might believe what I had told you regarding the temple she enjoins you to build in the place she asks that you should erect it. And, furthermore, I said that I had given my word to bring here some sign and proof of her will, as you asked. She met your request and with graciousness accepted your condition concerning the sign you must have before her will might be accomplished. Very early this morning she told me to come to see you again. So I asked for the sign that would make you believe and that she has said she would give me. Instantly she complied with my petition. She sent me to the top of the hill where I had previously seen her pick Castilian roses. Although I well knew that the summit of the hill is not a place where flowers grow, nevertheless I doubted nothing. And when I arrived at the top, I saw that I was in a terrestrial paradise, where every variety of exquisite flowers, brilliant with dew, flourished in abundance. These I gathered and carried back to her. With her own hands she arranged them and replaced them in my robe in order that I might bring them to you. Here they are. Behold and receive them."

Until that moment, Juan had kept the folds of his *tilma* closely drawn, guarding his roses zealously. Now, with a sudden movement, he released them. They fell on the floor in a colorful cascade, scattering perfume about them. Looking down at them, he felt waves of exultation sweep over him. He had delivered his burden, he had accomplished his mission, he had fulfilled his trust.

But his triumph had not yet reached its pinnacle. As he stood still, his heart pounding and his eyes fixed on the flowers, still bright with dew, that lay at his feet, he was suddenly aware that the bishop had been moved by some miracle even greater than that of the roses. Zumárraga had descended from his throne and had dropped on his knees. His lips were parted in prayer, and in his eyes glistened tears, as bright as the dewdrops on the roses. His transfigured gaze was turned not downward but upward, and with astonishment that knew no bounds, Juan saw that this was fixed with fervor upon his own humble person. Increasingly bewildered, he himself glanced toward the *tilma* from which the mass of brilliant bloom had so recently been released.

Its coarseness was completely concealed. On it, in glorious tones, was painted the image of the Blessed Virgin, exactly as she had appeared to him on the heights of Tepeyac.

'This Turbulent Priest'

A Conversion of Heart Cost St. Thomas Becket His Life

King Henry II of England thought himself more clever than words when he appointed his close friend Thomas Becket (1118-1170) archbishop of Canterbury. Becket, chancellor of England but not yet ordained a priest, thoroughly enjoyed the high life he shared with the king, and was only too eager to help his royal friend enrich himself at the expense of the Church. By naming him to the country's most important Church position, Henry envisioned nothing but clear sailing ahead.

What the king failed to foresee was the change of heart that would come over Becket after his ordination and installation — a conversion that would ultimately cost him his life. Becket, bolstered by an infusion of inner strength, decided to be as perfect a churchman as he could. In the process, he became a new man — selling his possessions, helping the poor, feeding the hungry. Most important, he wanted no more part of the king's evil schemes, daring to stand up to his royal master when no others would.

The frustrated king ultimately called out, "Who will rid me of this turbulent priest?" And four of his knights gave him an answer that will live in infamy.

Selection from *Lives of the Saints You Should Know*,
by Margaret and Matthew Bunson, Our Sunday
Visitor, Inc., 1994.

Henry II fretted and raved until a series of events took place that brought matters to a head between him and Thomas. For one thing, a parish priest was accused of a crime by one of the English barons, who promptly hunted the priest down and killed him. That action was against the law, as only the Church had the right to discipline priests and nuns in those days. Thomas appeared before Henry II, demanding that the baron be punished for his crime. King Henry, of course, almost fell off his throne when he heard Thomas's demand. His old friend Thomas à Becket was gone, and now he faced the archbishop of Canterbury, a formidable, stern enemy who was not awed by royal titles.

In order to get rid of Thomas and his defense of the Church, Henry II plotted with other foes of the archbishop and managed to exile him in shame. It did not matter that the accusations made were false. Thomas Becket was thrown out of England. He went immediately to Rome, but the English bishops had already visited the pope, Alexander III, and had filled his ears with their side of the dispute.

When asked about the various charges against him, Thomas Becket admitted that he had not been given the see of Canterbury in a proper way, and he also admitted that he was not qualified for the position. Taking off his ring and his cross, he tried to give them to the pope, who refused them. The Holy Father told him not to abandon Canterbury because that would mean abandoning the honor of the Church. He did advise, however, that it would be wise for Thomas to enter a monastery for a time.

Thomas and a companion happily did just that. They stayed in a French monastic house for some time, content to be there. The see (or archdiocese) of Canterbury remained empty, because the pope would not allow Henry II to replace Thomas Becket without an investigation and a decision from Rome.

Finally, on December 1, 1170, Becket returned to England. He had made a friend in France, King Louis VII, who believed in the conversion of Thomas Becket and wanted to see him reconciled with his own monarch. The French king also knew that he would face political problems if Thomas remained in France as a guest. Louis made peace between Henry II and his former friend, and Thomas took up his work once again as the defender of the faith in the isles.

The peace was short-lived, naturally, because the king felt betrayed by Thomas's careful watch over events. By the end of 1170, in fact, Henry II once again was ranting and raving around his castle, because his plots were being stopped at every turn by Thomas, whose sharp mind was capable of seeing through them. No matter what Henry tried, Thomas countered with some brilliant defense. In desperation one night, Henry II, seated with some of his mindless knights, asked: "Who will rid me of this turbulent priest?"

On December 29, 1170, Thomas Becket entered the cathedral of Canterbury with his trusted companion and started preparations for the Mass. Four knights of Henry II appeared in the sanctuary with swords drawn and with murder on their minds. The archbishop told them that they were violating the cathedral and ordered them to put away their swords. The knights only laughed. They had come to take care of Henry II's problems, and they had no intention of allowing the archbishop of Canterbury to leave the altar alive.

Thomas Becket, dying of wounds inflicted by the knights, sighed and asked for the prayers of St. Denis and St. Alphege of Canterbury, two martyred bishops. Praying and giving his soul to God, Thomas Becket fell silent at the altar of the cathedral. The archbishop's companion, a young monk, perished trying to defend him.

When word of the murders raced across England, Henry II was horrified. His rash words, his unreasonable hatred, and his ambitions had put him into a terrible political position. The pope and other Christian leaders in the world were even more horrified. Henry II and his knights were excommunicated, and the king had to make a public penance in order to restore peace and his own standing in the Church and in the country.

In the meantime, a shrine had been erected to Thomas at Canterbury. Many stories were being told throughout the land about miracles happening there, especially among the poor, whom Thomas Becket had cared for while he was archbishop.

The four knights who had murdered Thomas suffered excommunication for a time, but it is not recorded that they were punished for the murder. The blame fell clearly on the shoulders of King Henry II, and the public penance fell there as well. After putting off the ceremony as long as possible, King Henry had to appear as a penitent and sinner at the shrine of Thomas Becket in July 1174. There, in front of the English people and the representatives of the Church, he was stripped of his shirt and lashed by stout monks. He then made his way to Thomas's tomb and there he suffered more.

In life Thomas had always been the brightest one, the best. In death he triumphed not only for himself but also for the honor of the Church.

Thomas Becket was canonized by Pope Alexander III in 1173, and his shrine remained a site for pilgrims through the centuries.

Gentle Giant

The Scope of St. Thomas Aquinas's Mind Matched the Size of His Body

Even when he was a young man, it was clear that St. Thomas Aquinas (c. 1224-1274) was destined for intellectual greatness. They called him the gentle giant, since he presented an imposing figure. But he impressed his teachers and his fellow students even more with his mind than he did with his girth.

In time, his writings would cover virtually the entire body of Church doctrine, and he would be recognized as one of the greatest thinkers in the long history of the Church. But those who had been his fellow students still probably thought back to his days at school, when his large and slow-moving frame occasioned typical schoolyard insults. Too, they might have remembered the wise observation of his teacher, Albertus (or Albert) Magnus — the redoubtable Albert the Great: "You call this lad a dumb ox, but I tell you the whole world is going to hear his bellowing!"

Story from *Saints and Their Stories*, by Mary Montgomery, Harper & Row, 1988.

In a mountainside castle in southern Italy, the count of Aquino and his noble French wife welcomed their son into the world. This was their seventh child, and they named him Thomas. Long before Thomas was old enough to have any say about his life, his parents had it planned for him.

Near the castle where Thomas was born stood the great Benedictine Abbey of Monte Cassino. "Thomas will study at Monte Cassino and become a monk," said his mother.

"Yes, indeed," agreed his father. "But Thomas won't remain a monk all his life. He'll follow in the footsteps of his Aquino relatives. Just as they rose to become abbots of Monte Cassino, so will our son."

Thomas was five years old when his parents sent him to Monte Cassino to study. He proved to be a bright child with an inquiring mind. A few days after his arrival, he went to the abbot and asked, "What is God?" The abbot could not give him a satisfying answer. Thomas spent a lifetime trying to answer the question for himself.

Life inside the monastery was quiet and peaceful. But outside its high walls, there was much trouble and fighting. The emperor of Italy and the pope were in a struggle for power. The emperor's troops succeeded in taking over the monastery and turned it into a fortress. That ended the peaceful life at Monte Cassino. All the monks were forced to leave, and Thomas went to the university in Naples to continue his studies.

Thomas was fourteen then, and already he had grown to be a young giant. He was so tall he had to stoop to go through doorways. He had huge hands and feet, and his head was so large no ordinary hat would fit. His neck was thick and his chest round and firm as a barrel. Wherever he went, people stared at him and made rude remarks. Thomas was so strong he could have silenced anyone with a bone-breaking punch. But throughout his life, he never did anything violent to anyone. He was a sensitive man, extremely shy and quiet. He was a gentle giant.

While Thomas was in Naples, he began going to the Dominican church. He liked the simple way the Dominicans lived. They took vows of poverty and lived together as a family. They begged for what they needed and went about preaching the Gospels and bringing people to God. Just before Thomas finished his studies, he quit the university and joined the Dominican begging friars.

The Aquino family was stunned when they heard what Thomas had done. "Has he lost his senses?" stormed his father. "How can a son of noble birth join a religious order that has no monasteries or money? The friars actually *beg* for their food!"

"If we can get Thomas home, we can reason with him," said his mother. "We can make him see that he must choose a life that is in keeping with the family tradition."

Turning to her oldest son, she said, "Rinaldo, you are to kidnap Thomas and bring him back here."

Rinaldo did as his mother asked. For two years Thomas was locked in a room in the family castle. During this time, he memorized most of the Bible and began the writings that would make him famous. Nothing his family said or did could make Thomas change his mind about what he wanted to do with his life. Finally, one of his sisters helped him escape, and he rejoined his fellow Dominicans. They sent Thomas to Paris to study, and then to Cologne, Germany. There he studied under Albert Magnus, who was the most famous professor of his time. He is the man we now know as St. Albert the Great.

Day after day, Thomas sat in class with his huge body slumped in a chair. The other students were anxious to be heard, but Thomas just sat deep in thought. Before long, he had the nickname the Dumb Ox. One day a classmate took pity on Thomas and began to explain a difficult lesson to him. Thomas listened gratefully until the student got to the point where he could go no further. Then Thomas amazed him by finishing the most difficult part of the lesson.

It didn't take long before the great teacher Albert Magnus discovered that Thomas had a giant mind as well as a giant body. Thomas knew several languages. He could speak and write clearly. He had knowledge of astronomy, geometry, and music. "You call this lad a dumb ox," said the teacher Albert, "but I tell you the whole world is going to hear his bellowing!"

Even though fellow students recognized that Thomas had a brilliant mind, they still liked to tease him. Maybe it was because he was so gentle and trusting and always fell for their pranks. One day they told him to look out the window because there was a cow flying in the sky. Thomas slowly got his big body out of his chair and went to the window. The other students broke out laughing and one asked, "Why did you fall for the joke?"

Thomas replied, "I would rather believe that a cow could fly than that my brothers would lie."

The university gave Thomas a doctorate, which was the highest honor possible. It meant that he had learned his subjects so well he was able to teach them. Thomas soon became an even greater teacher than the great Albert Magnus.

Pastoral Lesson

Blessed John Duns Scotus Meets a Farmer in the Field

In the Middle Ages, pious legends abounded about holy men and women, the saints and teachers and preachers who set an example for others by what they did and what they said.

Here's a story about one of the most brilliant teacher-philosophers of his day. Blessed John Duns Scotus (c. 1266-1308), a Franciscan native of Scotland who was known as "the subtle doctor," developed a school that harmonized the thought of Aristotle with principles of Christian theology. A follower to a degree of St. Thomas Aquinas, he departed from Thomist teaching in some matters. He was also the first major theologian to endorse the doctrine of the Immaculate Conception.

Supporters of Duns Scotus might have used this little tale to humanize the man. It has the learned philosopher engaged in a brisk dialogue with a farmer in his field, making use of the encounter to teach a lesson about the knowledge of God.

Story from *Catechism in Stories*, by Rev. Lawrence G.
Lovasik, SVD, The Bruce Publishing Co., 1956.

The learned Franciscan Duns Scotus once heard a farmer uttering frightful curses and begged him not to damn his soul so thoughtlessly. The farmer answered, "God knows everything. He knows whether I shall go to heaven or to hell. If he knows that I shall go to heaven, why, to heaven I shall go; if he knows that I shall go to hell, why, to hell I shall go. What does it matter, then, what I do or say?"

"In that case," answered Duns Scotus, "why bother to plow your fields? God knows whether they will bear a good crop or not. If he knows that they will bear a good harvest, the harvest will be good whether you plow or not. If he knows that your crop will be a failure, why a failure it will be. So why should you waste your time plowing?"

The farmer then understood the real meaning of the omniscience of God.

Woman of Determination

Almost Single-handedly, Catherine of Siena Restored the Papacy to Rome

Even in that select company of extraordinary women produced by the Church down through the centuries, St. Catherine of Siena (1347-1380) stands out in a special way. From the time of her youth until her early death, she devoted her life to prayer and penance, and to caring for the sick and poor. A Dominican tertiary, she saw the face of Christ in all who sought her help, and none were turned away. Her spiritual life was exceptional; her wisdom and insights were such that she attracted a crowd of followers who accompanied her everywhere with cultlike devotion. So often did they occur that her visions seemed almost routine, her miracles matter-of-fact.

It took something of a miracle, in fact, to accomplish the feat for which most Catholics remember her: persuading Pope Gregory XI to return to Rome from Avignon, the French city where popes had resided as exiles for nearly seventy years. During this time (1309-1377) the reputation of the papacy nearly suffocated under the corruption and licentiousness of the Avignon court, and the decision-making power of individual popes gave way to the whims of the French cardinals.

What could be done? Catherine — never one to hide her light under a bushel — came up with the answer: she would convince this often indecisive pope that the good of the Church demanded his return to Rome. Immediately.

They corresponded. They met. Gregory was taken not only with her words but with her manner as well. And the four months Catherine spent in Avignon would ultimately change the face of the Church for all time.

Story adapted from *Catherine of Siena, A Biography*, by
Anne B. Baldwin, Our Sunday Visitor, Inc., 1987.

Peace, Catherine knew, could come to the Church only if the Holy Father returned to Rome. A strong pope in Rome could restore peace to Italy; a pope in Rome could free the Church of the corruption of Avignon; a pope in Rome was where God planned him to be, and therefore was in the best position to bring Christ's grace to his Church. Gregory XI agreed on the need to return to Rome; but knowing what had to be done was not the same as doing it, not for this pope.

Catherine was a woman of courage and action. She decided what was right, then she acted. She never stopped to consider what other people might think; other people's approval or disapproval was not important to her. God's approval was all she needed.

Pope Gregory XI, by contrast, was slow to take action. He listened carefully to the opinions of others, and cared very much whether they approved or disapproved of his actions. These were among the qualities for which he was made pope, according to many historians. The French cardinals who elected him wanted the power of the papacy to stay with them, so they chose a man who would weigh their advice and want their approval.

They did not approve of a move to Rome. They thought that in Gregory they had chosen a quiet, timid man, who took advice well. But they had elected a man who was made of stronger stuff than they realized, and that man found in Catherine of Siena the ally he needed to act in the best interests of all the Church.

When Catherine visited the pope in Avignon, she saw for herself the truth she had known intuitively: that the move from Avignon was as important as it was difficult. She saw with her eyes and smelled with her nose the unbelievable depth of sin and corruption that surrounded the pope. She saw the French cardinals who advised him, encouraging him always to think first of his own great need for security, and to think next of what he could do to please his family and friends. She saw the ladies of the court, the sisters, nieces, and mistresses of the cardinals, who spent their days in gossip and intrigue, and who treated Catherine's ecstasies like spectacles to be watched, and even stuck pins in her feet to see if she could respond during an ecstasy.

Avignon was exquisitely beautiful, a masterpiece of French architecture and landscaping, a city of a thousand splendors. It is doubtful that Catherine saw any of the splendors in her four months there. Her entire being was tuned to matters of the spirit and not of the material world. Catherine told her friends that the stench of sin in Avignon sickened her.

Catherine urged the pope to leave for Rome immediately so he could get on with the other tasks of his papacy. He listened and agreed with her, then listened to his Curia and agreed with them. Gregory knew what he had to do, but he found the arguments of the cardinals hard to resist, appealing as they did to his greatest fears.

He asked Catherine to pray for him, after Communion, and ask Jesus to send him a sign so he would know what to do.

Catherine prayed after Communion as requested, and then became silent and rigid, rapt in prayer. When she returned to herself an hour later, those in attendance heard her murmur, "Praised be God, now and forever." Later that day Catherine wrote to Pope Gregory that God showed her no impediment to the move, and that the greatest sign he would see would be the opposition the move would continue to arouse among his courtiers.

A few days later when they were talking together, the subject of Rome came up, and he asked her, as he had so often, what she would do if she were in his position. Catherine looked long and hard at him, gazing within to read the secrets of his heart.

"Who knows what ought to be done better than Your Holiness, who has long since made a vow to God to return to Rome?" she asked.

Gregory was astonished. He had never told anyone of that promise, made so long ago. How could Catherine know about it, unless God had revealed it to her? This was the sign he had longed for. Now he was ready to act.

He kept his preparations secret until the last possible minute. He had ships readied to take him to Genoa, and from there to Rome.

Gregory's reign in Rome never did bring peace. Though he made generous overtures to the Florentines, he did not reach agreement with them. He became disheartened, surrounded as he was with unhappy advisers, living in a land where he did not understand the language or the customs. He did not know where to begin on the reform of the Church that he knew was so necessary. He died in March of 1378, just a year and a half after he left Avignon. The one great accomplishment of his papacy was the move to Rome.

The Education of a Soldier

St. Ignatius Loyola: The Wounds of Battle
Led Him to a New Life

The sobering story of the conversion of St. Ignatius Loyola (1491-1556) is one of the best known among the lives of the saints. A soldier who had been severely wounded in battle, the young Ignatius began reading to pass the time while he recuperated, and the volumes that were chosen for him — a life of Christ, stories of the early saints — changed his life forever. After some years devoted to spiritual development, he realized that he needed a more formal education in order to serve the Lord to his full ability, and so he began the pursuit of wisdom in earnest.

In his early thirties by this time, he nonetheless plunged into his studies. Within a few years he and a group of followers started the steps that would lead to the establishment of the Society of Jesus — the Jesuits. Ignatius also went on to found the Roman College, which later became the Gregorian University.

Ever since their formation, the Jesuits — devoted to the Holy Father, the education of the young, and mission enterprises the world over — have been singularly recognized for their intellectual discipline in the service of Christ's Church. Their wise and determined founder could wish no more fitting memorial.

Here, based on Ignatius' own account of the incident, is the story of how it all began.

Adapted from *The Autobiography of St. Ignatius*, edited by
J.F.X. O'Conor, S.J., Benziger Brothers, 1900.

Ignatius' battle wounds had been extensive, and they took some time to heal. But once he was out of danger, he became bored and restless. How about something to read, he wondered; he enjoyed passing time with the light fiction of the day. But the household that had taken him in had nothing of the sort. They gave him instead two Spanish books of spiritual reading: *The Life of Christ* by Rudolph, the Carthusian, and another volume called *The Flowers of the Saints*.

The wounded soldier picked them up almost with a feeling of reluctance. Before long, however, he found that they had something to say to him. He read them — not only once, but again and again. And gradually, over a period of time, he found that his thoughts were turning, more and more frequently, to matters of the soul.

Frequently, perhaps, but not exclusively, Ignatius still found himself daydreaming of romantic conquests from time to time. He thought especially of one illustrious lady, and of different strategies that might impress her — and even as he did so he realized how farfetched these dreams really were.

In the meantime the divine mercy was at work, replacing these thoughts with others occasioned by his spiritual readings. He began to reflect on what he had read of the life of the Lord and the saints, asking himself:

"What if I should do what St. Francis did? What if I should act like St. Dominic?"

He pondered these things over and over in his mind, and more and more considered a course of action to follow:

"St. Dominic did this; I, too, will do it." "St. Francis did this: therefore I will do it."

The battle within his mind continued: heroic resolutions at one point, soon followed by vain and worldly thoughts. The sequence went on for a long while, thoughts about God alternating with those about the world.

But in these thoughts there was this difference: thoughts of worldly things entertained him for a while, but afterward he found himself dry and sad. When he thought of journeying to Jerusalem, though, and of living only on herbs and practicing austerities — well, that was different. He found that it was pleasant not only while he was thinking of them, but also long after he had ceased.

And one day, Ignatius would write, the eyes of his soul were opened. The difference became clear. He learned by experience that one train of thought left him sad, the other joyful. This was his first reasoning on spiritual matters.

From that point on, his future course was set, reaffirmed and strengthened by a vision of the Blessed Virgin. He felt a deep sense of contrition for past sins and made a promise that with the help of divine grace, he would pattern his life on the saints he had read about. His brother and all those who lived in the house weren't entirely sure what had happened, but they all recognized the profound change that had taken place in his soul.

St. Teresa of Ávila

Her First Journey for the Lord Was an Early One — And a Short One As Well

St. Teresa of Ávila (1515-1582) was adept at traveling between Carmelite convents, hearing the facts about one dispute or another, and settling the matter then and there. Her counsel was highly regarded and, it would seem, eagerly followed as well.

But that observation doesn't begin to hint at the turbulent lifetime of this great Spanish mystic, the first woman to be declared a Doctor of the Church. Her determination to bring strict reform to the Carmelite community upset many, men and women alike, and were it not for friends in high places — King Philip II of Spain, for example, as well as Pope Gregory XIII — she could easily have faced the threat of the Inquisition.

As it was, her counsel lived on through her writings, notably in The Way of Perfection, a guide to prayer and virtuous life composed especially for the Carmelites. Her other works — including her autobiography and her reflections on interior spiritual life — constitute one of the greatest collections of mystical writings in the history of the Church.

Back to her travels for a moment. They formed an integral part of her mission but often had to be made under rugged conditions. On one particularly difficult journey, with her carriage mired in mud, Teresa was said to have wondered aloud toward the heavens: "If this is how you treat your friends, what do you do to your enemies?"

Teresa's first journey has a place in all her biographies. She was just six when she slipped away from home with her brother Rodrigo, ten, heading off, she thought, for the land of the Moors — and the glory of martyrdom. Here's how it ended.

Story adapted from *Popular Life of Saint Teresa of Jesus*,
translated from the French by Annie Porter, Benziger
Brothers, 1884.

Little Teresa had no closer friend or more constant companion than her brother Rodrigo. He was older by four years, but her imagination was so rich and her personality so lively that he willingly let her take the lead in their activities. Together they both played and prayed, and took particular delight in reading the lives of the saints.

Teresa especially was fascinated with the special privilege that God seemed to afford martyrs for the faith: a few moments of suffering, and then instant entrance into heaven. She envied their fate.

When the idea came to her, then, it seemed only natural to invite Rodrigo to be her companion: let's go to the land of the Moors, she said, where we can preach the Gospel of Jesus. They will capture us, take us prisoner and kill us, and we will immediately be in the presence of the Lord. She was six and he was ten, and to Rodrigo it seemed a perfectly reasonable plan.

They kept their intentions secret, and a few days later, early in the morning, stole away from their parents' home. They carried a bit of food, wrapped in a napkin tied on the end of a stick, but mostly planned to sustain themselves by begging along the way. They left the city, and, crossing the bridge that spans the Adaja River turned their little steps toward the south.

Doña Beatriz, their mother, nearly collapsed when she found them missing, but her anguish was short-lived. The children's uncle discovered the little travelers near the Adaja Bridge and promptly brought them home. Doña Beatriz was torn between her relief at seeing them and her anger at them for exposing themselves to such danger. She saved most of her criticism for Rodrigo. As the older of the two, she said, he should have known better.

"It wasn't my fault," he protested. "The baby made me do it."

Play On!

St. Charles Borromeo's Advice Surprised His Priests

During the years of the Counter-Reformation, St. Charles Borromeo (1538-1584) was an esteemed adviser to popes and princes, but this little story shows him in another light: using an everyday situation to offer some sound advice to his own priests on an all-important matter.

Extending his influence far beyond his archdiocese of Milan, Charles Borromeo played a key role in organizing and shaping the third convocation of the Council of Trent (1562-1563). He was particularly instrumental in drafting the Roman Catechism that emerged from the Council and that would become familiar to generations of Catholics who followed him.

This great counselor was also a deeply revered archbishop. He worked unceasingly for the poor, managed to find food for thousands during a devastating famine in 1570, and pointedly stayed with his people during the lethal plague that struck Milan from 1576 to 1578. He lived on for some fifteen years after a would-be assassin nearly killed him in 1569, and on his deathbed he was heard to say, "Behold, I come. Your will be done."

Story adapted from *Anecdotes and Examples Illustrating the Catholic Catechism*, selected and arranged by Rev. Francis Spirago, Benziger Brothers, 1904.

Even the games Christians play can be meritorious in God's sight, as long as they take place with an eye to his glory. That's the message that comes through in this little anecdote about St. Charles Borromeo, archbishop of Milan.

On one occasion the saint, at the urging of several of his priests, joined them in a game of billiards. While the game was going on, one of the priests posed a question for his companions. "What would we do," he asked, "if we knew that the world was going to end in an hour?"

"I'd start praying right away," one of them answered, and another added, "I'd want to make a general confession covering my whole life." The others responded along similar lines. But St. Charles, who had a feeling that the question had been posed to see how he might answer, kept his silence. Finally one of the others put the question to him directly: "What would *you* do, Excellency, if the world were coming to an end within the hour?"

"Why, I'd just continue with the game of billiards," he told them. "After all, I began it with the full intention of honoring God."

The reply, as profound as it was unexpected, taught the priests a lesson — that even in our recreation it is possible to give glory to God.

Victory at Sea

The Battle of Lepanto Erased
a Serious Threat to the Church

The Battle of Lepanto (1571) was one of the most important naval engagements in history, culminating in the defeat of a Turkish fleet that had threatened the Church's presence throughout the eastern Mediterranean.

The Turks thought that the time had come to strike at the Christian nations of Europe, divided as they were by the turmoil of the Reformation. One ruler after another found it inconvenient to answer the call to arms, but eventually King Philip II of Spain, Emperor Charles V, and the Venetian Republic rallied to put together a fleet of some two hundred galleys under the command of Don Juan of Austria, Emperor Charles's son. Their victory at sea would be total: the Turks were routed and thousands of Christian galley slaves were freed from captivity. The death toll was staggering; fifteen thousand Turks and seven thousand Christians lost their lives. Uncounted numbers were wounded (including, interestingly enough, the Spaniard Miguel de Cervantes, who would go on to write Don Quixote*).*

In all, Lepanto turned out to be a pivotal event in the life of the Church. A Turkish victory would surely have made the Ottoman Empire supreme in the Mediterranean world. In thanksgiving for Lepanto, Pope St. Pius V instituted a feast in honor of the Virgin Mary, and to this day October 7 — the date of the battle itself — is observed as the Feast of the Rosary.

Down through the years many have told the story, but few have captured its rhythm and sweep as colorfully as G. K. Chesterton did in his epic poem — titled simply Lepanto. *Here it is in its entirety.*

Poem from *The Collected Works of G. K. Chesterton, Vol. X,
Collected Poetry, Part I*, compiled and with an introduction
by Aidan Mackey, Ignatius Press, 1994.

Lepanto

White founts falling in the courts of the sun,
And the Soldan of Byzantium is smiling as they run;

There is laughter like the fountains in that face of all men
feared,
It stirs the forest darkness, the darkness of his beard,
It curls the blood-red crescent, the crescent of his lips,
For the inmost sea of all the earth is shaken with his ships.
They have dared the white republics up the capes of Italy,
They have dashed the Adriatic round the Lion of the Sea,
And the Pope has cast his arms abroad for agony and loss,
And called the kings of Christendom for swords about the Cross,
The cold queen of England is looking in the glass;
The shadow of the Valois is yawning at the Mass;
From evening isles fantastical rings faint the Spanish gun,
And the Lord upon the Golden Horn is laughing in the sun.
Dim drums throbbing, in the hills half heard,
Where only on a nameless throne a crownless prince has stirred,
Where, risen from a doubtful seat and half-attainted stall,
The last knight of Europe takes weapons from the wall,
The last and lingering troubadour to whom the bird has sung,
That once went singing southward when all the world was
young.
In that enormous silence, tiny and unafraid,
Comes up along a winding road the noise of the Crusade.
Strong gongs groaning as the guns boom far,
Don John of Austria is going to the war,
Stiff flags straining in the night-blasts cold
In the gloom black-purple, in the glint old-gold,
Torchlight crimson on the copper kettle-drums,
Then the tuckets, then the trumpets, then the cannon, and he
comes.
Don John laughing in the brave beard curled,
Spurning of his stirrups like the thrones of all the world,
Holding his head up for a flag of all the free.
Love-light of Spain — hurrah!
Death-light of Africa!
Don John of Austria
Is riding to the sea.

Mahound is in his paradise above the evening star,
(*Don John of Austria is going to the war.*)
He moves a mighty turban on the timeless houri's knees,
His turban that is woven of the sunset and the seas.

He shakes the peacock gardens as he rises from his ease,
And he strides among the tree-tops and is taller than the trees,
And his voice through all the garden is a thunder sent to bring
Black Azrael and Ariel and Ammon on the wing.
Giants and the Genii,
Multiplex of wing and eye,
Whose strong obedience broke the sky
When Solomon was king.

They rush in red and purple from the red clouds of the morn,
From temples where the yellow gods shut up their eyes in scorn;
They rise in green robes roaring from the green hells of the sea
Where fallen skies and evil hues and eyeless creatures be;
On them the sea-valves cluster and the grey sea-forests curl,
Splashed with a splendid sickness, the sickness of the pearl;
They swell in sapphire smoke out of the blue cracks of the
    ground, —
They gather and they wonder and give worship to Mahound.
And he saith, "Break up the mountains where the hermit-folk
    may hide,
And sift the red and silver sands lest bone of saint abide,
And chase the Giaours flying night and day, not giving rest,
For that which was our trouble comes again out of the west.
We have set the seal of Solomon on all things under sun,
Of knowledge and of sorrow and endurance of things done,
But a noise is in the mountains, in the mountains, and I know
The voice that shook our palaces — four hundred years ago:
It is he that saith not 'Kismet'; it is he that knows not Fate;
It is Richard, it is Raymond, it is Godfrey in the gate!
It is he whose loss is laughter when he counts the wager worth,
Put down your feet upon him, that our peace be on the earth."
For he heard drums groaning and he heard guns jar,
(*Don John of Austria is going to the war.*)
Sudden and still — hurrah!
Bolt from Iberia!
Don John of Austria
Is gone by Alcalar.

St. Michael's on his Mountain in the sea-roads of the north
(*Don John of Austria is girt and going forth.*)
Where the grey seas glitter and the sharp tides shift
And the sea-folk labour and the red sails lift.
He shakes his lance of iron and he claps his wings of stone;
The noise is gone through Normandy; the noise is gone alone;
The North is full of tangled things and texts and aching eyes

And dead is all the innocence of anger and surprise,
And Christian killeth Christian in a narrow dusty room,
And Christian dreadeth Christ that hath a newer face of doom,
And Christian hateth Mary that God kissed in Galilee,
But Don John of Austria is riding to the sea.
Don John calling through the blast and the eclipse
Crying with the trumpet, with the trumpet of his lips,
Trumpet that sayeth ha!
Domino gloria!
Don John of Austria
Is shouting to the ships.

King Philip's in his closet with the Fleece about his neck
(*Don John of Austria is armed upon the deck.*)
The walls are hung with velvet that is black and soft as sin,
And little dwarfs creep out of it and little dwarfs creep in.
He holds a crystal phial that has colours like the moon,
He touches, and it tingles, and he trembles very soon,
And his face is as a fungus of a leprous white and grey
Like plants in the high houses that are shuttered from the
    day,
And death is in the phial and the end of noble work,
But Don John of Austria has fired upon the Turk.
Don John's hunting, and his hounds have bayed —
Booms *away* past Italy the rumour of his raid.
Gun upon gun, ha! ha!
Gun upon gun, hurrah!
Don John of Austria
Has loosed the cannonade.

The Pope was in his chapel before day or battle broke,
(*Don John of Austria is hidden in the smoke.*)
The hidden room in a man's house where God sits all the year,
The secret window whence the world looks small and very dear.
He sees as in a mirror on the monstrous twilight sea
The crescent of his cruel ships whose name is mystery;
They fling great shadows foe-wards, making Cross and Castle
    dark,
They veil the plumèd lions on the galleys of St. Mark;
And above the ships are palaces of brown, black-bearded chiefs,
And below the ships are prisons, where with multitudinous
    griefs,
Christian captives sick and sunless, all a labouring race re-
    pines
Like a race in sunken cities, like a nation in the mines.

Our Sunday Visitor's

They are lost like slaves that swat, and in the skies of morning
   hung
The stairways of the tallest gods when tyranny was young.

They are countless, voiceless, hopeless as those fallen or flee-
   ing on
Before the high Kings' horses in the granite of Babylon.
And many a one grows witless in his quiet room in hell
Where a yellow face looks inward through the lattice of his cell,
And he finds his God forgotten, and he seeks no more a sign —
(*But Don John of Austria has burst the battle-line!*)
Don John pounding from the slaughter-painted poop,
Purpling all the ocean like a bloody pirate's sloop,
Scarlet running over on the silvers and the golds,
Breaking of the hatches up and bursting of the holds,
Thronging of the thousands up that labour under sea
White for bliss and blind for sun and stunned for liberty.
Vivat Hispania!
Domino Gloria!
Don John of Austria
Has set his people free!

Cervantes on his galley sets the sword back in the sheath
(*Don John of Austria rides homeward with a wreath.*)
And he sees across a weary land a straggling road in Spain,
Up which a lean and foolish knight forever rides in vain,
And he smiles, but not as Sultans smile, and settles back the
   blade. . . .
(*But Don John of Austria rides home from the Crusade.*)

The Curé of Ars

As a Consoler of Penitents, St. John Vianney Had No Equal

When it comes to the life of St. John Vianney (1786-1859), the facts speak for themselves: no confessor in the history of the Church has been quite as renowned. Nor was there any equal to the counsel he was able to give sinners, since it came from God himself.

The numbers stagger the imagination, but they are accurate — twenty thousand visitors to the small town of Ars-en-Dombes, just to hear his words of advice; the Curé himself spending up to eighteen hours a day in the confessional, just to console struggling souls. Sound impossible? The accompanying story describes a typical day in his life — leaving the reader to wonder how the saint lasted as long as he did.

Understandably, perhaps, this kind of attention made some other priests a tad jealous, and they complained to the bishop that the Curé might be mentally unsound. Is that so? the bishop responded. In that case, he added, it's too bad that a few more priests didn't have a touch of exactly the same thing.

Story excerpted from *Portrait of a Parish Priest: St. John Vianney, the Curé d'Ars*, by Lancelot C. Sheppard, The Newman Press, 1958.

His day began at one in the morning. Just before that hour his flickering lantern could be discerned as he made his way across the courtyard that separated church from presbytery; shortly afterward the Angelus rang out, informing the parish and the pilgrims that Abbé Vianney was in church awaiting penitents. He would have found a certain number of them standing near the church or in the porch. After kneeling on the altar step for a little while he went off to the confessional in the chapel of St. John the Baptist. There he heard the women's confessions until six in summer and seven in winter.

It was then that he said Mass. Even while he was vesting, the pilgrims could not leave him in peace: men would be arguing about who should serve his Mass; others, men and women, came to ask his prayers for their intention. He acknowledged their requests by an inclination of the head.

After Mass he put on his rochet and stole and went to kneel before the altar. Here once more he was allowed no peace. Pilgrims came up to look at him. They would approach closely and stare, and went so far, sometimes, as to make remarks about him. When he had finished his thanksgiving, he returned to the sacristy, where numerous medals, rosaries, and objects of devotion were placed for his blessing and a pile of religious pictures awaited his signature. A sign of the Cross over the heap to be blessed, his initials scratched at the foot of the pictures (*J.M.B.V. Curé* was his usual method of signing), a word or two to those who came at this time to obtain his advice, and he hastened off to the *Providence* for the cup of milk ordered by the doctor after his illness of 1827. He was soon back again and established in the confessional in the sacristy where the men were queuing up to go to him.

At ten he managed to leave the penitents for a short time while he knelt on the sacristy floor and said the Little Hours of the breviary. He then returned to the men's confessions until eleven o'clock when he went down into the church to give the catechism lesson from a small pulpit specially reserved for the purpose.

Sometimes many of those present could not hear what he said, or could not understand, but in some extraordinary way the words told nonetheless. Perhaps it was the sight of him, the knowledge of what he was, his gentle smiling face that touched men's hearts. The congregation was a very mixed one. Priests and nuns, peasants, people of importance from all over the world rubbed elbows in the little church.

Sitting at his ease, resting against the rail of the small pulpit, in his long rochet and wearing a black *rabat* with its white piping, sometimes wagging an admonitory finger but generally sparing of gesture, a fleeting whimsical smile on his face, he gave these simple instructions without preparation — he had no time to prepare them — with no affectation or trick of oratory, and in his simplicity converted hundreds. A passing remark, the expression of his countenance, a sigh at the mention of sin, often sufficed to change a man's whole life. He repeated himself, he spoke in familiar language, sometimes he wept, but all that he did so artlessly was supremely effective.

At midday, kneeling before the altar, he said the Angelus and then left church to take his midday meal. In practice it was not as simple as that and sometimes the dozen yards from the church to the presbytery took him a quarter of in hour, for the way was lined on either side by pilgrims who wanted a blessing, a mother with a sick child to be healed, a cripple to be cured. They pushed and jostled, awaiting his appearance at the church door. Directly he was seen coming through the door there was a moment's silence as he let his eyes fall on them, embracing the whole crowd with a glance. Then the babble broke out.

"Holy father, bless me!"

"Pray for my son!"

"Cure this poor little child!"

"Convert my husband!"

He could not reply to all. With a word here and there, he started to make his way across to the presbytery, laying his hands sometimes on a child's head, answering a request for prayers with the gesture of a finger pointing to heaven consoling a poor woman with a few words: "Your husband is saved, but you must pray for him."

At last he was at the presbytery door and all that remained was for him to get through it alone; he kept this one hour of the day for himself. Sometimes when the crowd pressed round him he would take a handful of medals from his pocket and scatter them among them, slipping through the door and locking it behind him while attention was thus momentarily distracted.

Five minutes, at most ten, for his dinner, a few more minutes, ten perhaps, of sleep, and he was off to visit the sick of the parish, including any pilgrims confined to bed in one of the houses of the village. Certainly his "dinner hour" (from midday to one) was well filled — "between midday and one o'clock I've managed to have dinner, sweep my room, shave and sleep and visit the sick," he once explained to a questioner.

It was now one o'clock or after, and his penitents awaited him. Back in the church once more he finished the day's office saying Vespers and Compline, kneeling on the stone floor in front of the high altar, and then went straight to the confessional where he heard the women. At five o'clock he moved to the sacristy to deal with the men and remained there until nearly eight o'clock when he said night prayers from the pulpit for the assembled congregation. This done he went across to the presbytery where, possibly, further interviews awaited him: visiting clergy, his curate, the Brothers who had come to work in the parish — they all took this opportunity to have a word with him and might keep him half an hour or even an hour. At last he was able to go up to his room.

There he said Matins and Lauds of the next day and read a little of the lives of the saints. And now he could go to bed, but in all likelihood it was not to sleep. He was prone to a troublesome cough that obliged him to sit up in bed, often several times in the hour, but above all he was a prey to all the human misery, the sins, and conflicts of all sorts and conditions, which were poured into his ears throughout the greater part of his long day.

So the short night passed. However bad it proved, however little sleep he managed to obtain, punctually at one o'clock the Angelus rang out — earlier sometimes, even at midnight, if the crowd of penitents was exceptionally great — and all the village and its hundreds of pilgrims knew that Abbé Vianney was back in his confessional.

The Little Flower

St. Thérèse of Lisieux Took Her Case Directly to the Pope

St. Thérèse of Lisieux (1873-1897) knew what she wanted at a very early age: she wanted to enter the Carmelite convent, even though she was barely in her teens. Her chances seemed remote, however; she was turned down by her family, by her parish priest, even by the bishop of Bayeux. To the determined young Thérèse Martin, that meant only one thing — she would have to go directly to Pope Leo XIII.

Improbable as that might seem, she got her chance during a pilgrimage to Rome, one that would include a personal audience with the Holy Father. This story is about that meeting. Despite the pope's mild words of encouragement, it was several months before Thérèse began her brief life as a Carmelite — one that would lead to the world knowing her as the Little Flower, and make her the most beloved saint of modern times.

On the eve of her new life, her pastor promised his prayers but warned that she might live to regret her decision. Her confessor, on the other hand, knew better. "This child is privileged," he said, "and destined for great things."

Selection from *Thérèse of Lisieux: A Biography*, by Patricia O'Connor, Our Sunday Visitor, Inc., 1983.

The climax of the trip was the audience with His Holiness, Pope Leo XIII. As she prepared for the pilgrimage Thérèse had a single thought in mind — to take this chance to speak to the pope about entering the Carmel. If "the Holy Father," who would surely be able to read her soul, said yes, the canon and the bishop must agree. As the moment neared, the nuns back in the Carmel became more tightly linked with Thérèse in her determination. At times nearly daily letters passed between the pilgrims and the nuns back home, with Pauline finally writing emphatically that Thérèse must speak to the pope. "Pay no attention to the crowd that will be around you. What does it matter if they hear you? *Not the least bit.*" And not only Mother Gonzague but also Mother Geneviève, the foundress of the Lisieux Carmel, agreed. Speak up, Pauline coached, even if he passes by, speak up to the pope, but "let M. Révérony know nothing about this letter." As the day of the papal audience drew near, one thought blanched out the sights of Rome — "I had to *dare* to *speak to the pope* in front of everybody," Thérèse wrote. "This thought made me tremble."

On the appointed Sunday the Martins dressed according to instructions. "The style of dress for the pontifical audience is as follows: for men, a black suit, tie and white or black vest, no gloves. . . . Women should be in black silk or woolen dresses, a black veil covering the head, no gloves." Thérèse first glimpsed Pope Leo XIII at the Mass. Afterward she and Céline took their places at the end of a long line of darkly clad pilgrims that slowly inched its way toward the papal chair. Thérèse described the scene:

"Leo XIII was seated on a large armchair; he was dressed simply in a white cassock, with a cape of the same color, and on his head was a little skullcap. Around him were cardinals, archbishops, and bishops, but I saw them only in general, being occupied solely with the Holy Father. We passed in front of him in procession; each pilgrim knelt in turn, kissed the foot and hand of Leo XIII, (and) received his blessing. . . ."

Standing next to the pope was none other than Abbé Révérony. As Thérèse neared the papal chair Abbé Révérony — who had heard Louis Martin tell Bishop Hugonin that Thérèse intended to take her case to the pope — announced that no one was to speak to the Holy Father.

As Thérèse knelt in front of the pope and kissed his foot he stretched out his hand for her to kiss his ring as everyone in the long line had done. But Thérèse did not kiss the ring. She grabbed his knees and blurted out her much-rehearsed question: "Most Holy Father, I have a great favor to ask of you. . . . Holy Father, in honor of your Jubilee permit me to enter Carmel at the age of fifteen!"

There was silence, an embarrassed pause, for Pope Leo XIII at the age of seventy-seven was nearly deaf. Since he couldn't make out what this young girl was saying he turned to Father Révérony to find out. "Most Holy Father, this is *a child*," Thérèse heard him say, "who wants to enter Carmel at the age of fifteen, but the Superiors are considering the matter at the moment."

Now Pope Leo spoke to Thérèse, but not the words she wanted to hear. "Well, my child, do what the superiors tell you!" he said. With nothing rehearsed beyond the simple words of her request, still kneeling, Thérèse leaned her hands right on the pope's knees and said, "Oh, Holy Father, if you say yes, everybody will agree!" The pope, Thérèse reported, "gazed at me steadily, and he said 'Go . . . go . . . *you will enter if God wills it.*' "

The Road Led to Rome

Newman's Long Journey Ended in a Tiny Chapel on a Storm-Tossed Night

"All roads lead to Rome," G. K. Chesterton once observed. "That is one reason why many people never get there."

One who did get there, and happily so, caused a sensation when he arrived. John Henry Newman (1801-1890) was a towering figure — leader of the Oxford movement, pillar of the Anglican Church, a philosopher, theologian, and preacher of the first rank. His decision to enter the Roman Catholic Church brought on a firestorm of controversy within the British establishment and set off shock waves around the world.

Newman's journey to Rome was slow and halting, but once he finally made his profession of faith on a stormy midnight before Father Dominic, an Italian Passionist, his heart was at ease. Some of his greatest works would follow: Idea of a University *(1852), outlining his vision for liberal education;* Apologia Pro Vita Sua *(1864), a religious autobiography, and* A Grammar of Assent *(1870), a study of the psychology of faith.*

When Pope Leo XIII named him a cardinal in 1879, Newman chose as his motto Ex umbris et imaginibus in veritatem *("Out of the shadows and images into the truth").*

Excerpt from *John Henry Cardinal Newman*, by George J. Donahue, The Stratford Co., 1927.

The homecoming of Newman to Rome was not all sunshine and music. He died a lingering death to Anglicanism. He was obliged to separate from men and institutions that were as dear to him as the ruddy drops that visited his troubled heart. When he came, there came with him Frederick Oakley, Ambrose St. John, and F. W. Faver.

"From the end of 1841," Newman testifies, "I was on my deathbed as regards my membership with the Anglican Church, though at the time I became aware of it only by degrees."

"Never was a man followed by more tender regrets from pure-minded friends than John Henry Newman," writes Sir Robert Falconer, "when in October 1845 he made the great renunciation of the world in that he had rich possessions, in order to save his soul by entering the Church of Rome. He said good-bye to the places he loved most on earth — Trinity, Oriel, St. Mary's, Littlemore. He kissed, so runs the legend, the very leaves in the gardens on taking farewell." His valedictory as an Anglican preacher was a sermon on "The Parting of Friends," delivered to a small and grief-stricken congregation in the church at Littlemore.

The details of his reception into the True Church were dramatic as well as pathetic. Father Dominic was expected in Oxford on October 1, 1845. On the afternoon of the day, Newman said in a low tone to Dalgairns, who was going to meet Father Dominic, "When you see your friend, will you tell him that I wish him to receive me into the Church of Christ?"

The genius of the motion picture world could not have inspired the setting with greater dramatic elements. The evening grew on dark and stormy, the wind blew in gusts, rain fell in torrents; that night Newman left Protestantism for the Church of Rome.

The midnight scene in the little chapel where Newman made his confession is a scene for those only who can see high color in human adventures, and only those who "amberize" in verse the tragic beauty of this world, can appreciate the sight of Newman, so overcome that he could not stand alone, led out of the tiny chapel by his companions. It was an incident that has not only registered its consequences since but will continue its influence for generations yet unborn. The things in life, which have an eternal youth, are the things done in the dark and cold. That tiny chapel has influenced more souls perhaps than the frozen music or poetry in stone of the great cathedrals.

G. K. Chesterton

His Intellect and Wit Found Their Home in Rome

The conversion to Catholicism of Gilbert Keith Chesterton (1874-1936) didn't cause quite the sensation as that of John Henry Newman nearly a century earlier, but it rocked the British world of letters nonetheless. One of the great intellects of his time, Chesterton was a brilliant literary and social critic who was a pillar of the London establishment. Many of his friends were stunned to learn that he had turned to Rome.

Not so, perhaps, with some of those who were closest to him, who knew that that intellect (and, to be sure, the wit that went with it) would not be satisfied until it had found a home.

If anything, both intellect and wit sharpened in their new surroundings, as the accompanying collection of his epigrams, aphorisms, and gentle comments (on a wide array of topics) might suggest. "It is the test of a good religion," he once wrote, "whether you can joke about it." And joke about it he did, as he did about almost everything else. He never wrote humorously just for the sake of being funny; rather he used humor to help make his case. If the joke were on him, all the better.

Chesterton delighted in retelling the story of the letter he wrote to the manager of a nearby factory, complaining that its excessive noise was interfering with his work. With no response forthcoming, his secretary had to deal directly with the factory manager. "You see," she told him, "Mr. Chesterton cannot write." Said the manager in reply: "Yes, we've seen his letter. We're aware of that."

Selections from *The Quotable Chesterton: A Topical Compilation of the Wit, Wisdom and Satire of G. K. Chesterton*, edited by George J. Marlin, Richard P. Rabatin, and John L. Swan, Image Books, Doubleday & Co., Inc., 1987.

On genius: "I think there is one thing more important than the man of genius — and that is the genius of man."

Art school: "An art school is a place where about three people work with feverish energy and everybody else idles to a degree that I should have conceived unattainable by human nature."

Human endeavor: "If a thing is worth doing, it is worth doing badly."

Blasphemy: "Blasphemy depends upon belief, and is fading with it. If anyone doubts this, let him sit down seriously and try to think blasphemous thoughts about Thor. I think his family will find him at the end of the day in a state of some exhaustion."

Great men: "The great man tries to be ordinary, and becomes extraordinary in the process." And: "A great man knows he is not God, and the greater he is the better he knows it."

Free love: "They have invented a phrase, a phrase that is a black and white contradiction in two words — 'free love' — as if a lover ever had been, or ever could be, free. It is the nature of love to bind itself, and the institution of marriage merely paid the average man the compliment of taking him at his word."

The Church: "Catholics know the two or three transcendental truths on which they do agree, and take rather a pleasure in disagreeing on everything else." And: "A century or two hence Spiritualism may be a tradition and Socialism may be a tradition and Christian Science may be a tradition. But Catholicism will not be a tradition. It will still be a nuisance and a new and dangerous thing."

Age of reason: "There is nothing very much the matter with the age of reason; except, alas, that it comes before the age of discretion."

Dining (under difficult circumstances): "Of all modern phenomena, the most monstrous and ominous, the most manifestly rotting with disease, the most grimly prophetic of destruction, the most clearly and unmistakably inspired by evil spirits, the most instantly and awfully overshadowed by the wrath of heaven, the most near to madness and moral chaos, the most vivid with deviltry and despair, is the practice of having to listen to loud music while eating a meal in a restaurant."

Gentlemen: "There is no such thing as being a gentleman at important moments; it is at unimportant moments that a man is a gentleman. At important moments he ought to be something better."

Faith: "Faith is always at a disadvantage; it is a perpetually defeated thing that survives all its conquerors."

Humility: "Humility is the mother of giants. One sees great things from the valley; only small things from the peak."

Madness: "Madness is the eccentric behavior of somebody else."

Man of the future: "The man of the future must not be taught; he must be bred. This notion of producing superior human beings by the methods of the stud farm had often been urged, though its difficulties had never been cleared up. . . . The first and most obvious objection to it, of course, is this: that if you are to breed men as pigs, you require some overseer who is as much more subtle than a man as a man is more subtle than a pig. Such an individual is not easy to find."

Gaelic: "I suspect that many names and announcements are printed in Gaelic, not because Irishmen can read them, but because Englishmen can't."

Silly opinions: "A little while ago the family of a young lady attempted to shut her up in an asylum because she believed in free love. This atrocious injustice was stopped; but many people wrote to the papers to say that marriage was a very fine thing — as indeed it is. Of course, the answer was simple: that if everyone with silly opinions were locked up in an asylum, the asylums of the twentieth century would have to be somewhat unduly enlarged."

Jokes: "Joking is undignified; that is why it is so good for one's soul."

Words: "What is the good of words if they aren't important enough to quarrel over? Why do we choose one word more than another if there isn't any difference between them? If you called a woman a chimpanzee instead of an angel, wouldn't there be a quarrel about a word? If you're not going to argue about words, what are you going to argue about? Are you going to convey your meaning to me by moving your ears? The Church and the heresies always used to fight about words, because they are the only things worth fighting about."

The Day the Sun Danced

A Throng of Seventy Thousand Saw It Happen at Fátima

The story of Fátima (1917) is as well known to Catholics as those of Guadalupe and Lourdes; at each place an appearance by Our Lady was received with prayer and piety and accompanied by miracles. All three sites — Guadalupe in Mexico, Lourdes in France, and Fátima in Portugal — continue to attract throngs of pilgrims to this day.

Too, each apparition was first greeted with official skepticism. In the case of Fátima, the doubts were directed at the three children — Lucy Santos, ten, and her cousins, Francisco Marto, nine, and his sister Jacinta, seven — who saw Mary six times that year in a field called Cova da Iria. She urged greater devotion to the rosary and to her Immaculate Heart, foretold the end of World War I and the events that would lead to World War II, foresaw the rise of godlessness in Russia and that country's eventual conversion, and looked ahead to an era of world peace. In particular, she urged Catholics to receive Communion on five consecutive first Saturdays with those latter goals in mind.

To the children themselves she pledged a miracle — one that would reward their steadfast piety and convince the skeptics, whose number was growing by leaps and bounds as word of the visions spread — that her presence was real indeed. To see if it would truly happen, a throng of some seventy thousand descended on the Cova da Iria on October 13, more than twice the number that had turned up a month earlier. This time they would not be disappointed.

Story from *Fátima: Pilgrimage to Peace*, by April Oursler Armstrong and Martin F. Armstrong, Jr., Hanover House, 1954.

Rain, relentless and cold, had set in the night before. The hard red clay of the roads turned to sludge. Sightseers jammed the Marto house, clambering with muddy feet on chairs and beds to gawk as Jacinta and Francisco dressed. When Lucy joined them to walk to the Cova they could hardly move through the throngs.

A bitter wind swept down from the northwest. The rain seemed to be specially sent to erase all thoughts of heaven and shining white ladies. Seventy thousand people, who had traveled for days from all over Portugal, stood patiently under stolid black umbrellas. As the morning grew old, the rain grew fiercer. It could not silence the voices praying the rosary, nor the hymns ringing out over the dismal mountain range.

Exactly at noon, Standard Time, the children fell to their knees in the mud. Rain dripped from their upturned chins. The Lady had come.

"I want a chapel built here in my honor. I want you to continue saying the rosary every day.

"The war will end within a year, and the soldiers will return to their homes. . . ."

"Yes," said Lucy. And remembering the promise made in May, she asked, "Will you tell me your name?"

"I am the Lady of the Rosary."

And a little later: "People must amend their lives, and ask pardon for their sins. They must not offend Our Lord any more, for he is already too much offended!"

Before the children's eyes, Our Lady of the Rosary rose slowly toward the dark heavens. And to them was given a vision of paradise. They saw her in a mantle of blue, and beside her St. Joseph with the Christ Child in his arms. St. Joseph, all in white, leaned from the clouds and three times blessed the earth. And then he was gone, and in the pale sun stood Christ himself, tall in his red cloak, and beside him, Mary in the traditional garb of Our Lady of Sorrows. Solemnly, lovingly, Christ blessed the people below. And as that vision passed, Lucy alone saw Mary poised for an instant in the figure of Our Lady of Mount Carmel.

But the miracle? The people in the Cova did not see those visions. Instead, at the instant of the vision they heard Lucy cry:

"Look at the sun!"

Instantaneously the rain stopped. The black clouds split asunder, racing to the corners of the sky. The sun alone stood in the heavens, a sun such as man has never seen before. Without blinking, the throngs could stare directly into it. It was the color of mother-of-pearl. Yet there was neither mist nor cloud to dim it.

The sun in the noonday sky began to tremble and spin, whirling in a frenzy of fire. From it spun a thousand colors, red and blue, green and yellow, and the infinite shades between. It turned on itself, thrilling and twisting, dancing in the sky.

For a moment it paused in balance. Then, as if the bonds of nature were loosed, as if the universe were split apart, it seemed to plummet to earth. Heat and destruction hurtled downward, driving people to their knees. At the last possible second the sun retreated.

The sky settled. Men blinked and turned away from the blinding rays. It was noon in a brilliant sheep pasture in the mountains of Portugal. The ground, the grass, the clothes of the crowd, even their hair, were dry.

That, in necessarily inadequate words, was the miracle of the sun.

Did it really happen? Every one of the seventy thousand who were there that day swore they saw it. Many are living now to testify to it. People many kilometers away, even some who through illness or monastic seclusion had not heard of the promise and did not expect anything unusual, reported they saw the sun dance. . . . Therefore, it could not have been due to mass hypnosis, nor a group delusion.

The phenomenon of the sun was not noted at any astronomical observatory. By the measurements of science it could not — and did not — happen. Therefore, it could not have been natural in origin.

It occurred at the precise moment that the children had predicted a month beforehand.

Given those facts, it is at least easy for a reasonable person to understand why millions of people of all faiths believe, as we do, that the whirling of the sun was indeed the miracle the Lady had promised, "the miracle that would enable all to believe."

'It Takes the Irish . . .'

MacArthur Salutes the Boys
of Father Duffy's Fighting 69th

Father Francis P. Duffy (1871-1932), a New York priest and chaplain of the famed "Fighting 69th" Regiment in World War I, emerged from that conflict as a national hero. The honors and the medals he garnered were all legitimate; time and again he helped rally the troops in the trenches, where they spent one hundred eighty days in contact with the enemy (and lost hundreds of officers and men in combat). The chief of staff of the 42nd (Rainbow) Division — none other than Douglas MacArthur, who was then a colonel — was so impressed with Father Duffy's leadership qualities that he wanted to have him appointed a regimental commander, an honor the priest politely declined. His role, he insisted, was primarily spiritual.

Father Duffy carried his honors lightly. Once when he was back home, and a master of ceremonies got carried away with an introduction, he joked that he'd write a book about the war and call it Alone in Europe.

In New York, in the years after the war — the Roaring Twenties — he was the toast of the town. Mr. and Mrs. Irving Berlin would have him over for "a small dinner" honoring Ethel Barrymore; Bernard Baruch and Franklin D. Roosevelt were among those at the twenty-fifth anniversary of his ordination.

From the Times Square parish where he delighted in the role of pastor, he kept up friendships begun in France. One was with Alexander Woollcott, the former war correspondent who went on to become one of America's leading men of letters. In a tribute written for The New Yorker *just after Father Duffy's funeral, he described the priest as the city's "first citizen," adding: "Father Duffy was of such dimensions that he made New York into a small town."*

The hero-chaplain did get around to writing that book, and its real title was simply Father Duffy's Story. *It was a book that captivated the city and the nation, brimming with pride at all that it meant to be Irish, Catholic, and a New Yorker. These vignettes capture something of its flavor — and something of the man himself.*

Adapted from *Father Duffy's Story: A Tale of Humor and Heroism, of Life and Death With the Fighting Sixty-Ninth,* by Francis P. Duffy, George H. Doran Co., 1919.

June 19th, 1918: Yesterday was New York "Old Home Day" on the roads of Lorraine. We marched out from Baccarat on our hunt for new trouble, and met on the way the 77th Division, all National Army troops from New York City. It was a wonderful encounter. As the two columns passed each other on the road in the bright moonlight there were songs of New York, friendly greetings and badinage, sometimes good humored, sometimes with a sting to it.

More often it would be somebody going along the lines shouting "Anybody there from Greenwich Village?" or "Any of you guys from Tremont?" And no matter what part of New York City was chosen the answer was almost sure to be "Yes." Sometimes a chap went the whole line calling for some one man: "Is John Kelly there?" — the answer from our side being invariably, "Which of them do you want?" One young fellow in the 77th kept calling for his brother, who was with us. Finally he found him and the two lads ran at each other burdened with their heavy packs, grabbed each other awkwardly, and just punched each other and swore for lack of other words until officers ordered them into ranks, and they parted perhaps not to meet again.

At intervals both columns would break into song, the favorites being on the order of "East side, west side, all around the town. . . ."

The last notes I heard, as the tail of the dusty column swung around a bend in the road, were "Herald Square, anywhere, New York Town, take me there." Good lads, God bless them. I hope their wish comes true.

July 15th, 1918. It was 12:04 midnight by my watch when it began. No crescendo business about it. Just one sudden crash like an avalanche; but an avalanche that was to keep crashing for five hours. The whole sky seemed to be torn apart with sound — the roaring B-o-o-o-m-p of the discharge and the gradual menacing W-h-e-e-E-E-Z of traveling projectiles and the nerve-wracking W-h-a-n-g-g of bursts. Not that we could tell them apart. They were all mingled in one deafening combination of screech and roar, and they all seemed to be bursting just outside.

I stood it about twenty minutes and then curiosity got the better of me and I went out. I put my back against the door of the hut and looked up cautiously to see how high the protecting sandbags stood over my head, and then I took a good look around. I saw first the sky to the south and found that our guns were causing a comfortable share of the racket. The whole southern sky was punctuated with quick bursts of light, at times looking as if the central fires had burst through in a ten-mile fissure.

I crawled around the corner of the shack and looked toward the enemy. Little comfort there. I have been far enough north to see the Aurora Borealis dancing white and red from horizon to zenith; but never so bright, so lively, so awe-inspiring as the light from that German artillery.

I wanted to see Anderson. He was only forty yards away by a short cut over ground. I took the short cut — we were not allowed to use it by day — and had the uncomfortable feeling that even in the dark I was under enemy observation. It was the meanest forty yards I had ever done since as a lad of twelve I hurried up the lane to my father's door pursued by an ever-nearing ghost that had my shoulder in its clutches as I grasped the latch. But I went in now as then, whistling. . . .

Then a gas-masked figure opened the door and announced that there were two wounded men outside. That came under my business and it was a relief to find something to do. [One of them] was Schmedlein — his folks were parishioners of mine — and he had it bad. I was puffing by now and blaming myself that I had not followed Major Donovan's rules for keeping in condition. As I bent to the task I heard Phil McArdle's voice, "Aisy now, Father. Just give me a holt of him. Slither him up on my back. This is no work for the likes of you. . . ."

There were anxious moments before the outcome of the day's battle was no longer in doubt, after 10:00 o'clock that morning — especially when many machine guns were put out of action, and the call for further fire from our artillery met with a feeble response. I dropped in on Anderson. True to his motto, "Fight it out where you are," he was putting the last touches to his preparations for having his clerks, runners, and cooks make the last defense if necessary.

"Do you want some grenades, Padre?" was his question.

"No, Allie," I said, "every man to his trade. I stick to mine."

August 2nd, 1918. At 4:00 A.M. our patrols reported no resistance. The whole division started forward and found that the main body of the enemy had gone. Our infantry hastened on through the Foret de Nesles, keeping in touch with neighboring regiments left and right.

The 4th Division was coming up to relieve us, but Colonel MacArthur wanted a last effort made by his division. He called on one regiment, then on another, for a further advance. Their commanders said truthfully that the men were utterly fatigued and unable to go forward another step.

"It's up to you, McCoy," said the Chief of Staff. Our colonel called Captain Martin Meaney, now in command of what was left of the third battalion.

"Captain Meaney, a battalion is wanted to go ahead and gain contact with the enemy; you may report on the condition of your men."

"My men are few and they are tired, sir, but they are willing to go anywhere they are ordered, and they will consider an order to advance as a compliment," was the manly response.

As the brave and gallant few swung jauntily to their position at the head of the division, Colonel MacArthur exclaimed, "By God, McCoy, it takes the Irish when you want a hard thing done."

The Four Chaplains

They Gave Up Their Life Jackets on a Sinking Ship

The World War I exploits of Father Duffy, the hero-chaplain of the "Fighting 69th" Regiment, thrilled young and old across the United States — affecting, in a particular way, Catholic boys who were feeling the first stirrings of a priestly vocation. So it was with a youngster in Newark, New Jersey, named John Washington (1910-1943), who saw in Father Duffy — the gallant priest riding up and down the lines to comfort the men, encouraging them to heroic deeds — the same kind of bravery his father had told him Irish priests exhibited long ago in the face of British persecution.

John Washington, who decided early on that he wanted to be a priest — and someday, perhaps, a chaplain as well — got his wish on both counts. Ordained for what was then the Newark diocese in 1935, he became an army chaplain soon after the U.S. entered World War II. Little did he know that his own name would go down in memory for a kind of valor every bit as inspiring as that of Father Duffy.

In January 1943, he climbed aboard a converted freighter called the Dorchester *that was carrying troops from Massachusetts to Greenland. His shipmates included three other chaplains: George L. Fox and Clark V. Poling, both Protestant ministers, and a Jewish rabbi, Alexander D. Goode.*

The Dorchester *never made it to Greenland. Neither did Father Washington and his companions. Here is their story, one of the most stirring to come out of the war — the story of the Four Chaplains.*

Selection from *Sea of Glory, The Magnificent Story of the Four Chaplains,* by Francis Beauchesne Thornton, Prentice-Hall, Inc., 1953.

The Arctic night was beautiful, but it was also deadly. Like a toy being dragged by a loitering child the *Dorchester* made her way through the early hours of the darkness — a darkness overcast with an eerie glimmering of whiteness. She zigged and zagged and seemed to stumble from one crest to another, being punished by each in turn, yet staggering slowly on.

The ship's bells struck twice. It was one o'clock in the morning. They never sounded again.

A minute or so later a torpedo smashed into the *Dorchester*, well below the waterline amidships.

The stricken ship staggered from the explosion. Men lying fully clothed in their bunks were tossed to the decks like walnuts from an upset basket. Others were catapulted against the bulkheads.

Blackout lights went out instantly, plunging the entire ship into darkness and leaving the men to grope in terror as they fought their way topside.

The German submarine skipper had caught the freighter fair on his periscope's crossed hairs. The torpedo, running swift and true, ripped open the tender skin of the ship and exploded in all its fury in the engine room.

Steam lines burst, letting their vapor escape to kill and scald and torture the engineers and oilers. Fuel tanks split open, spewing their oily contents over the scene of terror, making each ladder and catwalk a place of peril.

In thirty seconds a hundred men were dead, scalded, mutilated, or drowned like rats in a trap.

Soldiers scrambled toward the companionways, already leaning crazily as the *Dorchester* listed to port, and fought their way, cursing and screaming, to the windy deck.

Abandon-ship drills, lectures on survival in torpedoings, and the military discipline so newly acquired by civilians-suddenly-turned-soldiers went by the boards. In each man's mind was the single thought of how to save himself.

Then out of chaos came brief signs of order as men conquered the fear that had short-circuited their thinking. Doctors and medics snatched up their kits and headed below, bucking the tide of men seeking the open decks. If they sensed their own danger they brushed it aside and went on to rescue the injured.

Life rafts went over the side as frantic men hacked at their lashings. Some bobbled away in the darkness before anyone could reach them. Others were so crowded with survivors that men died struggling to get a grip on their handlines.

Men shouted and men wept. Soldiers made their way out of the hold without their life jackets and went back to get them, dying in the smothering holds.

Hysteria compelled weak men to jump into the Atlantic with mad words upon their lips, but the bitter cold of the ocean stilled their cries as if the words thickened in their throats.

Through this scene of terror moved a few strong men: purposeful, calm, and seemingly unafraid.

Captain Greenspun was everywhere, encouraging the soldiers,

helping the crew to launch anything that would float, and issuing the few commands there were left to issue on a foundering, mortally wounded ship.

Army surgeons and medics behaved as though participating in a briefing session on how to care for the wounded at sea. Injured men were brought topside, bandaged, and helped into life boats when these were available. Men who might have died lived because of their ministration.

And everywhere about the ship, in the terror-ridden interior and on the crazily tilted deck, the four chaplains moved among the men with helpful words, giving some the strength to live and some the courage to die.

Knowing that the life expectancy of a man in such frigid waters was somewhere between eighteen and forty minutes, the three men with Crosses on their collars and the one with the Tablets of the Law on his, urged the soldiers to stay aboard as long as possible after the small boats had been cast off.

"Take it easy, soldier. It will be all right."

Strange how such simple, meaningless words could ease panic in a man's heart. Stranger still how they could inject starch into a coward's spine.

The *Dorchester* by now had lost all way and was lying dead in the water. Fitful winds plucked spume from the wave crests and whipped it into the faces of the men on deck.

Suddenly the ship shivered and men everywhere cried out.

"She's going down! She's going down! We'll be sucked under!"

The chaplains sensed the threat.

"Over the side, men, make it fast!" The wind tore the words from their lips.

"Swim to the life boats," they cried. "Get away from the ship!"

Men looked at the four chaplains with new wonder. They saw them move together as though that way they could be of greater help.

Soldiers lifted their eyes to them as if for a sign, some symbol to carry with them into the valley of death.

A man — more boy than man — made his way to the group at the rail.

"Padre, I've lost my life jacket. I can't swim. I'll . . ."

One of the chaplains tore off his own and put it about the boy's shoulders.

"Take this. I'm staying. I won't need it."

The soldier tied the jacket's strings, mounted the rail, and slipped into the sea, now almost level with the deck.

Of the three hundred or so men who survived, not one can remember which chaplain it was who first voiced the decision to stay with the ship.

Was it Father Washington, who couldn't swim across a duck pond? Was it Fox, survivor of one war and victim of another? Poling, heir to a great name in preaching? Or Goode, the Rabbi from the Pennsylvania Dutch country?

What does it matter now? If the first had not spoken, another would. Catholic, Jew, and Protestant: each proved that night that courage knows no distinction of creed, bravery no division of caste.

Violent squalls confused the dying moments of the freighter. Flares on the bridge revealed the deck, now awash, at an ugly slant. Men fought for places on the last raft, and the losers cursed and wept.

The four chaplains stood with arms linked, each one without a life jacket. Somewhere off in the seething seas four other men were cheating death, supported by the chaplains' gifts.

Icy waters reached their knees as their lips moved in prayer.

"Our Father, which art in heaven, hallowed be thy name. Thy kingdom come, Thy will be done . . ."

The troopship labored to rise from a trough and staggered on. Water sluiced along the sloping deck.

". . . *Ego te absolvo a peccatis tuis, in nomine Patris, et Filii, et Spiritus Sancti* . . ."

A soldier, bleeding through his bandages, crawled to where the four were standing. His voice was barely audible.

"God bless you," he said, and crawled into the sea.

A wave breached clear across the tilted deck.

"Hear, O Israel, the Lord Our God, the Lord is one . . ."

For an instant the light of a flare cast an effulgence upon the four of them for all who were left aboard to see.

". . . Forgive us our trespasses, as we forgive those who trespass against us . . ."

Once more the ship labored to breast the next wave. There was a great noise of water and air churning in the darkness.

The *Dorchester* fought to right herself, failed, and plunged beneath the surface.

The Beginning of Boys Town

Father Flanagan Thought
Every Youngster Deserved a Chance

The boy's name was Ismael, a tough Hispanic kid from Brooklyn, and the people at Boys Town — the Omaha, Nebraska, institution that's been a haven for troubled youngsters since its founding in 1917 — had gotten him sprung from a Bronx detention center to give him a chance at a new life. There was just one problem: Ismael wanted no part of it.

"He was a holy terror," said Father Val Peter, director of the Nebraska institution and the present-day successor to its legendary founder, Father Edward Flanagan (1886-1948). "He'd only been here for two days and said he couldn't stand it. 'I'd rather go back to lockup,' he said."

Father Peter continued the story: "One of our staff people told Ismael we weren't going to keep him here against his will, but advised him that this was no time to give up. Before he headed back to New York, how about spending a little time in the chapel to think it over? Ismael didn't like it that much, but he said okay.

"An hour later he came back, and he was a changed kid. He apologized. 'I want to stay,' he said. 'I know I can do it.' Our staff man couldn't believe it, and wanted to know what had happened in the chapel. Well, Ismael said, 'Father Flanagan' had stopped by and had a talk with him while he was there. 'Give Boys Town a try,' the priest had said. 'You'll like it here.' There was something in the way he said it, the youngster added, that made him decide to stay.

"The staff member smiled at the mention of 'Father Flanagan.' He described a couple of priests who might have dropped by at the chapel while Ismael was there. It must have been this priest, he told the boy, or that one. But the descriptions sounded off-base to Ismael. No, he said, it was Father Flanagan, and then he pointed to a portrait behind the interviewer's desk. 'That's him,' Ismael said. 'That's the priest who talked to me.'

"And indeed the portrait was one of Father Flanagan — who had died nearly fifty years before.

"That's a true story," Father Peter declared matter-of-factly. "In *fact, it's just one in a series of very curious coincidences. We really believe that Father Flanagan is up in heaven taking care of us."*

Ismael not only stayed, he became one of Boys Town's leading citizens. And it all adds to the luster of Father Flanagan, who — long before Spencer Tracy immortalized him by portraying him in the 1938 film Boys Town (with Mickey Rooney as the tough kid who was eventually reined in) — was a legend in his own time.

Father Flanagan, born in County Roscommon, Ireland, followed an older priest-brother to Omaha and was ordained himself in 1912. After a brief parish assignment he operated a thriving shelter in Omaha for vagrants, parolees, and other people down on their luck. At some point he came to realize how vulnerable children were when grown-ups' lives were in such disarray, and vowed to pay more attention to their plight. One day he was present in court when a gang of teenage toughs seemed headed for jail — until he decided to intervene. What happened next eventually led to the founding of Boys Town.

Selection from *Father Flanagan of Boys Town*, by Fulton
Oursler and Will Oursler, Doubleday & Co., Inc., 1949.

There was a "crime wave" current in the Omaha of that day. The entire city was aroused over outbreaks of store looting, housebreaking, and senseless, unprovoked attacks on pedestrians. Behind the outbreak was a gang of youths from South Omaha.

According to the police, it was a typical, tough, street-corner gang, of shifting membership. Often some member would be shipped off to reform school, to return a year or so later with added glamour because he had "done a stretch." . . .

Parents in the neighborhood, living in fear that their own children might come under the influence of the gang of hoodlums or become victims in one of the vicious street fights, were demanding that the gang be broken up. . . . The ringleaders, the parents insisted, had to be put away. . . .

Special [police] squads assigned to the case collected evidence against the ringleaders — enough evidence to send them to the reformatory until they were twenty-one.

Father Flanagan was in the court the morning the police brought in the seven leaders of the gang. He was fully aware of the public attitude. These were "really bad boys"! At the hands of the law they deserved no mercy.

There was scattered booing, and the judge had to rap for order as the young terrorists were brought in. They stood in a line in the prisoner's box. The priest leaned forward to scan their faces, and sat back, astonished.

Not one in this group of "gangsters" could have been more than fifteen years old.

The papers had pictured them as arrogant young criminals, defiant of all authority. But there was no arrogance on their faces now. They were seven frightened boys. . . . That fear was the clue he sought; they were still only boys; they could still be reached.

The judge told the prisoners to stand up. As he started to pronounce the sentences, Father Flanagan also stood up. The judge hesitated, glanced over at the priest, then asked: "Is there something you want to say about this case?"

"Yes," came the voice, like the crack of a rifle. "Yes, Your Honor. I would like to ask that these boys be paroled to my care."

There was a buzz of hostile comment in the courtroom, and the judge pounded for order as he called the priest to the bench. While the judge was well aware of the success Father Flanagan had won with his parolees, he also knew that they had all been comparatively minor cases.

"Do you realize," he asked, "what you would be taking on with these boys? Have you seen the records of what they've done?"

"I know the records," Flanagan answered. "And I know also, from what I've read and seen myself, the conditions under which they live. The temptations, the lack of supervision — "

"And you believe you could do something with boys such as these?"

The seven "incorrigibles" were standing close by. For the judge, the decision was not easy. An angry and frightened public opinion was demanding that the boys be punished. Political interests in the city would have no desire to outrage the community by letting the culprits go free. Yet the judge was a fair man and he had seen the skill this priest had with boys. At last he said:

"Father, I am going to give you the chance you ask. I hope you will be able to cure these boys. I am going to parole them in your charge."

His Honor turned to the prisoners.

"Now you are getting a chance," he told them. "I don't know if it will do you any good or not. Father Flanagan thinks he can help you. I hope that you'll remember that had it not been for him, all of you by now would be on your way to reform school."

Most stunned of all in that courtroom were the boys themselves. They looked at one another and then at the priest with bewilderment. Until this moment they had been expecting prison bars.

If Father Flanagan was aware of how startled they were, he gave no hint of it. He walked over and asked them to follow him.

Numbly, silently, they obeyed. Every eye in the courtroom was watching as Father Flanagan herded his new charges from the prisoner's box and followed them, Indian file, down the center aisle of the court and out to the street.

Light One Candle

A Priest's Timely Counsel
Helped Father Keller Do Just That

In this brief selection from his autobiography, Maryknoll Father James Keller (1900-1976) describes the counsel a priest gave him at a pivotal moment in his life — when he was trying to decide whether to return to the seminary to continue studying for the priesthood. If Father Ryan hadn't walked into the store in San Francisco where young James Keller was working, ordered a sundae, and then dispensed some timely advice, would things have turned out differently?

No one will ever know. But because of what Keller did hear from Father Ryan — that thousands of others might depend on what he could do for them as a priest — he decided to continue his priestly studies.

And how prophetic Father Ryan's counsel proved to be. As founder and longtime director of The Christophers, Father Keller would reach millions with his books, his radio and television programs, and the talks he gave from coast to coast — never forgetting to pass on his own counsel along the way: "It is better to light one candle than to curse the darkness."

Excerpt from *To Light a Candle*, by James Keller,
Doubleday & Co., Inc., 1963.

For years — even though they had been boyhood ones — I had definitely looked forward to becoming a priest. I could still plainly see that priestly work offered a unique opportunity, as the curate had said when I was six or seven, "to do some good for the world." And gradually I began to realize that, when all was said and done, my vocation in life was to be a priest.

One evening, during the period of struggle with myself, a priest came into the store and ordered a sundae. I didn't know him personally, but I had seen him and knew his name. He was Father Ryan, and had been ordained only a few years. Probably because I felt more troubled than ever, I approached him and introduced myself.

There weren't many customers in the store and apparently he was in no hurry, so we talked for some time. I told him that I had attended St. Patrick's Preparatory Seminary for three and a half years but had decided to leave a few months earlier. When he had finished his sundae, I followed him right out to the sidewalk to continue our conversation. The scene comes back to me vividly.

It was about nine o'clock and Market Street, broad and brightly lighted, had very little traffic on it. About fifty yards away, a Powell Street cable car was being pushed around on its little turntable, with four or five potential passengers lending a hand. Across the way, the show windows of the Emporium were bright, and on our side of the street the passersby paid little attention to the hatless fellow in earnest conversation with the priest.

Left to himself, Father Ryan would probably have long since been on his way. But I kept the conversation going because the thought was nagging at me that perhaps I should make another try at the priesthood. Since I was halfway resisting the thought, I may have been hoping that Father Ryan would tell me to "stay put."

"I've about decided," I told him, "not to go back."

And then, in the hope that he would back me up, I asked him if he didn't agree that my decision was wise.

To my surprise, he emphatically replied: "No, I'm not going to take it on my conscience to tell you not to go back to the seminary! After all, in God's plan, there may be thousands of people whose salvation depends on what you may do for them as a priest."

He may have said more, but that statement was enough. I don't remember our parting, and I never had another chance to talk intimately with him before he died two or three years later. But the point he emphasized left a deep and deciding impression on me. In the words of Our Lord, it was: "You have not chosen me, but I have chosen you" (John 15:16). I began to see that failure on my part to be an instrument of the divine plan could, in a minor way at least, deprive others of blessings that rightfully belonged to them and that were to be sent through one person like myself.

This profound thought has continued to affect me ever since. I have repeatedly referred to it in Christopher talks, writings, and broadcasts, stressing that "there is no substitute for you in fulfilling the mission in life that Almighty God has assigned to you and you alone."

'They Are My Brothers'

The Day a Dying Black Sister Electrified the Nation's Bishops

Sister Thea Bowman (1938-1990), a Franciscan Sister of Perpetual Adoration, left an indelible imprint on everyone she met. An impassioned speaker, she campaigned tirelessly for the cause of women and fellow African-Americans, in the Church and in the world — long after cancer had begun to ravage her body.

One of her most unforgettable appearances took place on June 17, 1989, during the spring meeting of the American bishops at Seton Hall University in South Orange, New Jersey. Confined to a wheelchair because of her illness, she brought the bishops to tears with the eloquence of her words and the love that so obviously flowed from her heart.

This account combines the reports of two Catholic News Service writers — Cindy Wooden and Jerry Filteau — who were there that memorable day. In an interview after the emotion-filled address she had given, Sister Thea assured reporters about her health by quoting from a spiritual: "I keep so busy serving my master, I ain't got time to die."

Adapted from dispatches of Catholic News Service,
June 19, 1989.

The U.S. bishops did things Sister Thea Bowman's way on June 17.

After telling the U.S. bishops what she thinks it means to be black and Catholic in the United States, Sister Bowman had them stand up, cross arms, hold hands, sing "We Shall Overcome" — and sway while they were doing it.

The brilliant, impassioned, loving testimonial of African-American Catholic faith given by Sister Bowman — a dying black nun whose grandfather was a slave — was the unquestioned highlight of the bishops' meeting.

Fifty-one-year-old Sister Bowman, keynote speaker in a two-hour study session on evangelization of African-Americans, brought tears to the eyes of many bishops and observers as she spoke and sang to them and, at the end, had them all join her in singing "We Shall Overcome."

Sister Bowman — a Franciscan Sister of Perpetual Adoration, teacher, gospel singer, author, lecturer, and faculty member of the Institute for Black Catholic Studies at Xavier University in New Orleans — enthralled the bishops with her half-hour speech. She spoke to them about black sufferings and hopes, contributions and needs, history and future, and, above all, faith in the U.S. Catholic Church.

Her talk itself witnessed the richness of African-American culture. To describe the feeling of many black Catholics about the Church she sang the black spiritual "Sometimes I Feel Like a Motherless Child." At times she used the ringing cadences of the black Baptist preacher, at times the scolding or cajoling tone of the black wife or mother.

Dressed in an elegant African-American gown, her voice clear and resonant, eyes sparkling and hands animated, Sister Bowman's only betrayal of the advanced bone cancer ravaging her body was the wheelchair she sat in as she spoke and sang.

Cardinal Bernard F. Law of Boston told the bishops afterward that in his many years of bishops' meetings it had been the first time "I was moved to tears of gladness in this assembly."

"The Church is Catholic because she is universal, because she's multicultural, because she's multiethnic," Sister Bowman told reporters after her presentation. The interview took place in a dorm room where Sister Thea was resting. Cancer diagnosed in 1984 has spread to her skull and most of her other bones, requiring her to use a wheelchair. She had radiation treatments a week earlier and was to begin a chemotherapy regimen in four days.

"I have pain. Pain is a constant," she said.

A well-known evangelizer, Sister Bowman said she travels as much as she can even with the pain because "I might not get better."

From under the blanket and quilt in the already warm room, the nun quoted a spiritual: "I keep so busy serving my master, I ain't got time to die."

"I feel grateful for the opportunity to speak to the Church assembled," she said. "Since I was a child, people have said I have a mouth."

Being one of the few women to have addressed a general meeting of the National Conference of Catholic Bishops didn't faze Sister Bowman.

"They are my brothers — they are my pastors; they are the

hierarchy of my Church — but they are my brothers and I thank God for them," she said.

"One of the gifts that African-Americans bring to a Catholic Church that is universal is a closeness," she said when asked about getting the bishops to stand close to each other and hold hands.

"Our houses were crowded. . . . Our churches were crowded and our neighborhoods were crowded. We like to touch," she said.

"We need to find a way to reach out and touch our clergy and our hierarchy . . . being in solidarity and holding on to one another. There are so many forces trying to divide us."

Too often, she said, Catholics leave their bishops and clergy alone. "We isolate them. We need to love them into life."

Sister Bowman said she and other black women were raised "to care for our men" — fathers, husbands, brothers, churchmen.

"They need my encouragement. . . . Sometimes they need my chastisement in order to be the men they need to be," she said.

"When men and women walk together in unity . . . when the lines of communications are truly open, whatever the question we have to consider, we'll make better decisions."

"I truly believe in integration," she said. "Real integration is people coming together fully functioning, bearing their gifts."

"For so long we remained in our own little camps; we need to learn to walk together. . . . We've come a long way, but we have a long way to go," she said.

Strength and Faith

Together, They Defined the Character of César Chavez

There were two things that impressed anyone who got to know César Chavez: his strength and his faith. The faith part of it, often on public display, was genuine. It helped to inform and define almost everything he did for La Causa, The Cause, *as leader of the United Farm Workers. These people,* his *people, needed deliverance from an evil system that exploited their labor and stole their dignity as men and women. His grounding in the Church's social teaching helped convince Chavez that his mission to lead them out of their misery was a holy one, and only his enemies thought otherwise.*

The strength of the man was almost tangible. Not the physical strength, necessarily, because that faded with the years. But the inner strength was something to experience—the conviction, the determination. It never quit — not when he was bargaining, not when he was striking, not when he was fasting. Where did it come from? This passage, from a biography by a reporter who covered the early Chavez years, suggests a likely source.

Selection from *Chavez and the Farm Workers*, by Ronald B.
Taylor, Beacon Press, 1975.

For some within the farmworker movement, the nonviolence of César Chavez was a tactic that had been tried, and found wanting; these young men and women felt it was time to return to the tactics of Pancho Villa and Emiliano Zapata. The Mexican revolution had been violent and romantic, and they wanted the struggle of the farmworkers to follow the same course. Older people began to listen to the talk, and to nod their heads. Such undercurrents worried Chavez, and, in late February of 1968, he called an unexpected meeting of the membership to announce that he had started on a personal fast on February 15. The fast was an act of penance, because the union was moving toward violence; but the fast was also an act of militancy on Chavez's part, started in the hope that it would counter the violent rhetoric.

Chavez said, "You reap what you sow; if we become violent

with others, then we will become violent among ourselves. Social justice for the dignity of man cannot be won at the price of human life. You cannot justify what you want for *La Raza*, for the people, and in the same breath destroy one life. . . . I will not compromise. Racism is wrong, racism is not the way, nationalism is not the way."

For his fast, Chavez walked to the Forty Acres. He had a cot installed in a small storage room within the adobe service station building. The room became a monastic cell; just outside, and across a narrow breezeway, there was a larger room that was turned into a combination chapel and administrative office.

In the second week of the fast, news of what was happening was leaked to reporters from the *Los Angeles Times*, *Time* magazine, and TV newsmen. Overnight the fast became a national news event. For twenty-five days, Chavez drank only water. As word of the fast spread through the farmworker communities of California and Arizona, the people started coming to Delano. They stood in line for hours waiting for their turn to meet and talk to this man who, by the act of religious fasting, became a symbol of their suffering.

The twenty-five-day fast came to an end on March 11, 1968, in the public park in Delano. Senator Robert Kennedy was there to break bread with Chavez, and to lend his support to the farmworker cause. There were four thousand farmworkers in the Delano park that day, and when Kennedy arrived he found them on both sides of a mile-long processional path, waiting for him. The crowds, the photographers, and TV crews were swept up in the turmoil.

There was an ecumenical Mass — ministers, rabbis, and priests participated — then speeches and the ceremonial breaking of the bread ended the fast. After Chavez and Kennedy had broken bread, the senator mounted the platform and talked to the workers. He advocated inclusion of farm labor under the NLRA, he urged a crackdown on the use of green-card aliens and illegal aliens as strikebreaking workers, and he brought cheers when he said, "Farmworkers need equal rights under the laws."

Chavez had prepared a statement, but was too weak to read it himself. An aide read: "Our lives are really all that belong to us . . . only by giving our lives do we find life. I am convinced that the truest act of courage, the strongest act of manliness, is to sacrifice ourselves for others in a totally nonviolent struggle for justice. To be a man is to suffer for others. God help us be men."

A Story of Faith

Illness Ended an Empty Life and Led to Understanding

More often than not, our leading preachers and speakers excel at storytelling too, and in this case two of the best come together to present an unforgettable tale about the gift of understanding.

Father William J. Bausch is a priest of the Trenton (New Jersey) diocese whose many books include several about the role of stories and storytelling in sharing the faith. Here he relates a story as told by Jesuit Father John Powell, whose books have sold more than fifteen million copies. It's about "Tommy," a one-time rebellious student of Father Powell's who gains a profound insight and understanding through the illness that would take his life.

*In another book (*More Telling Stories, Compelling Stories, *Twenty-Third Publications, 1993), Father Bausch had this to say about what's involved in the "ancient Christian enterprise" of storytelling:*

". . . Taking the truths and enfleshing them in life: desperate, riotous, mysterious, noble, grace-racked life as witnessed in men and women of all ages. Sometimes, of course, it happens that the story obscures the Gospel, gets in its way. Sometimes it illumines a point, and sometimes it does what a story is supposed to do: leave a lingering aura floating in the mind and imagination, suggesting possibilities of grace and conversion."

Grace and conversion. That suits the story of "Tommy" to a T.

Story from *Storytelling: Imagination and Faith*, by William J.
Bausch, Twenty-Third Publications, 1984 (originally in *The
Wisdom of Accepted Tenderness*, by Brennan Manning,
Dimension Books, 1978).

Some years ago, I stood watching my university students file into the classroom for our first session in "The Theology of Faith." That was the day I first saw Tommy. My eyes and my mind both blinked. He was combing his long hair, which hung all the way down to his shoulders. It was the first time I had ever seen a boy with hair that long. I guess it was just coming into fashion then. I know in my mind that it isn't what's on your head but in it that counts; but on that day, I am unprepared and my emotions flipped. I immediately filed Tommy under "S" for strange . . . very strange.

Tommy turned out to be the "atheist in residence" in my Theology of Faith course. He constantly objected to, smirked at, or whined about the possibility of an unconditionally loving Father-God. We lived with each other in relative peace for one semester, although I admit he was at times a pain in the back pew. When he came up at the end of the course to turn in his final exam, he asked in a slightly cynical tone: "Do you think I'll ever find God?" I decided on a little shock therapy. "No!" I said emphatically. "Oh," he responded, "I thought that was the product you were pushing." I let him get five steps from the classroom door and then called out: "Tommy! I don't think you'll ever find him, but I'm absolutely certain he will find you!" He shrugged a little and left my class and my life. I was a bit disappointed that he had missed my clever line.

Later, I heard that Tom had graduated, and I was duly grateful. Then a sad report. Tommy had terminal cancer. Before I could search him out, he came to see me. When he walked into my office, his body was badly wasted, and the long hair had all fallen out as a result of chemotherapy. But his eyes were bright and his voice was firm, for the first time, I think.

"Tommy, I've thought about you so often. I hear you are sick!" I blurted out.

"Oh, yes, very sick. I have cancer in both lungs. It's a matter of weeks."

"Can you talk about it, Tom. . . ?"

"Sure. What would you like to know?"

"What's it like to be only twenty-four and dying?"

"Well, it could be worse."

"Like what?"

"Well, like being fifty and having no values or ideals, like being fifty and thinking that booze, seducing women, and making money are the real 'biggies' in life."

I began to look through my mental file cabinet under "S" where I had filed Tom as Strange. (It seems everybody I try to reject by classification God sends back into my life to educate me.)

"But what I really came to see you about," Tom said, "is something you said to me on the last day of class. I asked you if you thought I would ever find God and you said, 'No!' which surprised me. Then you said, 'But he will find you.' I thought about that a lot, even though my search for God was not at all intense . . . at that time.

"But when the doctors removed a lump from my groin and told me it was malignant, I got serious about locating God. And when the malignancy spread to my vital organs, I really began banging

192

bloody fists against the bronze doors of heaven. But God did not come out. In fact, nothing happened. Did you ever try anything for a long time with great effort and with no success? You get psychologically glutted, fed up with trying. And then you quit. Well, one day I woke up, and instead of throwing a few more futile appeals over that high brick wall to a God who may or may not be there, I just quit. I decided that I didn't really care . . . about God, about an afterlife, or anything like that.

"I decided to spend what time I had left doing something more profitable. I thought about you and your class, and I remembered something else you had said: 'The essential sadness is to go through life without loving. But it would be almost equally sad to go through life and leave this world without ever telling those you loved that you had loved them.' So I began with the hardest one, my dad.

"He was reading the newspaper when I approached him."

"I said, 'Dad?' "

"Yes. What?" he asked without lowering the newspaper.

"Dad, I would like to talk with you."

"Well, talk."

"I mean . . . it's really important."

The newspaper came down *three slow inches*. "What is it?"

"Dad. I love you. I just wanted you to know that."

Tom smiled at me, and said with obvious satisfaction, as though he felt a warm and secret joy flowing inside of him: "The newspaper fluttered to the floor. Then my father did two things I could not remember him ever doing before. He cried, and he hugged me. And we talked all night, even though he had to go to work the next morning. It felt so good to be close to my father, to see his tears, to feel his hug, to hear him say that he loved me.

"It was easier with my mother and little brother. They cried with me too, and we hugged each other and started saying real nice things to each other. We shared the things we had been keeping secret for so many years. I was only sorry about one thing, that I had waited so long. Here I was, in the shadow of death, and I was just beginning to open up to all the people I had actually been close to.

"Then one day I turned around, and God was there. He didn't come to me when I pleaded with him. I guess I was like an animal trainer holding out a hoop, 'C'mon, jump through. C'mon, I'll give you three days . . . three weeks.' Apparently, God does things in his own way and at his own hour.

"But the important thing is that he was there. He found me. You were right. He found me even after I stopped looking for him."

"Tommy," I practically gasped, "I think you are saying something very important and much more universal than you realize. To me, at least, you are saying that the surest way to find God is not to make him a private possession, a problem-solver, or an instant consolation in time of need, but rather by opening yourself to his love.

"Tom, could I ask you a favor? Would you come into my present Theology of Faith course and tell them what you have just told me? If I told them the same thing, it wouldn't be half as effective as if you were to tell them."

"Oooh . . . I was ready for you, but I don't know if I'm ready for your class."

"Tom, think about it. If and when you are ready, give me a call."

In a few days Tommy called, said he was ready for the class, that he wanted to do that for God and for me. So we scheduled a date. The day came, but he never made it.

"Truly, he who loses his life for my sake will find it" (cf. Matthew 16:25, Mark 8:35, and Luke 9:24). Triumph grows out of suffering.

Introduction to Section 3:
The Corporal Works of Mercy

Mark down the seven corporal works of mercy as a handy guide to living out the Christian message. If the cardinal virtues give us the *power* to do good and avoid evil, and the gifts of the Holy Spirit *dispose* us to follow God's will, the corporal works of mercy are something else: a list of instructions, a how-to book, if you will, with specific directives that open the door to a Christian way of life.

Who remembers all seven? As a set of obligations, it takes in a lot of territory:

1. Feeding the hungry.
2. Giving drink to the thirsty.
3. Clothing the naked.
4. Visiting the imprisoned.
5. Sheltering the homeless.
6. Visiting the sick.
7. Burying the dead.

(Some lists combine two of these commands to form "visiting the sick and imprisoned" and add yet another — "ransoming the captive.")

Whether or not they can recite all seven by rote, most American Catholics are on familiar ground here. The corporal works of mercy are alive and well. The responsibility to help others still comes through loud and clear at the parish level — in Sunday homilies, in bulletin announcements that promote soup kitchens and food pantries and clothing drives, chapters of the Legion of Mary or the St. Vincent de Paul Society, and on and on and on.

Catholic students are getting the message, too. Many if not most Catholic high schools have service programs — in some cases mandatory — in which students go forth to work directly with the poor, the disabled, the elderly. Catholic college students have an extraordinarily high rate of volunteer service with the needy.

And those Catholics unable to perform these tasks directly tend to be generous with their financial support.

All of this is a healthy sign, because when Catholics perform the corporal works of mercy, they follow a lesson taught by Jesus himself.

But first: even though the words come from Jesus, the spirit is deeply rooted in Old Testament tradition — the tradition that reminds the faithful that the Lord is less interested in empty sacrifice and automatic ritual than he is in works that help those who need it. We find that in Micah, for example: "You have been told, O man, what is good, and what the Lord requires of you: only to do the right and to love goodness, and to walk humbly with your God" (Micah 6:8). Or again, in Tobit: "Give alms from your possessions. Do not turn your face away from any of the poor, and God's face will not be turned away from you" (Tobit 4:7).

And the great prophet Isaiah puts the matter quite explicitly: "This, rather, is the fasting that I wish: releasing those bound unjustly, untying the thongs of the yoke; . . . Sharing your bread with the hungry, sheltering the oppressed and the homeless; clothing the naked when you see them, and not turning your back on your own" (Isaiah 58:6-7).

Finally comes Jesus, who turns this thought into an intensely personal one for his disciples. Matthew's Gospel records his conversation with them, shortly before the Last Supper, as he explains that at the final judgment the king will welcome those on his right hand, the righteous, into the kingdom: "For I was hungry and you gave me food, I was thirsty and you gave me drink, a stranger and you welcomed me, naked and you clothed me, ill and you cared for me, in prison and you visited me" (Matthew 25:35-36). The righteous, of course, recall no such instances of helping their king. But he promptly clears it up for them: "Amen, I say to you, whatever you did for one of these least brothers of mine, you did for me" (Matthew 25:40).

It is a breakthrough kind of thought, a keystone of what would become the new faith: the idea that the Lord himself is present in all people. All of us, the poor included, are made in the divine image — the poor no less so simply because they *are* poor, or homeless, or disabled, or in prison. And therefore they are entitled to our works of mercy — a mercy that stems not so much from *justice*, even the demands of social justice, as it does from *love* — because when we look into the faces of the poor we see the face of God.

This is precisely the mercy that has been in the hearts of the great saints and heroes of the Church, from St. Bernard to Mother Teresa, from St. Vincent de Paul to Dorothy Day.

Retelling their stories here will remind us all of a glorious past — and, in the light of present-day needs, of our obligation to follow their example today wherever we can. They have something to teach us about each of the works of mercy that Our Lord spelled out.

Feeding the hungry. It was Jesus, again, who taught us to remember that most basic of prayers, representing the most basic of needs: "Give us this day our daily bread." How many around us are deprived of that bread? How many never hear the message of Jesus, our own Bread of Life?

Through the years Jesus' people have responded to his call in heroic measure: St. Genevieve, defying a blockade to bring food to the besieged people of Paris; St. Margaret of Scotland, a queen who managed to feed hundreds each morning before she had her own breakfast. And, in our own lifetime, there is Dorothy Day, whose soup kitchens inspired so many others — and who could find in each guest, no matter how challenging, something of the presence of the Lord.

Giving drink to the thirsty. The image is rich in Old Testament history. Here, once again, is Isaiah, promising the Lord's favor: "I will pour out water upon the thirsty ground, and streams upon the dry land; I will pour out my spirit upon your offspring, and my blessing upon your descendants" (Isaiah 44:3).

The old legends tell of saints whose gifts of water turned miraculously to something more substantial. Others, such as Blessed Jeanne Jugan, answered the call of those poor elderly people who thirsted for relief. She set in motion an instrument of tender mercy — the community known as the Little Sisters of the Poor — that continues to flourish today.

Clothing the naked. In the old stories of the saints, familiar patterns would emerge. One was of the gift of clothing to a needy person who, in time, turned out to be Jesus, or an angel, in disguise. That happened, for example, in the well-known story of St. Martin cutting his cloak in half for a shivering stranger, or the tale of St. Zita giving her borrowed coat to an old man in a church doorway. These and other legends helped to reinforce the need to give generously, even to share from meager resources.

On a larger level, consider the amazing story of Pauline Jaricot, the young French woman who almost single-handedly launched what would become the Society for the Propagation of the Faith — the international mission aid agency that helps people all over the world to put on the mantle of Christ's Church.

Visiting the imprisoned. Few Catholics today carry out this injunction in a direct fashion, and indeed few are in a position to do so. Those who do — family members and personal friends of prisoners, chaplains and advocates, those in the organized prison ministry of the Legion of Mary — know how difficult it can be. And yet it is listed right there along with all of the other corporal works of mercy we are enjoined to perform. How to go about it?

With our financial support, for one thing. The groups that carry out prison ministries are chronically underfinanced, and can use all the help they can get. Too, we can join Church and/or community efforts for better prisons, for humane treatment of prisoners. Even those convicted of serious crimes retain their human dignity, and must not be treated in a way that will cause them to lose all hope.

None of this should be done, of course, in a way that minimizes the *victims* of crime, our first concern in this regard. How to balance the two interests?

The moving story of Pope John Paul II visiting the prison cell of his would-be assassin, Mehmet Ali Agca, provides the answer. The pope wanted his assailant to know that he was forgiven — not in some impersonal way, but with a face-to-face encounter that would erase all doubt. Presumably the Holy Father had a second motive: to help Agca develop a sense of repentance, to offer him a sign of hope. But note that Pope John Paul did not suggest that Agca be freed, or that his sentence be lightened. Implicit in that is the recognition that the needs of justice must be served.

Significantly, the pope ensured that the visit received media attention. That was not to call attention to himself, of course — but rather to remind the world of the need to forgive, and of our obligation to visit those behind prison walls.

Sheltering the homeless. In the United States of the late twentieth century, this is no abstract concern. The scope of the problem of the homeless, particularly in cities, is staggering — an irony in view of personal fortunes that are being made by some, and the generally comfortable style of living that most Americans enjoy. Further, the problem is likely to worsen before it improves, as government cutbacks in programs for the poor will mean that more and more have to be replaced by charitable works.

The church community has responded generously. Many Catholic parishes support shelters in addition to soup kitchens, either on their own or in cooperation with other churches. And many, many individual Catholics have joined the effort in a heroic way.

Still — how much more there is to be done! And what exemplars the Church has to offer! Among them are St. Bernard of Manthon, whose thousand-year-old hospices for lost travelers still stand today; St. Charles Borromeo, the archbishop of Milan who turned over all his money to the poor, hungry, and homeless, keeping only enough to buy his bread and water, and straw on which to sleep; St. Vincent de Paul, the apostle of charity, whose spiritual descendants — the Vincentians of the Congregation of the Missions, and the Sisters of Charity — carry on his work today, more than three hundred years after his death.

Visiting the sick. If few of us are able to visit the imprisoned personally, almost all of us can take time to call on the sick. And, in fact, most of us do. Apart from personal visits to ailing family members or friends, many take part in parish ministries that include nursing home visits, hospice programs, and so forth. It's an ideal way to observe Jesus' teaching that we show mercy to others by our actions. There's an unspoken but very clear message that comes through when somebody makes a sick call. "I care," that person says. "You're not going through this alone."

Caring for the sick and being with them in their time of need is one of the oldest and noblest traditions of the Church, as indicated in the many stories here. One of the most gripping is that of the heroic nuns and priests of Memphis, Tennessee, as they responded to lethal outbreaks of yellow fever more than a century ago. When others fled, the priests and nuns stood fast, helping the sick and the dying as best they could. Their courage and their sacrifice — twenty-one priests and fifty nuns gave up their lives as they worked to save others — will stand forever as a symbol of Christian love.

Burying the dead. The final corporal work of mercy, burying the dead, testifies to the Christian conviction that the body is the temple of the spirit and the dwelling place of the soul. Proper burial provides a measure of dignity and respect, just as it did for the ancient Hebrew people. In the biblical book that bears his name, Tobit lists among the charitable works he had performed "for my kinsmen and my people" (Tobit 1:16) his practice of burying the dead.

Down through the centuries, few have carried out that task with greater devotion than Father Damien de Veuster, Hawaii's famed "Leper Priest." When he first arrived on the island of Molokai, he found that those who had succumbed to the dread illness were carelessly tossed aside; one of his first duties was to bury them — in coffins he constructed himself. Before his work was finished, he would build more than two thousand of them.

One more coffin would be made as well — his own. The priest who served the lepers so selflessly had contracted leprosy himself. In his final days the only place he could find solace was in the cemetery he had lovingly marked out, walking among the graves of so many that he had buried, graves that he himself had helped to dig. Here he found some consolation in all that he had been able to do. And, perhaps, in the thought of the glory that lay ahead.

'Your Valentine'

A Legend of Love Lives On in Young Hearts Everywhere

Legend is the best we can do when it comes to telling the story of St. Valentine (d.c. 269), since most of the facts of his life are lost in the mists of history. But somehow the basics survived: the amiable priest who defied Roman law to join young Christian couples in marriage; the steadfast visitor of prisoners who, when found out, was forced to become one of them himself; the captive who managed to get a message out from his cell signed with those magic words, "Your Valentine."

On the Church calendar, February 14 is not St. Valentine's Day; it's reserved for those great Apostles to the Slavs, Sts. Cyril and Methodius. But the connection is there nonetheless. Official or not — all fact or all legend, or something in between — the blissful spirit of St. Valentine seems destined to remain etched on young hearts all over the world, not just on February 14 but every day of the year.

Story excerpted from *Saints and Their Stories*, by Mary
Montgomery, Harper & Row, 1988.

Valentine had been born into a noble Roman family. He lived in a home with servants and many comforts. When he was a young man, he became a physician. Valentine liked his work, but he felt there was something missing in his life. He found what he was looking for in the new religion called Christianity. It was a religion that said you were to love your neighbor as yourself and that when you died you rose to a new life with God. Valentine loved his new faith so much that he became a priest.

Being a priest was something Valentine had to do in secret. In public he was a respected physician. As part of his work, he visited the sick in the city's jails. Prisoners in the jails were treated very badly. Christians were treated worst of all.

Valentine did what little he could to help his Christian friends. He smuggled food to them and slipped them medicine from his supply. This put him in great danger because Claudius, the Roman emperor, had spies everywhere. In time, Valentine was caught helping his friends. The soldiers arrested him and demanded that he offer sacrifices to the pagan gods. When Valentine refused, he was thrown into jail with the prisoners he had tried to help.

In jail, Valentine became friends with the jailer's daughter. Legend tells us she was blind and that Valentine cured her of her blindness.

Valentine knew that he was soon to die, so he wrote a letter to the jailer's daughter. He told her how much her friendship meant to him and thanked her for her kindness. He signed the letter, "Your Valentine."

Soldiers came and took Valentine to Palatine Hill where there was an altar to one of the pagan gods. On that hill, on the fourteenth day of February, Valentine was beheaded. He was buried in Rome, where a gate was once named in his honor. It was called *Porto Valentini.*

Almost two hundred years after Valentine's death, the Church of St. Praxedes was built over the place where he was buried. About that same time, the pope declared February 14 St. Valentine's Day. It was already a day on which there was a Roman festival to celebrate love. As part of the festival celebration, young men and women chose partners by drawing names from a box. The partners danced together and exchanged gifts as a sign of their affection. Some of the young people continued to see each other after the festival and many of them married. As Christianity spread, Church officials wanted to give Christian meaning to the pagan festival, and so it was named St. Valentine's Day.

These many years later, the greetings we send on February 14 are called "valentines." Giving these cards is a way to let people know that we care about them. The cards remind us of St. Valentine who died because of his love and concern for others.

Clothed in Glory

The Hair of St. Agnes Miraculously Grew About Her as a Cloak

The story of the martyrdom of St. Agnes (d. 304) is one treasured by Catholics down through the centuries — especially by Romans, since she was a Roman herself, and by young women, since she represented youth, virtue, and courage at its finest.

Born into a noble family, she lived in a time when Christians were fiercely persecuted under the Emperor Diocletian. It was also a time when young women — very young women — were expected to choose a husband. The pious Agnes had other plans, however, and the tortures she underwent as a result — and the miracles that for a time thwarted her captors — are the stuff of which legends, and saints, are made. In this case, the legend is retold exactly as nineteenth-century Catholics would have read it, the formal language of the day lending it an aura of mystery, devotion, and faith.

Story from *A Handbook of Christian Symbols and Stories of the Saints* by Clara Erskine Clement, Ticknor and Co., 1886 (republished by Gale Research Co., 1971).

St. Agnes was a Roman maiden of great beauty, and a Christian from her infancy. She was not more than thirteen years old when the son of the prefect Sempronius saw her, and so loved her that he sought her for his wife. But she refused his request, saying that she was already affianced to a husband whom she loved, meaning Jesus.

The young man knew not to whom she referred; and his jealousy and disappointed love made him sick, almost unto death. Then the physicians said, "This youth is sick of unrequited love, and our art can avail nothing." When the prefect questioned his son, he told his father of his love for Agnes, and that unless she would be his wife he must die.

Then Sempronius begged of Agnes and her parents that she should marry his son; but she replied, as before, that she preferred her betrothed to the son of the prefect. When he had inquired her meaning, and found that she was a Christian, he was glad; for there was an edict against the Christians, and he felt she was in his power. He then told her that since she would have no earthly husband, she must become a vestal virgin.

But she refused with scorn the worship of vain images, and declared that she would serve none but Jesus. Sempronius then threatened her with the most horrid death, and put her in chains, and dragged her to the altars of the gods. But she remained firm.

Then he ordered her to be taken to a house of infamy, to suffer the most fearful outrages. The soldiers stripped off her garments; but when she prayed, her hair was lengthened till it was as a cloak about her, covering her whole person, and those who saw her were seized with fear. So they shut her in a room; and when she prayed to Christ that she might not be dishonored, she saw before her a shining white garment, which she put on with joy, and the room was filled with great light.

The son of the prefect, thinking she must be subdued, now came to her. But he was struck blind, and fell in convulsions. Agnes, moved by his sufferings and the tears of his friends, prayed for his recovery, and he was healed. When Sempronius saw this, he wished to save her; but the people said, "She is a sorceress; let her die."

So she was condemned to be burned; but the flames harmed her not, while her executioners were consumed by them. Then they cried out the more, "She is a sorceress: she must die." Then an executioner was commanded to ascend the pile, and kill her with the sword. This he did; and gazing steadfastly toward heaven, she fell dead upon the pile.

She was buried on the Via Nomentana, and the Christians were accustomed to visit her tomb to weep. But she appeared to them, and forbade that they should sorrow for one who was happy in heaven.

Prisoner of Faith

St. Barbara Is Invoked in Praying for a Happy Death

St. Barbara (third century) is the saint whose name has traditionally been invoked by those seeking the grace of a happy death — a gesture, one assumes, to the cruel circumstances of her own life and the tragic way it came to an end.

Many of the factual details of her story are somewhat clouded, but the basics — her imprisonment by her father, her conversion, her torture and martyrdom — all seem to be historically verifiable. The legend of her father being struck by lightning at the moment of her death is another matter, however. That part of the story didn't make an appearance until the seventh century.

Still, St. Barbara, one of the Fourteen Holy Helpers, developed a devoted following, especially among those who asked for her help in preparing for their own death, and for safety during violent storms. Further, she is the patron saint of firefighters — and of artillerymen as well!

Story from *Mary, Help of Christians and the Fourteen Saints Invoked as Holy Helpers*, by Rev. Bonaventure Hammer, OFM, Benziger Brothers, 1909.

Nicomedia, a city in Asia Minor, was St. Barbara's birthplace. Her father, Dioscurus, was a pagan. Fearing that his only child might learn to know and love the doctrines of Christianity, he shut her up in a tower, apart from all intercourse with others. Nevertheless Barbara became a Christian. She passed her time in study, and from her lonely tower she used to watch the heavens in their wondrous beauty. She soon became convinced that the "heavens were telling the glory of God," a God greater than the idols she had been taught to worship. Her desire to know that God was in itself a prayer that he answered in his own wise way.

The fame of Origen, that famous Christian teacher in Alexandria, reached even the remote tower, and Barbara sent a trusty servant with the request that he would make known to her the truth. Origen sent her one of his disciples, disguised as a physician, who instructed and baptized her. She practiced her new religion discreetly while waiting for a favorable opportunity of acquainting her father with her conversion.

This opportunity came in a short time. Some workmen were sent by Dioscurus to make another room in the tower, and when they had made two windows she directed them to make a third. When her father saw this additional window, he asked the reason for it. She replied, "Know, my father, that the soul receives light through three windows, the Father, the Son, and the Holy Ghost, and the three are one." The father became so angry at this discovery of her having become a Christian that he would have killed his daughter with his sword, had she not fled to the top of the tower. He followed her, and finally had her in his power. First he wreaked his vengeance on her in blows, then clutching her by the hair he dragged her away and thrust her into a hut to prevent her escape. Next he tried every means to induce her to renounce her faith; threats, severe punishments, and starvation had no effect on the constancy of the Christian maiden.

Finding himself powerless to shake his daughter's constancy, Dioscurus delivered her to the proconsul Marcian, who had her scourged and tortured, but without causing her to deny the faith. During her sufferings, her father stood by, exulting in the torments of his child. Next night, after she had been taken back to prison, Our Lord appeared to her and healed her wounds. When Barbara appeared again before him, Marcian was greatly astonished to find no trace of the cruelties that had been perpetrated on her body. Again she resisted his importunities to deny the faith, and when he saw that all his efforts were in vain, he pronounced the sentence of death. Barbara was to be beheaded. Her unnatural father claimed the privilege to execute it with his own hands, and with one blow severed his daughter's head from her body, on December 4, 237.

At the moment of the saint's death a great tempest arose and Dioscurus was killed by lightning. Marcian, too, was overtaken by the same fate.

Burial in the Desert

Two Lions Were There to Help
as St. Anthony Abbot Dug a Grave

Legend has outstripped life when it comes to St. Anthony Abbot (251-356), as a reading of the accompanying story will make clear. St. Anthony (also known as St. Anthony of Egypt) did indeed live a life that was legendary in the figurative sense, but embellishments certainly added to the tale.

Not that there was much need for embellishment, for St. Anthony played a significant role in the development of the Church. Considered the patriarch of all monks, he is generally regarded as the founder of Christian monasticism, and he vigorously defended the Church against the heresy of Arianism.

The St. Paul mentioned in this story is also someone of note historically; he is revered as the first true Christian hermit. The lone source-reference on St. Paul's life describes his meeting with St. Anthony, and says that Anthony buried him in a cloak given him by St. Athanasius. As to the help Anthony was said to receive from two lions — perhaps that's another question for faith to resolve.

Story adapted from *A Handbook of Christian Symbols and Stories of the Saints*, by Clara Erskine Clement, Ticknor and Co., 1886 (republished by Gale Research Co., 1971).

Born in Alexandria, Egypt, Anthony was a man of great rank and wealth. But he was thoughtful as well, and early in life determined to seek a state of spiritual perfection. He gave some of his possessions to his sister, others to the poor, and then joined a company of hermits in the desert.

Satan was angered by the purity of his life, and sent demons to tempt and torment him.

Anthony remained steadfast through a series of trials, even including physical attacks that left him all but dead. When he revived himself, he returned to his cave and called out to Satan: "Did you really think I had fled? I, Anthony, have strength to fight on!" Then Satan, by now enraged, unleashed wild animals to attack the saintly hermit.

Suddenly a great light from heaven appeared in their midst, and the animals vanished. Anthony, looking up, cried out: "Lord Jesus! Where were you in my moments of anguish?" And Christ said gently, "Anthony, I was here beside you all the time, and rejoiced to see you contend and conquer. Be of good heart, for I will make your name famous throughout the world."

Anthony, now thirty-five years old, went further into the desert, living a life of complete solitude for twenty years. Then he began his public preaching — telling everyone of God's love, comforting the sick and afflicted, expelling demons. Thousands were converted and came to the desert, many of them staying on to join Anthony in lives of quiet prayer.

After living in the desert for seventy-five years, a voice called out to him: "There is one holier than you, for Paul the hermit has served God in solitude and penance for ninety years." Anthony resolved to seek out Paul, and at length found the holy man's cave. At first Paul would not receive him, but finally relented. They held communion together and as they sat, a raven brought them a loaf of bread. Paul blessed it and said: "For sixty years, this raven has brought me half a loaf of bread every day. But because you have come, my brother, the portion is doubled — and we are fed as Elijah was fed in the wilderness."

He continued: "My brother! God has sent you here in order to receive my last breath and bury me. Go, return to your own dwelling, and then bring back the cloak that was given to you by the holy Bishop Athanasius. Wrap me in it and lay me in the earth."

Anthony was amazed; no one had known of the gift from Athanasius. But off he went, wondering if Paul would still be alive when he came back. As it developed, he was about three hours' journey from Paul's cave on his return trip when he heard heavenly music. Looking up, he saw the spirit of Paul, as a star, borne by prophets, apostles, and angels to heaven. A mournful Anthony hastened to the cave and found the body of Paul, slumped over in an attitude of prayer. Anthony wept over him, recited the office of the dead, and wondered how, in his own weakened condition, he would manage to dig a grave for Paul.

Then came two lions across the desert, roaring as if in sympathy, and with their paws they dug a grave. Anthony laid the body of Paul — wrapped in the cloak of Athanasius — in the hollowed-out place. He later told of these things, which were believed by the whole Church, and Paul was canonized.

Some years later Anthony, by now one hundred four years old, told his friends that his own time had come. After going to a lonely place with a few Brothers, he charged them that they should keep secret the site of his burial. Gently his spirit passed away, and angels carried it to heaven.

St. Martin's Sacrifice

He Cut His Cape in Two for a Beggar —
Who Was Jesus Himself

The delightful story of St. Martin of Tours (c. 316-397) giving away half his cloak to a shivering beggar — who turned out to be Jesus himself — is one of the most familiar in the annals of the saints. Less well known is the fact that as bishop of Tours St. Martin went on to become one of the most influential figures in the fourth-century Church, especially in the development of Western monasticism.

Here's a fascinating sidelight connected with St. Martin's life. His cloak was venerated as a sacred relic in a relatively short time after his death, and was kept by the king's soldiers in a small private church. Since the cloak was known by its Latin name, capella, that became the name of the little church housing this important piece of clothing — the capella. In time, the name was applied to any small building with an altar intended, to some degree, for private worship — capella, in Latin, or, as we know it in English, the chapel. Further, those who had been responsible for guarding the relic in the capella were known as — what else? — chaplains. And finally, since the typical capella was too small to contain an organ, music that came "from the chapel" was always unaccompanied — or, to use the more familiar phrase, a capella.

And to think we owe it all to St. Martin of Tours!

Story adapted from *Catholic Anecdotes*, by the Brothers of the Christian Schools; translated from the French by Mrs. J. Sadlier; D. & J. Sadlier & Co., 1885.

Martin was first attracted to the faith as a young soldier, and while preparing for his baptism became known for helping anyone in need. He was generous with what little he had, keeping only enough of his salary to live on from day to day.

One day when Martin was eighteen — in the depth of a winter so severe that many perished from the cold — he met a poor man at the city gate of Amiens. The man was half naked and seemed totally abandoned, certainly in danger of death. Martin felt sure that somehow the Lord had placed this poor man in his care, but on this day he had no money at all — only his military uniform, to which was attached a sort of cloak.

At once an idea came to him. With his sword he cut the cloak in two, giving half to the miserable beggar and covering himself as best he could with the other half. The following night Martin had a miraculous vision while he was sleeping: he saw Jesus Christ clothed in the half-cloak with which he had covered the poor man. Then he heard the divine Lord saying to the angels at his side: "It was Martin, who is yet but a catechumen, who covered me with this cloak."

The dream left Martin in an inexpressible state of joy, and from that point on he prepared for his baptism without delay.

St. Januarius

The 'Miracle of the Blood' Continues to Amaze — And Attract the Faithful

The story of St. Januarius (early fourth century) resembles those of many other early martyrs of the Church: a frequent visitor of fellow Christians who were imprisoned, he eventually was taken prisoner himself before offering the supreme sacrifice of his life.

What's different about St. Januarius — or, as Italians have lovingly known him for centuries, San Gennaro? The difference is this: the glass vial that contains his blood. The blood continues to liquefy many times each year, as it has done since 1389 — defying scientific explanation, mystifying the public, attracting the faithful.

Story adapted from *Little Pictorial Lives of the Saints*,
Benziger Brothers, Inc., 1925.

Bishop of Benevento during the murderous persecutions of the Emperor Diocletian, St. Januarius often stayed with imprisoned fellow Christians to lift their spirits. He was visiting a holy deacon named Sosius — whose impending martyrdom had been foretold to Januarius in a vision — when he was arrested as well, along with other members of the clergy.

Wild animals were set upon them, but when they did no harm, the prisoners — Januarius among them — were ordered beheaded. A Christian woman named Eusebia collected the bishop's blood in a vial and brought it to nearby Naples, where today it rests in the cathedral. Since 1389 the blood has liquefied on special occasions — eighteen times each year, accompanied by ceremonies that feature tumultuous prayer. To date no scientific explanation has been advanced for this continuing phenomenon.

The Seven Sleepers

A Strange and Fascinating Tale
About Living and Dying for the Faith

Here's a fascinating story that's all but unknown to Catholics today — a shame, since it combines all the dramatic elements any listener might want. Take the old Rip Van Winkle legend, make it seven men instead of one, have them fall asleep nearly two hundred years instead of twenty, add a powerful Christian message — and you begin to get the idea.

The tale of the Seven Sleepers of Ephesus was widely known and enormously popular during the Middle Ages. It's about seven young Christians who were sealed up, supposedly as martyrs, during the persecutions of the Emperor Decius (c. 230), and miraculously were found alive during the reign of Emperor Theodosius (408-450).

What happened next? Let the storyteller take it from there.

Story adapted from *A Handbook of Christian Symbols and Stories of the Saints*, by Clara Erskine Clement, Ticknor and Co., 1886 (republished by Gale Research Co., 1971).

The story of the Seven Sleepers of Ephesus belongs to antiquity. It was being circulated within fifty years of the events described, and it spread rapidly through the civilized world, in a variety of languages.

It all began in the city of Ephesus during the reign of Decius, around the year 230. Seven young men — named Maximian, Malchus, Marcian, Dionysius, John, Serapion, and Constantine — found themselves on trial simply for being Christians, and when they refused to worship pagan gods were quickly condemned. They were able to flee to Mount Caelian, where they hid in a cave, but their Roman pursuers had seen them enter it. Rather than search the cave to capture them, they simply rolled great stones in front of the mouth of the cave, leaving the Christian youths inside to die of starvation.

Seeing what had happened, the brave young men resigned

themselves to their fate. Looking forward to their new life in the Lord, they prayed, embraced each other, and went to sleep.

Time rolled on until one hundred ninety-six years had passed — to the reign of Theodosius, a period in which a heresy had arisen that denied the resurrection of the dead. The emperor, grieving to see how rapidly the heresy had spread, retired to his palace to do penance. And it was just at this time that the Lord, in his wisdom, restored the seven sleepers to life.

A man from Ephesus, intending to build a stable, went to Mount Caelian and found some large stones in front of what appeared to be a cave. When he rolled the stones away and light entered the cave, the sleepers awoke — but thought they had slept for only a night! They determined that among the seven Malchus should venture into town to try to find some food, and off he went — with fear and trepidation.

Malchus was amazed to discover the changes that had taken place. First of all, the gates of the city were surmounted by crosses. Within the city walls the name of Christ, once only whispered among Jesus' followers, was heard everywhere. Malchus wondered if he might be dreaming.

He asked for a loaf of bread in a baker's shop, and offered in payment a coin from his pocket — a coin that dated from the time of Decius. The shopkeeper and other customers regarded the stranger with astonishment, wondering if he had robbed some secret treasure. He was taken off to appear before the bishop.

It was there that Malchus was able to tell what had really happened, and how his six companions still awaited him in the cave. Off to the mountain to see this miracle went an entourage — Malchus, the bishop, the governor, the shopkeeper, and hordes of people, even the Emperor Theodosius himself. One of the seven spoke directly to Theodosius:

"Believe in us, O Emperor! We have been raised *before* the Day of Judgment, that you might trust in the resurrection of the dead!"

Then all seven bowed their heads, lay down, and finally went home to the Lord and to eternal glory.

To the Rescue

St. Genevieve Risked Her Life to Feed Besieged, Starving Parisians

France's indomitable St. Genevieve (c. 422-c. 500) not only performed a work of mercy by feeding the hungry, but she displayed true fortitude as well: she had to run a blockade in order to do it. As the story indicates, Childeric, king of the Franks, decided to starve out the city of Paris with a siege, but Genevieve foiled his plans for a time by delivering food by way of barges that she floated down the River Seine.

Parisians had other reasons to be grateful to St. Genevieve, who, at a later time, took on none other than Attila the Hun. Miraculous rescues continued even years after her death. In 1129 a deadly illness swept Paris and killed some fourteen thousand people, but the plague stopped as swiftly as it had come once the shrine of St. Genevieve was carried in solemn procession throughout the city. For this and other favors granted down through the years, she continues to be honored as Paris's patron saint.

Story adapted from *Lives of the Saints You Should Know*, by Margaret and Matthew Bunson, Our Sunday Visitor, Inc., 1994.

Genevieve was just a teenager, newly consecrated to life with Christ as a nun, when her beloved Paris was put under siege. Childeric and his forces had blockaded the city, cutting off its supply of food from nearby farms. The king of the Franks was threatening to starve the city's inhabitants if they didn't surrender to his army.

Seeing the suffering around her, and knowing that many would die, Genevieve decided to take a great risk. With some companions she secretly escaped Paris and made her way to a fertile farming area. There she and her friends loaded up several barges with food and, eluding the blockade, sailed them down the River Seine. They gave away the food to the starving people of Paris, which — for a time, anyway — gave them the strength to endure the siege for a while longer.

Eventually, though, the superior forces of King Childeric prevailed, and finally they entered the city as conquerors. But the force of Genevieve's personality still made a difference. The Frankish king, who had heard of the young woman's bravery and daring, summoned her and listened thoughtfully to what she had to say. As a result of their talks he spared many Parisians, and even directed that a church be built in honor of St. Denis, once the city's beloved archbishop.

Some years later Parisians woke up to discover another threat, one even more deadly than that of the Franks, right on the city's doorstep. Once again it was Genevieve to the rescue, this time by a strategy that astonished the people of Paris.

Attila the Hun, "the scourge of God," was rampaging all over Europe, terrifying people and wrecking the countryside. The Huns had come from the wastelands of Asia, and had ravaged so many Christian countries that people — mistakenly — began to think that these barbarians had been sent to punish them for their sins. Word came that Attila and his marauders were on their way to Paris, and the people panicked. Throwing their belongings together, they started to stream out of the city.

Genevieve tried to convince them not to go. Our prayers can save the city, she told them; remain with me and ask for the Lord's help. Most people simply hooted and kept on running, but a few did stay with her and began to pray. So did Genevieve. And their prayers were heard. Just at the last moment, Attila and the Huns turned away from Paris and the city was saved. The scoffers felt foolish as they crept back to Paris, but soon all the people of the city were celebrating its deliverance from Attila the Hun — and giving thanks once more that Genevieve was one of their own.

The Merciful Queen

Each Morning, Margaret of Scotland
Waited On and Fed the Poor

Solicitude for the poor comes through first and foremost in every bio-graphical sketch of St. Margaret of Scotland (c. 1045-1093), and tak-ing care of those who needed food seems to have been at the top of her agenda. One classic account has her going through an elaborate routine every morning: feeding nine orphans first, and then three hundred other poor people; on to prayers in the church, then waiting on another twenty-four of the poor — and all of this before her own breakfast!

Margaret's abiding concern for the poor manifested itself in other ways. Her court reforms speeded up the judicial process for all people, and her insistence on proper observance of the Sabbath guaranteed at least one day of rest for the poor. Her "sweetness of temper" capti-vated all who came in contact with her, according to an early biogra-pher, and all Scotland rejoiced when its patroness was canonized in 1250.

None of what she accomplished would have been manageable without the blessing of her husband, the redoubtable — and quite uneducated — King Malcolm. Here's the story of how she managed to win him over.

Story adapted from *Married Saints*, by Selden P. Delany, The
Newman Press, 1950; copyright 1935 by Longmans Green
and Co., (first printing 1935; reprinted 1950).

Margaret's first goal was to civilize her husband, and this proved to be no easy task. Malcolm was primarily a warrior, and he could neither read nor write. His ruthless raids into the north of England had spread havoc, and he dragged into captivity multitudes of fair-haired Saxons. The queen sought to beautify his gloomy dwellings with tapestries and dinnerware for the royal table, and even pro-cured panes of glass for the windows of his castle in Edinburgh.

In time she was able to mold him like wax in her hands. Yet he was intensely jealous of her, and his suspicions sometimes made him ridiculous.

In the forest of Dunfermline was a secret cave to which she often retired for prayer. An evil-minded courtier suggested to the king that she went there for no good purpose. The king resolved to see for himself what went on in this secret place, so one day he followed her stealthily at a distance. As he approached the cave he heard her voice in tones of entreaty.

He seized his sword and was about to break through the bushes at the entrance to the cave when he caught her words more distinctly. She was praying for the conversion of his soul. Filled with remorse, he threw himself at her feet and begged to be forgiven.

Gradually Malcolm learned from her example how to pray, as he also learned to show mercy to the poor. The rough soldier repented of his sins and became so devout that his name is included in some Scottish calendars among the saints. Sometimes he followed her into the dark church where together they would spend the night in prayer and vigil. After a time he came to stand in awe of her innate goodness. Rather than risk offending someone so pure, he simply obeyed her wishes and took her counsel to heart.

Alpine Haven

Snowbound Travelers Found
a Shelter, Thanks to St. Bernard

Here is one case, happily, where the facts of the story pretty much confirm everything in the legend — and the legend is formidable indeed.

St. Bernard of Manthon (c. 996-1081) was in fact a priest in the Alpine regions near the Italian-Swiss border, where he had grown up. As a boy, with the help of his dog, he had saved a hiker who was dying in the snow, and as a priest he built two large hospices — still standing! — that would serve as havens for lost and/or snowbound travelers. He helped develop the breed of dog that bears his name today — the outsized St. Bernard, known for its courage, tenacity, and strength. Almost all that St. Bernard did in his priestly ministry, in fact, was motivated by his concern for endangered travelers in need of shelter, and his conviction that Christians had an obligation to help them.

Just about the only aspect of the St. Bernard story that isn't based on fact is that little cask of brandy supposedly strapped to the neck of each rescue dog. That, it turns out, was the figment of an artist's imagination. No harm done, though. It adds a little luster to the legend — and it's kept a legion of cartoonists in business for years.

Excerpt adapted from *Saints and Their Stories*, by Mary
Montgomery, Harper & Row, 1988.

Bernard's family lived near one of the most dangerous passes in the Swiss Alps.

Snowstorms came up suddenly, and many times travelers got caught in them. Some lost their way. Others were buried by snowslides. Bernard and his dog often found travelers in need of help. When he brought them home, his parents always took them in. They gave them food and a warm place to stay until they were ready to be on their way once more.

"Someday I'll see to it that there are churches and schools

throughout the valleys," Bernard told his parents. "And there will be swinging bridges joining the lower peaks so that people have an easier time getting from place to place."

"Those are big plans for a young man," said his father.

"And I have even more of them," Bernard answered. "I want to see that there are lookouts on the mountain summits and shelters built where climbers can rest. Perhaps I will even build a hospice run by monks who are trained to care for the lost and injured."

"I think you'll see to it that these are not just dreams," Bernard's father told him proudly. "I believe you'll make them come true."

Even though Bernard loved living in the mountains, it was lonely sometimes. There were no young people close enough to play with, so Bernard's dog was very special to him. He was like a good friend. Bernard's dream for his hospices included dogs. They would be powerful but gentle animals with a heavy coat of fur so they could withstand the cold. They would also have a keen sense of smell so they could pick up the scent of anyone lost in the snow.

Bernard went to France to study for the priesthood. When he was ordained, he returned to the mountains just as he had planned. Then he began working on his dreams.

Bernard served in the Swiss mountains for forty years. During that time, he saw to it that many churches and schools were built in the valleys. He also had swinging bridges built between the lower peaks of the Alps. Bernard's biggest project was the building of hospices along two of the mountain passes. The large gray stone buildings have been warm and safe places for travelers for nearly a thousand years. Anyone who visits Switzerland today can still visit these hospices. They are named St. Bernard Great and St. Bernard Little.

In the winter there is so much snow in the Alps that the road to the hospices is only open part way. For many years, monks had to carry food supplies and mail to the hospices. Today helicopters do some of the work the monks once did. Still, life at the hospices is difficult. Only young monks are called to serve. Most of them are excellent mountain guides, climbers, and skiers.

When the hospices were built, Bernard had a kennel attached to each of them. There he bred the dogs that helped the monks rescue people. The dogs that Bernard bred were big and powerful. Even though the dogs were large, they were very gentle. And they had an especially keen sense of smell. Their sense of smell was so good they could even sniff out someone buried under several feet of snow. Dogs were trained to bark when they found lost travelers. They were also trained to guide travelers over dangerous trails and to bark a warning when the footing was unsafe.

The Alps still stand as tall and get as snow-covered as they did when Bernard was a boy. The difference between then and now is that now there are many cities and villages and farms on the slopes of the mountains and in the valleys. The monks and their dogs are not called upon to rescue people as often as they were in Bernard's time. But the hospices Bernard built remain as a reminder of the man who cared about rescuing the weak and the lost.

The Rose Queen

Flowers Were the Symbol of the Generous Elizabeth of Hungary

The stories of the saints tell of no more devoted wife than St. Elizabeth of Hungary (1207-1231), who would travel with her husband, Louis, for a day or two whenever he was starting off on a journey and then rejoice at his return, and who was inconsolable when he died on his way to join the Crusades. A tender love story under any circumstances — all the more so, since theirs was an arranged marriage, set in place when Elizabeth was only four!

The roses that are a symbol of her life recall a miraculous manifestation of her generosity, which had become evident at a tender age. She was just three years old when she began giving away her clothes and her toys to the poor. Her final years as a widow were difficult, but her good works continued. She founded a hospital that cared for those who had no one else to look after them. Her exceptional charity was rewarded when she was named a saint in 1235, only four years after her death.

Story adapted from *A Handbook of Christian Symbols and Stories of the Saints*, by Clara Erskine Clement, Ticknor and Co., 1886 (republished by Gale Research Co., 1971).

Louis hardly knew what to make of his beautiful wife, Elizabeth. At times he feared she was too pure and holy to be any other than the bride of heaven, and indeed his parents had tried to head off the marriage because they thought her piety and devotion a bit too intense. But the wedding did take place, when Elizabeth was twenty. Even though she felt compelled to keep many of her charities a secret, afraid that Louis might object, she loved him deeply and managed a happy household.

Tradition has it that once, when visiting the poor people in the village near their castle, she found a child so sickly and covered with sores that no one would care for him. Elizabeth took the infant home and laid him in her own bed, enraging her mother-in-law —

who promptly told Louis what had happened. He stormed into the bedroom — only to find a beautiful and healthy child, who smiled and then vanished from sight even as Louis was looking at him. Those who told and retold this old legend insist that the infant was none other than Jesus himself.

Whenever Louis was away, Elizabeth devoted almost all her waking hours to caring for the poor. One winter day, not realizing that Louis was nearing their home as he returned from a journey, she set out for the village with her robe full of food for poor families. The path was icy, and she was quite bent over with the weight of her burden. Just then, Louis came around a bend in the pathway. Seeing the stooped figure of his young wife, he demanded to know what she was carrying in her robe. Elizabeth hesitated, drawing the robe more tightly about her. But Louis insisted, and Elizabeth had no choice.

She opened her mantle, and when she did, Louis saw only roses — red and white roses, lovelier than those that grow in summer, and here it was the dead of winter. Louis reached out to embrace her, but such a glory surrounded Elizabeth that he dared not touch her. He simply picked up one of the roses and placed it on his own cloak, dazzled by the wonder of what he had seen.

Angels in the Kitchen

St. Zita Appeared to Have Heavenly Help
in the Baking of the Bread

They told some remarkable stories about St. Zita (c. 1218-c. 1272), who spent forty-eight years in the service of the Fatinelli family. There's the one repeated here — that once, when she had overstayed her time at prayer, angels turned up in the kitchen to bake the bread she was supposed to have made. Another tells us that a large container of beans miraculously replenished itself because she kept dipping into it to pass some along to the poor, who showed up at the kitchen door every day. And then there's the one about the secret cache of food she had saved for the poor — inexplicably turning into roses when she was questioned about it by her suspicious master.

Still another, also recounted here, recalls the time she gave away a cloak to an old man sitting in the church doorway. There was a problem, though: the cloak she gave away wasn't her own, but belonged to none other than Signore Fatinelli himself. Its return under circumstances that seemed to be miraculous (there's that word again) only added to the legend of this remarkable woman.

What is known definitely about Zita is this: she made a model of her life of servitude, all the while retaining an independence all her own, and whatever her state in life, she never lost sight of her obligation to feed the hungry and care for the poor. That's a legacy worth remembering.

First story adapted from *Little Pictorial Lives of the Saints*,
Benziger Brothers, Inc., 1925; second story adapted from
Lives of the Saints You Should Know, by Margaret and
Matthew Bunson, Our Sunday Visitor, Inc., 1994.

1. Heavenly Helpers

For all the years that Zita worked for the Fatinelli family, her daily routine varied very little. She arose early, while the household was still asleep, to attend Mass each day. She spent the rest of the day cooking, cleaning, sewing — whatever chores were required to serve the family's needs. She continued working until late at night.

One day Zita, absorbed in prayer, remained in church past her usual hour — past the time that she usually spent baking the bread so it would be ready for the breakfast table. She hastened home, upset because she felt she had let the family down. Would she be punished?

As soon as she returned to the Fatinelli home, though, her mood changed from one of worry to one of astonishment — for the bread was already made and ready for the oven. Zita assumed that one of the other servants had done her this favor, but as she went to express her thanks they each politely declined the honor. None of them had made the bread. Zita wondered: could it possibly have been the mistress herself? Timidly she asked, but Signora Fatinelli said that she had no hand in making the bread.

In fact, no human hand was involved at all. The singularly beautiful aroma that arose from the bread once it was baked confirmed the truth: that angels had made it for Zita while she had been transfixed in prayer.

2. The Old Man and the Cloak

Once on a Christmas Eve, when Zita was on her way to church, her master Fatinelli gave her a fine cloak to keep her warm in the cold night air. When Zita arrived at the parish, St. Frediano's, she saw an old man in rags, shivering in the church doorway. She knew in a moment that he needed the cloak more than she did, and off it went to be wrapped around his shoulders. Eyes brimming with gratitude, the old man told her he knew it was only a loan, promising that the cloak would be returned.

Fatinelli was furious when Zita returned without the cloak. He was fairly used to her do-gooder ways, but this time, he ranted, she had gone too far. In the middle of his tirade came a knock at the door. It was the old man, coming to return the cloak with thanks and a blessing.

Word of the incident spread through town, as such things often do, and after a time the townspeople began to speak of the man as an angel. Indeed, the name of the doorway where the man received the cloak was renamed the Angel Portal — just as it's still called today.

'Where Are the Sick?'

St. Roch Went From City to City, a Pilgrim to the Ailing

When St. Roch (c. 1295-c. 1378) was born in the French town of Montpelier, his parents were amazed to discover a mark in the form of a cross on his chest, and they saw in it the sign of a great and holy life.

How right the years would prove them to be! St. Roch — also known as Rock, Roque, or Rocco — left his home to travel in Italy, and while there, in the town of Aquapendente, healed several victims of the plague. He went on doing the same thing in one city after another, always seeking out the sick and working his miracle cures. He devoted himself to them to such an extent that he constantly endangered his own health — until finally he fell ill himself. The years of unhappiness that followed would have tested the faith of lesser men, but St. Roch bore his trials with patience, humility, and — recognizing it all as God's will — a vow of silence.

The people of Italy and France revere him to this day, and his name continues to be invoked to help those threatened with serious illness.

Story adapted from *A Handbook of Christian Symbols and Stories of the Saints*, by Clara Erskine Clement, Ticknor and Co., 1886 (republished by Gale Research Co., 1971).

St. Roch spent many years traveling from one place to the other, wherever he heard of any dreadful disease that left people suffering. He constantly prayed that God might one day find him worthy to die as a martyr to this care for others.

At length he himself was struck down — in the town of Piacenza, where an epidemic of some unknown disease was raging. It happened after he fell asleep in a hospital, where he was weary after tending to the sick both night and day. When he awoke, he found himself with a horrible ulcer, the mark of the plague, on his thigh. Its pain was so severe that he shrieked out loud.

Rather than disturb others Roch crawled into the street, but because of his condition was not permitted to remain there. At that point he dragged himself to a wooded area outside the city, and lay down to die. But his time had not yet come. The same little dog that traveled with him in all his wanderings stayed by his side to care for him, bringing him a loaf of bread each day. Before long Roch was well enough to travel again, and this time he set out for home.

As fate would have it, he had been away so long and was so changed in appearance that no one from his old hometown had any idea who he was. There was definitely something about the stranger that was suspicious, the people agreed, so they eventually brought him before the judge as a spy. Even the judge, who was Roch's uncle, failed to recognize him, and wound up condemning him to prison. St. Roch, regarding it all as the will of God, said nothing, and was cast into a dungeon. No one took up his case, and Roch himself kept to his vow of silence. He remained in the lonely dungeon for five years.

One morning when the jailer went to his cell it was filled with a glory of light, and there on the cold floor lay Roch's body. Next to it was a paper on which he had written his name along with these words: "All those who are stricken by the plague, and who pray for aid through the merits and intercession of St. Roch, the servant of God, shall be healed." When the judge was shown the paper, he wept and was filled with remorse, as were many townspeople. The saint was honorably buried with the prayers of the whole city.

Nearly a hundred years later a severe plague broke out in Constance, where a great church council was taking place. A monk who recalled the promise of St. Roch suggested that his name be invoked to rid the city of plague, and indeed an image of the saint was carried through the streets in solemn procession, accompanied by prayers and litanies. The plague ceased, and before long the name of St. Roch was being venerated in many lands.

The Holy Helpers

An Old Legend Honors Fourteen Saints Who Respond to Special Pleas

By any reckoning, the story of the Fourteen Holy Helpers is one of the most fascinating in the long history of the Church. The names of these early Christian saints and martyrs, whose assistance was considered invaluable in times of crisis, were especially invoked when serious illness was involved — particularly in overcoming the "Black Death" that ravaged Europe from 1346 to 1349.

Some of the fourteen are well-known saints, and others less so. A few are quite obscure. The full list includes St. George, St. Blase, St. Pantaleon, St. Vitus, St. Erasmus, St. Christopher, St. Dionysius, St. Cyriacus, St. Achatius, St. Eustachius, St. Giles, St. Catherine, St. Margaret, and St. Barbara.

Why these fourteen? When the Black Death struck, its effects were sudden and violent. A victim's tongue would turn black. Then a high fever would set in, accompanied by an unbearable headache. Typically a victim would lose his mental faculties and die within hours — which meant that many died without the last sacraments of the Church. In the midst of a plague, people sought divine help through the intercession of the saints.

The Fourteen Holy Helpers all had an association with healing. St. Blase, of course, is revered for guarding against illnesses of the throat; St. Giles against the plague itself. St. Giles, St. Barbara, and St. Catherine were appealed to for protection against a sudden death, St. Pantaleon was the patron of physicians, and so on. Their heavenly assistance was widely credited with halting the devastating effects of the Black Death, and faith in the power of the fourteen saints spread rapidly throughout Europe.

Only two U.S. parishes adopted the name of the Holy Helpers, and devotion to this select group seems to be on the wane. Here's a charming story of how the Helpers once appeared to a shepherd in the Bavarian countryside.

Story adapted from *Mary, Help of Christians and the Fourteen Saints Invoked as Holy Helpers*, by Rev. Bonaventure Hammer, OFM, Benziger Brothers, 1909.

On a September evening in 1445, a young shepherd boy named Herman Leicht was gathering his flock for the homeward drive on a farm owned by the monks of Langheim Abbey, in the diocese of Bamberg. He heard what sounded like a human cry, and looked around to find a young child sitting in a nearby field. Herman was about to approach when the child disappeared from view.

Mystified, the shepherd returned to his flock. When he turned his head for another look, the child had come back — this time sitting in a circle of light, between two candles. By now, Herman was quite terrified and made the sign of the Cross. The child smiled as if to encourage him, but vanished when Herman took his first step in that direction. There were no more unexpected incidents that evening, and Herman drove his flock home. When he told his parents what had happened, they dismissed it as a delusion, but the Fathers in the monastery seemed more interested. If the child should ever appear to you again, they told Herman, find out what it wants.

It took several months, but the child did appear to Herman one more time — again at sunset, but now with thirteen other children, all in a halo of glory. More curious than afraid, the shepherd approached and asked the child he had seen the previous September — "in the name of the Father, and of the Son, and of the Holy Ghost" — just what it desired.

"We are the Fourteen Helpers, and desire that a chapel be built for us," the child replied. "Be our servant, and we shall serve you." Then all the children disappeared, and Herman was filled with a feeling of heavenly consolation.

That would not be the end of his visions. On the following Sunday he saw two lighted candles descending from the sky, directly to the point at which he had seen the group of children. This time he ran straight to the monastery with his news. The abbot and the community at large thought the young shepherd was simply letting his imagination run wild, but when extraordinary favors began to be granted to people who prayed at the site of the apparition, the monks had a change of heart. They built a chapel there, and when it was completed in 1448 they dedicated it to the Blessed Virgin Mary and the Fourteen Holy Helpers. Over the years it became a favorite shrine of pilgrims, helping to spread devotion to the Helpers throughout Italy, Austria, Hungary, Bohemia, and Switzerland.

The Sacred Heart

The City of Marseilles Credited Prayer
for Its Rescue From the Plague

Devotion to the Sacred Heart of Jesus began in the Middle Ages and, as an earlier story recounted, reached a flowering at the time of St. Margaret Mary Alacoque (1647-1690). In between was a remarkable procession of saints — among them Bernard of Clairvaux, Bonaventure, Gertrude, Catherine of Siena, Julian of Norwich, Frances of Rome, and Francis de Sales — who helped to develop and popularize it.

The faithful saw in the Sacred Heart a perfect symbol of Christ's divine love and mercy, especially as it applied to the very human problems they faced all the time. That was true in a particular way of the problem of devastating illnesses — such as the plague — for which no cure other than heavenly intervention seemed possible.

So it was with the plague that struck the French city of Marseilles in 1722, throwing its inhabitants "into the greatest consternation," in the words of this nineteenth-century report. City and Church joined forces to mount a procession in honor of the Sacred Heart, vowing to repeat it each year — and miraculously, the story states, "That very day all the sick were cured, and no one was ever after attacked by the plague."

Story from *Catholic Anecdotes*, by the Brothers of the
Christian Schools; translated from the French by Mrs. J.
Sadlier; D. & J. Sadlier & Co., 1885.

The devotion to the Sacred Heart of Jesus is entirely French; it dates from the close of the seventeenth century, but it is especially since the famous plague of Marseilles that it spread through the provinces.

In the month of May 1722, this plague, which had been supposed quite extinct, broke out again in that city, and threw it into the greatest consternation. The Heart of Jesus, which had already protected it once, was again the happy resource of the bishop, the celebrated Belzunce.

At his solicitation, the magistrates, in a body, made a vow to go every year in the name of the city, to the Church of the Visitation, on the Feast of the Sacred Heart, there to honor that worthy object of our love, to receive Holy Communion, to offer a white waxen taper four pounds in weight, adorned with the arms of the city, and, finally, to assist in the general procession which that prelate proposed to establish in perpetuity on that same day. This vow was pronounced publicly before the altar of the Cathedral Church, by the first of the municipal magistrates, in the name of all, on the day of the Fête-Dieu, before the procession of the Blessed Sacrament. The bishop held the Sacred Host in his hands, and the magistrates knelt before him. All the people united in a vow from which they expected such happy results. It was heard in a manner that excited the admiration as well as the gratitude of all Marseilles.

That very day all the sick were cured, and no one was ever after attacked by the plague. Fear, which in those fatal plagues does often more injury than the malady itself, gave place to entire confidence; the inhabitants of Marseilles believed themselves safe in the protection of the merciful heart of the Savior. The disease died out so completely that, six weeks after, the bishop of Marseilles, in a pastoral that he wrote exciting the people to gratitude, said to them: "We now enjoy such perfect health, that we have not had for some time in Marseilles either deaths or diseases of any kind, a thing wholly unprecedented in a city so large and populous, and which goes to prove the miracle."

It was in remembrance of this second favor, which appeared still more sudden and miraculous than the first, that the bishop of Marseilles established in perpetuity a general procession on the Feast of the Sacred Heart of Jesus. All these facts are established by the pastorals of that prelate, and by the official deliberations of the municipal body of Marseilles. The procession was interrupted for some time by the Revolution; but it now takes place again with as much faith and piety as in the eighteenth century.

The Emperor's Premonition

Charles V Foresaw His Own Death — And Prepared for It in a Coffin

As emperor of Germany and king of Spain, Charles V (1500-1558) was one of Europe's mightiest monarchs, generally considered the greatest Habsburg of them all. He is remembered for many things — including one unusual, even eerie, story involving a funeral. His own.

His role in history was an enormous one. It was Charles who rejected Martin Luther — and also Charles who helped block England's Henry VIII from obtaining a marriage annulment, leading directly to the king's break with Rome.

There's more, much more to the story. In the convoluted combination of religion and politics that prevailed at the time, Emperor Charles and Pope Clement VII were often at loggerheads — so much so that in 1527 the emperor sacked Rome, keeping the pope a virtual prisoner in the Castel Sant' Angelo. And significantly, it was Charles, historians say, whose interference kept the pope from responding more effectively to one of the greatest challenges the Church ever faced: the Protestant Reformation.

When Charles did retire to his monastery in 1556 (as accurately depicted in the accompanying story), he did so with much of Europe in turmoil and disarray. Thus did he begin preparing for his own death — which came about, strangely enough, in a way he appeared to have clearly foreseen.

Story from *Catholic Anecdotes*, by the Brothers of the
Christian Schools; translated from the French by Mrs. J.
Sadlier; D. & J. Sadlier & Co., 1885.

Charles V, emperor of Germany and Spain, may serve us as a model on the article of preparation for death. He was only fifty-five years old when he abdicated the crown, and renounced all his titles and dignities to consecrate his last years to the great work of preparing to appear before God.

He retired to the monastery of St. Just, on the frontiers of

Spain and Portugal, and gave himself up to the same exercises as the monks. By night, he rose like them to sing the Office; by day, he divided his time between prayer, reading, and study. His sole recreations were a short walk in the fields and the culture of a small garden. There was all that remained to him of so many states and provinces that he had once possessed.

But this is not all; he contented himself with the simplest and coarsest food, and often fasted with the rigor of a cenobite. Every Friday in Lent, he gave himself the discipline till the blood almost flowed, in order to obtain more efficaciously the pardon of his sins.

But he did something more extraordinary still. In order to familiarize himself with the thought of death, so salutary for a Christian, he would have his obsequies celebrated as though he were already dead. He laid himself then in a coffin, and was borne to the church. The walls were hung with black, tapers were lit, the bells were rung, prayers recited, and the Office of the Dead sung, precisely as if Charles V had been really dead.

However extraordinary this ceremony might be, the event showed that it was by a sort of presentiment he had had it solemnized. The very next day he was seized with the malady of which he died. His death was most edifying, for he had remembered the words of Our Lord, "What will it profit a man if he gain the whole world, and lose his own soul?"

Graveside Conversion

The Sight of the Empress's Body
Turned St. Francis Borgia to the Faith

From time to time unusual occurrences have accompanied the ceremony of burying the dead, few of them quite as striking as that of St. Francis Borgia (1510-1572). As this story indicates, he was so moved at the sight of the body of Empress Isabella that he decided to forsake the ways of the world and devote his talents to the Lord alone. (Coincidentally, he was commissioned to oversee the burial by the monarch who was the central figure in the previous story — Charles V.)

The conversion might not have been quite as instantaneous as suggested here. Isabella died in 1539, and Francis did not enter the Jesuits until 1546 — following the death of his wife. His priestly career would prove to be significant, however. He was instrumental in developing the Jesuits' mission program, and ultimately became the order's third general. Pope Clement X canonized him in 1671.

Story from *Catholic Anecdotes*, by the Brothers of the
Christian Schools; translated from the French by Mrs. J.
Sadlier; D. & J. Sadlier & Co., 1885.

Death is an eloquent preacher, who gives us continual lessons on the nothingness of earthly things. The very sight of a grave or a corpse has sometimes sufficed to make saints. Here is a striking example of the kind.

St. Francis Borgia, before quitting the world, was duke of Gandia and one of the most illustrious grandees of Spain. The Empress Isabella having died in 1539, Charles V, emperor of Germany and king of Spain, deputed Francis to convey and accompany her body to Grenada, where was situated the tombs of the kings of Spain. This mission was very honorable, and yet God made use of it to make the duke of Gandia a humble religious.

When the body had reached its destination and was about to be lowered into the royal vault, Francis Borgia had to open the coffin, in order to swear upon it that those were really the mortal remains of his sovereign, the Empress Isabella. What was his horror and disgust on beholding, instead of a beautiful princess, a foul and disgusting corpse!

"What," cried he, "is this all that remains of my gracious sovereign? Where, then, is her smooth white brow, her fresh fair cheeks, her smiling lips, and her radiant eyes?"

This thought and these reflections acted so promptly on his mind and heart that he resolved to consecrate himself wholly to God. Accordingly, having accomplished his mission, arranged his temporal affairs, and provided suitably for his children, he entered the company of Jesus and became a great saint.

Deathbed Triumph

His Guardian Angel and the Voice of Mary Calmed St. Andrew Avellino

An earlier story described the devotion to St. Barbara among those who pray for a happy death. So it is with St. Andrew Avellino (1520-1608), a Neapolitan priest who endured a lifetime of suffering but was comforted by heavenly aid as he lay dying.

The legends of the deathbed scene grew to remarkable proportion, even beyond those described here. According to one, when "a particularly ferocious demon" threatened St. Andrew, an angel appeared, grabbed the offender by the neck, and tossed him out the door.

By any measure, though, the lesson of St. Andrew's rescue was clear to the young listeners who heard this story: those who remain united with the Lord in life will surely be with him at death.

Story from *Little Pictorial Lives of the Saints*,
Benziger Brothers, Inc., 1925.

After a holy youth, Lancelot Avellino was ordained a priest at Naples. At the age of thirty-six he entered the Theatine Order, and took the name of Andrew, to show his love for the Cross. For years he was afflicted with a most painful rupture; yet he would never use a carriage.

Once when he was carrying the Viaticum, and a storm had extinguished the lamps, a heavenly light encircled him, guided his steps, and sheltered him from the rain. But as a rule, his sufferings were unrelieved by God or man.

On the last day of his life, St. Andrew rose to say Mass. He was in his eighty-ninth year, and so weak that he could scarcely reach the altar. He began the "Judica," and fell forward in a fit of apoplexy. Laid on a straw mattress, his whole frame was convulsed in agony, while the fiend in visible form advanced to seize his soul.

Then, as his brethren prayed and wept, the voice of Mary was heard, bidding the saint's guardian angel to send the tempter back to hell. A calm and holy smile settled on the features of the dying saint, as, with a grateful salutation to the image of Mary, he breathed forth his soul to God. His death happened on the tenth of November 1608.

An Example to His Priests

St. Charles Borromeo Taught the Duty of Caring for All

St. Charles Borromeo (1538-1584) was no ivory-tower bishop — although that style of life could have been his had he wanted it. After all, as an earlier story pointed out, his intellectual and theological influence made itself felt all over Europe, and his organizing genius helped shape the direction of the Council of Trent.

But Charles's first concern was for the people of his own archdiocese of Milan — the poor, the homeless, the hungry, and the unwanted. He made the corporal works of mercy his own. Even as a youth he cared little for his own comfort, giving generously to the poor instead. The pattern would continue throughout his lifetime, and if anything was growing in commitment as he himself grew in years.

Nor was he a mere armchair gift-giver. Others may have fled the city in panic, but — as the following story shows — when a death-dealing plague threatened to devastate Milan he waded right in. His courageous action had a double effect: not only did he bring comfort to the sick and dying, but his example inspired his priests to join him.

"If you wish to make any progress in the service of God," he once wrote, "we must begin every day of our life with new ardor." His life story makes one thing clear: no one followed that advice better than St. Charles Borromeo himself.

Story adapted from *A Handbook of Christian Symbols and Stories of the Saints*, by Clara Erskine Clement, Ticknor and Co., 1886 (republished by Gale Research Co., 1971).

Only twenty-three years old when he became archbishop of Milan, St. Charles Borromeo set a high standard right from the start. He dedicated all his income to the welfare of the people, keeping for himself just enough to buy his bread and water, and straw on which to sleep. He accompanied the missionaries that he sent to every part of his vast diocese, simply to make sure that the people who lived there were well cared for.

What was surely one of his finest hours came when a deadly plague struck the city of Milan in 1576. All who were able to do so had fled to the countryside, but Charles, convinced that his place was with the people, stayed on. He ministered to the sick and dying, saw to the needs of the poor, and provided spiritual comfort to all who were left behind in the ravaged city.

His action had a striking effect not only on Milan's citizens but on his own clergy as well. Some twenty-eight of his priests decided to join him in caring for plague victims despite the deadly risks involved. All of them — along with St. Charles himself — survived the long ordeal.

Not all the priests of the time were so taken with the bishop's example. Many had fallen into a great laxity of discipline, and were in the habit of using Church revenues for their own indulgence. St. Charles restored in many the zeal for service that had inspired them in the first place, but others scorned the sacrifices to which he urged them. One of the disaffected priests struck the bishop as he celebrated Mass, dealing what first appeared to be a mortal blow. But St. Charles quickly recovered from his wound, convincing his followers that they had witnessed a miracle.

He died on November 4, 1584, and with his last breath called out, *"Ecce venio"* — "Behold, I am coming."

He Wore a Red Cross

St. Camillus Sought Out the Dying
on the Back Streets of Rome

St. Camillus de Lellis (1550-1614) had something of a slow start on the road to sainthood. He loved to gamble, so much so that it became the passion of his life. He finally realized that it was destroying him instead of making him happy, and knew that he had to change his ways. Coming under the influence of the redoubtable St. Philip Neri, he decided to devote himself to those who were sick and destitute.

Camillus did that with a passion, so much so that he is now honored as the patron saint of Catholic nursing. Even after establishing a hospital and founding a religious community to care for the sick, he prowled the nighttime streets of Rome, always on the lookout for those who were dying and deserted. When he did so, incidentally, he proudly wore on his cassock a symbol of his concern: a large red cross. He made that symbol enduring, of course; even today it signals our care for those who need help.

Story adapted from *Little Pictorial Lives of the Saints*,
Benziger Brothers, Inc., 1925.

It was chance, in more than one way, that turned around the life of Camillus de Lellis. The games of chance that had left him penniless forced him to turn to menial labor, and by chance he ended up as a workman's helper — building a Capuchin convent. Inspired by the friars he saw each day as the work went on, and especially by the words of one friar who often stopped to speak to him, Camillus resolved to enter religious life. Three times he entered the Capuchin novitiate, but each time he went on medical leave because of an old leg wound.

Traveling to Rome for medical treatment, he was blessed to find as confessor and spiritual director none other than St. Philip Neri. But he was appalled at what he encountered in the hospital at which he was a patient: the indifference of both chaplains and medical personnel to the suffering of the sick. The experience helped determine his future. If he were to be a priest, he decided, his would be a priesthood devoted to the sick. Indeed he was ordained, and in 1586 the community he founded, the Servants of the Sick, was approved by the pope.

From that day forward his devotion never wavered. Called out at all hours of day and night, Camillus attended to the needs of patients with unmatched tenderness. He wept with them, consoled them, and prayed with them. He knew miraculously the state of their souls, and St. Philip Neri himself saw angels encouraging two Servants of the Sick who were attending a dying patient.

One day a sick man said to Camillus, "Father, I beg you to make up my bed. It is very hard."

"You beg me?" Camillus replied. "God forgive you, brother. Don't you know that you are to *command* me, for I am your servant?" And he added, "Would to God that in the hour of my death one sigh or one blessing of these poor creatures would fall on me."

His prayer was heard. Death came to him quietly after a brief illness, just as the attending priest was praying over him these words: "May Jesus Christ appear to you with a mild and joyful countenance."

Turning Point

A Single Homily by Vincent de Paul
Launched a Global Work of Charity

Few people in the long history of the Church have had as much impact on its care for the sick and the poor as St. Vincent de Paul (c. 1580-1660), the great "priest of charity." The conscience of France during his lifetime, he set a standard of commitment to God's poor that remains something to aim at today, more than three hundred years after his death.

One of his early fields of ministry was that of chaplain to navy rowers, the sailors with the demanding job of manning the oars on French galleys. He brought a certain sympathy to the task: as a young priest he was captured by Barbary pirates and spent two hard years behind the oars himself as a slave.

As his work among the destitute and the homeless grew and became well known, so did the legends about the man himself. As one early biographer reported: "He went through the streets of Paris at night, seeking the children who were left there to die. Once robbers rushed upon him, thinking he carried a treasure, but when he opened his cloak, they recognized him and his burden, and fell at his feet."

St. Vincent de Paul is deservedly remembered for founding both the Congregation of the Missions — the priests we know as the Vincentians — and, with the help of St. Louise de Marillac, the Sisters of Charity. (The Sisters' designated mission was revolutionary for its time — their convent the sickroom, their cloister the streets of the city.)

But even before those two enduring communities got started, Vincent had launched yet another: the Ladies of Charity, an organization of laywomen who devoted themselves to the care and solace of the sick and the poor. It all began one day, with a single stirring homily.

Story adapted from *The World of Monsieur Vincent*, by Mary Purcell, Charles Scribner's Sons, 1963.

The village people of Chatillon, near Lyons, welcomed their new curé in 1617, not knowing quite what to expect. It took them only a short while to find out.

One Sunday as he was vesting for Mass, Abbé Vincent de Paul, the new priest, received word that one of the families in the parish was in dire need. The entire household, it seemed, had fallen ill, with no one well enough to take care of another. Abbé Vincent decided to tell the worshipers there that day of the tragic situation and invite them to help out. He described their plight so movingly that the congregation took immediate action.

That very afternoon no less than fifty housewives set off to visit the stricken family, bringing with them food and wine. When the priest himself went to pay a call he was surprised to encounter so many groups of women carrying food baskets — full baskets on the way to the stricken family, empty ones returning. And when he arrived at the family's home, he was even more astonished: every table and chair was piled high with food and other gifts.

It was, to be sure, a marvelous outpouring of charity — but just as surely, far too much for any single family to consume. So, he later wrote: "I suggested to all these dear kind people whose charity had moved them to visit that family that they should take turns to visit them and cook for them, and not only for the family in question but for similar cases that might arise."

For the next two days Vincent drew up some ground rules to get the project going, and on Wednesday of that week seven women of the parish accepted his invitation to an organizational meeting. There were some temporal considerations on Vincent's blueprint: the qualifications for membership, the division of the organization into groups that would be limited to twenty women each, the fundraising responsibilities. But the heart of these Ladies of Charity would be charity itself.

Having prepared a meal, the guidelines read, each volunteer would take it herself to the sick person. Then:

"On entering she is to greet him cheerfully and charitably, arrange a tray on the bed, then invite him to eat for the love of Jesus and his holy Mother. . . . She will try to cheer him up if he seems unhappy. Having started him on his meal she will leave him if there is someone in the house to attend to him and go seek another whom she is to deal with in like manner. She is to remember always to begin with one who has somebody with him and finish with one who lives alone, so as to be able to stay a little longer with those who have no one."

Thus a great work of charity had its beginnings in a parish church in the village of Chatillon. It spread — at first to other villages nearby, eventually throughout France. The work goes on today all over the world, inspired, to begin with, by that single sermon. One may reasonably wonder just what it was that Abbé Vincent said on that Sunday, said so movingly that fifty of his listeners decided to undertake a personal errand of mercy. As it happens, there is no record of it. St. Vincent de Paul never wrote out his sermons.

But he left the world a clue in later years, when someone asked about that particular homily, the one that had led to the formation of the Ladies of Charity.

He couldn't answer exactly, he said, but it was the plight of that unfortunate family that had moved him so deeply. And all he did from that point on was speak from the heart.

St. Rose of Lima

She Opened Her Own Home
to the Poor, the Hungry, the Thirsty

Miraculous events took place throughout the lifetime of St. Rose of Lima (1586-1617), even from the time of her infancy. Her parents originally named her Isabella, but changed it to Rose after a rose blossom mysteriously appeared in the air over her cradle. As a young girl she was gifted with visions of Jesus and the Virgin Mary, and her neighbors claimed that a supernatural child was sometimes seen playing with her — one who left silver footprints on the road.

Growing up in Lima, Peru, Rose was as horrified at the plight of the downtrodden Indians as she was sad to see the excesses of her family's well-to-do neighbors. To say she was hard on herself hardly begins to describe her extreme self-imposed penances. Her mother, María, barely knew what to make of this unusual child, who made herself unattractive rather than face the prospect of marriage. The penances Rose endured and the hints of the supernatural that surrounded her eventually attracted the attention of a theological investigative team, but its members concluded that Rose was acting under God's guidance, living as God wished her to live. She moved on from personal acts of mortification to ceaseless works of charity, caring for the poor, the hungry, and the thirsty —first in a hut in her garden, then in her own home.

Word of her good deeds spread, and when she died, the entire city mourned. Miracles of healing and conversion continued after her death, however, and she was declared a saint in 1671. This brief story describes the way in which all the people of Lima poured out their love for Rose, even after her death — and why they felt as strongly as they did.

Story adapted from *Saints of the Americas*, by Rev. M. A.
Habig, OFM, Our Sunday Visitor, Inc., 1974.

When Rosa de Santa María died in 1617, all the people of Lima, Peru, felt as if they had lost someone from their own family. For St.

Rose of Lima — as later generations would know her — had endeared herself to the whole city.

She was to be buried after a Mass in the cathedral, but the crowd that turned out was so large and so torn by grief that the funeral was postponed to the next day. But that ceremony, too, had to be postponed — for the same reason. The crowds were simply too large to handle. There was only one solution, and Church authorities quickly realized it: Rose was buried on the third day, following a quiet, private funeral Mass in the cloister of the Dominican priory.

What caused such an outpouring of affection? The people of Lima — the poor Indians, especially, but all the others as well — knew that her love for them was genuine. It wasn't simply the way she cared for the sick, opening her family's home to them, or the countless personal works of charity she performed in their midst. It was the spirit of hope she gave to them all — for impoverished Indians, the hope of a future with justice; for her fellow Hispanic settlers, hope for redemption in the Lord.

As if that weren't enough, there was the way she had saved their city — not once, but three times. Twice she did it with her prayers and penances: one time when rebellion threatened the city, and another when earthquakes rocked the area but Lima itself was spared.

And then, in 1615, there had been the frightening raid of the Dutch pirate George Spitberg, which almost brought Lima to its knees.

Spitberg, commanding a squadron of seven ships, had passed through the Straits of Magellan at the southern end of South America and had ravaged the coast of Chile. He was now on his way to Callao, the port of Lima. The viceroy sent out three warships to meet them, but they suffered a sad defeat at the hands of the intruders. Many people sought refuge in the churches of Lima. Rose, too, went to the Church of Santo Domingo, determined to defend the Blessed Sacrament with her life.

Soon the pirates entered that very church. But they were so struck with awe and fear when they saw Rose, a radiant figure in white and black standing in front of the tabernacle, that they quickly fled back to their ships and abandoned their plan to plunder the city. Once again, Rose was hailed as the savior of Lima.

St. Peter Claver

The Prisoners He Visited Came Here in the Hold of a Ship

What possessed the spirit of St. Peter Claver (1580-1654)? Could it have been his family background? Might it have been the training he received at the hands of St. Alphonsus Rodríguez? Whatever it was, once he left his native Spain to become a missioner in South America, in Colombia, he found his calling — and pronounced himself "the slave of the Negroes forever."

Not only did he bring food and comfort to the imprisoned slaves arriving from West Africa; he gave them hope and the gift of faith as well. Canonized by Pope Leo XIII in 1888, he is the patron of Catholic missions among black people.

Story from *Lives of the Saints You Should Know* (Vol. 2), by Margaret and Matthew Bunson, Our Sunday Visitor, Inc., 1996.

In 1610 Peter Claver volunteered for the missions and was sent to Cartagena, in Colombia, then a Spanish territory. When he arrived there, he started his last training session before ordination to the priesthood, and he also learned a truly dreadful lesson about human beings. He discovered just how brutal and vile the human race could be when power and greed ruled over all.

The Spanish decided upon importing boatloads of black slaves that were available from the continent of Africa. Such men and women could be brought aboard ship, chained in the hold, and fed only the minimum to keep them alive during the voyage. Those that managed to make the long journey with their bodies and souls intact could be put to work. The survival of the fittest was the rule here, and the Spanish did not worry about the black men and women who perished on board the dreadful slave ships. They paid only two ecus (the monetary standard at the time) for each slave, and they could sell each one for two hundred ecus in Cartagena.

Peter Claver, being trained in the Jesuit seminary by Father Alphonsus de Sandoval, a true apostle of charity, saw the slave ships and the hideous pens and dungeons in which the imported men and women were kept in the city. He declared himself "the slave of the Negroes forever." This was no idle boast or romantic fancy. He was timid and humble by nature, but the agony of the slaves, so heartrending, so hideous, transformed him into a whirlwind of activity and strength.

Peter Claver was ordained a priest in 1615 and given a free hand with his mission, although he was probably cautioned by older, more experienced priests about the arrogance and cruelty of the Spanish aristocrats. He started out in a well-organized fashion, going in the pilot boat to meet each arriving slave ship. There he forced the ship's crews to open the hold, exposing the human cargo that had been so brutalized by the hardships of the long voyage, the darkness, and cramped space. The slaves were half crazed by the time they reached Cartagena, and Peter Claver went to each one of them personally, giving them food and water, binding their wounds, and soothing them with kindness. In order to make even more direct and personal contact, he used translators who were familiar with the various African dialects.

In the city's holding pens, he brought food, medicine, brandy, and tobacco to the slaves. Peter even went into the mines and plantations to inspect conditions and care for the slaves held there. It is recorded that he converted more than three hundred thousand in his ministry and heard five thousand confessions a year. He is also reported as having baptized as many as three million souls.

When a particular landowner or mine director refused to ease his treatment of the slaves under his control, he found himself face-to-face with Peter Claver. The saint moved into the mine or plantation owned by the tyrant, living with the slaves and confronting the Spanish hour by hour.

Now this type of behavior did not win him many friends among the Spanish, as his older religious companions had probably warned him. Not only the landowners and mine directors hated the sight of him. He had enemies even in the Church, where some accused him of blasphemy. These odd churchmen actually declared that the slaves scarcely possessed souls and were therefore unworthy of the sacraments that Peter so lovingly lavished on them.

The saint also saw society matrons leave a church when he arrived on the altar. They were displaying their sensitivity to his work, declaring by their actions that he had become infected with all sorts of terrible diseases through his contact with the slaves. He responded to this sort of mindless hysteria by redoubling his efforts.

Sailors and travelers found him a welcome patron when they arrived in the city port. Peter Claver nursed lepers and victims of St. Anthony's fire, a painful skin disease of the area. He also performed miracles for those in his care and announced prophecies that were proven genuine. As a result of all this increased work, and the obvious signs of God's favor, the Spanish of Cartagena slowly came to realize the mission of Peter Claver. Some even admitted that Cartagena was a cesspool of cruelty and vice, a city spared God's wrath only because Peter Claver lived within its borders. He was called the "Oracle of Cartagena," as more and more of the high-ranking Spanish flocked to aid him in his work.

Then the plague of 1650 struck in the region, and Peter Claver went among the thousands of stricken to bring comfort and medical care. He caught the disease and tried to keep working but was soon confined to his small cell, where a single slave took care of him. For four years the saint suffered alone, as the people of Cartagena, busy rebuilding their lives, forgot all about him. He died alone on September 8, 1654, and suddenly everyone in the city recognized the loss.

A massive civic funeral was held, attended by thousands, and Peter Claver was laid to rest in Cartagena. Canonized by Pope Leo XIII in 1888, St. Peter Claver was declared the patron of all Catholic missions to the Negroes, or blacks. His feast day is celebrated on September 9.

Begging for the Poor

Blessed Jeanne Jugan Went
Door-to-Door for Her Elderly Friends

For Blessed Jeanne Jugan (1792-1879), it all began when she gave up her own bed to an elderly, blind, and ailing neighbor who had no one to care for her. Before long there was a second old woman. Then four and five more, then twelve . . .

Jeanne Jugan devoted her extraordinary life to taking care of the elderly poor, forming an equally extraordinary community — the Little Sisters of the Poor — to join her in that work. They supported their heroic efforts by begging — asking for anything, turning away nothing. The story that follows recounts some of Jeanne's earliest efforts in that direction as she went door-to-door, basket in hand.

Even before Jeanne Jugan died, the community she founded had spread far beyond her native France. Today the Little Sisters, selfless as always, continue the work that Jeanne Jugan began, in almost every part of the world. And, now as then, the begging goes on as well.

Selection from *Jeanne Jugan: Humble So As to Love More*, by
Paul Milcent, Darton, Longman and Todd, 1979.

"Sister Jeanne, go out instead of us, beg for us." This was what the old women said. By this, they emphasized the very heart of this activity of begging. Jeanne Jugan substituted herself for the poor, identified herself with them; or rather, guided by the Spirit of Jesus, she recognized that the poor were her "own flesh." Their distress was her distress, their begging was her begging. This was how God loved us in Jesus.

Practical considerations led her to do the begging herself: if she had allowed the *good women* to go the rounds of the town, as they used to before she had given them shelter, she would have exposed them to many evils, especially those of them who were given to drink. So, she respectfully asked each to give her the addresses of her benefactors and then did the rounds herself instead. She used to explain, "Well, sir, the little old woman won't be coming anymore. I shall be coming instead. Please be so kind as to go on giving us your alms." Note the *us*.

It was not an easy decision to take. Jeanne was proud; in spite of knowing how admirably the women of Cancale came to one another's help, this was not sufficient to make her cheerfully take to begging. In her old age, she would still recall the victory over self that this had frequently required. "I used to go out with my basket, looking for something for our poor. . . . It cost me a lot to do this, but I did it for God and our dear poor."

Jeanne asked for money but also for gifts in kind: food — the remains of meals, or *leftovers*, were often particularly appreciated — things, clothes. "I should be very grateful if you could give me a spoonful of salt or a small amount of butter." "We could do with a copper for boiling the sheets." "A little wool or filasse (i.e., hemp) would be useful to us." She was not shy of putting into words what she lived by faith. If she happened to be asking for some wood to make a bed, she would be specific and say, "I should like a little wood to relieve a member of Jesus Christ." She accepted whatever she was given. Later she was to advise the novices, "Never throw anything away that comes by way of begging, until you have seen if you can't find some use for it." One day, in the village of La Froulerie, a gardener who knew about the adventure to which she had just committed herself, said, "Jeanne, what are we to call you now?" "The humble servant of the poor." "Then, this way please, humble servant of the poor!" and he gave her some vegetables.

She was not always so well received. In the course of one round, she rang a rich and miserly old man's doorbell. Knowing how to get on the right side of him, she persuaded him to give her a good contribution. Next day, she called again. This time, he was angry. She smiled, "But, sir, my poor were hungry yesterday, they are hungry again today, and tomorrow they will be hungry too." He gave again, and promised to go on giving. Thus, with a smile, she knew how to invite the rich to think again and discover their responsibilities.

Sometimes she was treated as a cadger. "Why don't you go and do an honest day's work?" "I do this for my poor, sir." Many times, she was turned away; she said, "Thank you." "You're mad to say thank you when shown the door." "It's for God."

One incident has become famous. An irritable old bachelor struck her. Gently she replied, "Thank you; that was for me. Now please give me something for my poor!"

She often used to apply for help at the Welfare Office and in the early days she was treated as a member of the organization. But one day a woman employee was rude to her and told her to take her place in the queue with the beggars. She obeyed. She was a beggar after all; it was the right place for her.

She was careful never to make any comment about those who had given her a bad reception. This was the advice she used to give the young when she was old herself:

"There will be people who will swear at you and send you away. The neighbors will say, 'You had a very poor reception next door,' but you must never show resentment. Whenever this happened to me, I used to say, 'Oh, no, those people treated me very well.' For, you see, when we are given a hostile reception, this is good for us and something we can offer to God."

Even her friends would reproach her from time to time. Mme. de La Mettrie, her old employer who was very fond of her, would say, "My dear Jeanne, you weigh yourself down with this horde of old people. You can't feed them! Our resources are limited; I have four children. What with your old folk, you'll reduce us to sleeping on the floor!" She never answered back, and went on as before.

Sometimes things went badly. Then she would drum up her courage. She would say to her companion, "Let's go on for God!" Or, one feast day at Saint-Servan, with one of those half-smiles characteristic of her, "Today, we're going to make a good collection. Our old folk have had a good dinner, so St. Joseph ought to be pleased at seeing his dependents being well looked after. He is going to bless us!"

A Penny a Week

A Card Game Scorepad Helped a Young French Woman Assist the Missions Worldwide

Pauline Jaricot (1799-1862) was swept up in the fervor of her times — and exciting times they were. The Church in her native France had been persecuted and repressed, first during the cruel years of the French Revolution and later under the empire of Napoleon. But then it burst forth in a flowering of creative zeal — rediscovering its own glorious heritage of faith, developing new religious communities, turning its eyes overseas, and producing heroic missionaries and saints.

Pauline was still in her teens when she first began her plans for a mission aid organization. A young woman who came from a privileged background, she had once been carefree and frivolous. That all changed with a sermon that she heard on vanity — a sermon, she later said, that was the turning point in her life. She began doing volunteer work in hospitals, bringing rosary beads to patients and chatting with those who needed a friend. People gave her small amounts of money, which she sent along to the missions.

Then one night came a vision, one that gave her an even broader view of the Church's needs. She began thinking. A penny a week from enough people, she reasoned, could help mission efforts all over the world — and thus was born the Society for the Propagation of the Faith. Today, more than one hundred seventy-five years after her initial efforts, the Society is busier than ever — not only feeding the hungry and giving drink to the thirsty but also clothing countless souls with the garment of their new faith.

Selection from *Difficult Star: The Life of Pauline Jaricot*, by
Katherine Burton, Longmans, Green and Co., 1947.

One evening after dinner, when the Perrins were their guests, her father suggested they all play cards, but Pauline, pleading a cold, said she would prefer to stay by the fire and warm herself for a while. She sat there, half listening to their talk of trumps and tricks, half thinking of problems of her own, especially that of help for the missions. Finally she stopped listening and thinking to concentrate on a prayer to God that he give her some plan for a work so needed in the world.

Suddenly into her mind came a plan, clear and complete. She reached quickly to the card table for a score sheet and wrote down the whole scheme before she could forget it.

When she reread what she had written, it was so simple that she wondered why no one had thought of it before. The groups needed to develop it were already at hand, she thought, and only an overall organization would be necessary. Every one of those who had so far aided her would be asked to find ten new associates and each of them would give a sou a week for the missions. In charge of these groups of ten would be someone to receive the collections. There would then be a chief collector for each group of ten hundred, that is, for a thousand. Among the most capable one could choose leaders to collect the thousands, who would take the sum collected to a common center.

For want of better words to designate the groups she wrote down *tens* for the first group; *hundreds* for the second, and *thousands* for the third. She saw how easy it would be for each person to find in his immediate circle ten persons, including himself, each to give a sou.

Anxious to put the scheme into action as soon as possible, Pauline decided to seek some authority with whom to discuss it. She went first to a priest who sometimes heard her confessions, M. Guichardot at Saint-Polycarpe, and he approved the idea. Later she went to consult the Abbé Würtz, now living outside Lyons, and he was delighted with the plan. He was amazed that Pauline had originated it. "You are not smart enough to have invented that, Pauline," he said. "Not only do I give you my permission, but I earnestly urge you to carry it out."

So Pauline, thinking she had the necessary permission, proceeded to begin the new work.

'We Must Go to the Poor'

A Taunting Challenge Inspired the Lifework of Blessed Frederic Ozanam

It was the kind of question quite likely to come up in a college debate, especially if the discussion happens to swing around to a social problem: "Okay, friend, if you feel that strongly, what are you doing about it?" That's pretty much the way the challenge was put to a young student at the Sorbonne in Paris, Frederic Ozanam (1813-1853), and it hit him smack between the eyes. But in a moment he realized that he knew the answer: "We must go to the poor."

Ozanam, a thoughtful Catholic in an often hostile setting, vigorously defended the faith whenever other students attacked it. He was a passionate advocate of greater generosity toward the sick, the poor, and the hungry. But it wasn't until he was really challenged that he rolled up his sleeves and went to work. With a group of friends he began visiting the poor people of Paris, bringing food, clothing, and words of cheer, dedicating the task to the patronage of St. Vincent de Paul.

The work begun by Frederic and his friends continues today through the St. Vincent de Paul Society, which still distributes food and clothing to the poor, and helps them with a variety of other programs. Here's the story of how it all got started, beginning with Frederic's early student days at the Sorbonne.

Story adapted from *Ten Christians*, by Boniface Hanley,
OFM, Ave Maria Press, 1979.

It was the unhappy lot of Catholics at the university that first drew Frederic into student affairs. Certain Sorbonne faculty members made it a practice to distort and mock Catholic teachings. Catholic students sat silent and helpless during these lectures, fearing these teachers would fail them or expel them if they objected. Young Ozanam, a born leader, appealed to all Sorbonne students' sense of fair play, and mounted petitions demanding the opportunity to reply to the charges against the faith. So effectively did Frederic rally the students' assistance that he could gleefully write home, "Every time a professor raises his voice against our faith, Catholic voices are now raised in protest." The mocking soon stopped.

In another effort to revitalize the Sorbonne's dispirited Catholics, Frederic joined a revered professor, Monsieur Bailly de Surcy, in reviving a defunct Catholic discussion club. This venture was to have an outcome that neither Bailly nor Ozanam, in their wildest imaginings, could foresee. The club, encouraging free discussions, attracted professors, scholars, and students of every religious and nonreligious conviction. But as the club debates grew increasingly volatile, atheists and doubters often bested their Catholic hosts. No matter what arguments Catholics raised, their opponents replied: "True, the Church was once a great force for good in this world. But what, my friends, is it doing now?"

One night during a hot debate, the articulate Frederic marshaled a finely honed argument concerning Christianity's role in civilization. His adversary waited patiently for Ozanam to conclude and then responded: "Let us be frank, Mr. Ozanam; let us also be very particular. What do you do besides talk to prove the faith you claim is in you?"

The question hit hard and hit home. Frederic, long ago, had promised he would dedicate his talents and energies to defending his faith. So far, the only talent he had really used was his mind, tongue, and ability to lead student protests.

The more Frederic pondered the bitter challenge, the more he determined to answer it. He just did not know how. One evening in early spring, 1833, Frederic finally had his answer. He was convinced God's blessing would not be on his writings, speaking, or organizing until he went to he poor with works of love. He had to back up his words with deeds. "We must do what Our Lord Jesus Christ did when preaching the Gospel," he told his friend Le Taillandier; "we must go to the poor." That very night, Frederic and Le Taillandier took their own meager winter wood supply and carried it to a poor family.

Little did the two students realize they were forerunners of a movement that would touch the lives of millions and spread the teachings of Christ far more effectively than any student protest or intellectually stimulating discussion club.

Frederic's heart burst with enthusiasm. Every instinct he possessed told him he had found in the service of the poor the only sure way to fulfill his teenage promise to defend his Catholic faith. His joy was infectious. Five other students joined him and Le Taillandier.

From the very beginning, the little band put their work under the patronage of the great French apostle of charity, St. Vincent de Paul. After all, they were doing the same work Vincent had done nearly two centuries before for their beloved French poor.

The Leper Priest

A Dying Father Damien Found Solace
With Those He Had Buried

"The Leper Priest." "Hero of Molokai." "Father Damien." Not all that long ago, any one of those phrases would have instantly identified Blessed Damien de Veuster (1840-1889) for any Catholic schoolchild in the country. Father Damien was a genuine missionary hero, one whose work among the abandoned lepers on the Hawaiian island of Molokai made him a true legend.

Sadly, his name is not all that widely recognized today, even though his beatification ceremony in 1995 helped to restore it in the public eye. It's a name that should be more widely known, because the heroism in the man was genuine, and every word of the legend happens to be true.

When the Belgian-born priest volunteered to serve the victims of leprosy (known formally as Hansen's disease) on Molokai, conditions were appalling. Damien changed all that. He gave the patients care they had never before received, provided ailing children with a ray of hope by educating them for the first time, and tended to the dying, who had long been ignored. The dead were finally given a touch of dignity by being buried in wooden coffins, built by Father Damien himself. He would have to make two thousand of them before he was through.

One day, instead of beginning his sermon at Mass by saying, "My dear brethren. . . ," he said instead: "We lepers. . . ." Father Damien, as he had feared, had contracted the disease himself. Here is the story of his final days. It was a time of suffering, but also one in which he found incomparable solace in the company of those he had laid to rest.

Selection from *Father Damien: The Man and His Era*, by
Margaret R. Bunson, Our Sunday Visitor, Inc., 1989, 1997.

The activity that saved Damien's mind and soul was a simple and customary one for him. Each night, when the tears came down his scarred cheeks, when he shook because of his sobbing, Damien went out into the Garden of the Dead to keep his beloved corpses company there. He himself had placed almost all of these corpses into their narrow graves, as he had also erected markers to ensure that future generations would remember them in their humanity. With his rosary in hand, he walked among their final resting places and prayed for them, perhaps even asking them to intercede for him as he started on the last lap of the same torturous journey that they had taken.

He spent nights among the graves and yet managed to work the next morning as if he had been given hours of sound rest on a comfortable bed. Leprosy was starting to transform his fleshly shell into a mask of torment. He was becoming one of the disintegrating half-dead creatures he had cared for in his early days in the settlement. No one had abandoned him by the side of the road to perish alone, but he was fast making his way to the same pitiful state.

He started going blind as a result of the infection of his eyes, and his companions were asked to read to him at night. Damien continued to pray his Breviary, or Divine Office, which linked men like Father Damien to other priests and religious throughout the world.

His right hand was now swollen beyond recognition and badly infected, and his face was disfigured horribly. He had acute diarrhea all of the time and was starting to cough excessively as the disease ravaged his lungs more and more. He could no longer lie flat, and he spent time propped upon the floor or walking about with a cane in the Garden of the Dead. When he went about, he had to protect his eyes from direct sunlight. His right arm was in a sling and his left foot was bandaged. The bridge of his nose had collapsed, and his glasses hung clumsily on his rotted ears.

On March 19, 1889, on the Feast of St. Joseph, his patron, Damien fell ill and became bedridden. Some of his companions discovered him on the floor of his bedroom, on a simple pallet, with only a thin blanket, shivering as bouts of fever wracked his body. He had never used a bed in the settlement, because he had not used one in the seminary. His companions, however, insisted upon his accepting a cot in order to facilitate their care for him (people could not crawl around on the floor in order to tend to his needs). He accepted a bed, and one was carried into the room for him. He made a rather odd comment once about the two companions who remained at his side in his room. No one else saw them, and Damien did not elaborate on their appearance and did not identify them. His companions, whom he recognized, kept unseen and silent vigil at his side.

On April 13, a fever rose in Damien again, reportedly rising to

105 degrees Fahrenheit. He had to forgo the pleasure of sitting up in a chair, as everyone around him knew that the end was near. He received Communion one last time, and two days later, early on the morning of April 15, he died. Those around him stated that he simply gave up his life, like a child, with a slight smile on his face. Typical of his fellow lepers, Damien's countenance took on a gentle repose in death, as the ravages of the disease receded. By the time his body had been dressed in a fresh soutane, the cleric's garb, all leprous signs were gone from his face.

Shrine of Healing Waters

St. Bernadette's Example Has Led Millions to Lourdes

No place of healing is as well known as the shrine to Our Lady of the Immaculate Conception at Lourdes, France, where millions of pilgrims from all over the world have come to pray for miraculous cures. Many prayers have been answered; cures have appeared without any reasonable medical explanation — leaving doctors and Church officials alike to conclude that miracles of healing do indeed take place at this blessed shrine.

Lourdes has been a holy site since the Blessed Mother first appeared here in 1858 to St. Bernadette Soubirous (1844-1879), then an unsophisticated and somewhat sickly girl of fourteen whose parents were extremely poor. This account is Bernadette's own, written down by a friend who had heard it from her own lips many times. Bernadette, her sister, and a friend had gone to look for firewood, and the other two had crossed a shallow river near a grotto without waiting for her. As she tried to hurry to join them, she heard an unsettling noise and looked up. What happened next would change her life, and the lives of many others.

Story from *The Sublime Shepherdess: The Life of Saint Bernadette of Lourdes*, by Frances Parkinson Keyes, Julian Messner, Inc., 1940.

I had just begun to take off my first stocking when suddenly I heard a great noise like the sound of a storm. I looked to the right, to the left, under the trees of the river, but nothing moved; I thought I was mistaken. I went on taking off my shoes and stockings; then I heard a fresh noise like the first. I was frightened and stood straight up. I lost all power of speech and thought when, turning my head toward the grotto, I saw at one of the openings of the rock a rosebush, one only, moving as if it were very windy.

Almost at the same time there came out of the interior of the grotto a golden-colored cloud, and soon after a Lady, young and beautiful, exceedingly beautiful, the like of whom I had never seen, came and placed herself at the entrance of the opening above the rosebush. She looked at me immediately, smiled at me, and signed to me to advance, as if she had been my mother. All fear had left me, but I seemed to know no longer where I was. I rubbed my eyes, I shut them, I opened them; but the Lady was still there continuing to smile at me and making me understand that I was not mistaken.

Without thinking of what I was doing, I took my rosary in my hands and went on my knees. The Lady made a sign of approval with her head and she herself took into her hands a rosary that hung on her right arm. When I attempted to begin the rosary and tried to lift my hand to my forehead, my arm remained paralyzed, and it was after the Lady had signed herself that I could do the same. The Lady left me to pray all alone; she passed the beads of her rosary between her fingers but she said nothing; only at the end of each decade did she say the "Gloria" with me.

When the recitation of the rosary was finished, the Lady returned to the interior of the rock and the golden cloud disappeared with her.

As soon as the Lady had disappeared, Jeanne Abadie and my sister returned to the grotto and found me on my knees in the same place where they had left me. They laughed at me, called me imbecile and bigot, and asked me if I would go back with them or not. I had now no difficulty in going into the stream, and I felt the water as warm as the water for washing plates and dishes.

We bound up in three fagots the branches and fragments of wood that my companions had brought; then we climbed the slope of Massabielle and took the forest road. Whilst we were going toward the town I asked Jeanne and Marie if they had noticed anything at the grotto.

"No," they answered. "Why do you ask us?"

"Oh, nothing," I replied indifferently.

However, before we got to the house, I told my sister Marie of the extraordinary things that had happened to me at the grotto, asking her to keep it secret.

Throughout the whole day the image of the Lady remained in my mind. In the evening at the family prayer I was troubled and began to cry.

"What is the matter?" asked my mother.

Marie hastened to answer for me and I was obliged to give the account of the wonder that had come to me that day.

"These are illusions," answered my mother; "you must drive these ideas out of your head and especially not go back again to Massabielle."

We went to bed, but I could not sleep. The face of the Lady, so good and so gracious, returned incessantly to my memory, and it was useless to recall what my mother had said to me; I could not believe that I had been deceived.

The Heroes of Memphis

A Lethal Yellow Fever Outbreak
Made Martyrs of Priests and Nuns

Stories of heroic sacrifice abound in the annals of the Church in the United States, but for the sheer scope of its drama and the martyrs it would call forth, few can match that of the yellow fever outbreak in Memphis, Tennessee, during the 1870s. Never has the Church acquitted itself more heroically; rarely have so many answered a cry for help with such selfless devotion.

Memphis was on the move in 1870, a growing city that seemed on its way to prosperity. But sanitary conditions were deplorable, so much so that travelers described it as the dirtiest city in the country. When lethal disease struck — as it did with a yellow fever outbreak in 1873, followed by another five years later — the results were devastating.

Yellow fever, or yellow jack, got its name from the yellowish color it gave its victims. They became violently ill and suffered from a fever that reached its peak in four or five days. The mortality rate was about fifty percent.

Medical science didn't know it at the time, but the disease was caused by the bites of certain mosquitoes that thrived in swampy areas — just the type found close to the city. The swamps, the mosquitoes, and the unhealthy state of municipal sanitation combined to turn the epidemic into a deadly plague.

What Memphians did know was that fleeing the city seemed to be a reliable way of avoiding yellow fever, and understandably they did so in great numbers. Not so with the city's priests and nuns, however. Not only did they stand by their posts to help the ill, but they had the volunteer aid of others from around the state. Their Christian concern cost many of them their lives. Here is a moving account of their heroic sacrifice.

Excerpts from *The Catholic Church in Tennessee*, by Thomas
J. Stritch, Catholic Center, 1987.

When word of the 1873 fever got around, the City of Memphis dropped from a population of forty thousand to one of only fifteen thousand in a month, a nigh-incredible exodus. Of these fifteen thousand, five thousand caught the fever. Two thousand of them died, at least half of them Irish Catholics.

The Catholic clergy and the Sisters who ran the schools and the orphanage remained at their posts, nursing the fever victims, bringing them the last rites of the Church, dispensing the help that the departed Memphians, as well as other cities and the United States governmental agencies generously gave, and being the bright light of witness to the Gospel that all Christians are supposed to be. Not only that, but priests from other parts of the diocese came to take the places of the fallen ones, and many more volunteered. And considering all this, perhaps the most heroic of all was Bishop Feehan, who could have ordered most of the priests elsewhere, and besought the Sisters to return to their motherhouses. From his correspondence it is clear that he tried to encourage the religious not to volunteer recklessly, but that he applauded and assisted those whose duty kept them at their posts. It must have been a difficult decision, as it was a heartrending task, to orchestrate a tragedy so hopeless and so desolate.

Never did an event call forth the best in the priesthood as these dreadful plagues. No less heroic were the Sisters. It is impossible to estimate how many Sisters in all there were in Memphis during the 1870s; but fifty are said to have died of the plague. Twenty-one priests died, a well-nigh incredible number, considering there were only twenty-five in all in 1880. The priests newly incardinated into the diocese in the 1870s just about equaled those who died of the fever.

After the plague of 1873 many Memphians who had fled it seeped back into the city. But many did not, and the place was never the same. All the indices of growth and prosperity fell, and the bright promise Memphis had given in 1869 and 1870 as a rival to St. Louis and Chicago faded forever. But the ill-fated city had more horrors to suffer. In July of 1878 the yellow jack struck again. Another mad exodus from the city took place. It is estimated that twenty-five thousand left town, by rail, water, on foot, in wagons, any way they could. Another five thousand took refuge in the camps on the high ground east of the city. These camps were set up by various relief organizations.

One of the best known was the Catholic camp named after Father Theobald Mathew, the Irish priest who was the apostle of the temperance movement among the Irish, in the mother country, in Great Britain, and in the United States. This camp was organized by Father William Walsh, who had watched his predecessor at St.

Brigid's Church die of the fever. This fixed his determination to prevent more deaths if he could, and he gathered all he could from his and the other Memphis parishes and established the camp. Not a single life was lost at it during the three months of its life, and many a tale is told of its charity and spirituality.

Memphis had shrunk to a population of nineteen thousand, fourteen thousand of whom were blacks, no longer immune to the yellow fever. Most of the rest were Irish. Their condition was like that of the plague-ridden towns of Europe in the fourteenth century: forlorn, terror-stricken, living with death as one normally does with breath.

"Deaths to date 2250," read a telegram from the excellent Central Relief Committee to its New York supporters on September 20, 1878; "Number now sick about 3,000; average deaths, 60% of the sick. We are feeding some 10,000 persons, sick and destitute . . . 15 volunteer physicians have died, 20 others are sick, and a great many nurses have died." The Central Relief Committee, the Howard Association, and the Catholic Church carried most of the enormous and horrible burden of care. The plague pursued its terrible course till the frost killed the larvae of the mosquitoes in the middle of October, but before it was gone it had killed sixteen more.

Prisoner 16670

St. Maximilian Kolbe Gave His Life
for a Fellow Inmate at Auschwitz

Countless stories of heroism came out of World War II, and many more will probably never be known. Few of those that did emerge from the flames are as moving as that of Father Maximilian Kolbe (1894-1941), who traded his own life for that of a fellow prisoner at Auschwitz — and in time was canonized as a saint by the Church he loved so much.

Father Maximilian, a Conventual Franciscan priest from Lodz, Poland, was distinguished by his devotion to Mary. He established a monthly publication in her honor. The City of Mary Immaculate, a center of Marian devotion that he founded in 1927, was becoming known on an international level only a few years later.

But by then the Nazis were coming to power in Germany, and he turned his journalistic attention to the threats they posed. That led him to be marked for arrest, and the Nazis took him into custody soon after they overran Poland in September 1939. As Prisoner 16670, he was sent to the infamous concentration camp at Auschwitz, where a date with destiny — and sainthood — awaited him. Here is a gripping account of his final tortured days on earth.

Story adapted from *Six Modern Martyrs*, by Mary Craig, The Crossroad Publishing Co., 1985.

One broiling hot day — either the last of July or the first of August 1941 — the wailing camp sirens announced the escape of a prisoner. The sound struck terror into the hearts of all who heard it: with the iniquitous rule of collective responsibility, for every man who escaped, ten of his fellows must die. And this was the most terrible and the most feared way of death: a long, slow starvation, buried alive in specially constructed airless concrete underground bunkers.

That evening the prisoners were summoned as usual to the Appel (the twice-daily roll call that meant hours of standing under a merciless sun or exposed to bitter winds). Lined up in the passage-way between Blocks 14 and 17, the prisoners learned that three men — one of them from Block 14 — had escaped. (One of them was found later, drowned in a latrine.) Everyone knew what that meant, and few could have slept that night.

Early in the morning they stood again on the Appel ground. All day long they stood at attention, without food or drink, each one dreading what might be in store.

At 7:00 P.M. the camp's deputy commandant Karl Fritzsch appeared, accompanied by Gestapo chief Gerhardt Palitzsch. Two archetypal, jack-booted Nazi supermen: Fritzsch had personally supervised the first mass murder of prisoners by means of the Cyclon B gas that had originally been manufactured for the extermination of vermin; while Palitzsch, a torturer of some renown, proudly boasted that he had executed twenty-five hundred prisoners with his own hands.

Slowly, wordlessly, they passed down the lines, their elegant uniforms contrasting starkly with the scarecrow rags of the men. Fritzsch pointed a finger, an SS man pushed a hapless man out of line, and Palitzsch noted the man's number in his book, while another SS man began to form a new line of victims.

Seven . . . eight . . . nine. As the ninth man was selected, he uttered an agonized cry: "My wife, my children, I shall never see them again." His choking sobs pierced the silence, while the scare-crows looked at him unmoved. For them the ordeal was almost over. Nine down, only one to go. They held their breath.

For what happened in the next few minutes we have the sworn testimony of several witnesses, and their accounts are remarkably consistent. Suddenly a small slight figure detached itself from the ranks, walked briskly toward the group of SS men, and stood at attention before Fritzsch. The man removed his regulation cap as he did so. It was number 16670 — a prisoner whose cheeks had an unhealthy flush and who wore round spectacles in wire frames.

Something like animation stirred at last among the men. This was unheard of. That anyone should dare to step out of line during an Appel was unthinkable. Surely the crazy fool would be kicked senseless or shot out of hand by the Gestapo. They watched and waited.

The moment passed. The crazy fool remained alive. Perhaps Fritzsch's sheer astonishment inhibited his usual responses. Prisoner 16670 pointed to the distraught man who had cried out, and asked, very calmly, in correct German, if he might take his place. The prisoners gasped. Perhaps Fritzsch gasped too, for he asked in amazement: "Who are you?" (He did not normally enter into conversation with subhumans.) "A Catholic priest," came the reply, as though that was all that needed to be said.

Incredulously, and indeed incredibly, Fritzsch nodded assent, gestured to the reprieved man, one Franciszek Gajowniczek, to return to his place in the line. Palitzsch replaced one number by another, ordered the condemned men to remove their shoes, and sent them off, to be stripped of their rags and buried alive. Next to the last in line went Raymund Kolbe, Father Maximilian, number 16670. As he was flung naked onto the concrete floor of that grisly cell, did he recall that centuries ago St. Francis had asked one of his friars to lay him naked on the bare earth to die?

In the tense days that followed, the whole camp waited for news and prayed for the doomed men. For almost two weeks they waited, but not with the despair that might have been expected. With a kind of renewed hope. The effect of 16670's self-sacrifice was like a shaft of light in the darkness.

Down below ground, in Block 13, the jailers knew that this time was different. They were accustomed to screams, groans, and curses, but in their place they now heard prayers and hymns. Prisoner 16670, it seemed, had not only taken the place of one victim but was helping the other nine to die as human beings. Feebly but distinctly prisoners in other cells joined in the praying.

As death overtook them one by one, the voices grew feebler and the prayers descended to a whisper. Prisoner 16670 had not once complained or asked for water, but had spent all his energies consoling the others. While they lay "like heaps of rags," he was still to be found, at each inspection, propped against the wall, looking calmly into the faces of his persecutors. "Lower your eyes," commanded the SS. "Do not look at us like that." This man was beyond their comprehension, they were heard to admit; they had never met anyone like him.

Almost two weeks passed. Only four remained alive, and of these only Father Kolbe was conscious. The authorities were becoming impatient: they wanted the bunker for a new batch of victims and they were not disposed to wait. Bringing in the head of the camp hospital, they ordered him to dispatch the prisoners with an injection of carbolic acid. Seated on the floor, still moving his lips in prayer, Father Kolbe held out his left arm for the fatal injection.

A janitor later found him "still seated, propped up against the corner, his head slightly to one side, his eyes wide open and fixed on one point. As if in ecstasy, his face was serene and radiant."

To the prisoners in Auschwitz camp, news of his death came like the announcement of a victory. It had the force of an electric shock, arousing them to take a fresh look at their fate.

Friends tried in vain to save his body from the crematorium

fires. It went up in smoke and his ashes were scattered over the surrounding fields. Years later, when his cause was being introduced in Rome, Karol Wojtyla, bishop of Kraków, the future Pope John Paul II, was asked to send a relic of Father Kolbe to the Vatican. "But I had nothing to give them," he said sadly, "nothing but a grain of Auschwitz soil."

A Frightening Friend

Dorothy Day's Soup Kitchens Provided a Welcome for Every Guest

How many hungry people have been fed over the years in Catholic Worker soup kitchens? The number is surely beyond counting. Feeding the hungry is one of the basic activities of the Catholic Worker movement, founded by Dorothy Day (1897-1980) and continued in her name in centers all over the country.

The movement stands for an unwavering commitment to peace and nonviolence as well as dedication to the poor, and in all these things Dorothy Day was a model unsurpassed in her time. That's one of the reasons she is seriously being considered as a candidate for sainthood.

Many followers think that that is especially fitting in view of the deep connection that Miss Day — herself a convert — felt with the Church. At a 1997 conference at Marquette University in Milwaukee, historian David O'Brien of the College of the Holy Cross, Worcester, Massachusetts, put that aspect of her life in focus. "How Dorothy Day loved the Church, its traditions and odd structures, its rich assortment of persons and personalities, its saints and its martyrs!" he said. "So much so did people like Dorothy love the Church that, like Daniel Berrigan, they could not recognize themselves apart from it."

Again: how many people have been fed in Dorothy Day's soup kitchens? No one will ever know. But here — in her own words, as told to the noted psychiatrist and Pulitzer Prize-winning author Dr. Robert Coles — is the story of one of them.

Excerpt from *Dorothy Day: A Radical Devotion*, by Robert
Coles, Addison-Wesley, 1987.

I remember times when I kept holding on to my rosary beads; when I prayed as hard as I could; when I talked to myself, pleaded with myself, to be more understanding of the people who come to us. There are times when nothing seems to work, though, when the energy and conviction seem to have fled, gone elsewhere. I would find myself in tears, but wouldn't know why the tears were there. "Your eyes are watering," I would hear, and I would say yes, they are. I have a bad cold. I guess I did. I guess I was shivering because the world seemed so bleak for all these poor folks, and I had begun to see things from their point of view. When I caught myself thinking it was a terrible shame that our guests weren't doing as I was — seeing the world through *our* point of view, *my* point of view — I began to realize that I was in real trouble. I'd pick up the Bible and read and read, sometimes spend hours on one page, going over and over a passage. The sin of pride, I keep repeating to myself, is the worst of all sins, and it lurks around every corner.

I was thinking back to some of the really wild and crazy times we all lived through. Oh, we've had some very troubled people here, some men and women who have been — as we say it — "way out in left field." I'm sure you would have had the proper psychiatric names to apply to them, if you would have been there. Some were dangerous. They came armed. They had knives and guns. They had been drinking a lot. They were agitated and noisy, so noisy, they quieted everyone else down. In a strange way, they could be a relief. They made all the others so frightened, so *respectful*, that they stopped *their* noise, the everyday loud talking that made such a commotion for our ears.

I was recalling the time when a very drunk sailor, who was a notoriously angry man, came to us, and he told all the people in the room to shut up, and he told a few men if they didn't get out of the room, he'd kill them. I was serving soup and bread, and I went to him and told him he was a great friend to us that day, and we were grateful, *very* grateful. He looked at me. I'll never forget those blue eyes of his; they were moving away from me, then closing in on me; they were dancing all over, then they were so still and penetrating I was more afraid of them than any knife or gun he may have had. His hair was long, for those days, and he would move his right hand through the thick, curly hair and then he'd wipe the hand on his trousers, as if he'd touched something dirty. Mind you, his trousers were fairly dirty themselves. He saw me following that hand, looking at his trousers, and he bellowed, "What are you looking at?" There were some swear words in the question. I knew our only hope was to be as quick and decisive and as honest with him as I could possibly be. I said, "At you." He shouted back, "Why are you looking at me?" I answered, "Because I'm standing here talking with you." He shouted back, "Well, who are you?" I gave him my name and asked him who he was. He told me — his first name, at least, Fred. I offered my hand to him, and he offered his, but before he let us shake, he asked me if I was worried that he was dirty. I said no, and besides, I hadn't washed my own hands, and there was all sorts of crud on them, from the kitchen, and would he excuse me, and he said yes, and then we shook.

Then I took the initiative. I thanked him. I said he had just been a lifesaver. He gave me a strange look. He lowered his eyes, stared at the floor, and talked to me without looking at me. He said he *didn't* want to be called a lifesaver, I must not call him that. He was growling, and I was more frightened then than I had been earlier, when he was shouting, and the whole room was terrified. I decided *not* to explain my use of the word, the phrase. This was no time for a lecture on colloquial English. I asked him if I could give him some soup. He asked me what was in it. I told him lots of good vegetables. He asked me if I would have some. I said I was hungry, and I sure would. So we sat down, and he wouldn't start until I did. He watched me swallow a few tablespoons, and then he was about to start his, when all of a sudden he changed his mind and asked me if he could have *my* soup. I said sure, and he gobbled it up!

Meanwhile, I had a flash of an intuition, because I saw him staring at his soup! I asked him if I could have that soup. He said yes, that he *wanted* me to have it, as a matter of fact. He was growling again. I took the bowl and slurped it up, hungrily. I *was* hungry. He sat there watching me, as intently as I had ever been watched. The whole room was silent — the strangest silence I think we had ever had in any Catholic Worker soup kitchen. As I was finishing the bowl I began to realize what was going on in his head. I put the bowl down. His eyes moved from me to the bowl. I asked him if there was anything else he wanted. He didn't answer me. I told him I was very happy to meet him, and then I turned to another man, sitting nearby, and asked him how he was doing. Before he could answer, the big man I had just been talking to had come nearer to me, and it must have seemed to some people in the room that he was going to attack me, to hurt me.

He was growling a bit, making noises like a dog does. I looked at him, and he stared at me. I remember what took place as clearly as if it happened yesterday. I could only think of one thing — what I had learned long ago, reading the Bible, years before I became a Catholic, the King James Version: "Be not overcome of evil, but overcome evil with good." They are the last words of the twelfth chapter of Paul's letter to the Romans. That chapter is one of my favorites. I read it at least once every few days, sometimes over and over again. I spoke those words to myself — "Be not overcome of evil, but overcome evil with good" — and I smiled at that man. He didn't smile back. I picked up a piece of bread, broke it in half, took part of one half in my mouth, and offered him the other half — and he took it. He said thank you, and I said (trying to appear as relaxed and casual as possible), "Oh, do come here, anytime; we'd love to have you as our guest." Then I excused myself. I said I had to go get us some vegetables for tomorrow's soup. He sat down and finished his bread. As I left, I could hear the room getting noisier and noisier, and I'll tell you, I was never happier to hear all that rattle, all that racket in that dining room of ours. Do you know what? The next day that man came early in the morning with bags full of celery and carrots and onions and potatoes. I asked him, please, to come and have lunch, taste the soup with his vegetables in it, and he said he would. He became one of our regulars.

'If I Could Go to the Grotto Now...'

A Dying Dr. Tom Dooley Thinks Back to His Days at Notre Dame

The revisionists have been having a field day with Dr. Tom Dooley (1927-1961), the legendary American "jungle doctor" of Southeast Asia in the 1950s. He was a shameless self-promoter, his critics now conclude; his personal life was full of sexual secrets and he worked as a shill for the CIA.

These are serious complaints, and perhaps time will tell how seriously they deserve to be taken. It is worth remembering, though, that the record shows an extraordinary list of accomplishments for Tom Dooley — not the least of which is the awareness he developed for a forsaken corner of the world. Even the critics concede that his work for the sick in Laos and South Vietnam was selfless in nature, that his humanitarian efforts were genuine, and that there was never a hint of self-aggrandizement — except, perhaps, in the celebrity it brought — in what became his worldwide fame.

There were Americans with him in Vientiane who were critical of his ego, zeal, and flair for personal publicity. A new arrival, who came to be Dooley's friend, did not say the criticisms were invalid. But he also wrote: "Most people did not make the effort, as I did, to look behind the Dooley façade. . . . He was a remarkable human being, full of deep love and pity for the suffering people of the world."

Dooley was a Notre Dame man, and he loved his school with a passion. Stricken at an early age with the cancer that would kill him, he wrote this deathbed letter to Father Theodore M. Hesburgh, CSC, then the university's president, in December of 1960. It is reproduced on an engraved plaque, still there for students and visitors to see, near the Grotto he loved so much.

Selection from *Promises to Keep: The Life of Doctor Thomas A. Dooley*, by Agnes W. Dooley, Farrar, Straus and Cudahy, Inc., 1962.

Hong Kong
December 2, 1960

Dear Father Hesburgh:

They've got me down. Flat on the back, with plaster, sandbags, and hot-water bottles. I've contrived a way of pumping the bed up a bit so that, with a long reach, I can get to my typewriter, my mind, my brain, my fingers.

Two things prompt this note to you, Father. The first is that whenever my cancer acts up a bit, and it is certainly "acting up" now, I turn inward a bit. Less do I think of my hospitals around the world, or of ninety-four doctors, fund-raisers, and the like. More do I think of one Divine Doctor and my personal fund of grace. Is it enough?

It has become pretty definite that the cancer has spread to the lumbar vertebra, accounting for all the back problems over the last two months. I have monstrous phantoms, all men do. But I try to exorcise them with all the fury of the Middle Ages. And inside and outside the wind blows.

But when the time comes, like now, then the storm around me does not matter. The winds within me do not matter. Nothing human or earthly can touch me. A milder storm of peace gathers in my heart. What seems unpossessable, I can possess. What seems unfathomable, I fathom. What is unutterable, I can utter. Because I can pray. I can communicate. How do people endure anything on earth if they cannot have God?

I realize the external symbols that surround one when he prays are not important. The stark wooden cross on an altar of boxes in Haiphong with a tortured priest, the magnificence of the Sacred Heart Bernini altar at Notre Dame — they are essentially the same. Both are symbols. It is the something else there that counts.

But just now, and just so many times, how I long for the Grotto. Away from the Grotto, Dooley just prays. But at the Grotto, especially now when there must be snow everywhere and the lake is ice glass, and that triangular fountain on the left is frozen solid, and all the priests are bundled in their too-large, too-long old black coats and the students wear snow boots. . . . If I could go to the Grotto now, then I think I could sing inside. I could be full of faith and poetry and loveliness and know more beauty, tenderness, and compassion. This is soggy sentimentalism, I know. (Old prayers from a hospital bed are just as pleasing to God as more youthful prayers from a Grotto on the lid of night.)

But like telling a mother in labor, "It's okay, millions have endured the labor pains and survived happy, you will too," it's consoling, but doesn't lessen the pain. Accordingly, knowing that prayers from here are just as good as from the Grotto doesn't lessen my gnawing, yearning passion to be there.

I don't mean to ramble. Yes, I do.

The second reason I write to you just now is that I have in front of me the Notre Dame *Alumnus* of September 1960. And herein is a story. This is a Chinese hospital run by a Chinese division of the Sisters of Charity (I think). Though my doctors are British, the hospital is as Chinese as shark's-fin soup. Each orderly, companion, nurse, and nun knows of my work in Asia, and each has taken it upon himself to "give" personally to the man they feel has given to their Asia. As a consequence, I'm a bit smothered in tender, loving care.

With a triumphant smile this morning, one of the nuns brought me some American magazines (which are limp with age and which I must hold horizontal above my head to read) — an old *National Geographic*, two older copies of *Time*, and that unfortunate edition of *Life*, and with these, a copy of the Notre Dame *Alumnus*. How did it ever get here?

So, Father Hesburgh, Notre Dame is twice on my mind, and always in my heart. That Grotto is the rock to which my life is anchored. Do the students ever appreciate what they have, while they have it? I know I never did. Spent most of my time being angry at the clergy at school: 10:00 P.M. bed check, absurd for a nineteen-year-old veteran, etc., etc., etc.

Won't take any more of your time, did just want to communicate for a moment, and again offer my thanks to my beloved Notre Dame. Though I lack a certain buoyancy in my bones just now, I lack none in my spirit. I must return to the states soon, and I hope to sneak into that Grotto — before the snow has melted.

Tom Dooley

On History's Stage

Mother Teresa's Worldwide Mission Began on a Train Ride in India

When she died in 1997, the whole world mourned. That was because the whole world had come to admire and love Mother Teresa of Calcutta (1910-1997), celebrated as one of the century's greatest figures for her work with the poorest of the poor.

Oh, there were a few exceptions here and there, people who complained she did nothing to attack the root causes of poverty. But while critics carped, Mother Teresa continued doing just what she had been doing all along: caring for those who found care nowhere else, soothing the pain of those who were destitute and dying, burying those who had breathed their last. To all of these — because in each she saw the face of Jesus — she gave that most precious of commodities: human dignity. If that wasn't enough for her handful of critics, it was more than enough for the world at large — which gave her its love in return.

The first of the brief vignettes that follow describes how her decision to serve the poor came about — a magical moment in which she heard the voice of God calling her to, of all places, the slums of Calcutta. From that day, going back more than 50 years, her Missionaries of Charity have grown to more than 4,000 (representing 79 nationalities) serving in 199 countries around the world. And they still serve the poorest of the poor.

Stories 1 and 3 excerpted from *Ten Christians*, by Boniface Hanley, OFM, Ave Maria Press, 1979; stories 2, 5, 7, and 8 excerpted from *Love Without Boundaries: Mother Teresa of Calcutta*, by Georges Goreé and Jean Barbier, translated by Paula Speakman. Veritas Publications, 1974, and Our Sunday Visitor, Inc., 1980; stories 4 and 6 excerpted from *A Simple Path*, by Mother Teresa, compiled by Lucinda Vardey, Ballantine Books, 1995.

1. A Call From the Spirit of God

Sister Teresa's young pupils at St. Mary's High School in Calcutta were aware of the problem of poverty and discussed it with her. She was very happy teaching, but God was to lead her from the classroom and the great vocation of teaching to another classroom as wide as the world and crammed with pupils who hungered and thirsted from a different type of need. It all happened when Sister Teresa was on her way to her annual retreat in 1946.

"The Spirit of God," Scripture tells us, "breathes where he wills." The Spirit of God touched the heart of this Sister as she sat on a little train that was huffing and puffing its way up to the tea country of Darjeeling. Sister was looking forward to the peace and rest of the annual retreat. While she sat watching the countryside roll by the train window, as she said later, "I heard the call to give up all and follow him into the slums to serve among the poorest of the poor." It is impossible to describe the movement of God within the human heart. The only term we can use, and the only term Sister Teresa could use, was the word "called." But it was a call as old as that of Abraham to leave his father's house. She was asked to leave her own religious community and enter the strange and frightening world of India's poor.

2. The First Candidate

All she needed now were candidates. Along came one of her former pupils, a pretty Bengali girl from a good family. Her name was Shubashini; she had a brown complexion, white teeth, and wore a magnificent sari. "I want to become one of your Sisters," she said.

"You are going to have to renounce everything, even yourself," said Teresa. "Your life will have to be one long self-denial. Think it over!" "I have thought about it," replied Shubashini. Teresa looked at her carefully. The qualities she was looking for in her future missionaries were in the first place health of mind and body, the ability to learn, common sense, and above all a natural gaiety and unfailing good humor. Shubashini had all of these. "Come and see me again on St. Joseph's Day."

The young girl came back on the appointed day. She took off her beautiful sari and put on the coarse garment, and took the name of Agnes, which had been Teresa's before she entered the convent. Other young girls joined Sister Agnes. Soon there were twelve of them, and so a new congregation came into existence.

3. A Home for the Dying

One day, while on the streets of Calcutta, Mother Teresa saw a dying lady who had been half eaten by rats and ants. She picked her up and brought her to a hospital, but the hospital could not do anything for the lady. Undaunted, Mother Teresa took the poor woman to the city hall and asked the authorities to give her a place where she could bring these dying people who filled the streets.

The city health officer asked if she would accept an empty temple where, in former times, Hindus would worship Kali, the goddess of death, usually done in preparation for burying their own dead. She said, "I was very happy to have that place for many reasons, but especially knowing that it was the center of worship and devotion of the Hindus."

Within twenty-four hours she had patients in there, and she started the work of the home for the sick and destitute dying. Since that day the Sisters have picked up thousands of people from the streets, many of whom have lived as the result of their care.

4. The Simple Path

An Indian admirer of Mother Teresa, a businessman, once had five lines printed for her on small yellow cards. These she calls her "business cards" and she offers them freely to people because they clearly explain the direction of her work, her simple path. It is composed of six essential steps: silence, prayer, faith, love, service, and peace. Familiarity with one will naturally lead on to another. If one surrenders to the nature of the process, life will inevitably run more smoothly, more joyfully, and more peacefully:

The fruit of silence is *prayer*. The fruit of prayer is *faith*. The fruit of faith is *love*. The fruit of love is *service*. The fruit of service is *peace*.

5. A Timely Call

Sister Francis-Xavier telephoned Mother Teresa from Agra: she was urgently looking for fifty thousand rupees to start a children's home. "Impossible," Mother Teresa answered. "Where do you think we would find that much money?"

A few minutes later the telephone rang. It was the editor of a newspaper: "Mother Teresa, the Philippine government has just awarded you the Magsaysay prize for all your work. A sum of money comes with it."

"How much?"

"Fifty thousand rupees."

"In that case," said Mother Teresa, "I suppose God wants a children's home started in Agra."

6. 'Come On In, Father'

There are so many stories about the power of prayer and how God always answers us. A priest, Father Bert White, visited us in

Calcutta because he was interested in our work. He came at just the right time:

"I was on my way to see the work of Mother Teresa and the Missionaries of Charity and decided to attend Mass at the motherhouse. Arriving at the front door, I was greeted by a Sister who said to me, 'Thank God you're here, Father; come on in.' I said, 'How do you know I'm a priest?' because I was not wearing my clerical clothes, and she answered, 'The priest who usually says Mass couldn't come so we prayed to God to send us another.' "

7. 'They're Here to Help'

In Amman, Jordan, Mother Teresa founded a community to help the refugee camps after the Six-Day War. Archbishop Pio Laghi, apostolic delegate in Palestine, and Monsignor John G. Nolan of the Pontifical Mission for Palestine crossed the lines from Jerusalem to Amman to welcome her, after the battle had ceased. Monsignor Nolan went with the Sisters to Djebal El Jaufa, the poorest area of the town.

During the crisis between the Jordanians and the Fedayeen, the latter surrounded the Sisters' house, ordering the nuns to line up against the wall, and prepared to shoot them. At that moment a Muslim came into the room and shouted, "Stop! These nuns came to care for our poor people." The Fedayeen left, apologizing.

8. Mother Teresa's Final Blessing

"Finally, I have only one message of peace and that is to love one another as God loves each one of you. Jesus came to give us the good news that God loves us and that he wants us to love one another. And when the time comes to die and go home to God again, we will hear him say, 'Come and possess the kingdom prepared for you, because I was hungry and you gave me to eat, I was naked and you clothed me, I was sick and you visited me. Whatever you did to the least of my brethren, you did it to me.'

"God bless you. Mother Teresa."

Papal Visit

In a Rome Jail Cell, John Paul II
Forgives His Would-be Assassin

Mehmet Ali Agca, the man who tried to assassinate Pope John Paul II (1920-) on May 13, 1981, came terrifyingly close to succeeding. A single bullet from his 9mm Browning Parabellum struck with devastating impact, ripping apart the pope's abdominal organs and narrowly missing his central aorta. When doctors began what would become more than five hours of surgery, they found that the pope had lost three fourths of his blood, and that his blood pressure was so low as to be nearly undetectable.

But just as John Paul had prayed the moment he was hit ("Mary, my mother . . ."), the world prayed that he would survive. And recover he did, the swiftness of it astonishing his physicians. Two things were uppermost in the pope's mind at that point. First was gratitude to God and to the Blessed Virgin for his survival. (He particularly credited Our Lady of Fátima for saving his life, and made a pilgrimage to her shrine in Portugal on the first anniversary of the assassination attempt — also the feast day of Our Lady of Fátima.) And five days after the shooting — his sixty-first birthday — he had a special message for the would-be assassin: "I am praying for the brother who wounded me and whom I sincerely forgive."

Those words caught the attention of people everywhere, surprising many. Is it really possible, they wondered, to forgive someone who has just tried to kill you? The pope would underscore his message three-and-a-half years later. That's when he expressed his forgiveness on a uniquely personal level, paying a dramatic face-to-face visit to Agca in his jail cell. Here is an account of that visit — one the Holy Father hoped would be a model the whole world might follow.

Selection from *Keepers of the Keys*, by Wilton Wynn,
Random House, 1988.

No doubt John Paul's most spectacular exploitation of the mass media was achieved not on a voyage abroad but in Rome itself —

his meeting two days after Christmas, 1984, with the man who had gunned him down three years before, Mehmet Ali Agca. In mid-December the pope decided to pay a Christmas-season visit to Rome's Rebibbia prison, following the example of his predecessors Paul VI and John XXIII (the only previous pontiffs who had visited prisons). Agca was one of the inmates of Rebibbia, where he was serving his life sentence for the near-fatal shooting of the pope. When the Turk heard that the pope would visit the prison, he told the chaplain, "I would like him to come to me, because I am sorry." A meeting was arranged.

The encounter took place in Agca's bare white-walled cell in the maximum-security wing of Rebibbia, a large penal complex on the outskirts of Rome. Four persons entered the cell with the pope — his secretary Monsignor Dziwisz, two security men, and a cameraman of the Vatican television service. These four stood far back near the door while pope and assailant sat on black plastic chairs in a corner of the cell with their heads together. Agca bowed to kiss the pope's hand as they met, and John Paul's first words were, "Do you speak Italian?" Agca does. The conversation was conducted in Italian.

During the meeting, the pope often held one hand to his forehead with eyes tightly closed while Agca spoke to him. At times he grasped the Turk's arm in what looked like a gesture of support. The unshaven Agca laughed now and then, but the smile would fade quickly. Nobody ever revealed the full text of that conversation, but the TV tape picked up faint phrases:

Agca: "First of all, I wish to ask your forgiveness."

Fragments from what the pope said: "Jesus. . . Perhaps one day. . . We remember. . . The Lord give you grace. . . A small gift. . ." (a rosary in silver and mother-of-pearl).

This scene was shown on television screens around the world. Photos ran on front pages of newspapers everywhere, and on the cover of *Time* magazine. Luigi Accattoi, Vatican correspondent of Milan's *Corriere della Sera*, observed: "The decision of the pope to meet Agca was audacious. But even more audacious was his wish to have the meeting photographed and filmed."

John Paul easily could have met Agca privately, with no press or cameramen around. It was his decision to make the meeting a media event, a decision that showed he meant to use this dramatic meeting to communicate to all the world, more effectively than words could, the message he had chosen for 1984, which he had proclaimed a Holy Year. The theme of that Jubilee Year was "Penance and Reconciliation."

Introduction to Section 4:
The Spiritual Works of Mercy

The spiritual works of mercy flow quite naturally from their counterparts, the corporal works of mercy. The distinction is easy enough to remember: the corporal works (feeding the hungry, giving drink to the thirsty, clothing the naked, and so on) deal with the body, while the spiritual works are directed toward the soul. We know that we are obliged as followers of Jesus to assist people who need our help. The spiritual works of mercy remind us to regard their spiritual well-being as attentively as we do their physical needs.

The spiritual works of mercy are seven:
1. Counseling the doubtful.
2. Instructing the ignorant.
3. Admonishing sinners.
4. Comforting the afflicted.
5. Forgiving offenses.
6. Bearing wrongs patiently.
7. Praying for the living and the dead.

At first glance, they lack the dramatic appeal of the corporal works. Most of us are inclined to pitch in, for example, if by "feeding the hungry" or "sheltering the homeless" we're able to ease the plight of others. But "admonishing sinners"? That sounds as if it might be something for someone else. Too, the spiritual works carry something of a passive tone. "Bearing wrongs patiently" somehow lacks the attraction of the active call to give drink to the thirsty, visit the sick, or bury the dead.

Still, the two categories are intertwined. In a real sense, the corporal works are incomplete without the spiritual works — which are not only complementary but which also *fulfill* them. Both are extensions of the Christian love to which all followers of Jesus are called.

That comes from the Gospel itself. Do you remember Jesus' reply when one of the Pharisees asked him which commandment is the greatest? "He said to him, 'You shall love the Lord, your God, with all your heart, with all your soul, and with all your mind. This is the greatest and the first commandment. The second is like it: You shall love your neighbor as yourself. The whole law and the prophets depend on these two commandments' " (Matthew 22:37-40).

The teaching could hardly be clearer, nor could its significance: *The whole law and the prophets depend on these two commandments.* Love for our neighbor is bound inseparably to our love for

God. Each of us is obliged to demonstrate that love, and we do so most obviously by helping our neighbor when the need arises. Jesus gave us the model for this in Luke's Gospel, when he read aloud from Isaiah (61:1-2) in the synagogue at Nazareth:

"He unrolled the scroll and found the passage where it was written: 'The Spirit of the Lord is upon me, because he has anointed me to bring glad tidings to the poor. He has sent me to proclaim liberty to captives and recovery of sight to the blind, to let the oppressed go free, and to proclaim a year acceptable to the Lord.' Rolling up the scroll, he handed it back to the attendant and sat down, and the eyes of all in the synagogue looked intently at him. He said to them, 'Today this scripture passage is fulfilled in your hearing' " (Luke 4:17-21).

In applying Isaiah's prophecy to himself, Jesus was spelling out his mission — helping the poor, the captive, the oppressed, the forgotten, all of those troubled in any way. Today we are called to carry on that mission in *his* name as members of *his* Church, extending *his* love to the world. What kind of love is it? More than a simple feeling of affection, even more than the material gifts represented in the corporal works of mercy, vitally important though they are.

And here is where the spiritual works come in. This is the next level. God calls us to love our neighbors by being present to them, giving away to others what is truly good in our own lives — our faith. We are to do so generously, not out of self-interest but in the spirit of unselfish love that will ultimately bring us perfect fulfillment in the Lord. That's the kind of love you'll find in the stories that follow.

Counseling the Doubtful. From its beginnings, the Church has produced extraordinary counselors whose words or example were able to sway the doubters of their day. Stories of a few of them appear here — all the way back to St. Dominic, who discovered the secret of bringing heretics back into the fold, up to the contemporary ministry of Archbishop Fulton J. Sheen.

The story of St. Dominic shows clearly that it was his eloquent preaching that figured so prominently in his success with the Albigensians, that strange and sacrificial cult. And when it came to eloquent preaching, few if any contemporaries were able to match the skills of Archbishop Sheen. Reaching millions through his top-rated television program or dealing with potential converts on a one-to-one basis, he proved to be one of the most influential counselors of our time.

Instructing the Ignorant. What an array of teachers the Church has given the world! Again, the tradition goes back to the roots of Christianity — when in spreading the faith the earliest missioners instructed those who were ignorant of God — and continues to this day, with so many people still searching for the truth that Christ's Church can provide.

There are teachers of great renown here, such as St. Thomas Aquinas. Most of us probably remember St. Elizabeth Ann Seton as a teacher first and foremost, but she was also a widow and a mother — and had some serious domestic problems on her mind.

Then, too, there's St. Lucy Filippini, a whirlwind of an educator in eighteenth-century Italy who was light-years ahead of her time. She defied prevailing tradition not only by daring to provide an education for women, of all things, but by taking in prostitutes off the streets so they could be trained to make a living respectably. In the process, one would hope, she erased the ignorance of some of her critics as well as that of her students in class.

Admonishing Sinners. The stories of the saints demonstrate that there's more than one way to set a sinner on the right path. St. Simeon Stylites did it with stern warnings and calls to repentance, issued from his curious tower high atop a desert plain. St. Raymond of Peñafort was able to accomplish it — at least as far as one sinful king was concerned — with a dazzling miracle at sea.

It fell to Pope St. Gregory VII, however, to admonish one sinner of note — namely, Emperor Henry IV — in a way that eventually would add a new phrase to the language. The pope made the excommunicated emperor wait for three days in the snow at Canossa before relenting and granting him pardon. "Going to Canossa" became another way of saying "submitting to Church authority." New phrase or not, however, this was one story that had no happy ending.

Comforting the Afflicted. "To comfort the afflicted and afflict the comfortable." That's an old way of summing up one of the primary duties of religious people. It still applies, just as it did years ago, because it still makes sense. The self-satisfied, the comfortable, do indeed need a jolt of reality every now and then. Afflicting them with a reminder of their Christian duties is scarcely harsh punishment; it's a service to their spiritual well-being.

Comforting the afflicted, now — that's even more a work of mercy. And there's no end to the afflictions around us that need attention.

One of the most remarkable stories in that regard is that of Father Titus Brandsma, a Dutch Carmelite who was taken prisoner by the Nazis during World War II. He not only proved to be a tower of strength to his fellow prisoners, comforting them as they endured torture and the constant possibility of death. In addition to that, he tried to instill some sense of right and wrong in their German captors, who were suffering — for whatever reason — from the affliction of moral blindness.

Father Brandsma's prison companions were terrified of what this might mean — an extra beating, perhaps, or ridicule at the very least. The Dutch priest persisted.

"Who knows?" he told them. "Perhaps something will stick."

Forgiving Offenses. Here is a spiritual work of mercy that any of us can perform, at least once every day — and, probably, then some. For offenses crop up all the time, from the simplest traffic indignity — what about that guy who cut in front of us at the toll booth? — to serious libels that damage reputations. It is a hard teaching, but our faith tells us that such insults must be pardoned.

If the teaching seems *too* hard, consider the stories of some of the Christians reported here. St. Paul Miki, for example, who imitated Jesus by pardoning his executors as he died — on a cross. Or, in our own day, a New York City policeman named Steven McDonald, paralyzed for life by a teenager's bullet. Not only did McDonald personally forgive the young man, but he goes out to schools and youth groups to preach the message of reconciliation.

Then there is the late Cardinal Joseph Bernardin of Chicago, whose reputation was smeared by a false accusation of sexual misconduct. The cardinal pressed for a meeting with his accuser, heard his confession, and granted him absolution — not long before he himself would go to his eternal reward. How could the Lord not have been pleased with this selfless act of sacrifice and love?

Bearing Wrongs Patiently. Again, modern living offers endless examples of wrongs that must be borne. Patiently. The job promotion that never came. The big part in the school play that went to someone else's child. Dreams unrealized and hopes still unfulfilled, in spite of all the best efforts and plans and prayers.

The "wrongs" are simply part of life. It's the way people deal with them that helps to measure their commitment to the teaching of Jesus.

St. Monica despaired of her son Augustine, who ignored the example she set and squandered his obvious talents. She bore this wrong for years — with prayers and tears, to be sure, but also with patience. She was no longer alive when, in later years, he became one of the greatest spiritual teachers the Church would ever produce. But she did live long enough to see the future St. Augustine embrace the faith, and for Monica that was enough. The eulogy he delivered for his mother testifies eloquently to the depth of his conversion.

St. Gerard Majella answered a false accusation with silence and prayer until the accuser's confession finally cleared him. Prayer was the answer, too, for Maryknoll Bishop James E. Walsh, jailed by the Chinese communists for twelve years. The rosary, prayed almost constantly, became his daily companion, and somehow he held on to his gentle humor as well. "To say the rosary one needs nothing at all but time," he said, reflecting on his experience after his release, "and now you have plenty of that. . . ."

Praying for the Living and the Dead. Almost from the time they learn their earliest prayers Catholics are taught to pray for others, both living and dead. It should be no surprise, then, that many holy people are remembered for their prayers for others.

There was St. Catherine of Ricci, for example, whose personal holiness enabled her to assume the suffering of a soul in purgatory. Among our near-contemporaries revered for the power of their prayers are two twentieth-century Capuchin priests, both of whom are candidates for sainthood. One was an American — Father Solanus Casey. His superiors entrusted him with only limited priestly faculties when he was ordained, so concerned were they about his fitness to preach and hear confessions. So they gave him a humble assignment: opening the door and answering the phone. In that role he would affect the lives of thousands with his warmth, his words, and his prayers.

In Italy, Padre Pio astounded the crowds who came to see him with his mystic otherworldliness and the stigmata — the signs of Christ's wounds — that he bore. His prayers for others were legendary, said to work wonders. And what an extraordinary wonder is the one reported here: the tale of a tortured soul who came back from purgatory, seeking the release he knew he would find in Padre Pio's prayers.

Beyond the Legend

In Converting the Irish, St. Patrick
Left an Enduring Legacy for the World

Anyone writing about the life of St. Patrick (c. 389-461) has to leave a good bit of it to chance. The date of his birth is uncertain, that of his death only slightly less so. He could have been born in Wales — or perhaps Scotland, or Britain. In youth he was definitely taken captive and held in slavery in Ireland; when he escaped he ended up — probably — in France. We're not sure when, or exactly how, he became a bishop.

The legends about him have taken on lives of their own, but they, too, have question marks attached. For example: driving the snakes out of Ireland while he was fasting on Croagh Patrick? Probably not. Did he use the three-leafed shamrock to explain the doctrine of the Trinity? Maybe. And maybe not.

What Patrick did do, beyond a doubt, was to bring the faith to a people living in pagan ignorance — to bring it to them in a way they could, and did, make all their own. It endured to a degree that it would in few other places. Patrick was nothing less than one of the greatest missionaries of all time. His stamp remains today on all things Irish, especially its people — no matter how far they may have strayed from their native land. Patrick's presence, then, is with us today, all over the world.

Here are two traditional stories, the first about Patrick's run-in with the high king at Tara, and the fire he lit — the one that wouldn't go out — on the Hill of Slane. An anonymous poem, from the Gaelic, celebrates the event. The second tale tells how the saint ended his fast on Croagh Patrick, which had lasted for forty days and forty nights, by bargaining with an angel.

The great prayer attributed to him — the Breastplate of St. Patrick — may not really bear his personal touch. Its language and style seem to be those of the seventh or eighth century, rather than of his own time. But as Thomas Cahill writes in his extraordinary book, How the Irish Saved Civilization *(Nan A. Talese/ Doubleday, 1995): "If Patrick did not write it (at least in its current form), it surely takes its inspiration from him. For in this cosmic incantation, the inarticulate outcast who wept for slaves, aided common men in difficulty, and loved sunrise and sea, at last finds his voice."*

The Breastplate of St. Patrick, a traditional lyric prayer, often appears in shortened form. Here it is published in full, representing the saint's utter confidence in God's presence and protection all about him.

Items 1, 2, and 3 are from *Patrick: Sixteen Centuries With Ireland's Patron Saint*, compiled and edited by Alice-Boyd Proudfoot, MacMillan Publishing Co., Inc., 1990. "The Lighting of the Fire" is originally from *The Improbable Irish*, by Walter Bryan, Ace Books, 1969; "The Rune of Saint Patrick" is an anonymous poem from the Gaelic; "Climbing Croagh Patrick" is from *In Search of Ireland*, Methuen & Co., Ltd., 1930. Item 4, "The Breastplate of St. Patrick," is reprinted from traditional sources.

1. The Lighting of the Fire

Patrick made straight for the citadel of Tara and arrived at the Hill of Slane, ten miles away, on the evening of Easter Saturday. This was the day of the year on which it was his duty to light the paschal fire. But it was also a pagan festival to celebrate the beginning of summer, this being symbolized by the extinguishing of all fires throughout the country; a ceremonial fire was then lit by the Druids, from which all the other fires were reignited. It was a crime punishable by death to allow any fire until this was done, as Patrick well knew.

Preparations for the Druid ceremony were in full swing when a light was seen on the distant Hill of Slane, rapidly becoming a great glow in the darkening sky. The Druids ran to the king in anger, crying with a strange foreboding, "If that fire be not put out, it will burn forever."

The king and his Druids, in eight chariots, sped to Slane, where a great crowd of people had already gathered. Patrick came through them to meet the king, singing: "Some in chariots and some on horse, but we in the name of the Lord." The words were from the Bible, but the tune was his. The king was impressed by Patrick's courage, the people were charmed by the song, the Druids conceded defeat, and the Church had entered into its estate in Ireland.

2. The Rune of Saint Patrick

Tara today in this fateful hour
I place all Heaven with its power,

and the sun with its brightness,
and the snow with its whiteness,
and fire with all the strength it hath,
and lightning with its rapid wrath,
and the winds with their swiftness along their path,
and the sea with its deepness,
and the rocks with their steepness,
and the earth with its starkness:
all these I place,
by God's almighty help and grace,
between myself and the powers of darkness.

3. Climbing Croagh Patrick (Patrick's Hill)

When Lent came in the year A.D. 441 St. Patrick retired to a great mountain in Connaught to commune with God. He fasted there for forty days and forty nights, weeping, so it is said, until his chasuble was wet with tears.

The medieval monks possessed detailed accounts of St. Patrick's fast. They said that to the angel, who returned to him every night with promises from God, the saint said:

"Is there aught else that will be granted to me?"

"Is there aught else thou wouldst demand?" asked the angel.

"There is," replied St. Patrick, "that the Saxons shall not abide in Ireland by consent or perforce so long as I abide in heaven."

"Now get thee gone," commanded the angel.

"I will not get me gone," said St. Patrick, "since I have been tormented until I am blessed."

"Is there aught else thou wouldst demand?" asked the angel once more.

St. Patrick requested that on the Day of Judgment he should be judge over the men of Ireland.

"Assuredly," said the angel, "that is not got from the Lord."

"Unless it is got from Him," replied the determined saint, "departure from this Rick shall not be got from me from today until Doom; and, what is more, I shall leave a guardian there."

The angel returned with a message from heaven:

"The Lord said, 'There hath not come, and there will not come from the Apostles, a man more admirable, were it not for thy hardness. What thou hast prayed for, thou shalt have . . . and there will be a consecration of the men of the folk of Ireland, both living and dead.' "

St. Patrick said:

"A blessing on the bountiful King who hath given; and the Rick shall now be departed therefrom."

As he arose and prepared to descend from the mountain, mighty birds flew about him so that the air was dark and full of the beating of wings. So St. Patrick stood, like Moses on Sinai, and round him all the Saints of Ireland, past, present, and to come.

4. The Breastplate of St. Patrick
I arise today
Through a mighty strength, the invocation of the Trinity,
Through belief in the threeness,
Through confession of the oneness
Of the Creator of Creation.

I arise today
Through the strength of Christ's birth with his baptism,
Through the strength of his crucifixion with his burial,
Through the strength of his resurrection with his ascension,
Through the strength of his descent for the judgment of Doom.

I arise today
Through the strength of the love of Cherubim,
In obedience of angels,
In the service of archangels,
In hope of resurrection to meet with reward,
In prayers of patriarchs,
In predictions of prophets,
In preaching of Apostles,
In faith of confessors,
In innocence of holy virgins,
In deeds of righteous men.

I arise today
Through the strength of heaven:
Light of sun,
Radiance of moon,
Splendor of fire,
Speed of lightning,
Swiftness of wind,
Depth of sea,
Stability of earth,
Firmness of rock.

I arise today
Through God's strength to pilot me,
God's might to uphold me,
God's wisdom to guide me,
God's eye to look before me,

God's ear to hear me,
God's word to speak for me,
God's hand to guard me,
God's way to lie before me,
God's shield to protect me,
God's host to save me
From snares of devils,
From temptations of vices,
From everyone who shall wish me ill,
Afar and anear,
Alone and in multitude.

I summon today all these powers between me and those evils,
Against every cruel merciless power that may oppose my body
    and soul
Against incantations of false prophets,
Against black laws of pagandom,
Against false laws of heretics,
Against craft of idolatry,
Against spells of witches and smiths and wizards,
Against every knowledge that corrupts man's body and soul.

Christ to shield me today
Against poisoning, against burning,
Against drowning, against wounding,
So that there may come to me abundance of reward,
Christ with me, Christ before me, Christ behind me,
Christ in me, Christ beneath me, Christ above me,
Christ on my right, Christ on my left,
Christ when I lie down, Christ when I sit down, Christ when I
    arise,
Christ in the heart of every man who thinks of me,
Christ in the mouth of everyone who speaks of me,
Christ in every eye that sees me,
Christ in every ear that hears me.

I arise today
Through a mighty strength, the invocation of the Trinity,
Through belief in the threeness,
Through confession of the oneness,
Of the Creator of Creation.

Our Sunday Visitor's

Faith and St. Blase

He Prepared for Martyrdom Even as the Sick Were Brought Before Him

We know that St. Blase (d. 316) stood up heroically under persecution, even curing those who were brought to him while he was a prisoner — including the young boy with a fishbone caught in his throat. And somehow, the candles we use in his memory for the blessing of the throats each February 3 are arranged in an X-fashion, after the Cross of St. Andrew.

What are we to make of this? Cardinal John O'Connor of New York suggests an answer in his column, "From My Viewpoint," which appears regularly in Catholic New York. This particular column recalled the tortures of the old-fashioned mustard plaster as a guardian against sore throats, and then considered the intriguing situation of St. Blase:

"It all goes to make up this wondrous faith of ours, which is at least as much mystery as it is knowledge, and more often than not a mix of each. As the Letter to the Hebrews puts it, 'To have faith is to be sure of the things we hope for, to be certain of the things we can not see.' It's the faith to which I will be grateful to my mother and father all the days of my life, the faith that made it possible for me to reconcile mustard plasters with the blessing of throats, the faith that I may not live fully enough, but which I love ever so deeply.

"And on days like the Feast of St. Blase, I'm reminded of the countless numbers who have died for that faith, and I'm glad to be in church on these feast days, to think about them, to hope some of their goodness will rub off on me. Even that is a good reason to get my throat blessed — just to hobnob with St. Blase and be blessed through his intercession. As the blessing itself says, deliverance from every evil is asked, so even if my throat does bother me there are a lot of more important evils I'd be happy to get rid of.

"And whatever else, with the help of Colman's English Mustard my father gave me a very healthy respect for hell. If St. Blase does nothing but remind me of the same, it's worth putting my throat between the candles."

Story adapted from *Mary, Help of Christians and the Fourteen Saints Invoked as Holy Helpers*, by Rev. Bonaventure Hammer, OFM, Benziger Brothers, 1909.

St. Blase, born in Sebaste, Armenia, was a physician whose every act in life was guided by his Christian faith. His virtue was so widely known and deeply admired, by clergy and laypeople alike, that he was elected bishop of his native city. From that day on, he was as devoted to healing souls as he had been to curing bodily ills, and to all he served as a shining example of virtue.

During his years as bishop a cruel persecution of Christians broke out, while Licinius was serving as emperor. The persecutors first went after the bishops, knowing full well that if they bowed before the empire's threats, their flocks would be sure to follow. Listening to the pleas of his people — and bearing in mind the words of Matthew's Gospel, "When they persecute you in one town, flee to another" (Matthew 10:23) — St. Blase hid himself in a cave. Before long, however, the holy bishop was tracked down, and he was brought in shackles to be tried for crimes against the empire.

During his trial Blase remained steadfast in the faith, to such a stirring degree that even some of the attendants were moved. His captors, frustrated by the bishop's refusal to yield to their threats, tied him up and tortured him before throwing him into prison. A long jail sentence, they thought, would wear down his endurance and lead him to make sacrifices to Roman idols. Time would prove that they had the wrong man.

Because his jailer permitted Blase to have visitors in prison, the bishop was able to continue his ministry to the troubled and the sick, consoling those with problems and curing many who were ill. One day a mother brought her young boy to see Blase. The lad had swallowed a fishbone while eating, and it had lodged in his throat — not only causing great pain but threatening to choke him to death. St. Blase prayed and made the sign of the Cross over the boy, who was instantaneously cured. From that day to this, the name of St. Blase has been invoked by those seeking relief or protection from troubles of the throat.

Once his captors saw that they were making no progress with Blase, they brought him again before the court and commanded him to make sacrifices before their pagan idols. But the bishop looked at the judge and said:

"You are blind, because you are not illuminated by the true light. How can a man sacrifice to idols, when he adores the true God alone? I do not fear your threats. Do with me according to your

Our Sunday Visitor's

pleasure; my body is in your power. But God alone has power over my soul. You seek salvation with the idols; I hope and trust to receive it from the only true and living God whom I adore."

The prefect responded by sentencing the prisoner to death. St. Blase was beheaded, becoming a martyr for the faith on February 3, 316.

The Doctor's Dream

How St. Augustine's Friend Gennadius
Resolved His Doubts

An earlier story described the way St. Augustine (354-430) resolved his own doubts about the faith. He then went on to become one of the most influential figures in the history of the Church.

The story here, adapted from a letter written by St. Augustine, describes the experience of a friend — the physician Gennadius — and in the process hints at the scope of the saint's prodigious literary output. In addition to his 218 letters, he wrote 113 books and 500 sermons — in each of them achieving a remarkable clarity of expression and brilliance in thought.

When it came to resolving the doubts of others, Augustine had few equals. In this tale, however, he's content to take a bystander's role — and let the story tell itself.

Story adapted from *Catholic Anecdotes*, by the Brothers of
the Christian Schools; translated from the French by Mrs. J.
Sadlier; D. & J. Sadlier & Co., 1885.

Can our dreams prove the existence of the soul, and its distinctness from our body? St. Augustine himself considered this intriguing question in a letter written to Evodius about their mutual friend Gennadius.

Augustine wrote that Gennadius, who had practiced medicine in Rome and later settled in Carthage, began having doubts about his faith — specifically about the resurrection, and about eternal life. Simply put, he just could not understand how these things could be.

As he was otherwise a good Christian, the letter continued, God was pleased to enlighten him. One night Gennadius dreamed that a young man approached him and said, "Follow me." They set out and soon arrived in a strange city, where they heard music of the most ravishing sweetness. "The music that you're now hearing," Gennadius's guide told him, "is the singing of the inhabitants of the heavenly Jerusalem."

When he woke up, Gennadius paid little attention to the dream, thinking it nothing out of the ordinary. But that night when he had fallen asleep, the same young man appeared to him in another dream.

"Do you know who I am?" asked the visitor.

"Certainly," Gennadius replied. "I saw you in the dream I had last night, and we journeyed together."

"Yes," the guide said. "You spoke, heard, and acted during your sleep, but your body was in bed — motionless, your eyes closed. It wasn't your body, then, that journeyed and heard and saw; it was your *soul* that did all that. And so it will be after your death. Your soul will do all these things."

With that, Gennadius awoke, with a fresh understanding of what he had questioned. And once he understood, he no longer doubted.

A Mother's Tears

St. Monica's Patience Helped Her Bear the Faithlessness of Her Son

It took patience, tears, and prayers to get St. Monica (331-387) through the ordeal of coping with a faithless son. She knew that the youth — who would one day be the incomparable St. Augustine — had unique talents that he was thoughtlessly squandering. At the same time she knew she could never abandon him, and so the prayers — and the tears — continued.

Finally, of course, her patience was rewarded. She lived to see Augustine embrace the faith, and even though his rise to greatness would come after her death, she could not help but be reminded of the prophecy of a bishop to whom she had once confided her worst fears: "It is impossible that the son of so many tears will be lost."

Here, in the eulogy he wrote for her (which appears in his Confessions), Augustine reveals the depth of his love for his mother. He lavishly praises her forbearance — for putting up so patiently with a difficult husband and meddling servants — and her gentle ways ("she showed herself a peacemaker between any differing and discordant souls"). She loved everyone as if she were the mother of all, Augustine said, and served everyone as if she were the child of all.

In the conclusion of the eulogy printed here, Augustine speaks to Our Lord of his final day with his mother — of their consideration of the perfection of God's love and the beauty of eternal life, and of the peace with which she would go to her reward, knowing that she had seen her son "a Catholic Christian" before she died.

Selection from *Confessions*, Augustine of Hippo, Book IX.

She was brought up modestly and soberly, and made subject by You to her parents, rather than by her parents to You. When she had arrived at a marriageable age, she was given to a husband, whom she served as her lord. And she busied herself to win him over to You, preaching You by her actions. By this, You made her beautiful, and reverently lovable, admired by her husband. For she so bore the wronging of her bed as never to have any dissension with her husband on account of it. For she waited for Your mercy upon him, that by believing in You he might become chaste.

Besides this, as he was earnest in friendship, so he was violent in anger. But she had learned that an angry husband should not be resisted, neither in deed, nor even in word. But so soon as he was grown calm and tranquil, and she saw a fitting moment, she would give him a reason for her conduct, should he have been excited without cause.

In short, while many matrons, who had more gentle husbands, carried the marks of beatings on their dishonored faces and would privately blame the lives of their husbands, she would blame their tongues, admonishing them, but with jest, that from the hour they heard the marriage vows read to them, they should think of them as instruments whereby they were made servants; so, keeping in mind their condition, they ought not oppose their lords. They knew what a furious husband she endured, and so they marveled that it had never been reported, nor appeared by any indication, that Patricius had beaten his wife, or that there had been any domestic strife between them, even for a day. When they asked her confidentially why this was so, she taught them her rule, which I have mentioned above. Those who observed it experienced the wisdom of it, and rejoiced; those who did not were kept in subjection, and suffered.

Overcoming Gossip. By submission, persevering with patience and meekness, she also won over her mother-in-law, who was at first prejudiced against her by the gossip of ill-disposed servants. She told her son about the tongues of the meddling servants, and how it had disturbed the domestic peace between herself and her daughter-in-law, and she begged him to punish them for it. He complied with his mother's wish, restoring discipline to his family and ensuring future harmony, by correcting with lashes those she had exposed. She promised a similar reward to any who, in order to please her, should say anything evil to her about her daughter-in-law. Now, none dared to do so, and they lived together with a wonderful sweetness of mutual goodwill.

This great gift You gave — my God, my mercy — to Your good handmaid, from whose womb You created me: that, whenever she could, she showed herself a peacemaker between any differing and discordant souls. She would hear, on both sides, the most bitter things — the sort that arises from growing and unsettled discord, when the crudities of enmity are exhaled in bitter speeches to a present friend against an absent enemy. And then she would disclose nothing about the one to the other, nothing but what might avail to their reconciliation. This would have seemed a small good thing to me, if I did not know (to my sorrow) countless persons, who, through some horrible and far-spreading infection of sin, not only disclose to enemies mutually enraged the things said in passion against each other, but even add some things that were never spoken at all. Whereas, to a generous man, it ought to seem a small thing not to incite or increase the enmities of men by ill-speaking, unless he tries, by kind words, to extinguish them. That is how she was — You, her most intimate Instructor, teaching her in the school of her heart.

Inspiring Conversions. Finally, toward the end of his earthly life, she won over her husband to You. Yet she did not complain to him, as one of the faithful, about the things she had endured before he had found faith.

She was also the servant of Your servants. Whoever knew her would praise and honor and love You in her. By the testimony of her holy conversation, they perceived You in her heart. For she had been the wife of one man, had repaid her parents, had guided her house piously, was well spoken of for good works, had brought up children, laboring in birth for them each time she saw them swerving from You. Lastly, O Lord (since it is by Your permission we speak), she loved all of us, the baptized, who lived together before she rested in You, as if she had been mother of us all, and she served us as if she had been the child of all.

As the day approached on which she was to depart this life (a day You knew, though we did not), it happened — that is, You, by Your secret ways, arranged it — that she and I stood alone, leaning in a certain window, from which we looked upon the garden of the house we occupied at Ostia. There, away from the crowd, we rested for the voyage, after the fatigues of our long journey. We were conversing alone very pleasantly and, "forgetting what lies behind but straining forward to what lies ahead" (Philippians 3:13), we were, in the presence of the truth You are, discussing the nature of the eternal life of the saints, which eye has not seen, nor ear heard, neither has entered into the heart of man. We opened wide the mouth of our heart, after those supernal streams of Your fountain, "the fountain of life," which is "with You" (Psalm 36:10), that being watered by it according to our capacity, we might in some measure consider so high a mystery.

A Glimpse of Glory. Our conversation arrived at this point: that the highest bodily pleasure, in the brightest earthly light, seemed unworthy of comparison to the sweetness of that life. Lifting ourselves with a more ardent affection toward the Selfsame, we gradually passed through all bodily things, and even the heaven itself, whence sun, moon, and stars shine upon the earth. We soared higher still by inward musing, and conversation, admiring Your works;

and we came to our own minds, and went beyond them, that we might go as high as that region of unfailing plenty, where You feed Israel forever with the food of truth, and where life is that Wisdom by whom all these things are made, all that have been and are to come; and she is not made, but is as she has been, and so shall ever be; because to "have been" and "to be in the future" are not in her, but only "to be," since she is eternal; for to "have been" and "to be in the future" are not eternal.

While we were speaking, and straining after her, we slightly touched her with the whole effort of our heart; and we sighed, and there left bound the firstfruits of the Spirit (cf. Romans 8:23). We returned to the noise of our own mouth, where the word spoken has both beginning and end. But what is like Your Word, Our Lord, who remains in himself without becoming old, and who "makes all things new" (Revelation 21:5)? . . .

Lord, You know that, on that day, when we were talking this way, the world with all its delights grew contemptible to us, even while we spoke. Then my mother said, "Son, for myself, I no longer take pleasure in anything in this life. What I want now, and why I am here, I do not know, now that my hopes in this world are satisfied. There was indeed one thing for which I wished to wait in this life, and that was that I might see you a Catholic Christian before I died. My God has exceeded this abundantly, so that I see you despising all earthly happiness, for you have been made his servant. What am I doing here?"

The Height of Perfection

From His Tower, St. Simeon Stylites
Called on Sinners to Repent

St. Simeon Stylites (d. 460) took an unusual route in seeking the path to spiritual perfection: he spent most of his adult life perched atop a pillar, open to the elements, and there he contemplated the mysteries of life, and death, and what lies beyond.

If his calling seems strange to us today, it was no less so in his own time. Crowds pressed around to see this peculiar sight, disturbing Simeon so much that he extended the height of his tower from its original nine feet to about fifty feet. Still, people came from all over the land — in the area of modern-day Syria — not only to see Simeon for themselves but also to hear what this man of God had to say.

He did not disappoint them. He preached to the crowds, calling on sinners to repent — and the wisdom of his words, combined with the singular example of his sacrifice, led many of them to do just that.

Story adapted from *Little Pictorial Lives of the Saints*,
Benziger Brothers, Inc., 1925.

One winter's day, about the year 401, the snow lay thick around Sisan, a little town in Cilicia. A shepherd boy, unable to lead his sheep to the fields that day because of the cold, went instead to church, and there he listened to a sermon on the beatitudes. It was a message that would change his life.

Simeon — for that was the boy's name — asked how the wondrous blessings of the beatitudes might be obtained, and when he was told about the monastic life a thirst for perfection began to form in his soul. In time he would go on to become one of the wonders of the world, the incomparable St. Simeon Stylites.

He was warned that perfection would cost him dearly, and so it did. Entering the monastery while still a boy, he spent a dozen years in superhuman austerity — binding himself with a penitential rope, eating only once a week, eventually going on fasts that lasted as much as forty days.

Then he began his most amazing penance of all — living for thirty-seven years atop pillars in the desert, exposed to heat and cold, spending day and night adoring the majesty of God. Perfection was everything to St. Simeon; the hardships hardly mattered.

The hermits of Egypt were suspicious of this strange new wonder, and sent one of their company to coax Simeon down from his pillar to return to a normal way of life. In a moment the saint made ready to descend, and the Egyptian visitor was impressed with this show of humility. "Stay," he said, "and take courage. Your way of life is from God."

Obedience and humility marked Simeon's life, but so too — despite the rigors he forced on himself — did cheerfulness. The words that God put into his mouth brought crowds of nonbelievers to baptism, and sinners to penance. In the year 460 those who watched him from below noticed that he had been motionless for three full days. Someone climbed up to speak to him, but found the old man dead. His body was still bent in an attitude of prayer, but his soul was surely with God.

The life of St. Simeon Stylites teaches two important lessons: First, all of us must constantly renew within ourselves an intense desire for perfection, and second, we must use with fidelity and courage those means of perfection that God points out.

A Father's Plea

St. Benedict Restores a Peasant's Stricken Son to Life

As the patriarch of Western monasticism, St. Benedict (c. 480-c. 550) was one of the most influential figures in the history of the Church. The rule that he established for the men who lived around him in prayer was adopted for many of the religious communities that would follow, inspiring countless numbers of the faithful down through the centuries.

But that was the St. Benedict of history. In his day-to-day life he was always attentive to the needs of those around him. This tale recounts how, at the urging of a grief-stricken parent, he restored a child to life — recalling the story of Elijah and the widow's son, and her words of gratitude to the prophet for saving the boy's life: "Now indeed I know that you are a man of God" (1 Kings 17:24). Generations to come would say the same of Benedict.

Story adapted from *Little Pictorial Lives of the Saints*,
Benziger Brothers, Inc., 1925.

St. Benedict, noble in lineage and blessed by grace and in name, fled to a deep cave at Subiaco after being scandalized by the wicked behavior of his schoolmates in Rome. He remained there for years. The holy monk Romanus kept him fed and clothed him in the monastic habit, and eventually the word of his sanctity brought other monks to his side, to serve under his leadership. (His rule was too rigorous for some of his companions, one of whom once tried to poison his drink. When Benedict made the sign of the Cross over the tainted drinking cup, it broke and fell in pieces to the ground.)

At Monte Cassino Benedict founded the famous abbey that still stands today, the holy place where he wrote his rule and where he lived out his life. By prayer, he did all things: performed miracles, saw visions, and prophesied.

One day a peasant ran up to him in anguish. His boy had just died, and he pleaded for a miracle. "Give me back my son!" he cried out to Benedict.

"Such miracles are not for us to work, but rather for the blessed

Apostles," the saint replied. "Why do you place a burden upon me that my weakness cannot bear?"

But at length his compassion came to the fore. He went swiftly with the peasant to his home, knelt down, and prostrated himself on the body of the child. He prayed fervently for some time, then arose and called out:

"O Lord, behold not my sins but the faith of this man who mourns his son, and restore to the body that soul that has been taken away."

Hardly had he spoken when the child's body began to tremble. Taking the boy by the hand, he restored him alive to his grateful father.

A Blow for the Church

The 'Sacred Oak' Went Down,
But St. Boniface Was Still Standing

As he worked to bring Christ's message to the people of long-ago Germany, St. Boniface (680-754) labored under a double burden. Not only did he face every missionary's challenge of introducing the word of God to strangers, but he also had to contend with churchmen who were there before him — and who had become too lax and worldly in their ways. Boniface had come to Germany to convert pagan worshipers and to admonish sinners — and found many of the latter in his own midst.

Ultimately St. Boniface, the Apostle of Germany, would prevail. He scored one of his most notable successes by chopping down a tree revered by nature-worshipers as the Sacred Oak of Thor — and, despite the dire predictions of a large crowd gathered for the event, surviving to tell the tale. The people saw that their gods were no match for the Christian faith, and many witnesses were baptized as a result. Boniface's burial site at Fulda Abbey — which he had founded in 743 — is regarded to this day as one of Germany's holiest places.

St. Boniface's love for the Church was steadfast and unyielding. In this excerpt from one of his letters, some might even see a message for the faithful today: "In her voyage across the ocean of this world, the Church is like a great ship being pounded by the waves of life's different stresses. Our duty is not to abandon ship, but to keep her on her course. Let us stand fast in what is right, and prepare our souls for trial. Let us wait upon God's strengthening and say to him: 'O Lord, you have been our refuge in all generations.' "

Story adapted from *Saint Boniface*, by Godfrey Kurth,
translated by Rt. Rev. Victor Day with additions by Rev.
Francis S. Betten, SJ, The Bruce Publishing Co., 1935.

The crowd was spoiling for a good show. People had come from all over the Hessian countryside to this holy hill of Gudensberg, near Geismar, site of the Sacred Oak of Thor. They fully expected their god of thunder to destroy the Christian missionary from Rome, Boniface, who had boldly announced his plan to chop down the towering tree.

The people were outraged. Worshiping sacred trees and fountains was ingrained into the lives of these ancient Germans, and they would have taken matters into their own hands had it not been for one thing: the safe-conduct letter that Boniface held from Charles Martel. The Germans wisely decided not to test the Frankish ruler's patience by punishing Boniface themselves. At any rate, they reasoned, the great god Thor would certainly avenge the unspeakable desecration himself. Restlessly they awaited the next move.

They did not wait long. Boniface, personally given his mission (and a bishop's miter) by Pope Gregory II, struck the first blow with a powerful swing of his ax, and as the crowd gasped, his fellow monks joined him. What happened next left everyone speechless. A rustling sound was heard in the upper branches, and soon it became a whirlwind. Then, with an ear-piercing roar, the giant oak fell to the ground, split into four large parts.

The tree was down — but Boniface stood tall!

Only for a brief time did the crowd remain silent. Soon people began to come forward, dazzled by what they had seen, amazed at the courageous act performed by Boniface. Within moments many expressed a desire to become Christians, and in time belief in the power of the old Teutonic gods — who had so clearly failed to avenge themselves — was broken throughout the old kingdom.

Boniface and his companions put the wood from the sacred oak to good use. They cut it into planks and used them to build a chapel on the spot. They dedicated it to the memory of St. Peter, and for years afterward it stood there as an enduring symbol of the new faith.

The Limits of Power

King Canute Shows His Fawning Courtiers
That Only God Is Almighty

The wise King Canute (c. 995-1035) of this story ruled Denmark and Norway in addition to England. He established peace in the realm, restored the Church to a place of honor, and fostered friendly relations with the Holy Roman Empire, even traveling to Rome in 1027 for the coronation of Conrad II.

Some accounts have it that in the legend cited here Canute was actually attempting to hold back the tide as an indication of his own strength, but this version — in which the king manages to convince his obsequious courtiers that only God is all-powerful — seems much more in character.

Story adapted from *Catechism in Stories*, by Rev. Lawrence
G. Lovasik, SVD, The Bruce Publishing Co., 1956.

Long ago England was ruled by a wise and holy king named Canute. Some of his courtiers constantly flattered him, ever in search of special favors. One day their leader boldly approached him.

"O King," he said, "you are the greatest of all kings. You are even the master of the seas, which obey your voice."

Canute said nothing as he listened to these foolish words, but his head sank lower and lower as a sign of his discomfort. Finally he arose and ordered that his throne be taken to a nearby beach, and placed down on the sands just as the tide was coming in. When that was accomplished, he sat in the throne and called out in a loud voice to the waves as they crashed ever nearer to the shore.

"O waves," he cried, "I command you to go back, and not dare approach your royal master!" But, of course, the waves continued to roll in, and before long they left the king's feet soaking wet. With that he turned to his courtiers and said:

"Foolish men, behold how fragile is the power of a king. Only God can command the sea and say to it, 'Thus far will you go, and no farther!' Learn from what you have seen that God alone is almighty."

Our Sunday Visitor's

Going to Canossa

Henry IV Stood in the Snow for Three Days, Awaiting Forgiveness

Rarely has any sinner been admonished by having to stand in the snow for three days while awaiting forgiveness. Even more rarely did the sinner happen to be an emperor as well.

But that is what happened to Henry IV (1050-1106), who had been excommunicated by Pope St. Gregory VII (c. 1020-1085) and sought readmission to the sacraments. At issue was control over the appointment of bishops, and while the pope weighed his decision a penitent Henry stood outside the papal retreat at Canossa —for three full days, the story goes, and in the snow to boot.

Ultimately Pope Gregory relented and the excommunication was lifted, but there would be no happy ending: the old quarrel resumed, Henry was excommunicated again, and eventually forced the pope to flee from Rome. Pope Gregory died in exile, but his successors finally saw to Henry's abdication some twenty years later.

Not only did the struggle help to settle the issue of investiture, it would also add a phrase to the language. When Bismarck used the words "going to Canossa" centuries later, the meaning was clear: submission to the authority of the Church.

Story from *Great Moments in Catholic History: 100 Memorable Events in Catholic History Told in Picture and Story*, by Rev. Edward Lodge Curran, Grosset & Dunlap, 1937.

There have been two Roman Empires. One was the pagan Roman Empire that persecuted the Church.

The other Roman Empire began with the coronation of the Frankish King Charlemagne by Pope Leo III on Christmas Day in the year 800. The first Roman Empire was a pagan empire. The second Roman Empire was a Christian empire. That is why the second Roman Empire is called the Holy Roman Empire.

Certain emperors insisted that they and they alone should

choose men to be bishops. This led to many abuses, and the quarrel of the emperors with the Church is known in history as the "investiture quarrel." The selection of unworthy men against the wishes of the Church caused many scandals. For this the kings or emperors who selected unworthy men were to blame and not the Church.

In the eleventh century a great pope tried to stop these scandals. Pope Gregory VII (1073-1085) was born in 1020 and became a Benedictine monk. He led a holy life. Because of his learning, four popes kept him in Rome and followed his advice. As a monk he was known as Hildebrand.

One of his first acts upon becoming pope in 1073 was to prevent the Emperor Henry IV from interfering in the selection of bishops. Henry IV refused to obey. Then the pope excommunicated the emperor, but the people and kings of Germany agreed with the pope. They threatened to revolt against their emperor.

Henry IV came to Italy seeking the pope's forgiveness. He found the pope at the castle of Canossa. For three days the emperor stood outside the castle clad in the dress of a penitent. Finally convinced of his sincerity, the pope forgave him.

The repentance of Henry IV, however, was not sincere. He returned to Germany and began to oppose the Church all over again. Advancing on Rome, Henry IV forced Pope Gregory to flee to the Abbey of Monte Cassino. There he died.

His dying words were: "I have loved justice and hated iniquity; therefore I die in exile."

In 1122 the freedom for which Pope St. Gregory VII fought was won. Henceforth the Church was to be free in the selection of her bishops for Germany.

Miracle at Sea

St. Raymond of Peñafort
Changed the Ways of a Sinful King

Even as miracles go, this one was something special. Forbidden by Spain's King James from sailing home to Barcelona from Majorca, St. Raymond of Peñafort (1175-1275) defiantly fashioned a raft of sorts from his own cloak, and, using a staff for a mast and a fold of the cloak for a sail, made it safely home over the open waters. Since the king's sinful deception was the reason for Raymond's flight to begin with, the miracle had a very practical benefit: James, impressed beyond words, changed his ways for good.

Impressive it might be, but the story doesn't begin to hint at the intellectual breadth of this great saint. A trusted adviser to Pope Gregory IX and one-time master general of the Dominicans, he also wrote a manual for confessors that would have a lasting effect on the sacrament of penance. His codification of canon law remained the standard for the entire Church until its revision in 1917. Further, it was his suggestion that led St. Thomas Aquinas to write his Summa Contra Gentiles, *which helped theologians and missionaries in the effort to attract non-Christians to the faith.*

Still, the miracle of the cloak comes quickly to mind when St. Raymond's name is mentioned. That's probably as it should be, because — as noted above — even as a miracle it's something special. And as a story, it's worth reading again and again.

Selection adapted from *A Handbook of Christian Symbols and Stories of the Saints*, by Clara Erskine Clement, Ticknor and Co., 1886 (republished by Gale Research Co., 1971).

St. Raymond, whose family was allied with the royal house of Aragon, entered religious life with the Dominicans at an early age and before long was widely known for his devotion to the Church and his charity toward the poor. He became the spiritual director and confessor of King James of Aragon *(El Conquistador)*, and a miracle in which the king played a prominent role would later figure in his cause for canonization.

The king, it seems, was a gentleman of some accomplishment, but he was determined not to let his confessor interfere with his pleasures. At one point he became deeply involved with a beautiful woman of his court, and the affair continued despite every effort of Raymond to put an end to it.

A trip to Majorca was coming up, and the king ordered the priest to accompany him. Only if that woman stays behind, Raymond replied, and the king pretended to agree to that condition. But in reality — unknown to Raymond — the lady made the voyage too, disguised as a page. Raymond, furious when he discovered the deception, angrily told the king that he was leaving immediately to return to the mainland. King James, irritated by the priest's defiance, not only forbade any vessel from leaving port but threatened to put to death anyone who helped Raymond escape.

The standoff didn't last long. "An earthly king has deprived us of the means of escape," Raymond said, "but a heavenly king will supply them."

Climbing along a rock wall that projected into the sea, he spread his cloak upon the waters. Quickly he set his staff upright to serve as a mast, tying one corner of the cloak to it for a sail. Then, making the sign of the Cross, he boldly embarked on his incredible journey — and wafted over the ocean so rapidly that within six hours he was in Barcelona.

The five hundred people who saw him land were doubly amazed — not only to see this holy priest afloat to begin with but to watch in dumbfounded disbelief as he took up his cloak from the water perfectly dry, wrapped it around him, and with great humility retired to his cell.

King James, overcome by the miracle, repented the sinful ways he had followed, and from that point on governed both his kingdom and his own life in accordance with St. Raymond's advice.

Firsthand Lesson

St. Dominic Saw the Right Way
to Combat the Heresies of His Day

Traveling with his bishop at a time when heretical doctrines were rocking the Church and society at large, St. Dominic (c. 1170-1221) learned a valuable lesson.

The people, it seemed, were being lured by a sect that preached spartan living and an excessively demanding approach to the faith. But on his travels Dominic saw that the Church was attempting to counsel these doubters with preachers conspicuous for their high living and good times — exactly the wrong strategy to follow.

The experience led St. Dominic to gather others about him and preach God's word lovingly and simply, in the Gospel tradition. In time he formally organized the community of the Order of Preachers, known to us all as the Dominicans. The work of counseling the doubtful that St. Dominic began so many years ago still goes on today — still under his own name.

Selections adapted from *Saint of the Day*, Leonard Foley,
OFM, Editor, St. Anthony Messenger Press, 1990.

1. The Way to Spread the Word

If he hadn't taken a trip with his bishop, Dominic would probably have remained within the structure of contemplative life. But the trip changed all that; afterward he remained contemplative in spirit but active in doing the apostolic work of the Lord.

The journey in question, which his bishop invited Dominic to join, took them to Northern Europe, at the time a hotbed of heresy — in particular that of the Albigensians. The Albigensians (Cathari, "the pure") held to two principles — one good, one evil — in the world. All matter, they insisted, is evil; therefore they denied the Incarnation and the sacraments. On the same principle they abstained from procreation and took a minimum of food and drink. The inner circle led what must be called a heroic life of purity.

Dominic sensed the need for the Church to combat the heresy, and was commissioned to be part of the preaching crusade against it. It took no time at all for him to see why it wasn't working: the ordinary people admired and followed the ascetical leaders of the Albigenses. Their lives were lived in perpetual sacrifice, while the Catholics who traveled about were equipped with fine horses and retinues, kept servants, and stayed at the best inns. It was hardly a strategy designed to succeed.

Dominic chose another path. With three Cistercians who joined him, he began a life of itinerant preaching according to the Gospel ideal, converting countless people to the true faith. He continued the work for ten years, eventually gathering his fellow preachers around him in a community. In 1215 he founded a religious house at Toulouse, which was to be the beginning of the Order of Preachers — the Dominicans.

2. A Meeting of Brothers

Legend has it that Dominic saw the sinful world threatened by God's anger but saved by the intercession of Our Lady, who pointed out to her Son two figures. One was Dominic himself, the other a stranger.

In church the next day Dominic saw a ragged beggar enter — in fact, the other man in the vision. He went up to him, embraced him, and said, "You are my companion and must walk with me. If we hold together, no earthly power can withstand us."

Who was the beggar? None other than Francis of Assisi. The meeting of the two founders is commemorated twice a year, when on their respective feast days Dominicans and Franciscans celebrate Mass in each other's churches, and afterward sit at the same table — in the words of *Butler's Lives of the Saints*, "to eat the bread that for seven centuries has never been wanting."

The Wonder Worker

St. Anthony's Preaching Helped Lost Souls Find Their Way Home

Statues of St. Anthony of Padua (1195-1231), found in abundance here and abroad, generally show the saint with the Christ Child in his arms — for a reason: that was the way he was once seen in a vision by someone in his company. It was one of many miracles associated with St. Anthony, which is why he was acclaimed — in his own lifetime and far beyond — as "the wonder worker."

For reasons explained in the accompanying story, St. Anthony is also acknowledged as the classic finder of lost articles — including, not incidentally, the lost souls who found their way home by virtue of his incomparable powers of preaching.

A favorite St. Anthony story in that regard was told by Faith Abbot McFadden in St. Anthony Messenger *magazine not long ago. Her family, brought up in New York City, was taught not only the familiar "Tony, Tony, look around: Something's lost and must be found" when seeking the saint's aid in looking for lost articles, but also a variant when trying to flag down a taxi on busy Manhattan nights: "Tony, Tony, look around: Something hasn't yet been found."*

That ritual was employed on a particularly frigid evening outside Lincoln Center and, against all odds, an empty cab screeched to a halt right in front of them. The McFaddens settled down in the back seat, but the driver didn't take off right away. He turned around. He looked at them. And with a big smile he said, "Hi. My name's Tony."

You can call it a coincidence. But don't try to tell that to Ms. McFadden.

Story adapted from *Saints and Their Stories*, by Mary
Montogomery, Harper & Row, 1988.

Why do we pray to St. Anthony of Padua when we're looking for something that's lost? How did the custom begin? No one has the definitive answer, but a number of stories may help to explain it.

For example: once Anthony was missing his Mass book. It had been a gift from his mother and was very precious to him. After looking everywhere he could think of, with no success at all, he began to pray — and just then there was a knock on the door. A frightened young priest who was standing there held out the book to Anthony. "I'm very sorry for what I've done," he said. "Please forgive me." Anthony gladly accepted the book, and forgave the student at once.

Or this one: a poor woman was upset because she couldn't find some money she had saved. "Go home and sweep the bedroom of your house," Anthony told her. She did as he directed — and there was the missing money!

Or, perhaps best of all, this well-known tale of Anthony's introduction to preaching, and the results it would produce:

One day some young Franciscans who had been studying for the priesthood were to be ordained. At the last minute, a problem arose — the priest who was supposed to preach failed to appear. Who would give the talk? Confusion reigned. At the last minute, Anthony was told: "You're the one. We want you to speak."

"Whatever shall I say?" asked the surprised Anthony. "I have no time to prepare a sermon."

"Say whatever the Holy Spirit directs you to say," he was told.

Anthony spoke, and everyone at the ordination was amazed. "I didn't know Anthony was a man of such education and learning," one friar whispered to another. "How could anyone know?" the friar whispered back. "He's too modest to ever talk about himself."

News about Anthony's ability to speak spread quickly. He was asked to preach to people in other cities. Before long he was known throughout Italy and France. Audiences crowded the churches to hear him speak about God and how God wants us to live our lives. Some people spent all night in the pews, just to be sure they would have a place in the morning. Shopkeepers closed their shops to go and listen. When churches couldn't hold the crowd, Anthony spoke in the streets. When the streets filled, he led the crowd out to the hills.

All the while, he was bringing people closer to God. Some were already faithful Catholics, but many were people who had gone astray. They were wayward souls — lost souls. But Anthony's words had found them and brought them home again.

A Foretaste of Paradise

Thomas Aquinas's Heavenly Vision
Ended His Earthly Labors

Throughout his life, St. Thomas Aquinas (c. 1224-1274) gave over his soaring intellect to the instruction of others, learned and ignorant alike. "The Angelic Doctor," as he was known, covered the entire body of Church doctrine with his writings — including his greatest work, the Summa Theologica. *To this day he is honored as the patron saint of Catholic schools, colleges, and universities.*

But even this intellectual giant would come to realize that the sum of human knowledge is as nothing compared to what lies ahead in heaven. It came to him in a vision — one so breathtaking that he reached an astonishing conclusion: since everything he had written in his lifetime was no more than straw, as he put it, he would never take up his pen again. And he was true to his word. Here is the story.

Selection from *The Angelic Doctor: The Life and World
of St. Thomas Aquinas*, by Matthew Bunson, Our
Sunday Visitor, Inc., 1994.

This third part of the *Summa* was written sometime between October 1272 and early December 1273 while Thomas was still in Naples. The entire book itself, however, was never completed. The reasons are to be found in the increasing mysticism of the writer and growing periods of ecstatic union.

Thomas Aquinas had always displayed both the inclination and the temperament of a mystic. As a boy, his long periods of silent introspection were punctuated by his endless questioning of his teachers, at Monte Cassino and then again at Naples — "What is God?" His quest as a theologian, a philosopher, and a Dominican had been to answer that simple question. While his way had been to utilize logic and reason in examining the endless facets of God, the spiritual path of the mystic had also been traveled. But these journeys Thomas generally kept to himself, although many incidents, particularly in later life, were shared or witnessed by fellow friars.

Many people today think of Thomas as a dry, unimaginative, and rather unemotional figure — a thinking machine of theology and doctrine. Such a view is, of course, entirely wrong, for the ceaseless labors of Thomas were the result of his burning desire to explain in clear, rational terms the visions and visitations he had received all of his life, and to provide a profound explanation for the union in all of humankind: the Spirit and matter. Like all saints, Thomas's core was the search for Christ, and his pursuit of philosophical science was his means of making that discovery.

It is difficult to say precisely when his mystical episodes began. As has been seen, there were apparently the first stages of development in his youth, but probably the most notable of the early experiences were while in captivity by his family in the prison at Monte San Giovanni. There he was visited by angels, one of several visitations by these divine servants. Because of his abiding love for angelic hosts, Thomas would earn the title *Doctor Angelicus* (that is, the Angelic Doctor). Even in the *Summa* he examined the nature of angels, speculating whether an angel could travel from point A to point B without traversing the space between. He also discussed the now famous question as to how many angels could fit on the head of a pin. His answers, minus all the brilliant explanatory exposition: angels could go from point A to point B instantly, and all of them could fit on the head of a pin.

There were other visions, at Orvieto and Paris, and his superiors began to notice that these episodes were, from around 1268, growing in length and frequency. This was especially true in the years 1273-1274, his last on earth. After each of these events, Thomas was heard to say, "Oh, who will deliver me from this body of death?"

His daily life was also being more and more invaded by ecstasy. His writing was slowing as his mind was ceasing to focus on specific literary endeavors, passing instead into contemplative periods that stretched for hours at a time. A papal legate, in fact, was once witness to this. Sent to inquire as to Thomas's progress in Naples, this ambassador of Pope Gregory X found Thomas sitting staring off toward the window of the chamber, seemingly lost in thought. After waiting for some time and trying unsuccessfully to bring him back to the world in courteous ways — clearing his throat or tapping the floor — the legate finally tugged at Thomas's habit. On another occasion, the crucifix in Thomas's room was seen to move.

These events were only a precursor for the inevitable day when Thomas would behold a vision so beautiful that his life would never be the same. That day came on December 6, 1273. Thomas was saying Mass when he was gripped by a particularly long ecstasy.

Returning to his mortal senses, he finished the Mass and retired to his cell. Brother Reginald, who had been waiting for Thomas to return to work on the *Summa*, finally went to the cell and inquired if Thomas was ready to resume dictating, as there was still much to do on the book. Thomas, however, quietly declared that he had put down his pen and would write no more. Reginald pressed him as to why he was doing this and Thomas declared: "I can do no more. Such secrets have been revealed to me that all that I have written now seems like straw." He was good to his word. He never picked up another pen, leaving the *Summa* and other treatises, commentaries, and studies unfinished.

Exhausted and growing weaker by the day, Thomas spent his time in prayer and private devotion. The pleas of his fellow Dominicans that he go back to writing and teaching were gently but firmly refused. No power in the world could compel him to compose another hymn or to write another word.

On March 7, 1274, at Fossanova, Thomas closed his eyes for the last time, finally being delivered from "this body of death." He died amidst the prayers of the Cistercians and the tears of his Dominican companions. Word spread like an earthquake of sorrow throughout Christendom that Thomas Aquinas was dead.

The Sacred Seal

St. John Nepomucene Refused to Break the Confessional Bond — And Died a Martyr

The king placed an unconscionable demand on St. John Nepomucene (1345-1393), confessor to the queen: either reveal what the queen had told him in her confession, or forfeit his life. For St. John, a Prague priest and court preacher, there was no need to think it over. The seal of confession was inviolable, come what may. And so he became a martyr for the faith.

St. John Nepomucene not only passed along a legacy of courage in the name of sacramental integrity, he also left his name to the first American bishop to be canonized: St. John Nepomucene Neumann, fourth bishop of Philadelphia and a true American saint.

Story adapted from *Anecdotes and Examples Illustrating the Catholic Catechism*, selected and arranged by Rev. Francis Spirago, Benziger Brothers, 1904.

St. John Nepomucene, ordained to the priesthood in Prague, attracted many with the eloquence of his preaching — including no less than the royal family. King Wenzel appointed him court preacher, and his wife, the queen, was so pleased with him that she chose him as her confessor.

The king knew this, of course, and one day asked John to see him privately. He was anxious to know about something she had said in her confession, and asked the priest about it. John was taken aback. He refused to say a word on the subject to the king, pointing out that even under the pain of death, a priest cannot reveal what is said in the confessional. The king pressed on. Surely the rules might be bent a bit, he said, suggesting that a bishop's hat could well be John's if he chose to cooperate. Of course, King Wenzel was wasting his time; John dismissed the offer out of hand.

Now the king grew furious. He had the saint thrown into prison, where he was cruelly tortured. But still John said not a word. At length the queen succeeded in having him freed, and he immediately went to the shrine dedicated to the Mother of God near Prague, praying for strength to meet the crisis that he knew lay ahead. It was not long in coming.

King Wenzel summoned him once more, threatening to have him drowned in the Moldau River unless the priest revealed the queen's confessional secrets. But yet again John remained silent, and the king followed through on his threat. That very evening soldiers took the holy priest, bound and gagged, to the Karlsbrucke and tossed him over the side of the bridge into the Moldau. (A tablet still marks the site where the act of infamy was carried out.)

Immediately five lights appeared, shining like stars, on the surface of the water where the saint's body was floating. King Wenzel and his queen happened to be standing by a palace window overlooking the river at that instant, and they too were amazed by the lights upon the water. The king knew their meaning at once. Both conscience- and panic-stricken, he left Prague that same night in case an insurrection arose. Before long fishermen found the body of the saint, who was interred with great ceremony in the cathedral.

Famine conditions prevailed that summer in Bohemia following a prolonged drought, one so severe that people could cross the bed of the Moldau River without even wetting their feet. They were convinced that the king's unspeakable act was responsible for their troubles, and began praying for help at the tomb of St. John. Not much time passed before the tomb became a shrine, with many coming from far distances, including emperors and queens, to venerate his memory. Miraculous cures were reported by visitors to the tomb, and the fame of John's sanctity spread throughout the Christian world.

Several hundred years later, when John Nepomucene's cause for canonization was being studied, a team of bishops, doctors, and professors unsealed the saint's sepulchre. All that was left of his body were bones and dust, with one exception: his tongue was discovered whole and incorrupt, a sign of the priest's fidelity to the seal of confession. It is still kept in a reliquary in the Prague cathedral, incorrupt to this day, still venerated by the faithful.

A Final Note of Grace

St. Thomas More Died 'The King's Good Servant, But God's First'

Nearly five hundred years after his death, St. Thomas More (1478-1535) is to the present generation exactly what he was in his own lifetime: a giant of the faith. His brilliance was legendary, living on in his literary works, his speeches — and, to be sure, his wit. Yet all his worldly talents were solidly grounded in his Catholic faith. It enabled him to bear injustices with patience and a good heart, as he once took the trouble to explain: "Comfort in tribulation can be secured only on the sure ground of faith holding as true the words of Scripture and the teaching of the Catholic Church."

That faith would be tested to its limits. For many years a trusted adviser to King Henry VIII, as well as his good friend, Thomas reached the peak of his courtly career as chancellor of England. But he resigned that post after three years, in 1532, because of his irreconcilable opposition to Henry's divorce from Catherine of Aragon. When he later refused to take the Oath of Succession required by the king, he was arrested for treason, convicted in a trumped-up trial, and sentenced to death by beheading.

Once again his faith would sustain him, as his own words confirm: "I will not mistrust [God], though I shall feel myself weakening and on the verge of being overcome with fear. . . . I trust he shall place his holy hand on me and in the stormy seas hold me up from drowning."

This selection from Richard Marius's admirable biography of St. Thomas begins moments after his conviction and carries readers through his final few days, marked as they were by his unfailing good humor. There are also those memorable last words: "I die the King's good servant, but God's first."

Selection from *Thomas More: A Biography*, by Richard
Marius, Alfred A. Knopf, 1984.

So it was over, and More was led out to the Thames and into the boat that would take him downriver. Margaret was waiting for her father at Tower Wharf, "where she knew he should pass by before he could enter into the Tower — there tarrying for his coming home." When she saw him, she pushed through the crowd, through the encircling guard with its pikes and halberds, and threw her arms around his neck and kissed him. He gave her his blessing and comforted her, and they parted. But Margaret could not let him go, and she pushed her way back again and again and embraced him and kissed him, "and at last with a full heavy heart was fain to depart from him." Stapleton says that at Margaret's second embrace More said nothing because his voice was choked with tears. He also says that Margaret Giggs Clement and More's son John kissed their father as well.

Executions followed swiftly on judgments in those days. More lived five nights after his trial. The trial was held on Thursday; on Monday, More wrote to Margaret the last letter of his life. With it he sent the hair shirt that he had worn for so long. The letter itself is a little masterpiece, filled with affection for those he loved best. He does not mention Dame Alice, his wife; perhaps her hostility to his stand and her anguish over her poverty had worn away their love at last.

"Our Lord bless you, good daughter, and your good husband and your little boy and all yours and all my children and all my godchildren and all our friends. Recommend me when you may to my good daughter Cicily whom I beseech Our Lord to comfort, and I send her my blessing and to all her children and pray her to pray for me. I send her a handkerchief, and God comfort my good son her husband. . . . I cumber you, good Margaret, much, but I would be sorry if it should be any longer than tomorrow, for it is Saint Thomas Eve and the Utas of Saint Peter, and therefore tomorrow long I to go to God; it were a day very meet and convenient for me. I never liked your manner toward me better than when you kissed me last for I love when daughterly love and dear charity hath no leisure to look for worldly courtesy. Farewell, my dear child, and pray for me, and I shall for you and all you, friends, that we may merrily meet in heaven. I thank you for your great costs. . . . I pray you at time convenient recommend me to my good son John More. I liked well his natural fashion. Our Lord bless him and his good wife my loving daughter to whom I pray him be good, as he hath great cause. . . ."

Early in the morning on Tuesday, July 6, 1535, Sir Thomas Pope, one of More's friends, came from the king and the council to announce that he would die before nine o'clock. It is hard to tell if More's reply is ironic or not; the man preserved his mysteries to the end, and his spirit of irony daunted many of his contemporaries as it daunts us today.

"Master Pope," he said, "for your good tidings I most heartily thank you. I have been always much bounded to the king's highness for the benefits and honors that he hath still from time to time most bountifully heaped upon me. And yet more bound am I to his grace for putting me into this place, where I have had convenient time and space to have remembrance of my end. And so help me God, most of all, Master Pope, am I bound to his highness that it pleaseth him so shortly to rid me out of the miseries of this wretched world. And therefore will I not fail earnestly to pray for his grace, both here and also in another world."

"The king's pleasure is further," Pope said, "that at your execution you shall not use many words."

"Master Pope," More said, "you do well to give me warning of his grace's pleasure, for otherwise I had purposed at that time somewhat to have spoken, but of no matter wherewith his grace, or any other, should have had cause to be offended. Nevertheless, whatsoever I intended, I am ready obediently to conform myself to his grace's commandments. And I beseech you, good Master Pope, to be a mean unto his highness that my daughter Margaret may be at my burial."

"The king is content already," Pope said, "that your wife, children, and your other friends shall have liberty to be present."

The interview shows Henry wary of More's oratorical powers, even on the scaffold. The Carthusians and Richard Reynolds had preached as long as they had breath while they were being put to death, and More was doubtless a much better orator than they. His gift for public speaking was what made him best known to the citizens of London and the court; it is the part of him that we cannot recover.

When Pope had taken his departure in tears, More dressed himself in the finest clothes he had. He was, as always, ready to be at his best before an audience. The Lieutenant of the Tower was scandalized. As part of his fee, the headsman received the clothes of his victim, and the lieutenant said that the man was a rogue. Finally the argument of the lieutenant prevailed — probably because More did not wish to give anything of high value to one who might use it for immoral purposes. More changed into a rough gray cloak that belonged to his servant John a Wood, but he did send the executioner a gold coin called an angel.

So he was led out to the scaffold on Tower Hill. It was to be his last stage. More walked to his death carrying a small red cross, symbol of the blood of Christ and symbol, too, of those ancient and almost mythological crusaders who had gone to the Holy Land to fight the infidel. We have a legion of stories about his progress up the hill through the pressing throng who had come to see him die.

All are agreed on one thing: he kept his wit and his composure to the very end.

Hall tells of the woman who pushed through the crowd and beseeched him to release some evidence about a case of hers, evidence that she could not obtain after his arrest. He said, "Good woman, have patience for a little while, for the king is good unto me that even within this half-hour he will discharge me of all business and help thee himself."

The scaffold was old and tottering, and More needed a helping hand to mount its steps. He said to the Lieutenant of the Tower, "I pray you, Master Lieutenant, see me safe up, and for my coming down, let me shift for myself."

As tradition demanded, the executioner kneeled and asked More's forgiveness for what he was about to do. As tradition also demanded, More embraced and kissed him and gave him his blessing.

He was brief in asking all the people to pray for him. Roper says that he told them to bear witness with him that he should "now there suffer death in and for the faith of the Holy Catholic Church." A pamphlet called the *Paris News Letter* carried the report of the trial and execution to the Continent; it adds the eloquent detail that More said he died the king's good servant but God's first.

By the customs of executions of this sort, More would, after his speech, have taken off most of his clothes to give them as a fee to the headsman. Roper says that More told the executioner not to be afraid to do his work. His neck was short, More said; if the executioner cared for his reputation as a headsman, he should not strike awry. Fifty years afterward Stapleton wrote that More bound his own eyes with a linen band; he got the story from Margaret Giggs Clement, More's adopted daughter, who was the only member of the family to see More die.

The block on the scaffold was low and small. More, like Fisher before him, would have had to lie on his stomach to put his neck across it. He moved his tangled gray beard carefully out of the way; some remembered that he said it should not be cut in two because it had done no treason.

When he had arranged himself, he waited, doubtless reciting in his mind one of the ancient prayers of his beloved Church.

Apostle to the East

St. Francis Xavier Took to the Trees to Thwart Would-be Assassins

St. Francis Xavier (1506-1552) was so successful at instructing others in the faith that the Church honors him as patron of foreign missions. This Spanish-born priest, sailing under the flag of Portugal, baptized thousands in modern-day India, Sri Lanka, and Japan, at a time when travel was difficult and communication between peoples was often a challenge at best. Still, Francis persevered, with a determination that seemed boundless.

The scope of that determination, in fact, is still astounding today. Jesuit sources (Francis, a friend of St. Ignatius Loyola, was one of the first Jesuits) place the number of conversions for which he was responsible at seven hundred thousand. That remarkable figure testifies to his missionary zeal. Whether or not the number is accurate beyond question seems less important than the fact that in courageously bringing Christ's message to a distant corner of the world, St. Francis Xavier planted the seeds of Church communities that continue to flourish in our own time.

The enterprise, of course, was not without its dangers — some of them life-threatening. This tale, from Francis' days in India, tells how the saint once escaped a hellish fate by climbing a bit closer to the heavens.

Selection from *The Fire of Francis Xavier: The Story of an Apostle,* by Arthur R. McGratty, S.J., The Bruce Publishing Company, 1951.

Southern India contained those who resented Francis' coming, his introduction of new religious ways. "We must kill this foreigner," was the whispered agreement among some pagans. Francis smiled grimly when his Christians brought him word of occasional plots against his life.

"Perhaps," he said, "the devil resents my presence. But I will take care. Not for myself, for there is so much work yet to do. The work is only beginning."

One night a breathless Christian raced to the missionary's hut. "Father Francis," he panted, gesticulating wildly, "they are coming! Men — with clubs and knives. They have sworn to kill you tonight!"

The priest moved swiftly. He directed his informant to flee through the dense wood behind his hut. As soon as his benefactor was safely away, Francis extinguished his little lamp, then stepped outside the hut. The starless night folded everything in a great darkness. Francis moved a short distance away, then climbed quickly and silently high into the branches of a tall tree.

When his pagan assailants reached the little clearing, they whispered excitedly to one another. Francis, high above, listening and motionless, sensed rather than understood the import of the low sounds far below him. First, the instructions, the quickly arranged surrounding of the hut, the attack to follow, the flash of knives within, and the death of the priest. The incongruity of the moment crossed the hidden priest's features with an unseen smile. His arms clung to the smooth branch and, offering unspoken prayer for his assailants' welfare, Francis heard, rather than saw, the pathetic steps of the attempted murder's failure. It was all over and done within a few minutes. The low sounds of disappointment, coming from the attacking party as it left the empty hut, faded as the thwarted group moved away into the night.

Should he come down? Francis asked himself. One might as well be prudent. The men might return. Francis sighed, then found himself a suitable crotch of branches. Best to compose oneself as comfortably as possible for the remainder of the night. As the priest fell into a light sleep, the ghost of a smile stood on his face. What (his mind was asking) would your former students at the University of Paris, or indeed the Sorbonne faculty, think of Master Xavier, falling asleep in the branches of a tree in faraway India?

In the morning Francis descended, led his Christians in their devotions, and then set off again afoot for the nearest neighboring village. The fatigue of his daily journeyings, he admits, was ever present. He was the only priest at the time among the Parava native Christians. The faithful numbered some forty thousand. Working to the point of physical and emotional exhaustion frequently breaks a man's spirit and morale. But not in one in whose spirit flamed a desire for more, for more and more souls.

The Example of Jesus

A Crucified St. Paul Miki Pardoned His Persecutors Before He Died

Martyrs for the faith have endured death by almost every imaginable means, but few have been tested in exactly the same way as Jesus. That was the fate that persecutors had in store, however, for St. Paul Miki (1556-1597): he and twenty-five companions were crucified by Japanese authorities. Paul Miki would imitate Christ not only in the manner of death but also in responding to those responsible for his execution. He forgave them, and asked others to do the same.

The Church in Japan, flourishing not long before as a result of the pioneering mission efforts of St. Francis Xavier, was nearly extinguished by a series of persecutions under rulers who feared the inroads of Christianity on their ancient culture. Not only would martyrs such as Paul Miki and his companions forfeit their lives, but all missioners were expelled from the country. Not until the mid-nineteenth century did the Church regain a foothold in Japan, but the sacrifice of the Japanese martyrs was never forgotten.

St. Paul Miki, a Jesuit Scholastic, died with the example of Jesus in his heart and on his mind. As life ebbed away from him on the cross, he said: "After Christ's example I forgive my persecutors. I do not hate them. I ask God to have pity on all, and I hope my blood will fall on my fellow men as a fruitful rain."

Story from *The Book of Saints*, by Michael Walsh,
Twenty-Third Publications, 1994.

The city of Nagasaki in Japan is now infamous for the devastation caused by the dropping of the atomic bomb upon it in 1945. But it had been revered by Christians in Japan since 1597 because of the deaths there, on "the holy hill," of twenty-six priests and laypeople, the first martyrs of the Japanese Church. They died by crucifixion like their Master, being tied to the crosses as they lay upon the ground and then, when the crosses were set upright, planted in the ground alongside each other, they were put to death by the thrust of a lance, each by a separate executioner.

Christianity came to Japan with Francis Xavier in 1549. By the time he left in the hope of going to China, there had been some two thousand converts. After his departure the numbers had continued to grow rapidly, partly at least because of the conversion of a group of the feudal lords who, for reasons of their own, were opposed to the power of the Buddhist monks. Perhaps the great growth in Christianity alarmed Hideyoshi, the ruler who ordered the persecution. Some of the incoming missionaries had little understanding of the particular situation in Japan; the Jesuit superior in the country was, to say the least, imprudent; and the Japanese had a very real fear of invasion by Portuguese soldiers. For these and several other reasons, partly religious, partly to do with the internal politics of Japan, Hideyoshi first ordered the destruction of some churches and other foundations, and then condemned the Christians to death.

Of the twenty-six who died in 1597 six were Franciscans, one of whom was born in India, another in Mexico City; the rest came from Spain. Three were Jesuits, all Japanese, and there were seventeen Japanese laymen. Collectively they are known as Paul Miki and Companions — Paul Miki was a Jesuit Scholastic.

Paul, born in 1556, came from a noble family in Kyoto that converted to Christianity; he was baptized when he was five years old. He went to the Jesuit-run seminary at Anzuciana when he was twenty, but two years later entered the Jesuit noviceship. Though the Jesuits had attempted to adapt the faith to fit in with Japanese culture, in many ways they remained incurably European in outlook: Paul had to learn Latin to study theology, and he found it very difficult. But he also spent a great deal of time studying Buddhism, especially in the form it was found in Japan, and that knowledge became invaluable when he was able to preach and to debate with the Buddhist bonzes. His arguments drew many of his fellow-countrymen and women into accepting the Gospel. It was partly that his sermons were especially persuasive. One Franciscan said of him that he was the most devout of the preachers of the day, and that no one had such great success, but that his success depended at least as much upon Paul's own evident holiness as upon the words that he spoke.

When the persecution broke out, Paul was arrested in Osaka, the day after Christmas, 1596. He was imprisoned together with two Japanese Jesuit novices: John Kisal, who was sixty-four years old, and John Soan de Goto, who was not yet twenty; both were received into the Society of Jesus before they were put to death upon their crosses. After their arrest they were taken to Kyoto where each had part of his left ear cut off, and paraded around the city to be scoffed at by the populace. From Kyoto they were sent for execution to Nagasaki, where they died together on February 5, 1597, though their feast is now celebrated by the Church on February 6.

Of the martyrs who died that day each gave his own example of heroism. St. Paul Miki, who had preached so effectively during his life, still on the cross encouraged the many bystanders to embrace Christianity. Just before he died he pardoned those who had put him to death, an act that moved many who heard him. He died saying, "Into your hands, O Lord, I commend my spirit." John Soan's father was among those who saw the martyrdom. He encouraged his son to endure to the end, saying that both he and John's mother would also willingly die for their faith. This was no empty promise because one of the onlookers who confessed himself a Christian was seized and executed on the spot. One of those who died was only twelve years old; another, Anthony Dojuku, who was thirteen, intoned a hymn.

Many more Christians died in the years that followed, two hundred five of whom have also been beatified. The twenty-six who were martyred in 1597 were beatified for their heroic witness to the message of the Gospel in 1627, and were canonized by Pope Pius IX in 1862.

St. Paul Miki's words to Christians who tried to get him released: "Is that your way of showing your love for me? Did you wish to deprive me of the immense privilege that God has given me? You ought to rejoice, and praise his goodness for it."

Answered Prayers

St. Catherine of Ricci Assumed the Suffering of a Soul in Purgatory

The reputation for holiness of St. Catherine of Ricci (1522-1590) spread far beyond the walls of her Dominican convent at Prato, in the Tuscan region of Italy, and pilgrims by the hundreds regularly visited to ask her blessing and her prayers.

Their confidence was hardly misguided. She was a woman of learning, corresponding frequently with the leading Church reformers of her time. But in addition, Catherine was one of the most amazing visionaries the Church has known. She experienced on a weekly basis the pain and sorrow of Christ's passion, an ordeal that would last from noon each Thursday until four o'clock the following afternoon. Witnesses swore she also possessed the gift of bilocation, and that she often visited her friend St. Philip Neri in this fashion.

Catherine's prayers for the living and the dead were eagerly petitioned, and never turned away. This story tells of the miraculous way in which she "prayed into heaven" a soul from purgatory — by gladly accepting the suffering he had borne.

Story adapted from *Little Pictorial Lives of the Saints,*
Benziger Brothers, Inc., 1925.

She was originally Alexandrina of Ricci, the daughter of a noble Florentine, but she took the name of Catherine — after her patron, St. Catherine of Siena — when she entered the Third Order of St. Dominic at Prato when she was just thirteen. It would not be long before the name of Catherine of Ricci was one to reckon with.

Her special attraction was to the passion of Christ, in which she was permitted to participate in a miraculous way. When she was twenty-one, she had a vision of the crucifixion so intense that she was confined to bed for three weeks, and was only restored — on Holy Saturday — by an apparition of St. Mary Magdalene and Jesus risen. For twelve years she spent each Friday in an ecstatic state and bore signs of the stigmata — a wound in her left side, the marks of the crown of thorns.

Catherine's sufferings linked her closely to the souls in purgatory, and on their behalf she offered all her prayers and penances. Her love for them was so well-known, in fact, that family and friends of those who had died beseeched her for her special prayers for a departed loved one. She knew by revelation of the arrival of a soul in purgatory and the hour of its release, and at times was able to converse with the saints in glory.

On one occasion it was revealed to Catherine that a certain man for whom she had been praying was indeed in purgatory, and such was her love for others that she offered to assume all the punishment that would be his. Her prayer was granted, and the suffering soul entered heaven. But for the next forty days Catherine suffered indescribable agonies of the body. Through it all she was calm and joyful, declaring that she wanted only the release of souls from purgatory so they might see and praise their Redeemer.

One Fervent Prayer

The 'Memorare' Turned Life Around
for a Youthful Francis de Sales

A good friend of St. Francis de Sales (1567-1622) once paid him a supreme compliment. "If God the Father is as loving as de Sales," the friend said, "no one should have any fear of him." People indeed found Francis de Sales to be warm in his affection for others, a trait reflected in the generosity of his prayer life. He regularly prayed not only for the material well-being of friends and strangers alike but for their spiritual health as well. For those already committed, he asked a strengthening of faith; for those outside the fold, the grace of conversion. His legendary efforts in that direction, which relied so much on a loving approach, made him a forerunner of today's spirit of ecumenism and interfaith cooperation.

Prayer was at the heart of all he did, for a reason. As the first brief story indicates, it was his recitation of the Memorare — the prayer that begins, "Remember, O most loving Virgin Mary . . ." — that lifted him from a deep depression and helped him understand the meaning of salvation.

The second selection describes the zeal with which he converted the Chablais region — how he found "only six or seven" Catholics when he arrived and increased their number to thousands. The account is by his faithful coworker, St. Jane Frances de Chantal, and is taken from her testimony in 1627, five years after Francis' death, in hearings for his canonization.

As priest and bishop, he taught others of the serenity contained in a life of prayer. "Divine love, enlightening our soul and making us pleasing to God, is called grace," he wrote. "Giving us power to do good, it is called charity. When it reaches the point of perfection where it makes us earnestly, frequently, and readily do good, it is called devotion."

First story from *The Book of Saints,* by Michael Walsh,
Twenty-Third Publications, 1994; second selection from *St. Francis de Sales: A Testimony by St. Chantal,* introduction
by Elisabeth Stopp, Institute of Salesian Studies, 1967.

1. The Right Prayer at the Right Time

Of all the books that have helped Christians in their search for closer union with God, few have been more important, and more widely read, than the *Introduction to the Devout Life,* that appeared first at the very end of 1608, and the *Treatise on the Love of God,* published in 1616. They are complementary, the first being for beginners, the second for those more advanced. Both were written by Francis de Sales, a saint who, from the number of his publications, was declared by Pope Pius XI to be the patron of all authors.

He was born on August 21, 1567, the oldest of thirteen children. His family was noble, and he was born in the château de Sales, though his family name was de Boisy. He went to school in Annecy and then, at the age of fourteen, to the University of Paris, where he lived in the Jesuit college. He stayed in Paris for six years, studying rhetoric and philosophy, though he also found time for Scripture and theology.

It was toward the end of his time in Paris, when he was nineteen, that the event occurred which set the tone for his devotional life and for the spiritual teaching he passed on to others. When Francis was born, the Calvinist belief that people were predestined by God for heaven or hell, and the greater part of the human race was predestined for hell, had also affected Catholics. Francis was no exception. He feared that he had lost God's friendship and that he would be damned for all eternity. He fell into a despair so deep that his health began to suffer.

One day, in this anguish, he prayed that, whether or not he was to be damned, he would never give in to cursing or blaspheming. Shortly afterward, when he was kneeling before a statue of the Virgin Mary and saying the prayer that begins "Remember, O most loving Virgin Mary. . . ," the despair left him, never to return. He became overwhelmingly conscious that God wished not the damnation of all except a handful but exactly the opposite: that God wanted the salvation of everybody.

There were others of the period who said the same. What was different about Francis was that he wrote down his advice in a manner that was intensely personal. The books, though distributed widely, were originally composed as advice to particular friends of the saint. It was that sense of friendship in his writings on the devout life that made the books so effective.

2. From 'Six or Seven' Catholics to Thousands

I declare it to be public knowledge that our blessed prelate was sent to the Chablais to convert the people there who had been heretics for about seventy years. When the late Bishop de Granier gave him this assignment, the blessed prelate was silent for a while and then answered as I have already reported when he was first told to preach: "At your word I will cast forth the nets."

I seem to remember him saying to me in this connection that relying only on God and on obedience, he set to work in the town of Thonon where there were at first only some six or seven Catholics. He made this town his center and preached and taught there before his small flock in exactly the same way as he would have done for a large congregation. And as a reward God sent him a special joy, for when he was giving a sermon on the invocation of saints on the Feast of St. Stephen, one of these seven Catholics who was greatly distressed by doubts on this point and in his general belief in the Catholic apostolic and Roman Church was completely won back to his faith, and he afterward told the holy prelate what had happened. This confirmed him in his practice of never leaving out the sermon just because there were only very few people to listen.

He spent three whole years on this mission and often went in great peril of his life, as one can easily judge from the attitude of the heretics, for they often rose up in rebellion against this different doctrine that was being preached among them. I have been told this by a very trustworthy eyewitness. This same person told me that a Capuchin called Father Esprit one day went to listen to a heretical sermon at Thonon and began a fierce argument with the minister, our Blessed Father [Francis de Sales] being also present. A number of people picked up stones ready to let fly at them. The late Madame de Vallon, who was there and was at that time one of the most hardened opponents of the faith, has since said that it was only the presence of the Blessed Father that finally put an end to the uproar, for when they turned to look at his friendly face it calmed down their fury. And indeed, this is just how it would affect people, for his face was all gentleness and peace when he looked at you. And not long afterward this same Madame de Vallon was converted, and so wholeheartedly that she even put herself under his spiritual direction and he guided her so well that she lived in great holiness and perfection until her death a few years later.

Our Blessed Father went through untold danger, weariness, and labor while for three years he worked unremittingly for the conversion of these people, and he did it all at his own expense and for the most part alone. Sometimes, but only rarely, he was helped by the said Louis de Sales, his cousin, whom he also kept out of his own pocket. And when he went to visit his father from time to time, he left his cousin in charge and provided for his upkeep.

There was a marvelous increase in the number of Catholics, and this decided him to go to Turin to see His Royal Highness, the duke of Savoy, and petition his help to regain possession of the churches at Thonon; he also wanted to have more missionaries as well as funds for their upkeep, for he was no longer able to manage on his own. He got what he needed, and in a short space of time the whole region returned to the Catholic, apostolic, and Roman faith, to the number of several thousand converts. I heard all this from eyewitnesses; and the Blessed Father himself also told me some of these things personally.

And this is true, well known, and public knowledge.

Her Beauty Was Spiritual

Kateri Tekakwitha Bore Criticism and Insults With a Forgiving Smile

Blessed Kateri Tekakwitha (1656-1680), the young Mohawk woman whose conversion to Catholicism has inspired others for generations, dealt with more than her share of misunderstanding in a life that was all too brief.

An affliction with smallpox as a child left her face scarred and her body weak, and subjected her for years to the taunts of other children. Her otherworldly ways as an adolescent and young woman added to the puzzlement of those about her, who wondered why she couldn't simply act as the other villagers did. Finally came her conversion to the Christian faith, prompting others to poke fun at her and spread false rumors about her conduct.

Kateri remained above it all throughout her ordeal, quietly forgiving those who tormented her and focusing her thoughts on God. She clearly had more important things to do.

Selection from *Lives of the Saints You Should Know*
(*Vol. 2*), by Margaret and Matthew Bunson, Our
Sunday Visitor, Inc., 1996.

Kateri was much beloved by her own Mohawks, especially by the older women who admired her gentle kindness and her willingness to work without complaining. She was also noted for her skill in decorating shirts, mantles, and other pieces of clothing. She seemed to see the patterns in her heart, if not in her eyes.

In June 1677, Kateri's life was about to change. The arrival of the Blackrobes, as the Jesuit priests were called, started a long series of conversions among the people. The lovely feast-day celebrations, including the manger scenes of Christmas, attracted the Mohawks. Kateri attended some of these festivals, but she made no move toward entering the Church. She had refused to marry any of the young Mohawk warriors, however, a fact that made her people consider her odd, perhaps even unhealthy in the mind. Marriage was an honorable state in the Five Nations.

When the "Dawn of Day" — the name given to Father Jacques de Lamberville (the Jesuit who knew the Mohawks so well) — came to the village mission, life changed for the Indian maiden. He talked to Kateri one day and was startled to hear her ask for baptism. She was actually a high-ranked Mohawk, and her conversion would have a great effect on the others in the village. Also, Kateri seemed to understand prayer, penance, and the presence of God without formal catechism. Father de Lamberville told her she could begin studying the faith but was slow to speak about baptism. Her family agreed to the catechism lessons, and Kateri went to the priest's instruction courses, astounding the Jesuits with her knowledge of the spiritual life.

The day of her baptism, Easter Sunday, 1676, was very special in the village. The Mohawks decorated the chapel specially for the ceremony and many attended out of respect for Kateri. She began her new life in Christ as a true contemplative, which means simply that she experienced "the joyful gaze of her soul upon God." She appeared small and delicate, but in her spirit she was an eagle flying directly to God.

Her long hours of prayer and her continued refusal to marry brought about a response from her uncle and the other Mohawks. Rumors were started by those who did not understand, and one young Mohawk warrior told her to act normal or die. The situation became worse each day, and Father de Lamberville asked God to send him a solution, some way to give Kateri protection.

The answer came in the person of a powerful Oneida chief named Garonhiague but called "Hot Ashes" or "Hot Cinders" by the white man because of his ferocious temper and deadly skills in hunting and battle. Hot Ashes was a Christian, and he was asked by Father de Lamberville to help Kateri get away from her village and into a Christian Indian settlement. Hot Ashes agreed to have his companions take Kateri to the Sault Mission, which she reached in the fall of 1677. The mission was located on the beautiful Lake St. Paul, where the Portage River emptied into the mighty St. Lawrence. Officially the site was called the Mission of St. Francis Xavier of Sault St. Louis. The word *sault* was French for rapids, or white-water stretches, in the rivers.

Kateri was quite taken by the peace and joy of the community and by the beautiful chapel that was open to all of the Native Americans. Mass started at 4:00 A.M., when the stars were fading and the nearby lakes and forests were mantled by mists. Kateri attended two Masses each morning, with the congregation singing hymns in their own language. The rosary was also recited. In the afternoon they met for Vespers and Benediction of the Blessed Sacrament. Kateri attended all of these services and also prayed in a grove in the woods. At her side was Anastasia, an older woman who had known Kateri's mother.

Kateri received Holy Communion on Christmas Day in 1677, and again her companions decorated the chapel out of affection and love. As she approached the altar, however, many in the chapel were startled. Kateri's plain face took on a glowing light and a new beauty. She was already ill, but receiving Christ in Communion filled her with such joy that her whole being reflected what she was experiencing.

Another woman, Marie Thérèse Tegaiaguenta, came into Kateri's world as her spirit soared and her physical strength faded. Both women prayed together and even asked if they could become nuns. The priests laughed, of course, because it was unthinkable that a Native American might be called to the religious life, at least from a European's point of view. Kateri solved the problem by making a private vow that she would never seek comfort in the arms of a human being and would never depart from Christ. In her soul, Kateri was already far more advanced in prayer, understanding the presence of God and united to him in the way of the truly great mystics of the world.

Her prayers and acts of penance took their toll eventually, and Kateri took to her pallet, a thin, stuffed mattress. No longer able to go to the chapel, she was given holy cards by the priests and spent hours looking at them with joy. The other Native Americans, sensing that her spirit was about to break loose from the bonds of the earth, gathered around her. To their astonishment, Kateri told them the secrets of their lives, predicted the future, and warned those whose faith was lukewarm.

The time came, of course, when the priests announced that they would bring her the Church's last rites. Kateri admitted to Marie Thérèse that she was ashamed to greet Christ in her usual rags, so Marie Thérèse and the other Mohawk women brought her new garments and dressed her lovingly for her final journey. Kateri Tekakwitha died on April 17, 1680, at the age of twenty-four.

Six days after her death Kateri appeared to a priest of the Sault Mission to warn him of coming events. Anastasia, her friend, saw her, radiant and beautiful, and people discovered that the personal effects she had left behind had miraculous healing properties. Her personal items brought renewed strength, relief from pain, even lasting cures.

The Lily of the Mohawks was a mystic who needed no schooling in the art of love and prayer. She was declared Venerable, or worthy of special honor, in 1943, and thirty-seven years later, in 1980, she was declared Blessed. The prayer being recited by people all over the world for her canonization recognizes that Kateri Tekakwitha blossomed in the American wilderness in the company of God and his angels.

Ahead of Her Time

St. Lucy Filippini Saw the Education of Women as a Holy Calling

For most people in the Church — and in society at large — the education of young women was low on the priority list three hundred years ago. Not only did custom dictate that it was dangerous to educate the poor, especially women, but Church law — as pronounced at the Council of Trent — actually forbade the formal education of young girls.

Here and there, however, a few pushed forward against the tide. One of them was St. Lucy Filippini (1672-1732). Spurred by her mentor, Rose Venerini, and an encouraging bishop, Cardinal Mark Anthony Barbarigo, she conducted her first academy for girls in the Italian town of Montefiascone when she was just twenty. She went on to establish many more schools in her lifetime, and the educational work she began continues today — in Italy, in the United States, and in countries throughout the world — through the religious community she founded, the Religious Teachers Filippini.

St. Lucy was motivated by concern not only for the temporal well-being of young women but much more so for the state of their souls. Licentiousness and loose living were rampant in her day, and in addition to teaching students Lucy — light-years ahead of her time — even took in prostitutes to keep them off the streets until they could be trained for respectable professions.

This story, taken from a new translation of a biography written shortly after her death, describes her encounter with a group of confrontational women — and the way she converted them on the spot.

Story from *The Life of St. Lucy Filippini*, by Francesco Di Simone, translated by Edwin Bannon, FSC, Ottavia Publications, 1997.

An incident that occurred in the celebrated fortress town of Pitigliano, in Tuscany, was remarkable, so clearly did it demonstrate the power God had given his servant Lucy's words to convert souls and move hearts.

Very soon after arriving in Pitigliano she followed her usual custom of starting things by introducing her spiritual exercises to the women of the place. Now in cities where there is a large population, as in Pitigliano, there are always some loose-living females. A number of these came, in this instance, to Lucy's exercises, not to lament their sins but to make fun. They arrived all dolled up with local garlands and floral adornments.

Lucy took all this in with a glance but prudently hid her displeasure at seeing the pathetic women flaunting their foolish finery. She simply began, as usual, to make a meditation out loud.

Wonder of wonders! It was as if her words were so many fiery darts finding their target in the hearts of the frivolous ones. Before long they were sobbing bitterly; full of shame for their foolishness, they tore off and flung away their garlands and ribbons to the winds!

The Mothers' Saint

Gerard Majella Answered a False Accusation With Silence and Prayer

For reasons not entirely clear, mothers and mothers-to-be have made St. Gerard Majella (1726-1755) their patron. Perhaps it was because he was generous to his own mother; perhaps it was that a woman whose family had known him prayed to him while experiencing a difficult childbirth — and soon had a healthy baby boy. Whatever the reason, the connection is firmly established, and St. Gerard — to whom many miracles were attributed in life — continues to help those who turn to him today.

The miracles began early for this son of an Italian tailor. The infant Jesus was said to be his playmate while he was only a toddler, and while growing up he could see Jesus when the priest elevated the Host at Mass. Later in life, other tales abounded about his mystical powers: levitation, bilocation, the ability to read minds.

It was also early in life that he began to understand how to bear wrongs with humility before God. As a tailor's apprentice he worked long hours under a brutal foreman who constantly ridiculed and insulted him. As houseboy, he was employed by a notoriously bad-tempered bishop. Finally, as a Redemptorist Brother — during the time that the congregation was still being led by its founder, St. Alphonsus Liguori — St. Gerard suffered in silence and prayer through the pains of a false accusation.

It happened after the saintly ways of Brother Gerard had begun to attract public attention, and crowds were beginning to follow him. Perhaps it was resentment of this good man, perhaps a mere case of jealousy that caused a woman to come forward with a lurid tale. At any rate, here is the story of the accusation, an encounter with Alphonsus Liguori himself, Brother Gerard's strategy of silence — and his eventual vindication.

Selection from "The Mothers' Saint — Gerard Majella," by
Alicia von Stamwitz, *Liguorian* magazine, May 1994,
published by The Redemptorists.

Given human envy, perhaps it is not surprising that this good and favored religious was the subject of a malicious rumor. In 1753 a woman named Neria Caggiano accused Gerard of having had relations with a young woman. When Alphonsus Liguori received a letter informing him of the allegation, he promptly summoned Gerard.

Gerard had never before met the founder and superior general of the Congregation. He stood before him and listened as Father Liguori read aloud the incriminating letter. When he had finished, Father Liguori looked up, waiting for Gerard's explanation. Gerard remained silent: he was thinking of the congregation's rule that advised Redemptorists never to make excuses for themselves.

Father Liguori was bewildered. Although he doubted that this highly regarded Redemptorist was guilty of the reported sin, he was forced to take the allegation seriously. He prohibited Gerard from having any contact or communication with the outside world until the matter was settled. Furthermore, Gerard was forbidden to receive Communion.

For three months Gerard was in disgrace. His confreres urged him to clear his name. "It is in God's hands," Gerard answered. "If he wills that my innocence be proven, who can accomplish it more easily than he?"

Meanwhile, Neria Caggiano's conscience was tormenting her. She wrote a second letter to Father Liguori, admitting she had lied. Father Liguori summoned Gerard a second time. "You were innocent all the time," he said. "Why didn't you say anything?"

"How could I, Father?" Gerard replied. "Does not the rule forbid me to excuse myself, and does it not advise me to bear in silence whatever mortifications are imposed by the superior?" Father Liguori had never intended the order's rule to be taken to such a literal extreme. Nevertheless, he could not help but admire the simplicity and faithfulness of the young Brother.

A Mother First

Elizabeth Ann Seton, a Young Widow, Faced Challenges at Home

St. Elizabeth Ann Seton (1774-1821) is one of the towering figures of the American Church. Foundress of the Sisters of Charity in the United States, she is also credited with establishing the nation's Catholic school system and is the first native-born American saint.

But before she became a Catholic, before she became a teacher or a religious woman — and long before she became a saint — she was a mother. As a young widow rearing five children, Elizabeth Ann Seton faced uncommon challenges, meeting them with courage, determination, and prayer.

She had returned to America from Italy (where her husband had died), ready to join the Catholic Church even at the cost of forfeiting family financial support. For a time all she had were her children — and even that comfort, she found, could prove to be fleeting.

From 1809 on she was formally known as Mother Seton, after taking vows of poverty, chastity, and obedience before Archbishop John Carroll, and in March of that year oversaw the move — of both her family and her new religious congregation — to Emmitsburg, Maryland. As determined as she was to keep her children together even while directing her fledgling community, Elizabeth found the dual challenge daunting. Her daughter Anna — "still her mother's problem child," the author tells us — provided special problems, including a romantic entanglement doomed to failure. This story describes Anna's return to Elizabeth and, joy of joys, her own discovery of a religious vocation. But fate had an unhappy ending in store for mother and daughter.

Selection from *Mothers of the Saints: Portraits of Ten Mothers of the Saints and Three Saints Who Were Mothers*, by Wendy Leifeld, Servant Publications, 1991.

Despite Anna's teenage storms of emotion, the family was together and happy. Family gatherings were held weekly with the boys coming over from their school. Everyone would gather in the small dining room for a hearty meal and much laughter and fun. Richard was the clown, and Bec was lively and fun-loving. Kitty and William were more serious and sedate. They all got along very well together, though they had their spats.

Anna had decided to stay in Baltimore to try her wings, and Elizabeth allowed her to do so, though she had misgivings. The young girl soon realized that she was "almost" as unhappy in the city as she had been at the mountain. She missed her mother and wanted to come home after all. Anna realized that even though her mother had been kind and understanding, she never had really approved of the relationship. As it turned out, there was good cause. Within months Charles Du Pavillon wrote to tell her he had fallen in love with another girl and was marrying her. Anna, because Elizabeth had kept communication open and loving, was able to turn to her in her sorrow, and they became even closer.

Instead of finding the school and the Sisters' life unbearably boring as she did before, Anna took an interest in the youngest pupils. Mother and daughter took long horseback rides together, enjoying nature and each other's company. Anna was very quiet in her grief that autumn and then decided to join the Sisterhood. The dramatic touch was as evident here as in her romantic and clandestine love affair, but at the heart of it there was a genuine vocation.

Troubles with the superior, Father David, continued and threatened to split the community apart. The winter had been extremely hard on the women's health. Elizabeth had finally admitted that she had consumption. Tuberculosis was spreading through the Sisters. With organizational troubles, factions between Sisters, and ill health, Elizabeth was hard-pressed — but not enough to forget her children.

Just as Anna's heart was settled, her health gave way. The next few years would tax Elizabeth's emotional strength and trust in God considerably, as two of her girls suffered and died from tuberculosis, while her boys gave her increasing cause for concern. William was so sick that he could not be moved from Mount St. Mary's College. Anna was just as ill, and Elizabeth did not dare to leave her or the other sick Sisters for long.

All the bouts of tuberculosis in the family had left their mark on Elizabeth. She admitted, "[Anna] may not be as ill as I imagine, for never was anyone easier frightened, after so many hard trials." She came down with a painful case of boils and was nearly frantic with worry for her children. As always, it was to God that Elizabeth turned for her comfort and support. Fear gave way time and time again to trust and resignation to God's will.

Elizabeth began to prepare her daughter to die. Eternity was her steadfast hope and only lasting consolation, and it was a spiritual principle that she had passed on to her daughter. They talked as much of happy news, William's return to health, letters from home, as they did of her approaching death. Anna's growth in holiness after her return home nine months previously had been heroic. Her sufferings were horrible to witness: her lungs were consumed and her bones protruded in places. Every breath was an agony. Her mother sat by her side as often as she could. The two of them surpassed the merely human in their love for one another through this final crisis. Elizabeth would call on Anna to offer up her increasing suffering, while Anna would gently scold her mother for crying: "Can it be for me, should you not rejoice? It will be but a moment and [we shall be] reunited for Eternity."

As Anna entered her final agony Elizabeth wrote, "...the pain of her eyes was so great she could no longer fix them. She said, 'I can no longer look at you, my dear Crucifix, but I enter my agony with my Savior . . . yes, adorable Lord, your will and yours alone be done. I will it too. I leave my dearest Mother because you will it.' "

Elizabeth knelt beside the bed holding high the crucifix for her little girl, the "Child of her soul," to see. Finally, she was led by the hand to the chapel to pray before the Blessed Sacrament until her sixteen-year-old daughter died.

Elizabeth was dead to the world in her grief. Yet when the boys arrived sobbing hard, she rebuked them, "You are *men*, and Mother looks for support from you." Anna was buried in the "little sacred wood," the third Sister to be buried there, and the third Seton. When all was done at graveside, one tear only was seen on Elizabeth's cheek and the impassioned words uttered in a whisper, "Father, Thy will be done!"

Virgin and Martyr

A Youthful St. Maria Goretti
Forgave Her Attacker Before She Died

The story of St. Maria Goretti (1890-1902) is at once simple and profound, born of tragedy and ending in glory.

This young girl from an impoverished farm family in Italy was attacked by a teenage neighbor, then stabbed repeatedly when she fought off his sexual advances. Her wounds would prove to be fatal, but before she died she forgave him with a faith and fervor far beyond her years: "I forgive Alessandro, I forgive him with all my heart, and I want him to be with me in heaven."

Less than a half-century later she was canonized by Pope Pius XII in a ceremony attended by some two hundred fifty thousand people. One of them was Maria's attacker — now sixty-six years old, freed after a long prison term — who joined others in the throng crying tears of joy. Knowing that Maria had forgiven him, he had learned how to forgive himself.

Story from *Saint of the Day*, Leonard Foley, OFM, Editor, St.
Anthony Messenger Press, 1990.

The largest crowd ever assembled for a canonization — two hundred fifty thousand — symbolized the reaction of millions touched by the simple story of Maria Goretti.

She was the daughter of a poor Italian tenant-farmer, had no chance to go to school, never learned to read or write. When she made her First Communion not long before her death at age twelve, she was one of the bigger and somewhat backward members of the class.

On a hot afternoon in July, Maria was sitting at the top of the stairs of her cottage, mending a shirt. She was not quite twelve years old, but physically mature. A cart stopped outside, and a neighbor, Alessandro, eighteen years old, ran up the stairs. He seized her and pulled her into a bedroom. She struggled and tried to call for help, gasping that she would be killed rather than submit. "No,

God does not wish it. It is a sin. You would go to hell for it." Alessandro began striking at her blindly with a long dagger.

She was taken to a hospital. Her last hours were marked by the usual simple compassion of the good — concern about where her mother would sleep, forgiveness of her murderer (she had been in fear of him, but did not say anything lest she cause trouble to his family), and her devout welcoming of Viaticum. She died about twenty-four hours after the attack.

Her murderer was sentenced to thirty years in prison. For a long time he was unrepentant and surly. One night he had a dream or vision of Maria, gathering flowers and offering them to him. His life changed. When he was released after twenty-seven years, his first act was to go to beg the forgiveness of Maria's mother.

Devotion to the young martyr grew, miracles were worked, and in less than a half-century she was canonized. At her beatification in 1947, her mother (then eighty-two), two sisters, and a brother appeared with Pope Pius XII on the balcony of St. Peter's. Three years later, at her canonization, a sixty-six-year-old Alessandro Serenelli knelt among the quarter-million people and cried tears of joy.

Maria may have had trouble with catechism, but she had no trouble with faith. God's will was holiness, decency, respect for one's body, absolute obedience, total trust. In a complex world, her faith was simple: it is a privilege to be loved by God, and to love him — at any cost. As the virtue of chastity dies the death of a thousand qualifications, she is a breath of sweet fresh air.

A Calming Presence

Even in the 'Dark Tunnel' of Dachau, Father Titus Brandsma Saw an Eternal Light

In comforting the afflicted souls in the Nazi concentration camp at Dachau, Blessed Titus Brandsma (1881-1942) continued the lifelong mission of helping others that he had undertaken as a Carmelite priest. There was one major difference: he now consoled others as a fellow prisoner.

Father Titus was one of the Netherlands' best-known scholars and spiritual leaders. A journalist as well, he wrote and spoke out about the gathering Nazi menace during the '30s, toning down his criticism not a bit when the Germans occupied his homeland in 1940. "The dangerous little friar," as the Germans called him, was soon a marked man. When he was finally arrested on January 19, 1942, he composed this defiant response in his prison cell: "The Nazi movement is regarded by the Dutch people not only as an insult to God in relation to his creatures but also a violation of the glorious traditions of the Dutch nation. If it is necessary, we, the Dutch people, will give our lives for our faith."

It took only months before Father Titus wound up in Dachau. Before he finally met death by lethal injection in the camp "hospital," he amazed his fellow captives — many of them priests as well — with his courage, compassion, and depth of faith. His gentleness reached out not only to other prisoners but, astoundingly, to his brutal captors as well. "Who knows?" he said, explaining his concern. "Perhaps something will stick."

Father Titus was beatified in 1985. This gripping account of his final days is from an inspiring biography written by Father Joseph Rees, a priest of the archdiocese of Westminster, England.

Selection adapted from *Titus Brandsma: A Modern Martyr*,
by Joseph Rees, Sidgwick & Jackson, 1971.

On July 12, 1942, Titus wrote his last letter. It was addressed to Oegeklooster, the place where he was born and where his sister lived in their old farmhouse. For the last time he wrote his comforting stereotyped comment: "All is well with me." It was followed by: "One has to adjust oneself, of course, to new situations, that with God's help one manages here as well as elsewhere." He ended up asking the family "not to worry too much about me," and signed himself, "In Christ, your Anno."

After the war, De Coninck, a Belgian Jesuit, wrote an article about the priests in Dachau. He said that Titus went to his death "happy that he had been treated like the scourged Christ," though Titus himself would never have put it like this. Histrionics were not his line. But there is no doubt that his sense of inner peace, of joy almost, was so deep that he conveyed it to everyone around him.

It is extraordinary that during his short stay in Dachau, a matter of five weeks, Titus Brandsma should have left the profound impression he did. He was, after all, one of many who were suffering equal misery and degradation, where it was a terrible struggle merely to stay alive. But Dr. Kentenich, who knew him for only two or three weeks, remarked in 1954 that "his person and his words suggested such calm, such resignation and so much hope, that one does not easily forget it."

Without reserve he consoled, encouraged, heard confessions in the *Stube*, or wherever the chance presented itself, and encouraged others to keep in touch with God.

One evening there was a near panic. Titus had returned from work utterly exhausted. He got through the roll call only to find that it was one of those occasions when the priests had to stay on for another spell of exercise. Still, Titus got through, although it was obvious that he could barely manage to eat, polish the bowl, and wash. What they had all feared for some time was now going to happen.

On his return to Block 28, a guard inspected him and was patently not satisfied. He beat and kicked Titus as if he had gone mad. He was watched by others in an agonizing silence. With his spectacle case still pressed under his arm, Titus had managed to crawl toward the doorstep of Block 28 where the Dutch friar Raphael Tijhuis helped him to get back into his bunk. There was no need to console Titus. He waited until the guard was safely out of the way; then, smiling, he said: "I knew whom I had with me!"

He then suggested that together they should say the *Adoro te* and, with a barely perceptible gesture, he blessed the friar.

The following morning Tijhuis learnt that Titus had spent a poor night as far as sleeping was concerned and that those sleepless hours had been spent in union with God. Nothing, moreover, would stop him from trying to bring the guards back to God and their humanity, in spite of all his fellow prisoners did to dissuade him. He talked to the guards and tried to make contact with them. When Tijhuis attempted to dissuade him from doing so, as it was quite futile and he was only going to get an extra beating, Titus replied: "Who knows? Perhaps something will stick."

He prayed for them a lot, but he also seems to have considered it his duty to approach them in an attempt to bring them back to their sanity. More than once he encouraged his fellow prisoners by saying: "We are here in a dark tunnel. We have to pass through it. Somewhere at the end shines the eternal light."

He spoke as much for the guards in their spiritual darkness as for the prisoners under their charge.

It was evident to everyone who saw him that he could not go on much longer. He had already been pressed to go into the "hospital" but, as some of them remembered, was not keen on the idea. Many were suspicious as to what went on there. And events have proved them right, for Dr. Rascher had set up an experimental station there where high pressure and exposure experiments were practiced on defenseless prisoners. Another professor, Schilling, had his allotment of prisoners infected with malaria agents. Biochemical experiments were also carried out.

Father Kuyper was on the spot when Becker, the supervisor of Block 28, with his elbows leaning on the frame of an open window, bent down toward those inside. He seemed less maliciously humored than usual and told Titus that he looked pretty ill. Later, before he was executed in 1945 for his war crimes, this man was to reconcile himself with God. Who knows at what moment the seeds of this reconciliation began to grow? It is not impossible that the prayers that Titus offered up for him began at some stage to have effect.

Now, at any rate, having looked him over carefully, Becker suggested that Titus had better go to the "hospital." Titus, for the first time without an argument, agreed. Father Kuyper was amazed at how readily he accepted the suggestion this time. Possibly Titus himself felt that he could not go on any longer.

One hears nothing about any words of farewell. What we do know is that he could barely stand on his feet anymore, that he was exhausted and very ill, that he had been persuaded even by his own friends to go, that it must have seemed to him the only place left to go to. And so, on that cold, rainy morning, after having been beaten up, he was at the end of his tether and, supported by his colleague, he entered the camp "hospital."

He was to be there for only a matter of days, at the most a week. He lay there on a straw mattress on which so many had died before him. He had no room to himself, no crucifix at which to gaze. The care taken of him was minimal, but he was beyond human care.

A nurse has come forward of her own accord to bear witness to Titus Brandsma, to whom she administered the deadly injection that was to put him out of his misery with the same casual effectiveness as if he were a suffering dog.

From her we know that he had been disgracefully humiliated by the doctors who experimented on him. It is neither fitting nor necessary to describe these experiments. While the doctors used his body for their own ends Titus merely said aloud: "Not my will, but Thine be done."

Titus had seriously talked to the nurse and discovered that she came from Holland, and moreover from a Catholic home. "How is it," he had asked her, "that you ended up here? I shall pray for you a great deal."

He gave her his rosary, at which she protested: "But I can no longer pray."

To this Titus retorted: "Well, if you can't say the first part, surely you can still say, 'Pray for us sinners.' "

She tried to excuse herself, and muttered something about "so many bad priests." Titus responded to her remark and asked her to observe the sufferings of the imprisoned priests around her. He even told her that he was glad to undergo his own sufferings for God's sake.

This nurse, whose name and address are known in Rome only, as her identity must remain secret on grounds of possible reprisals, has never forgotten her encounter with Titus Brandsma. She has returned to the practice of her Catholic religion.

A prominent Austrian, Dr. Fritz Kühr, who survived the horrors of the camp, and was even given an administrative position at the "hospital," had a couple of times taken Communion to Titus. He fell completely under the spell of his personality, even in these distressing circumstances. Kühr had to be extremely careful, of course, as he had no business to be with the patients.

The other patients were constantly seen to be surrounding Titus who tried to encourage and console them and direct their attention to God. But, for the last day or two, he was unconscious. Dr. Kühr had twice slipped in to see if Titus could take Holy Communion, but he had found him beyond recall.

The nurse's final evidence concerns Titus's fatal injection. It was given on Sunday, July 26, at 1:50 P.M. Ten minutes later, at two o'clock, Titus Brandsma died.

There is nothing to be said for the sufferings of Dachau and camps like them, unless it is, perhaps, the compassion and understanding between men that they have generated in place of the hate that created them. There is little to remind us of the agony and desolation, the waste of human life and spirit, that they represent except in stories like those of Titus Brandsma. But although we may, perhaps, be fortunate enough never to experience their like again, they have not failed in human, as well as in spiritual, terms if they have served to show us how, in the most dire moments of sorrow, in the most agonizing moments of stress, there is always light at the end of the tunnel.

'Give Us This Day . . .'

Heroic World War II Chaplain Died
With the Lord's Prayer on His Lips

He was a chaplain quite by accident, but Father William Cummings's exploits in World War II were heroic by any measure and earned him a permanent place of honor in the annals of the military. The Japanese were advancing on Manila in the war's early days when Father Cummings hitched a boat ride with U.S. soldiers across Manila Bay to the Bataan peninsula. The school where he taught had been burned down, the American priest said, its students scattered. Besides, he thought the army might be able to use him in the days ahead.

How right he proved to be. All through the siege of Bataan and the final holdout on the island of Corregidor, he was a singular source of comfort and inspiration to overwhelmed GIs. His presence and that of other chaplains was needed more than ever in dangerous combat situations because, as he told a war correspondent so succinctly, "There are no atheists in foxholes." The correspondent flashed those words across the sea to home and around the world.

Then the real ordeal began: imprisonment by the Japanese, death marches, living conditions nothing less than inhumane. "There are so many men here," he said in a prison camp. "I cannot help them all, but if I can help a few, than maybe God will feel my life is justified. When I worry about their suffering, I don't have time to think of myself."

His final days were spent in the hold of a Japanese prison ship, still comforting the men he loved. This moving account of his death is by Sidney Stewart — a GI who survived and who, although not a Catholic, made Father Cummings the centerpiece of his engrossing memoir of those dark days.

Selection from *Give Us This Day*, by Sidney Stewart,
W. W. Norton & Co., Inc., 1956.

Each evening sanity returned to the men when Father Cummings began to pray. By now, almost all the other priests had died.

354   *Our Sunday Visitor's*

"There were eighteen, no, nineteen of us when we left Manila," he recalled one evening. "Now . . ." He didn't finish.

Each night the solace and the comfort that we received from the prayers was more than anything that anyone else could do for us. He gave us strength and hope.

I looked forward every hour for night to come, when Father Cummings stood and said his prayer again. I lived only for that prayer of faith and hope. It was the only strength I had. His voice was like the voice of God to me. I knew that Rass felt the same, Rass, who was always so much more religious than I. He was now so weak that it was all he could do to stand. Yet I knew he lived too for that prayer in the evening.

Men were dying at the rate of twenty and thirty a day. Every morning their bodies were wrapped with rope and drawn up through the hold and dropped into the sea. Each day I watched the bodies going up into the sky through the open hatch. The rope swung out across the deck and I heard the sound of the bodies as they splashed into the sea.

One afternoon Father Cummings crawled over to pray for a dying boy and did not come back. Rass went to look for him. He found him unconscious through exhaustion, so white and still that when he brought him back and laid him near me, I was frightened.

I knew I could not hold on without him. I was afraid to ask Rass if he was dead. Not saying a word, Rass shook his head.

"No." He laid Father Cummings beside me. I sat up and began to rub his arms and his hands and his face. Rass helped, and soon life returned. His eyelids flickered slowly and he opened his kind gray eyes.

"I'll be all right, boys." He smiled wanly.

But he wasn't able to walk anymore. Rass cared for the two of us now. Father Cummings had been passing blood many days with dysentery. He was so weak that he could not walk. His lips were parched and cracked and his hands moved convulsively up and down his throat. I knew that he couldn't make it much longer. I prayed silently to myself that I would die before he did, that I would not have to see him die.

But that evening, as it was growing dark down in the hold, and the faint light that came through the hatch was nearly gone, he begged me, "Can you lift your arm behind me? I can't stand, but my voice will carry. They will hear my prayer!"

I pushed my shoulder in behind him and put my arms around him and held him up. Faltering, he began to speak.

"Men! Men, can you hear my voice?"

Slowly he began to pray: "Our Father, who art in heaven, hallowed be thy name. . . ."

The cries of the men became still. I concentrated on the voice that soothed me and gave me strength and the will to live. Then I felt his body shiver and tremble in my arms. He gasped for air and there was a terrible pain written on his face. He gritted his teeth, sighed, and went on.

"Thy will be done — on earth — as it is — in heaven."

I felt him tremble again as if he wanted to cough. His hands fluttered and his eyelids almost closed. Then with superhuman effort he spoke again.

"Give us this day . . ."

I felt his body go tense all over. He relaxed and his hand fell by his side. I waited, but his eyes looked straight ahead. The eyelids no longer flickered. I knew he was dead, but I continued to hold him, afraid even to move. Rass crawled beside me. He lifted Father Cummings's hand and felt for his pulse.

"Lay him down, Sid," he said evenly. "He's gone. Lay him down. He's gone now."

I cradled his head against my shoulder. I didn't want to lay him down. I couldn't bear to face the fact that he was gone.

"Go ahead, Sid. Lay him down. Lay him down, he's gone," Rass said firmly.

I moved from behind him and laid his head gently on the floor. Then I noticed that the hold was quiet. The men had gone off into their exhausted, hungry sleep. Rass reached across the body and gripped my arm.

"Sid, he died like he would have wanted to die, praying to the God that he believed in, to the God that gave him strength."

"Why did he have to die, Rass? Why did he have to leave us?"

"Don't think about the fact that he is gone. Try to think of his last words. The last thing he tried to give us."

Rass went on calmly, "You know his last words were, 'Give us this day.' We must try only to live until we can see the sun up in the morning, you and I, and we'll make it. Live only for one day, for just twenty-four more hours."

'It Was the Pope...'

Romans Credited Pius XII With Saving the Eternal City During World War II

No single event during the lifetime of Pope Pius XII (1876-1958) was as personally challenging or distressing to him as the bloody carnage of World War II — nor was anything more damaging to his reputation, following his death, than the charge that he had failed to "speak out" on behalf of Europe's Jews during that conflict.

Sadly, the allegation gained a wide measure of credence — even though the record utterly fails to support it. He directed efforts to save Jews in Rome and throughout Italy; on a broader level he vigorously denounced Nazi policies and atrocities. He did so, even though such efforts courted disaster in the form of further reprisals, and after the war many Jewish organizations and individuals thanked him publicly for his work on their behalf.

All during the war Pope Pius labored tirelessly for peace, with particular concern for the safety of Rome and its people. These vignettes of his wartime activities by Frank J. Korn — author of Rome: The Eternal City (Our Sunday Visitor, Inc.) *— hint at the delicate task that fell to him as Vicar of Christ during history's bloodiest conflict.*

Selections from "Pope Pius XII: The Pope of Peace In
an Age of War," by Frank J. Korn, *Our Sunday
Visitor*, October 15, 1978.

1. Tears Amidst the Ruins

At about eleven in the morning of July 19, 1943, a hundred American bombers flew over the Tiburtina section of Rome and in their wake left horrible destruction of life and property. Among the victims was the venerable and beautiful sixth-century Basilica of St. Lawrence Outside the Walls, which suffered extensive damage. The noise and the tremors were heard and felt across the city, and the pope, who was talking to a small group in his study high upon the Vatican Hill, rushed to his window and, transfixed in grief, watched the ugly smoke clouds rising over Tiburtina. Concerned at once about innocent victims, the Holy Father telephoned Monsignor Giovanni Battista Montini, Secretary of Ordinary Ecclesiastical Affairs, and told him to go to the Vatican bank and draw out a large sum of money, take the first car he saw, and drive to the scene.

When the pontiff arrived at the site, terrified men, women, and children ran toward the tall white figure, their *Santo Padre*, to whom they now looked for comfort and strength.

Papa Pacelli, their fellow Roman, walked among the people, comforting the injured and dying, his white soutane smeared with blood where his spiritual sons and daughters touched and grasped his garment as children often do when scared. One lady thrust her infant into the Holy Father's hands. Tears welled in his eyes when he quickly realized the baby was dead. And those same eyes brimmed again when His Holiness was informed that a few bombs had struck a section of the Campo Verano, Rome's largest cemetery, and had destroyed the Pacelli family plot where the pontiff's parents had been interred.

But there were still works of mercy to be done, and Pope Pius, with Monsignor Montini ever at his side, began to distribute the money from the Vatican bank until it was all gone. Then, before he departed, he climbed up on the rubble of the Basilica of St. Lawrence to say some soothing and encouraging words to his flock and to lead them in prayer. On his return trip to the Vatican, Pope Pius sobbed all the way. Back in his study he dashed off a bitter letter of protest to President Roosevelt in which he described graphically the horror he had just viewed.

2. Appalled by the Nazis

Later that summer, after the Italian Army had surrendered, Nazi troops goose-stepped into Rome and ringed the Vatican "to protect the Holy Father and the Eternal City."

On November 6, at around eight in the evening, a German plane dropped four small bombs in the Vatican itself. It was the hope of the Nazis that the pope, now recognizing the Badoglio administration as the official government of Italy, would be intimidated, and secondly that the public would suspect the Allied Force as the villains in this air raid also.

When word of the treachery raced through Rome the next morning, many thousands of Romans converged on St. Peter's Square to gather beneath the pope's window. There for several hours they cheered their pontiff's courage and poured out their love for him. The German high command in the city offered to enter the Vatican and "investigate the whole matter." Pius coolly declined the offer. While vowing to respect the integrity of the Vatican, the German leadership also urged Pope Pius to let them escort him to a neutral country in the interest of his "personal safety." This offer was also coolly rejected. Rome's bishop had no desire, or intention, of neglecting his own diocese. Hitler began to contemplate the idea of hauling the pope off to captivity in Germany.

At this point the campaign of persecution against the Jewish minority of Rome, which had been launched with the Nazis' arrival, was accelerated.

One day back in September, Chief Rabbi Eugenio Zollo had been summoned to Nazi headquarters and informed that he would have to deliver to German authorities, by noon of the following day, one million lire in cash and a hundred pounds of gold, and that failure to do so would result in the dispersal of the Roman Jewish community. "Dispersal" was the Nazi euphemism for executions, imprisonments, and atrocities. In vain the poor Jewish people tried to raise the ransom. Chief Rabbi Eugenio appealed to Chief Priest Eugenio, who instructed the Vatican treasurer to raise whatever gold was necessary (even if it meant melting down sacred vessels).

Appalled by the Nazi programs across Europe and in his own city, the pope did not discourage the steady flow of those seeking asylum across the various Vatican border checkpoints. In fact, he fostered the flow by directing Rome's nuns, priests, monks, and Catholic laity to open the doors of their convents, churches, monasteries, and homes to their Jewish brethren. Even the ancient catacombs were pressed into service as secret shelters. Before long the Vatican, the papal villa in Castel Gandolfo, and nearly two hundred Catholic institutions in and around the Eternal City bulged with thousands of Jewish fugitives, including Chief Rabbi Zollo. As the tension in the city grew more unbearable, the pope flexed what little Vatican muscle there was. St. Peter's doors were ordered closed. Pope Pius took away the ceremonial halberds of his Swiss Guards and replaced them with machine guns.

3. A Jolly Good Fellow

In the waning hours of the fourth of June 1944, Allied troops at last penetrated the ancient Aurelian fortifications and entered *La Città Eterna*.

In the weeks to follow, the Holy Father was to grant countless audiences daily to large groups of American servicemen, of every religious persuasion. Some were awed by the natural charisma of Pope Pius XII, others fascinated by his special looks, all held in thrall by his high-pitched, gentle, and fatherly voice. Many were moved to tears of joy at being in the presence of Christ's vicar on earth.

Occasionally Pope Pius would receive smaller groups of the

men in audience in the various antechambers of the Apostolic Palace. These gatherings were considerably less ceremonial and *Papa Pacelli* delighted in exchanging a few light words with each sailor or soldier in the room. On some occasions, not out of disrespect but out of spontaneous joy and love, the pope's visitors would depart from protocol. Pope Pius's bony features burst into a boyish grin one day when at the conclusion of a small audience an overjoyed lieutenant called out, "Okay! Let's really hear it for His Holiness!" and then led his surprised but willing men in a rendition of "For He's a Jolly Good Fellow."

A Gift of Presence

When Father Solanus Prayed for Them, People Found That Things Got Better

It's often remarked that one of the greatest gifts a priest can give is that of presence — when there's a family crisis, when a loved one dies, whenever the situation calls for prayers and comfort. People often find that a priest, just by being there in a time of need, is a symbol of reassurance. And they appreciate it.

In that event, Capuchin Father Solanus Casey (1870-1957) was a gift-giver unlike any other. He was present to people day after day, year after year, welcoming with a glad heart the strangers who showed up at his door — by the thousands! Not only did he provide comfort for them with his words and his prayers, he often seemed to work miracles on their behalf as well.

When he was ordained in 1904, his superiors recognized his goodness but thought his abilities were somewhat limited, and so they made him a "simplex priest" — one who could offer Mass but was not able to hear confessions or preach on doctrinal matters. He didn't complain about that, or about the menial jobs he was given over the years, including doorkeeper. That simply meant he could meet more people — helping them, praying for them, giving them his blessing.

Word of this wonder worker spread —first in the Midwest, then throughout the country and beyond. Father Solanus is now a candidate for beatification and canonization, this "simplex priest" who preached sermons of incomparable eloquence as he spoke to that endless line of visitors.

His death didn't stop them, by the way. Every day dozens of written petitions cover his tomb in the chapel of St. Bonaventure's Monastery in Detroit, left there by visitors who still want his prayers. It's safe to assume that he's still listening, and still praying.

Selection from *Our Sunday Visitor's Father Solanus: The Story of Solanus Casey, O.F.M. Cap. (Updated)*, by Catherine M. Odell, Our Sunday Visitor, Inc., 1988, 1995.

After eighty-six years of life, including sixty years as a religious, Father Solanus Casey, O.F.M. Cap., had very little that could be called "personal effects." Several days after his death in Detroit, Michigan, on July 31, 1957, his Capuchin Brothers went to his small room at St. Bonaventure's Friary to collect his things.

There was a black-brimmed winter hat, a brown skull cap, some family photos, letters, a trunk, some books, a pair of wire-rimmed glasses, a pair of shoes, a winter overcoat, a second pair of sandals, some underclothes and nightshirts, a breviary, a violin with bow, several pictures of the Blessed Virgin, a rosary, two worn habits, and the red stole he'd worn each Wednesday at the 3:00 P.M. healing service. It was a poor man's holdings.

A much larger legacy of the man did exist. It was the kind that couldn't be counted or evaluated in terms of dollars and cents.

"Some years ago I was in utter despair and just wanted to die," confessed a tearful woman at the Capuchin's wake. "I spoke to him and began to live again."

"Fifteen years ago, my son was dying of polio," a parent reported. "Father Solanus blessed him and today he is in the best of health."

There were hundreds — even thousands — of such stories. They all had a common theme. Father Solanus had prayed, and things were never the same again. Many times, things changed for the better. People with cancer, paralysis, blindness, emotional illness, and tumors were among those who claimed healings through this priest. Others realized that Solanus was preparing them to accept death, the loss of a loved one, or continued suffering.

When Father Solanus prayed for others, his prayers were answered with unexplainable frequency. He was able to foresee future events and often shared his visions with others. In today's light, it seems evident that Father Solanus had been given the gifts of miracles, prophecy, healing, discernment, and other gifts of the Spirit described by St. Paul in 1 Corinthians 12. Father Solanus also had mighty gifts of faith, hope, and love that overflowed into all that he said and did.

His was a life that changed others, often after no more than a momentary meeting. His closeness to the Lord was so apparent that people of all ages, creeds, economic backgrounds, and cultures were drawn to him. An investigation of his cause for beatification and canonization is currently under way. As a result, he may one day be named as the first native-born American male canonized as a saint. Father Solanus himself might have blushed at the prospect. Throughout his life, he simply asked his friends to pray for his own conversion and salvation.

A Prayer for the Dead

The Night a Tortured Soul From Purgatory Made His Way to Padre Pio

Contemporaries have always flocked to the side of people they recognized for exceptional holiness — people, as previous stories indicated, ranging in time from St. Blase to Father Solanus Casey. That is no less true of Padre Pio (1887-1968), the Italian Capuchin mystic who bore the stigmata — the same wounds suffered by Jesus in the crucifixion — longer than anyone else in Church history. Throughout his long priestly career visitors appeared every day at the Capuchin Friary of Our Lady of Grace at San Giovanni Rotondo to confess their sins, worship with him, and ask for his prayers.

Americans came to know Padre Pio — whose given name was Francesco Forgione — after World War II, when GIs visited the priest by the thousands. Their accounts of his Masses — at which he seemed to bear the pain of Christ's crucifixion, oblivious to those around him — brought home to American Catholics what those in Italy and nearby countries already knew: that Padre Pio was a man of extraordinary gifts.

Fame brought some problems. Many questioned his activities, but various Church investigations turned up no evidence of wrongdoing — nor any medical explanation of his wounds. Pope John Paul II, who as a young priest had gone to confession to Padre Pio, seemed to give his cause a personal blessing by visiting his tomb (in 1987) and praising him as an exemplary priest.

Padre Pio repeatedly counseled visitors to pray for the living and the dead, even those whose holiness might seem not to require it. When Pope Pius X died, for example, he said, "I believe that his holy soul has no need of our intercessory prayers, but let us pray for his eternal rest just the same, since our prayers will never go to waste."

The list of his supernatural gifts is astounding, and he was beatified in May 1999 in recognition of his holiness. On one memorable occasion, he was able to follow his own advice and pray for the dead — in a personal way, under circumstances that appear to have no natural explanation. Here is his biographer's account of what happened.

Selection from *Padre Pio: The True Story (Revised and Expanded)*, by C. Bernard Ruffin, Our Sunday Visitor, Inc., 1991.

In May 1922, Padre Pio told the bishop of Melfi, Alberto Costa, and the superior of the friary, Padre Lorenzo of San Marco in Lamis, in the presence of five other friars, the account that one of them, Fra Alberto D'Apolito of San Giovanni Rotondo, wrote down. Padre Pio said that "in the middle" of the war, after a heavy snowfall, he was sitting by the fireplace one evening in the guest room, absorbed in prayer, when an old man, wearing an old-fashioned cloak still favored by southern Italian peasants at the time, sat down beside him. "I could not imagine how he could have entered the friary at this time of night. I questioned him: 'Who are you? What do you want?' "

The old man told him, "Padre Pio, I am Pietro Di Mauro, son of Nicola, nicknamed Precoco." He went on to say, "I died in this friary on the eighteenth of September 1908, in Cell Number 4, when it was still [a poorhouse]. One night, while in bed, I fell asleep with a lighted cigar, which ignited the [mattress] and I died, suffocated and burned. I am still in purgatory. I need a holy Mass in order to be freed. God permitted that I come and ask you for help."

According to Padre Pio: "After listening to him, I replied, 'Rest assured that tomorrow I will celebrate Mass for your liberation.' I arose and accompanied him to the door of the friary, so that he could leave. I did not realize at that moment that the door was closed and locked: I opened it and bade him farewell. The moon lit up the square, covered with snow. When I no longer saw him in front of me, I was taken by a sense of fear, and I closed the door, reentered the guest room, and felt faint."

A few days later, Padre Pio told the story to Padre Paolino, and the two decided to go to the town hall, where they looked at the vital statistics for the year 1908 and found that on September 18 of that year, one Pietro Di Mauro had in fact died of burns and asphyxiation in Room Number 4 at the friary, then used as a home for the indigent poor!

One of a Kind

Archbishop Sheen Captivated Audiences of Millions

Archbishop Fulton J. Sheen (1895-1979), quite possibly the most gifted preacher of his day, was beyond question the greatest television personality the Church ever produced. His style, his wit, and his faith-filled message captivated millions and won immeasurable friendship and respect for the Church.

A first-rate scholar, Archbishop Sheen had a rare gift: he was able to express complex theological distinctions in terms that everyday people could readily understand. It was a gift that would help him win many converts, including well-known personalities from the political and publishing worlds.

Partly as a result of that — and certainly as the result of his amazingly popular Life Is Worth Living *television program — he also became something of a celebrity. But no one ever had to take him down a peg. Fulton Sheen was quite capable of doing that himself, and, in fact, enjoyed nothing more. He loved telling a story on himself — like the one in which someone asked him about his formal title. "What is it like to be titular archbishop of Newport in Wales?" the questioner wanted to know. "Very much like being made a Knight of the Garter," he replied. "It's an honor to have the Garter, but it doesn't hold up a thing."*

The accompanying selection from Archbishop Sheen's autobiography gives something of the background of his television years — and suggests the ways in which his words of faith were able to influence millions of doubtful people. From time to time, as the U.S. bishops try to uncover a more effective communications strategy, someone invariably asks, "Why don't we get another Fulton Sheen?" The answer should be obvious. There isn't another Fulton Sheen. He was one of a kind.

Selection from *Treasure in Clay — The Autobiography of Fulton J. Sheen*, Doubleday & Co., Inc., 1980.

There was never any rehearsal for our television show, which meant a great saving for the producer. This was in part because I never use notes. *Time* magazine once sent a special writer to the theater to see what trick I was using week after week to give telecasts without the use of a TelePrompTer or idiot cards. The only prop that I used was a blackboard. It was on a swivel so that after writing on one side it could be turned over. I created the illusion that an "angel," who was one of the stagehands, would wash one side of the board as I moved away from one of the cameras' range. When the board was clean, I would perhaps use the blackboard again but always attributing its cleanliness to the angel, who became nationally famous. . . .

I appeared on television just as a bishop in black cassock and purple cloak called "ferriola." I was giving a lecture once in Longmeadow, Massachusetts. The auditorium was on the second floor. Some boys on the other side of the street on this warm night could see me on the stage and they shouted out: "Superman."

As a custom that started in kindergarten, I always wrote "JMJ" at the top of the blackboard, as I do on every piece of paper before I write — and which I hope someday will be put on my tombstone. In answer to many letters, the public finally recognized me and the words "Jesus, Mary, and Joseph."

Many televisions in bars were tuned to my program, which aired opposite Milton Berle. This was due in part to many taxi drivers who enjoyed my television show and who stopped working during that half hour. One taxi driver said to me one day: "Have you written a book?" I told him that I had. He said: "If I didn't already have a book, I'd buy yours."

The judgment of the viewing audience varied according to the way I appeared on their television screen. Assisting at an episcopal ordination in Brooklyn, I was marching into the cathedral with a number of other bishops when one woman on the sidewalk shouted: "You certainly look better on television!"

I would always have a large clock at the front of the stage when I spoke. This was in order that I might do my own timing. The television time that was without interruption lasted about twenty-seven minutes and twenty seconds. The trick to conclude on time without hurrying or without being cut was to assign an exact time to the conclusion. If it were two minutes or three minutes long, I would break off from my regular theme and begin the conclusion so there was never any hurried cutoff.

I would spend about thirty hours preparing every telecast, which meant that enough material was gathered to talk for an hour or more. As in breathing, there is always more oxygen outside of the body than that which is taken in by the lungs, so the knowledge that one has on a certain subject must be far greater than that which is imparted. Though I would forget this or that point which I intended to deliver, I could draw on the store of accumulated information to take its place. . . .

When I began television nationally and on a commercial basis, . . . I was no longer talking in the name of the Church and under the sponsorship of its bishops. The new method had to be more ecumenical and directed to Catholics, Protestants, Jews, and all men of good will. It was no longer a direct presentation of Christian doctrine but rather a reasoned approach to it beginning with something that was common to the audience. Hence, during those television years, the subjects ranged from communism, to art, to science, to humor, aviation, war, etc. Starting with something that was common to the audience and to me, I would gradually proceed from the known to the unknown or to the moral and Christian philosophy. It was the same method Our Blessed Lord used when he met a prostitute at the well. What was there in common between Divine Purity and this woman who had five husbands and was living with a man who was not her husband? The only common denominator was a love of cold water. Starting with that, he led to the subject of the waters of everlasting life.

A Mission Hero

The Rosary Sustained Bishop Walsh During His Chinese Captivity

The Church continues to produce its missionary heroes in our own day, few of them more courageous and faithful — not to mention modest — than Maryknoll Bishop James E. Walsh (1891-1981). One of the original students to enroll in the society, he was a pioneer in its China mission and later served (1936-1946) as Maryknoll's superior general.

Then he returned to China and in 1948 became head of the Catholic Central Bureau, a kind of clearinghouse for all Church groups in that nation. But by then the communists had taken control of the government, eventually ordering the bureau to suspend all operations and placing Bishop Walsh under investigation. In 1958 he was arrested and sentenced — as a spy, of all things — to a twenty-year jail term.

He later wrote that the rosary was chiefly responsible for sustaining him during his long years as a prisoner. "To say the rosary one needs nothing at all but time," he said, "and now you have plenty of that. . . . Moreover, it is a way to continue your ministry, come to think of it. You can pray now for all those troubled people of yours instead of just worrying about them all day long."

The bishop was seventy-nine when he was finally released in 1970, after being held for twelve years. Weak and frail, he met the press at the Maryknoll Hospital in Kowloon; his statement that day forms the story that follows. Despite his ordeal, he never lost his modesty or his gentle humor. When The Catholic University of America gave him its Cardinal Gibbons Award, he said only this:

"I am not aware that I did anything to deserve such an honor. True, I did spend twelve years in prison in China, and that is something unusual, no doubt. But in my case, the experience was just a routine part of my profession, and therefore, I consider it no great credit to myself. I was a Catholic priest and my people were in trouble. So, I simply stayed with them as all priests should at such times."

Selection from *Zeal for Your House*, by Bishop James E.
Walsh, Our Sunday Visitor, Inc., 1976.

I'm very happy to be free once again. I never thought I would ever see the day of my release. I felt that I would not live long enough to complete my sentence of twenty years, and that I would die in prison. It is a bit hard for me to believe even now that I have been released. I have no bitterness toward those who tried and condemned me. I just could never feel angry with any Chinese. I felt that way almost from the day I first set foot in China in 1918 and it has just grown stronger with the years, even during my imprisonment.

I love the Chinese people.

I must admit that I find it hard to justify the severity of the sentence meted out to me, for I was not a spy either for the U.S. government or for the Vatican. I came to China in 1918 as a priest and missioner for the purpose of preaching the Gospel of Jesus Christ to the Chinese people and tending to their spiritual and material needs. I can tell you in all honesty and sincerity that I have never spent a day during my forty years on Chinese soil in doing anything but that.

It should be obvious that from the time of my arrest until my release my experiences have been varied. It hasn't all been sweetness and light. There were periods of harassment and personal suffering. The monotony of daily confinement in a small room for twelve years; waking up each morning and trying to plan how I would occupy my day so as to maintain my sanity and ideals as a priest and missioner to the Chinese people was especially hard to bear. At the same time I'm grateful to Almighty God that for the most part I was treated with basic human dignity and given the basic necessities.

Right now I find myself rather weak physically and I tire quickly. My Maryknoll superiors have decided I should rest here in the hospital for a few weeks and then return to my homeland. I'm ready and willing to do as they ask. That has been a guideline for me all my life. I'd like to see my brothers and sisters once again and all of my old Maryknoll confreres who have borne the heat and burden of the missionary day with me for so long.

I'm beginning to suspect that many changes have taken place in all walks of life since I last had contact with the outside world. I feel a bit like Rip Van Winkle waking up after a long sleep.

I'd like very much to visit our Holy Father, my superior as Christ's vicar, and hope to do so when I can travel.

I'm more than grateful for all the love and care that has been given to me here in Our Lady of Maryknoll Hospital since I arrived a few days ago. I want to express my heartfelt thanks to the doctors and nurses and to all the hospital staff. I can't possibly answer them all individually, but I want to express my thanks to all those who have sent me telegrams and personal letters conveying their best wishes and joy.

I'm just a bit bewildered by all the fuss and attention that has followed my release. After all I was only doing my duty as a priest and shepherd by staying with my flock.

When the Best Die...

Cardinal Cooke's Example Inspired a Young Priest, Ordained on His Deathbed

As a friend, confidant, and later biographer of New York's Cardinal Terence Cooke (1921-1983), Father Benedict J. Groeschel, c.f.r., knew the cardinal well. Father Benedict was with him in his final days, when the mortal illness that was secret for so long finally became known to the world. Arguably, those days also constituted the cardinal's finest hours — when, in his own dying, he prayed not only for those who had died before him but also for all those in troubled places around the world, the living who so desperately needed his prayers as well. Father Benedict writes movingly of those last hours in Thy Will Be Done *(Alba House, 1990).*

The final prayers of Cardinal Cooke would come to rest in ways that even he might not have imagined — for example, on the cancer-wracked body of a New York seminarian named Eugene Hamilton, who, inspired by the cardinal, would press on with his studies, and would reach his goal of the priesthood only hours before his own death.

Here is Father Benedict's account of that moving moment.

Selection from *A Priest Forever*, by Fr. Benedict J. Groeschel, c.f.r., Our Sunday Visitor, Inc., 1998.

Someone asked me recently why the best die apparently long before their time. This is a mystery and will remain one till the end of the world. Why do those who have so much to give leave us so soon? And why do those who contribute little or nothing, or those who only take and demand more, go on so much longer? It is a mystery — but there are some answers.

By the grace of God, many of the real givers manage in the process of dying to make their leaving of this world a great gift to those they leave behind. Such a person was Cardinal Terence Cooke, the archbishop of New York who died of cancer and leukemia in 1983. Always known as a kindly, gentle, and most dedicated priest and a man of consistent humility and patience, he had secretly been terminally ill for nine years. During these years he worked tirelessly, exhibiting an almost mysterious energy and resilience while undergoing painful and debilitating chemotherapy. During the last six weeks of his life, when his imminent death was revealed, he used his last energies to write several powerful pastoral letters in defense of human life, especially of the unborn and the terminally ill. He pleaded for the poor, the handicapped, the aged. He also wrote about peace and justice in Northern Ireland, and even a letter of sympathy on the death of Cardinal Medeiros of Boston. His last words in defense of life will echo long after his death.

While writing the biography of Cardinal Cooke, I was fortunate enough to receive innumerable stories of his selfless service — far too many to use in his biography. His own writings and the account of his deeds became a series of lessons on how to live the eight beatitudes. After his death, his example and intercession became a chain of blessings that gives no sign of diminishing.

The lives of people of great generosity often become chains of blessings and of truly Christian attitudes for those they leave behind. Sometimes this phenomenon is recognized in the life of a well-known person like Cardinal Cooke, but often it is unnoticed in the life of an uncelebrated person. Perhaps if you think about it you can find some giver, someone of special goodness and generosity in your own past whose example lives on in others sensitive enough to have learned.

For thousands of people this phenomenon of lasting influence is true of Cardinal Cooke. Years after his death I find myself asking what he would have done in a troubling situation. A heart-moving example of the cardinal's power to deeply affect another person's life has recently come to light in the words of Father Eugene Hamilton, a young New York seminarian ordained a priest in the hour of death. Cardinal Cooke and this seminarian met only once, when Eugene as a child attended his father's ordination to the diaconate. But when Eugene — whose kindness, leadership, and friendliness resembled the cardinal's in so many ways — came down with cancer he immediately turned to the archbishop as a model and guide.

The following moving passage is taken from the manuscript of a book Eugene left in his computer and now published in my biography of this extraordinary young man (*A Priest Forever*, Our Sunday Visitor, Inc., 1998).

"Terence J. Cooke, archbishop of New York, became a model for my struggle with cancer and a model for my vocation. For [nineteen] years, Cardinal Cooke battled cancer and lived out his priestly vocation. His perseverance was admirable; his fidelity to his personal understanding of a priest was remarkable. Both were qualities that I had come to admire many years before I myself became sick. . . .

"I had thought of Cardinal Cooke often in my seminary years and the preceding years while I was contemplating my vocation. His episcopal motto, *Fiat Voluntas Tua* ('Thy Will Be Done'), highlighted my own desire to do the will of the Father. Throughout my life it was the Father's will that had drawn me in directions and led me to follow paths that I never would have dreamed of. . . .

"With my diagnosis, I became more familiar with the life of Cardinal Cooke and the man himself by reading everything I could on him. I would speak with him in prayer; he had cancer, he would understand. I would tell him of how much I wanted to be a priest, and I got a sense of his own love of the priesthood. While I would receive my chemotherapy treatments, I would whisper '*Fiat Voluntas Tua*' over and over. It became my prayer and my hope. Like a true saint, he drew me closer to God, to Mary, and to the Church. I asked one and all to pray for the cardinal's intercession and his ultimate canonization. Here was a New York priest with cancer; this was an individual who would realize what I was going through. My relationship with Cardinal Cooke brought me out of this physical world, yet the situation became more real. I was praying with and asking the intercession of someone in the spiritual world, yet I became more human as a result. My connection with Cardinal Cooke never took me out of this world but firmly planted me in it. After receiving my terminal diagnosis, I went to the crypt in St. Patrick's Cathedral to visit Cardinal Cooke's tomb. After praying with my family, I spent some time alone in that crypt. With each passing day, I was being drawn closer to him; the Father's will had become more urgent. Like Cardinal Cooke, I had now entered that mysterious category of persons known as the dying."

Eugene's great confidence in God led him to believe that he would be ordained so that he could participate in the Paschal Mystery of eternal life as a priest. With his family and friends he asked the intercession of the late cardinal whose cause for beatification was already in process. Gene and his family prayed that either he would be cured so as to be ordained with his class, or that he would be able to become a priest ahead of time. When Gene's medical situation deteriorated, Cardinal John O'Connor applied for a papal dispensation to ordain him three years before the end of his studies. This permission was given by the Holy Father "from my whole heart." A few days later — on January 24, 1997, when Gene unexpectedly started to slip away — Bishop (later Archbishop) Edwin O'Brien, then rector of his seminary, ordained Gene less than three hours before he left this world.

The gentle goodness of Cardinal Cooke and the youthful devotion and deep faith of Father Eugene came together to give many of us a profound example of the power of faith in very dark times. Already a great many have been blessed by this example sealed with the memory of a holy death. The cardinal and the very young priest come together to give a message of hope to those they left behind. Cardinal Cooke's episcopal motto was "Thy Will Be Done." Gene's second-to-last words to his brother, Tom, were "Pray for me that I will be able to do God's will." Thus a chain of wisdom, faith, and hope was forged that will extend through the years and will bring blessings to many who are not even born when these two dedicated followers of Christ completed their assigned tasks in this life so very well.

Martyrs in Another Land

Four Religious Women Gave Their Lives for the Poor in El Salvador

The bloody civil war that tore El Salvador apart took some seventy-five thousand lives before a peace treaty signed in Mexico in 1992 formally brought it to a close. Frequently its victims were targets of assassins rather than combat casualties. That was true in many cases involving Church personnel — most notably Archbishop Oscar Romero, shot to death while celebrating Mass in March 1980; six Jesuits at Central American University, murdered along with their housekeeper and her daughter in 1989; and four religious women from the United States, brutally assaulted and killed on December 2, 1980, as they were driving to their mission from the San Salvador Airport.

These four women — Maryknoll Sisters Ita Ford and Maura Clarke, Ursuline Sister Dorothy Kazel, and Jean Donovan, a lay missionary — were martyrs for their faith and for the poor people they served in Christ's name. Their killers — an army sergeant and four members of the National Guard — were eventually found guilty and sentenced to thirty-year prison terms, but other military officials knew of the murders and attempted to cover them up. The Commission on the Truth for El Salvador, meeting in 1993, also concluded that the arrest and execution of the churchwomen was planned prior to their arrival at the airport, and that the army sergeant carried out the orders of a superior to kill them.

During the twelve-year war, one million Salvadorans became refugees, many of them fleeing the country in order to survive. And the seventy-five thousand dead included four religious women from the United States, who were in El Salvador to help the poor. This story is mostly about one of them, Jean Donovan. Not long before her death, she wrote this: "Several times I have decided to leave El Salvador. I almost could except for the children. Who would care for them? Whose heart could be so staunch as to favor the reasonable thing in a sea of their tears and loneliness? Not mine, dear friend. Not mine."

Story by David Scott, in *The Evangelist*, the diocesan
newspaper of Albany, New York, 1993.

A crowd had gathered in the field along a country road outside San Salvador, El Salvador. The noontime air was still, as church workers and peasants removed a crude cross made of tree limbs from a mound of fresh earth. Then they began digging.

Three feet down their shovels hit upon the body of a woman. She was clad in blue jeans that had been pulled on backwards. They dragged the body out, placing it carefully on the ground near the cross. Her face was shredded beyond recognition, collapsed by a gaping gunshot wound.

It was December 1980, and Jean Donovan had already lain in her shallow grave for two days, atop the bodies of three nuns: Maura Clarke, Ita Ford, and Dorothy Kazel, friends and fellow church workers. Each had been raped, murdered, and secretly buried by members of El Salvador's National Guard.

"El Salvador is such a beautiful country," Jean had written in her diary the year before. "Where else would you find roses blooming in December?" It was a cruel irony that her life was choked off in its flower, only twenty-six Decembers after it began.

Jean had been born two months prematurely, as if so eager and full of life that she could not wait to leave the womb. She was raised in a close-knit Catholic family in the affluent Connecticut suburb of Westport, where her father worked as an executive for United Technologies, a defense contractor.

Following in her parents' footsteps, Jean early on set herself on the fast track of upward social mobility. By twenty-four, she had a master's degree in economics and landed an executive post in the Cleveland office of Arthur Anderson & Son, one of the country's largest accounting firms.

Still, there was an emptiness in the center of Jean Donovan's young life. In 1977 she returned to Ireland to visit a priest whom she had met when she was a foreign exchange student there.

"Don't laugh too loud," she told him. "I've come to talk to you because I think I have to change my life." During their discussion, the priest, who had spent a decade as a missionary in Harlem and Peru, told her: "You've got everything. You should think about giving a little back to God."

When she came home, she enrolled in a missionary program for laypeople run by the Cleveland diocese and the Maryknoll religious order.

"I have a gut feeling that my motivation to be a missionary is a true calling from God," she told her family and friends. "I want to get closer to him, and that's the only way I think I can."

Over the objections of family members, as well as the protests of her fiancé, she went off to work with the poor of El Salvador in 1979. Even as she left, she was consumed by self-doubts. "Why would God want me?" she asked in a letter to a friend. "I'm so inadequate and no good."

Jean aided children and families made homeless by the fighting of El Salvador's civil war. Entries from Jean's diary track the grim, steady rise in the number of bodies she and her colleagues helped bury — victims of government-sponsored terrorism and political murder.

"At times, I'm really scared for me as well," she confessed to a friend. "But mostly I know the Lord will protect me, so I'm certainly not looking over my shoulder."

As the violence continued to swell uncontrollably in El Salvador, she made a final visit home. Her friends and family, even her Irish priest-friend, pleaded in vain with her not to return.

She spent her last week visiting her parents, who said she seemed serene, confident, and carefree. As she set her face once more toward El Salvador, she was prepared for suffering, as if she believed that suffering was necessary if she was to get closer to Christ. "I think that the hardship one endures may be God's way of taking you into the desert and to prepare you to meet and love him more fully," she wrote to a friend.

Along a dark Salvadoran road, late on December 2, 1980, she endured violation, humiliation, and execution in order to meet her Lord.

Yet it is the Spirit of the Lord's resurrection that seems to speak from the bones of Jean Donovan's open grave. Jean's was the spirit of one who came to believe that the rich must go to the poor to meet Christ and share in his resurrection.

"I don't know how the poor survive," she once wrote. "People in our positions really have to die unto ourselves and our wealth to gain the spirituality of the poor and oppressed. I have a long way to go on that score. They can teach you so much with their patience and their wanting eyes."

A Message Worth Sharing

Crippled by a Youth's Bullet, a New York Cop Preaches Forgiveness

In one sense, the life of New York City Police Officer Steven McDonald (1957-) changed forever on the day in 1986 when he was wounded by a bullet from a gun fired by a teenager he was chasing in Central Park. Until that day, McDonald had a lot in common with many other New York cops: youth, boundless energy, family pride in the police department and an Irish heritage, a beautiful young wife expecting their first child — in short, a future without limit.

Then came the run-in with Shavod Jones. Jones's bullet hit with deadly effect, severing McDonald's spinal column and leaving him paralyzed. In their newspapers, New Yorkers followed the gripping story that came next: Steven's slow and courageous recovery; the birth of his son, Conor; his gradual resumption of public appearances; the ability to make use of a motorized wheelchair (controlled by puffs of his own breath, since he could no longer use his arms). And then, although his speech sounded hesitant at first, since he breathes through a ventilator, his own comments about what had happened. New Yorkers got beyond the words themselves to hear the message, which surprised many of them: McDonald was preaching forgiveness.

The Central Park incident had changed Steven McDonald physically, but nothing altered his spiritual outlook. In time he visited his assailant in prison, offering his forgiveness and urging him to use his God-given abilities to make something of himself.

But for Steven McDonald, there was more to do than forgive Shavod Jones. He began taking that message of forgiveness and nonviolence to the city's schools, youth clubs, church groups — anyone, he says, who will have him. He's still doing it now, as Detective Steven McDonald. In the process, he lends new meaning to the old phrase: he is, without a doubt, one of "New York's finest."

From "Hero Cop: Detective McDonald Urges Youth to Forgive, Frequent the Sacraments," by John Burger, in *Catholic New York*, the archdiocesan newspaper of New York, 1998.

He speaks softly and needs help in breathing, but Detective Steven McDonald's message to youth was loud and clear: go to church, pray, forgive.

The paralyzed New York City cop shared his story of faith and forgiveness at St. Catharine's Church in Blauvelt, where some two hundred fifty adults and teenagers gathered on March 31. Shot by a fifteen-year-old in Central Park in 1986, McDonald described his progress from "the most terrifying moment of my life" to a realization that God has a plan for everyone.

Leaving a poster-size "Pledge of Nonviolence" for display at the parish, McDonald attributed destruction of human life, such as the recent killings of students in Jonesboro, Arkansas, to a general lack of faith.

He urged the young people to hold on to their faith and realize that God has a plan for each of them. "God wants to use us to establish his peace on earth," he said. "Allow the Holy Spirit to work through you to overcome evil in the world."

Especially important, he told them, is regular confession and Communion. "I've been to a lot of churches that are not of our faith, and I have to say that they are spiritually empty without the Eucharist," he said.

Seeking God's forgiveness implies forgiving others, he continued. Forgiving Shavod Jones, the gunman who put him in a wheelchair, wasn't a one-time deal, he said. He has to keep forgiving him even as he asks God continually to forgive his own sins.

Forgiving Jones, he said, "put all the ugliness behind." Otherwise, he would have been too filled with anger, and nobody would be able to live with him, he explained.

Jones died in a motorcycle accident after being paroled in 1995. McDonald, who had wanted to bring him along on speaking engagements, believed in his potential to live a good life.

McDonald said his faith has grown since the shooting. Although his doctors said he would be paralyzed for the rest of his life, he chooses to say "for a very long time."

"I believe God has miracles for everyone," he said. He credited his wife and mother for pulling him through the troubled times with their strong faith and prayers.

He said his grandfather, also a New York City policeman, was shot in 1936. McDonald pointed out that while Jones was black, his grandfather's shooters were "the same skin color as him."

"Good and evil have nothing to do with the color of your skin but with the way we choose to live our lives," he said.

As he told his story in a quiet, labored voice, the silence in the church was punctuated only by the clicking of his respirator and, eventually, the soft sobbing of those moved by his tale of courage.

'I Knew That I Had to Seek Him Out'

How Cardinal Bernardin Forgave
the Man Who Falsely Accused Him

Few American bishops have been as widely loved and universally respected as Cardinal Joseph Bernardin (1928-1996), the late archbishop of Chicago. He was one of the country's most influential prelates as well, and will always be thought of first and foremost as a reconciler. As priest, bishop, archbishop, and cardinal, as parish assistant or bishops' conference official or head of a mighty archdiocese, Joseph Bernardin's goal was always to bring people together.

His skills of reconciliation were never tested as sorely as they were in his final years, after he was falsely accused of abuse by a one-time seminarian named Steven Cook. The charges had startled and devastated the cardinal, but he met them with prayer and forthright denials. If outwardly he was calm, however, his inner turmoil was constant. And so it would remain until the truth was finally made known. Finally, on February 28, 1994, a hundred days after the allegations, Cook appeared before a federal judge to request that the charges be withdrawn.

Others might have let the matter end there, relieved that an ordeal had been happily ended. Not Cardinal Bernardin. His own personal concerns aside — pancreatic cancer would claim his life on November 14, 1996 — he understood there was more to do. Of Steven Cook, he wrote: "He was the sheep who had been lost, and, as a shepherd, I knew that I had to seek him out."

Here is the cardinal's own account of what happened next. Following that, to conclude this book as it did his own, is his personal reflection of what heaven must be like.

Selections from *The Gift of Peace: Personal Reflections*, by
Joseph Cardinal Bernardin, Loyola Press, 1997.

1. A Mass of Reconciliation

More striking to me than the fact that a troubled priest at St. Gregory Seminary had unwittingly played a role in promoting my false indictment was what we gradually learned of Steven Cook's own difficult life. His brief, unhappy period in the Cincinnati seminary had been followed by an estrangement from the Church and a drift into a promiscuous lifestyle. He was suffering from AIDS and was being cared for by a friend at an apartment in Philadelphia whose address they kept secret. He was the sheep who had been lost, and, as a shepherd, I knew that I had to seek him out.

Indeed, after the case was dropped and my final press conference on the matter was covered by the same CNN that had played such a prominent part in publicizing the initial accusation, I plunged back into my crowded schedule. Nonetheless, I thought often of Steven in his lonely, illness-ridden exile from both his parental home and the Church. By mid-December, I felt deeply that this entire episode would not be complete until I followed my shepherd's calling to seek him out. I only prayed that he would receive me. The experience of the false accusation would not be complete until I met and reconciled with Steven. Even though I had never heard from him, I sensed he also wanted to see me.

Not knowing his address or phone number and not wanting to take him by surprise, I made contact with Steven's mother, Mary, through Father Phil Seher, her pastor in Cincinnati and a friend of mine. She sent back word that Steven was not only willing but also had a real desire to meet with me. I flew to Philadelphia with Father Scott Donahue on December 30, 1994. Monsignor James Malloy, the rector of St. Charles Borromeo Seminary, where the meeting was to be held, picked us up and drove us to its campus in suburban Overbrook.

I was a bit anxious as we entered the snow-patched seminary grounds. The campus, with its traditional granite structures, was quiet — the seminarians were on Christmas vacation. In the large, tall-windowed room on the second floor of the main building, we waited patiently for Steven and his companion. It was hard to refrain from asking myself an unwelcome question: Would Steven be able to keep the appointment or not?

Within a few minutes he arrived with his friend Kevin. We shook hands, and I sat with Steven on a couch as Father Donahue and Kevin sat in the wing chairs at either end of it. Steven looked only slightly gaunt despite his grave illness. I explained to him that the only reason for requesting the meeting was to bring closure to the traumatic events of last winter by personally letting him know that I harbored no ill feelings toward him. I told him I wanted to pray with him for his physical and spiritual well-being. Steven replied that he had decided to meet with me so he could apologize for the embarrassment and hurt he had caused. In other words, we both sought reconciliation. However, Steven said he wanted to tell me about his life before we continued.

With a tone and gestures that indicated Steven had bottled up his story for a long time, he told me that as a young seminarian he had been sexually abused by a priest he thought was his friend. He claimed that the authorities did not take his report of the priest's misconduct seriously. He became embittered and left the Church. Much later, he came into contact with a New Jersey-based lawyer with a reputation for bringing legal actions against priests accused of sexual abuse. This lawyer, Steven said, put him in touch with a priest in another state to advise him spiritually.

Although Steven was pursuing a case only against his seminary teacher, his priest adviser began mentioning me, Cardinal Bernardin, suggesting that, if I were included in the case, Steven would surely get back what he wanted from the Church. This "spiritual guide" pushed my name, urging Steven to name me along with the other priest in the legal action. He also urged Steven's mother to cooperate in this plan, sending her flowers as part of his effort to persuade her to support Steven's action. This was the very same priest who expressed his opinion during a Chicago radio talk show on November 12, 1993, that I was guilty.

It became difficult for Steven to explain how, with what he described as a poorly trained therapist, he thought that he had recaptured memories of my abusing him and went along with including me in the suit. He seemed confused and uncertain about this. His friend Kevin broke in to say that he was always suspicious of the lawyer and the priest-adviser.

I looked directly at Steven, seated a few inches away from me. "You know," I said, "that I never abused you."

"I know," he answered softly. "Can you tell me that again?"

I looked directly into his eyes. "I have never abused you. You know that, don't you?"

Steven nodded. "Yes," he replied, "I know that, and I want to apologize for saying that you did." Steven's apology was simple, direct, deeply moving. I accepted his apology. I told him that I had prayed for him every day and would continue to pray for his health and peace of mind. It became increasingly clear that he was in precarious health.

I then asked whether he wanted me to celebrate Mass for him. At first, he hesitated. "I'm not sure I want to have Mass," he said haltingly; "I've felt very alienated from God and the Church a long time." He said that on several occasions while in a hotel he threw a Gideon Bible against the wall in anger and frustration. "Perhaps," he said, "just a simple prayer would be more appropriate."

I hesitated for a moment after that, unsure of how he would react to the gift I removed from my briefcase. I told him that I would not press the issue but did want to show him two items I had brought with me. "Steven," I said, "I have brought you something, a Bible that I have inscribed to you. But I do understand, and I won't be offended if you don't want to accept it." Steven took the Bible in quivering hands, pressed it to his heart as tears welled up in his eyes.

I then took a hundred-year-old chalice out of my case. "Steven, this is a gift from a man I don't even know. He asked me to use it to say Mass for you some day."

"Please," Steven responded tearfully, "let's celebrate Mass now."

Never in my entire priesthood have I witnessed a more profound reconciliation. The words I am using to tell you this story cannot begin to describe the power of God's grace at work that afternoon. It was a manifestation of God's love, forgiveness, and healing that I will never forget.

Kevin, Steven's friend, asked if he, a non-Catholic, could attend, and I told him that it would be fine. We all went to the seminary chapel where, with great joy, and thanksgiving, Father Donahue and I celebrated Mass for the Feast of the Holy Family. We all embraced at the greeting of peace, and, afterward, I anointed Steven with the sacrament of the sick.

Then I said a few words: "In every family there are times when there is hurt, anger, or alienation. But we cannot run away from our family. We have only one family and so, after every falling out, we must make every effort to be reconciled. So, too, the Church is our spiritual family. Once we become a member, we may be hurt or become alienated, but it is still our family. Since there is no other, we must work at reconciliation. And that is what we have been doing this very afternoon."

Before Steven left, he told me, "A big burden has been lifted from me today. I feel healed and very much at peace." We had previously agreed to keep our meeting secret, but Steven now said to me, "I'm so happy, I want people to know about our reconciliation." He asked me to tell the story, which I did a few weeks later in *The New World*, our archdiocesan paper. When I read it to him beforehand on the phone, he told me, "Cardinal, you're a good writer. Go with it."

As we flew back to Chicago that evening, Father Donahue and I felt the lightness of spirit that an afternoon of grace brings to one's life. I could not help but think that the ordeal of the accusation led straight to this extraordinary experience of God's grace in our sacramental reconciliation. And I could not help but recall the work of the Good Shepherd: to seek and restore to the sheepfold the one that has been, only for a while, lost.

Steven and I kept in touch after that and, six months later, when I received a diagnosis of pancreatic cancer, his was one of the first letters I received. He had only a few months to live when he wrote it, filled with sympathy and encouragement for me. He planned to visit me in Chicago at the end of August, but he was too ill. Steven died at his mother's home on September 22, 1995, fully reconciled with the Church. "This," he said, smiling from his death-bed at his mother about his return to the sacraments, "is my gift to you." The priest in Cincinnati who attended him told this to me soon afterward.

2. A Glimpse of Heaven

Many people have asked me to tell them about heaven and the afterlife. I sometimes smile at the request because I do not know any more than they do. Yet, when one young man asked if I looked forward to being united with God and all those who have gone before me, I made a connection to something I said earlier in the book. The first time I traveled with my mother and sister to my parents' homeland of Tonadico di Primiero, in northern Italy, I felt as if I had been there before. After years of looking through my mother's photo albums, I knew the mountains, the land, the houses, the people. As soon as we entered the valley, I said, "My God, I know this place. I am home." Somehow I think crossing from this life into life eternal will be similar. I will be home.

Special Acknowledgments

Special thanks go to the following for the use of their material in this work:

Anecdotes and Examples Illustrating the Catholic Catechism, selected and arranged by Rev. Francis Spirago, Benziger Brothers, 1904.

The Angelic Doctor: The Life and World of St. Thomas Aquinas, by Matthew Bunson, Our Sunday Visitor, Inc., 1994.

The Autobiography of St. Ignatius, edited by J.F.X. O'Conor, S.J., Benziger Brothers, 1900.

The Book of Saints, by Michael Walsh, Twenty-Third Publications, 1994. This excerpt is reprinted, with permission from *Book of Saints,* copyright © 1994 by Michael Walsh (paper, 156 pp., $9.95), published by Twenty-Third Publications, P.O. Box 180, Mystic, CT 06355, toll-free 1-800-321-0411.

Story on Sister Thea Bowman, by Cindy Wooden and Jerry Filteau, adapted from Catholic News Service. Copyright © 1989 Catholic News Service / U.S. Catholic Conference; reprinted with permission.

Brother Francis, edited by Lawrence Cunningham, Harper & Row, 1972. Permission to use granted by author.

Catechism in Stories, by Rev. Lawrence G. Lovasik, SVD, The Bruce Publishing Co., 1956.

Catherine of Siena, A Biography, by Anne B. Baldwin, Our Sunday Visitor, Inc., 1987.

Catholic Anecdotes, by the Brothers of the Christian Schools; translated from the French by Mrs. J. Sadlier; D. & J. Sadlier & Co., 1885.

The Catholic Church in Tennessee, by Thomas J. Stritch, Catholic Center, 1987. Permission to use granted by Bishop Edward U. Kmiec.

Chavez and the Farm Workers, by Ronald B. Taylor, Beacon Press, 1975. *Chavez and the Farm Workers,* by Ronald B. Taylor; copyright © 1975 by Ronald B. Taylor; reprinted by permission of Beacon Press, Boston.

The Collected Works of G. K. Chesterton, Vol. X, Collected Poetry, Part I, compiled and with an introduction by Aidan Mackey, Ignatius Press, 1994.

Difficult Star: The Life of Pauline Jaricot, by Katherine Burton, Longmans, Green and Co., 1947.

Story on Jean Donovan, by David Scott, *The Evangelist,* the diocesan newspaper of Albany, New York, 1993. Reprinted with permission from *The Evangelist,* newspaper of the Albany (N.Y.) Roman Catholic Diocese.

Dorothy Day: A Radical Devotion, by Robert Coles, Addison-Wesley, 1987. From *Dorothy Day: A Radical Devotion*, by Robert Coles; copyright © 1989 by Robert Coles; reprinted by permission of Perseus Books Publishers, a member of Perseus Books, L.L.C.

The Earliest Life of Gregory the Great, by an Anonymous Monk of Whitby; text, translation, and notes by Bertram Colgrave, The University of Kansas Press, 1968. Permission to use granted by The University of Kansas Press, Lawrence, Kans.

Father Damien: The Man and His Era, by Margaret R. Bunson, Our Sunday Visitor, Inc., 1989, 1997.

Father Duffy's Story: A Tale of Humor and Heroism, of Life and Death With the Fighting Sixty-Ninth, by Francis P. Duffy, George H. Doran Co., 1919.

Father Flanagan of Boys Town, by Fulton Oursler and Will Oursler, Doubleday & Co., Inc., 1949. From *Father Flanagan of Boys Town*, by Fulton Oursler and Will Oursler; copyright © 1949 by Fulton Oursler and Will Oursler; used by permission of Doubleday, a Division of Random House, Inc.

Fátima: Pilgrimage to Peace, by April Oursler Armstrong and Martin F. Armstrong, Jr., Hanover House, 1954.

The Fire of Francis Xavier: The Story of an Apostle, by Arthur R. McGratty, S.J., The Bruce Publishing Company, 1951.

The Gift of Peace: Personal Reflections, by Joseph Cardinal Bernardin, Loyola Press, 1997. Used by permission of Loyola Press, Chicago.

Give Us This Day, by Sidney Stewart, W. W. Norton & Co., Inc., 1956. Used by permission of the copyright holder (Balkin Agency, Inc., P.O. Box 222, Amherst, MA 01004, agent for the estate of Sidney Stewart).

The Grace of Guadalupe, by Frances Parkinson Keyes, Julian Messner, Inc., 1941.

Great Moments in Catholic History: 100 Memorable Events in Catholic History Told in Picture and Story, by Rev. Edward Lodge Curran, Grosset & Dunlap, 1937.

The Great White Shepherd of Christendom, edited by Charles J. O'Malley, J. S. Hyland & Co., 1903.

A Handbook of Christian Symbols and Stories of the Saints, by Clara Erskine Clement, Ticknor and Co., 1886 (republished by Gale Research Co., 1971).

"Hero Cop: Detective McDonald Urges Youth to Forgive, Frequent the Sacraments," by John Burger, in *Catholic New York*, the archdiocesan newspaper of New York, 1998.

How the Irish Saved Civilization, by Thomas Cahill, Anchor Books, Doubleday & Co., Inc., 1995. Excerpt from *How the Irish Saved Civilization*, by Thomas Cahill; copyright © 1995 by Thomas

Cahill; used by permission of Doubleday, a Division of Random House, Inc.

The Improbable Irish, by Walter Bryan, Ace Books, 1969.

In Search of Ireland, Methuen & Co., Ltd., 1930.

Jeanne Jugan: Humble So As to Love More, by Paul Milcent, Darton, Longman and Todd, 1979. Taken from *Jeanne Jugan: Humble So As to Love More*, by Paul Milcent; published and copyright © 1979 by Darton, Longman and Todd Ltd., and used by permission of the publishers.

John Henry Cardinal Newman, by George J. Donahue, The Stratford Co., 1927.

John Ireland and the American Catholic Church, by Marvin R. O'Connell, Minnesota Historical Society Press, 1988. Permission to use granted by Minnesota Historical Society Press, St. Paul, MN 55101.

Keepers of the Keys, by Wilton Wynn, Random House, 1988. From *Keepers of the Keys*, by Wilton Wynn; copyright © 1988 by Wilton Wynn; reprinted by permission of Random House, Inc.

The Life of St. Lucy Filippini, by Francesco Di Simone, translated by Edwin Bannon, FSC, Ottavia Publications, 1997.

Life of the Most Reverend John Hughes, D.D., First Archbishop of New York, by John R. G. Hassard, D. Appleton and Co., 1866.

The Little Flowers of St. Francis of Assisi, St. Anthony Guild Press, 1958. Permission to use granted by The Franciscans, St. Anthony's Guild, Paterson, NJ 07501-2948.

Little Lives of the Great Saints, by John O'Kane Murray, P. J. Kenedy & Sons, 1910.

Little Pictorial Lives of the Saints, Benziger Brothers, Inc., 1925. Permission to use granted by Glencoe/McGraw-Hill, 21600 Oxnard St., Suite 500, Woodland Hills, CA 91367.

Lives of the Saints You Should Know, by Margaret and Matthew Bunson, Our Sunday Visitor, Inc., 1994.

Lives of the Saints You Should Know (Vol. 2), by Margaret and Matthew Bunson, Our Sunday Visitor, Inc., 1996.

Love Without Boundaries: Mother Teresa of Calcutta, by Georges Goreé and Jean Barbier, translated by Paula Speakman (translation copyright © 1974 by Paula Speakman). First published in English in 1974 by Veritas Publications (Dublin) and T. Shand Alba Publications (London); Our Sunday Visitor, Inc., edition published in 1980 by special arrangement with Veritas. Original edition, *Amour sans Frontière (mère Teresa de Calcutta)*, copyright © 1972 by Bayard / Le Centurion, Paris; permission to use granted by Bayard-Presse.

Married Saints, by Selden P. Delany, The Newman Press, 1950; copyright © 1935 by Longmans Green and Co., (first printing 1935; reprinted 1950). Permission to use granted by Paulist Press, Mahwah, N.J.

Mary, Help of Christians and the Fourteen Saints Invoked as Holy Helpers, by Rev. Bonaventure Hammer, OFM, Benziger Brothers, 1909.

Matt Talbot, The Irish Worker's Glory, by Rev. James F. Cassidy, Burns, Oates & Washbourne Ltd., 1934. By permission of Burns & Oates.

Mothers of the Saints: Portraits of Ten Mothers of the Saints and Three Saints Who Were Mothers, by Wendy Leifeld, Servant Publications, 1991. Permission to use granted by Wendy Leifeld.

"The Mothers' Saint — Gerard Majella," by Alicia von Stamwitz, *Liguorian* magazine, May 1994, published by The Redemptorists. Originally published in Liguorian magazine, May 1994; reprinted with permission from Liguorian, One Liguori Dr., Liguori, MO 63057.

Story on Sister Helen Mrosla, OSF, which first appeared in *Proteus: A Journal of Ideas*, Spring, 1991. Reprinted in the October 1991 *Reader's Digest* and in *Chicken Soup for the Soul*, by Jack Canfield and Mark Victor Hansen, Health Communications, Inc., 1993.

Our Sunday Visitor's Father Solanus: The Story of Solanus Casey, O.F.M. Cap. (Updated), by Catherine M. Odell, Our Sunday Visitor, Inc., 1988, 1995.

Padre Pio: The True Story (Revised and Expanded), by C. Bernard Ruffin, Our Sunday Visitor, Inc., 1991.

Patrick: Sixteen Centuries With Ireland's Patron Saint, compiled and edited by Alice-Boyd Proudfoot, MacMillan Publishing Co., Inc., 1990.

Pope, Council and World: The Story of Vatican II, by Robert Blair Kaiser, The Macmillan Co., 1963. Reprinted with the permission of Simon & Schuster, Inc.; from *Pope, Council and the World: The Story of Vatican II*, by Robert Blair Kaiser; copyright © 1963, and renewed 1991 by Robert Blair Kaiser.

"Pope Pius XII: The Pope of Peace In an Age of War," by Frank J. Korn, *Our Sunday Visitor*, October 15, 1978.

Popular Life of Saint Teresa of Jesus, translated from the French by Annie Porter, Benziger Brothers, 1884.

Portrait of a Parish Priest: St. John Vianney, the Curé d'Ars, by Lancelot C. Sheppard, The Newman Press, 1958. Permission to use granted by Paulist Press, Mahwah, N.J.

A Priest Forever, by Fr. Benedict J. Groeschel, c.f.r., Our Sunday Visitor, Inc., 1998.

Promises to Keep: The Life of Doctor Thomas A. Dooley, by Agnes W. Dooley, Farrar, Straus and Cudahy, Inc., 1962. Excerpt from "From Medical Corpsman to M.D.," from *Promises to Keep: The Life of Doctor Thomas A. Dooley*, by Agnes W. Dooley; copyright © 1962 by Agnes W. Dooley and Malcolm W. Dooley; reprinted by permission of Farrar, Straus & Giroux, Inc.

The Quotable Chesterton: A Topical Compilation of the Wit, Wisdom and Satire of G. K. Chesterton, edited by George J. Marlin, Richard P. Rabatin, and John L. Swan, Image Books, Doubleday & Co., Inc., 1987.

Saint Among Savages: The Life of Isaac Jogues, by Francis Talbot, S.J., Harper & Brothers Publishers, 1935. Permission to use granted by HarperCollins Publishers, Inc., New York.

Saint Boniface, by Godfrey Kurth, translated by Rt. Rev. Victor Day with additions by Rev. Francis S. Betten, SJ, The Bruce Publishing Co., 1935.

St. Francis de Sales: A Testimony by St. Chantal, introduction by Elisabeth Stopp, Institute of Salesian Studies, 1967.

St. Joan of Arc, by Margaret and Matthew Bunson, Our Sunday Visitor, Inc., 1992.

Saint of the Day, Leonard Foley, OFM, Editor, St. Anthony Messenger Press, 1990. Used by permission of St. Anthony Messenger Press.

Saints and Their Stories, by Mary Montgomery, Harper & Row, 1988. Five stories, as submitted from *Saints and Their Stories*, by Mary Montgomery, copyright © 1988 by Mary Montgomery, reprinted by permission of HarperCollins Publishers, Inc., New York.

Saints of the Americas, by Rev. M. A. Habig, OFM, Our Sunday Visitor, Inc., 1974.

Sea of Glory, The Magnificent Story of the Four Chaplains, by Francis Beauchesne Thornton, Prentice-Hall, Inc., 1953.

A Simple Path, by Mother Teresa, compiled by Lucinda Vardey, Ballantine Books, 1995. From *A Simple Path*, by Mother Teresa; compiled by Lucinda Vardey; copyright © 1995 by Mother Teresa; reprinted by permission of Ballantine Books, a Division of Random House, Inc.

Six Modern Martyrs, by Mary Craig, The Crossroad Publishing Co., 1985.

Storytelling: Imagination and Faith, by William J. Bausch, Twenty-Third Publications, 1984 (originally in *The Wisdom of Accepted Tenderness*, by Brennan Manning, Dimension Books, 1978). Copyright © 1978, 1997 by John Powell; published by Thomas More Publishing, 200 E. Bethany Dr., Allen, TX 75002; reprinted with permission of the publisher.

The Sublime Shepherdess: The Life of Saint Bernadette of Lourdes, by Frances Parkinson Keyes, Julian Messner, Inc., 1940.

Ten Christians, by Boniface Hanley, OFM, Ave Maria Press, 1979. Permission to use granted by Rev. Boniface Hanley, OFM, St. Joseph's Friary, 454 Germantown Rd., West Milford, NJ 07480.

Thérèse of Lisieux: A Biography, by Patricia O'Connor, Our Sunday Visitor, Inc., 1983.

Index

Note: For a number of reasons, this specialized index does not conform strictly to conventional styles; for instance, some entries appear in the usual way, that is, last names first, as in "Bausch, William J. (Rev.)"; while others, such as saints' names, appear with first names first, as in "Maximilian Kolbe (St.)." Other modifications are self-explanatory.